Descendants
Of
Hagar

Descendants
Of
Hagar

Nik Nicholson

authorHOUSE®

AuthorHouse™ LLC
1663 Liberty Drive
Bloomington, IN 47403
www.authorhouse.com
Phone: 1-800-839-8640

This is a work of fiction. All characters, organizations, and events portrayed
in this novel are either products of the writer's imagination, or are used
fictitiously. Every word written here is strictly for entertainment purposes.

Content Editor: Nik Nicholson
Grammar and Line Editor: Claudia Moss
Copy Editor: Nik Nicholson
Readers: Dorian Moreno, Angela Burgess, Shirley
Lavoile, Tammy James, Koweta Burgess
Cover Painting: Lam Lu

Published by AuthorHouse   07/23/2013

ISBN: 978-1-4817-7971-5 (sc)
ISBN: 978-1-4817-7970-8 (hc)
ISBN: 978-1-4817-7969-2 (e)

Library of Congress Control Number: 2013913106

This book is dedicated to my grandmother,
Shirley Bell Nicholson, whose fight to live
taught me not to waste my breath.

Acknowledgments

First, I thank all of the Clark County librarians who assisted my research, the majority of which came from books in my local library. I pray technology does not make libraries extinct.

Second, I thank all of the masculine-centered women who graciously answered my long questionnaire and added questions they felt were critical. Your responses assisted me in imagining Linny's character. I am grateful for your openness and honesty regarding the complexities of being masculine-centered. Thank you for sharing your frustrations about how you are portrayed and the lack of portrayals. I pray you know I attempted to create an honest expression of how much you must overcome to love yourselves and others. This is my love letter to you. I pray you receive it well.

Next, I thank Keith Brantley, also known as "The Griot" in poetry circles, for creating "The Poet's Corner." As a result of "The Poet's Corner," I found an artist family at the West Las Vegas Art Center. I thank all there—the poets, artists, actors, dancers and drummers, who taught me about community.

I wish Kianga Palacio was here in the flesh, to witness this dream realized.

I thank Dorian Moreno for offering to read me, unpublished. It was Dorian who introduced me to reader feedback as an integral part of the editing process. As a result, I also thank my additional readers: Angela Burgess, Koweta Burgess, Tammy James and Shirley Lavoile. Your input was an invaluable part of my journey in the self-publishing process, which, I've learned isn't wholly about "the self."

Finally, I'd like to thank Ms. Claudia Moss, also known as "The Siren" in poetry circles. Early on, Claudia became my writing mentor and encouraged me to self-publish. Claudia held my hand through this long process; by being motivation when I was lethargic after so many edits. More than a friend, she has been a one-woman support system. I am overwhelmed with gratitude for her presence as a safe space for my spirit.

I am also grateful for late night conversations where we talked shit, laughed ourselves silly and brainstormed about taking over the world, one book at a time. I am honored to witness how courageously and full Claudia lives life. Her light gives me courage; she is one of my main inspirations.

As with all things, I thank God. I also thank God for everyone mentioned here, and so many others that have been a lesson or blessing.

Love Is Life, Live.

Descendants
Of
Hagar

The spiritual man makes judgments about all things, but he himself is not subject to any man's judgment. 1 Corinthians 2:15

Chapter One

"Say dat gin," Miemay say squinting 'a eyes like it's too much sun in 'a face, leaning into 'a cane and spitting.

We both sitting on 'a porch. I'm on the big seat right outside the front door, she at the edge sitting on a stool. I'm reading 'a the Bible, this her seventh or eighth time going through this whole book I know bout.

Use to always have one of us grandkids reading it to 'a, til folks start saying she corrupting they children, by explaining the Bible and answering our questions. Zion ain't the kind of place where you can talk about the Bible like it's any other book and not be called crazy or hell bound. Miemay marked for all that, then some. A hell bound crazy witch what they call 'a, when they mad at 'a and she ain around.

I use to take up reading it to 'a, wherever the other grandkids left off. Now I'm the only one old enough to read it to 'a and not be corrupted. That's how I come to read this whole book almost four times myself. If we ain't reading the Bible, I'm reading books the Belangers loaned 'a, since she told 'em she like for 'a grandbabies to read to 'a.

I read 'a Oliver Optic's stories for boys, James Fenimore Cooper, Charlotte Bronte, Louisa May Alcott, Washington Irving and Mrs. A.D.T. Whitney. Two of Miemay's favorites are Bronte's, *Jane Eyre* and Cooper's, *Last of the Mohicans*. I think *Last of the Mohicans* is too wordy, I like Whitney's writing more, don't need no dictionary to understand it.

Feels like I'm reading this scripture wrong. So I point to the passage with my finger, and follow that finger with my eyes. "John 19:30," I announce, then wait for Miemay to tell me what's wrong.

When she don't speak, I repeat the scripture, "When Jesus therefore had received the vinegar, he said, 'It is finished:' then he bowed his head, and gave up the ghos-"

"Wouldn't have to read the Bible so much if ya come to church," Reverend Patrick shouts, interrupting, coming long side the house from the back and on up to the porch.

Rest of the men behind Miemay house, working in the clearing, building 'a new house. It's gone have electricity and plumbing.

He frown at Miemay chewing tabbaca. When she spit, he cringe. He don't chew neither, and think it ain't ladylike for women.

Reverend Patrick a big black man with jet black cotton hair patted close to his head. He look like an outsider cause his Daddy married a dark-skinned woman from Alabama. Now he and all his kin done had it hard. Most of 'em had to marry folks outside of Zion. Everybody here light skinned. Some of us look white, like Miemay. They ain't trying to get darker or have dark children. In Zion, marrying darker is marrying down.

"Cain't git ta hebin one day a week, few hours a Sunday. Wudn't hafta red it maself if ya red what it relly say. Cut all dat shoutin and goin on. Stop sayin what white folk tell ya say."

"Now you listen here-"

"Nall you. You the one gone listen," Miemay cut 'im off glancing at 'im, adjusting 'aself on 'a cane then looking off ahead. "Don't fagit cho place. I dah mama. Talk ta ya wife like dat. Truf hurt." She chew deep for his displeasure then scowl at 'im. "Nah what chu wont, boy?"

He fumble for the words then say, "What chu need two bafrooms in one house for? Don't make no sense. You just one woman, and all ya kids grown. Ain't got nobody stayin whicha," he protests, looking over at me. "I'm gone just build ya one. And ya ain't gittin no two story cause ya too old to be climbing steps. What chu need four bedrooms for? You ain't rich."

"It's five, ain neva been foe, since ya smart. It's what I wont, it's what I done paid fa. Nah do what I say, and git."

2

He look at 'a hard, his fist balled up, but Miemay don't even look at 'im. She said what she had to, and her word is "The Word" round Zion, even when nobody agree. They have to respect 'a, she the oldest person in Zion and own the most land. Miemay act like he ain even there, put some more tabbaca in 'a mouth.

After he standing there for a while, Miemay spit again then say, "Go on readin, chile."

When I pick up the Bible again, he storm off. I want to ask Miemay why she don't go to church, but it don't seem like it's my place to ask bout 'a relationship with the lord.

Chapter Two

"What ee say?" Miemay's voice cry out, breaking the silence of us waiting in the front room. Sound like this ain't the first time she done asked, cause she ain't never been one to holla outside a ritual. "It ma body! It ma body!" she scream, pleading, which push me to my feet and on to 'a bedroom.

I hear 'a door close, then the white doctor the Belangers sent tilt his hat at me as we pass each other in the hallway. I nod back, then come toe to toe with my Daddy.

He guarding Miemay closed bedroom door. We squared up, he fold his arms like a warrior or something, rock on his heels, like I come to fight.

I stay relaxed, look down at the ground. Don't want him to think wrong of me, don't want him to see no disrespect. This ain't no challenge, I just feel like I need to be in there with 'a.

"We done agreed not to tell 'a," he say sternly, "Nah, GIT!" I don't flinch, just keep my eyes to the ground and wait.

"Let 'a in hur!" Miemay cry louder.

Daddy face sour then he move slowly out the way breathing hard. If he say git, I got to git, but if Miemay say he got to git, he got to git. She his great grandmother. I'm in the fifth generation. Sometimes seem like Miemay only my great-great grandmother, way my cousins and nem treat 'a.

Most folks in Zion treat 'a like a stranger even though she all our mama some kinda way. She just don't do what everybody else do, or say what everybody else say. But when you see what happen, after what she do, you know why. Or when you stop and listen, think about what she saying, it always fall into place.

People don't listen to Miemay til somebody sick, bout to die, or having a baby. She birth more babies than any other woman here in Zion. Always mixing some herb potion for ailments and things, folks say she learned from being a slave. Miemay always tell me, what she know ain't come from being no slave. She say her mama was a root woman, and her mama's mama was a root woman. People swear Miemay stopped yellow fever fore it could move in Zion good, when doctors couldn't even figure it out. That's why, it's a big deal a real doctor done come to see about 'a.

When I open the door she crying, chest heaving and 'a hair ain't pinned up, it's all over the place. She look like a white lady with long white hair. It start off straight from the scalp, get wavy, then curl on the ends where its laying on 'a stomach, and below 'a elbows. Four of 'a seven daughters in the room, all of 'em looking like 'a and each other. They all over 'a bed, and the youngest standing by the dresser looking at 'a like she already dead. Miemay got 'a lip poked out, wiping 'a eyes, and throwing 'a hair like something bout to happen.

"Woe nah. Ain gone be no spells tonight," I tease, hurt deep in my soul she upset. Make me sick to see 'a crying, but I don't let on its bothering me. Iain seen 'a cry since my uncle was lynched, long with them strangers, and I was a child then. I'm trying to talk 'a down, outta meanness. Might not be no spell, but she been known to cuss 'a children when they done worked 'a last nerve.

"Linay?" Miemay say sweetly, but stern. Everybody else call me Linny, but she make my name sound almost like hers. Maybe cause I got 'a name. We both named Madelyn, she Madelyn Belanger, I'm Madelyn Remington. They call me Linny, cause her old masters, the Belangers, still call 'a Maddy.

"Yes, ma'am," I say real proper like, standing tall, cause that's how we play and it's my way of letting 'a know I'm at 'a service.

"Tell ya Miemay what the docta say nah."

"Well, Iain the one he talk to, Miemay." I smile, coming out the door way and taking my hat off so she can see my eyes. Ima have to dance with this ol girl, she ain't giving up that easy and I ain't neither.

"Dat ain what I ax ya, Linay." She stare at me, reading my soul. Never taking 'a eyes off mine, she moving slow cross the bed like a cat bout to pounce a bird, but Iain no bird.

When 'a daughter Matilda reach to help 'a, she heavy paw her like a wild animal. Iain never seen this part of 'a.

"Don't woncha hep, don't need it," she breathe hard then hiss at 'em. Now, I know she bout to show out.

Still Iain gone answer, she always be getting me in trouble with everybody. Zion ain't the type of place where you think for yourself. We all decide, well, they decide, Iain old enough to have a word in edgewise. I'm a woman, Iain got no house of my own, and Iain got no man to speak my piece in meetings.

"Know how many folk I den walked home? Know how many I brang the message it's dey time? How many come ta me afta dey out dis worl' ta tell dey people thangs? I speaks ta folk Iain neva knowed, bout thangs Iain neva heard of."

"Aw, Miemay!" Ondrea chastises 'a, standing and twisting 'a face. "You know it's the devil to be talking bout spirits and such."

"Aw, git on nah wit dat deva bidnis," Miemay snap back still looking at me, and they know she gone know what the doctor say. He ain say it to me, but I heard 'im. They really trying to break 'a focus, but what she got a mind to do, she got a mind to do. "How long I got, Linay?" she ask, turning 'a head and looking round at 'a daughters, disappointed and betrayed.

"Nobody but God know that, Miemay," I answer, sad and confident that that's the truth. Hating she asking me and I'm doing what they did to get 'a all upset by not just telling 'a what the doctor said.

"See! Dat's why you ain't pose to be in here!" Matilda screams, stomping 'a foot at me fussing.

I hear the folks in the hall sigh on the other side of the closed door, then slowly walk out the hall like I told 'a.

I don't feel like I just said, "He said in a few months you gone die." Plus, I think she already know. She could always tell when other folks gone die. Why she wouldn't know her time coming?

"You too young to be on somebody walk home," Ondrea say shaking 'a head at me and scowling.

"So, I on the walk home?" Miemay smile, almost satisfied.

Ondrea shake 'a head sadly, trying to catch a lip from trembling, realizing what she done said. The air so thick you could stab the tension with a knife. If Ondrea lip poke out, Miemay got 'a. Looking at 'a other sisters, they all looking back shaking they head at 'a, for 'a to hold it in, but she cain't. A single tear stream down 'a face.

Then Miemay slap 'a bed knowing.

I breathe relieved, glad Ondrea the one told 'a she on the walk home.

Over took with what she done, or that Miemay dying, more tears stream down Ondrea's face, which she try to catch fore they fall.

"It's all ova nah," Miemay say, satisfied and staring into Ondrea's eyes trying to comfort 'a.

Ondrea keep fighting what's already done. When she cain't stop 'aself, she storm out the room slamming the door. "Jet! She done tricked me into tellin 'a," we hear Ondrea tell 'a husband before breaking into loud sobs. Sound like she crying in his chest.

Chapter Three

———— ❦ ————

"Come on nah, cetch ma hand, Linay." Miemay holding a hand out while she stirring, trying to push 'aself up from the bed. I stop reading and rush to 'a side, pull 'a up to sitting position. "Wooo," she breath out hard, looking at me like it's the first time she seen me before. "Ya strong gull," she heaving, "as a ox."

"Don't talk, Mama Bird," I tell 'a concerned.

She fan off the warning, keep on coming.

I realize she getting up. Iain spect this so I'm clinging to 'a, trying to go with 'a movements. See where she trying to go.

Leaning on me, she scooting to the edge of the bed, pull the cover from 'a legs, place 'a feet on the wood floor then tap me and I know what it is now.

I pulls 'a up on 'a feet. Hold 'a real close, in a tight hug, case she fall.

She a tree though, she don't waiver, she push me away.

I let go slow, then move back looking at 'a.

She put 'a hand on my shoulder, steady 'aself. It's like we doing a dance, every step she take forward, I take one back.

"Tied of layin down. Gotta walk round," she say stubbornly, taking a step, while both us wait to make sure 'a strength don't fail.

I can already hear Daddy nem scolding me bout how I do whatever she say, and not what's right. Doctor say, she spose to be laying down. Ever since the doctor told us she had a few months to live, we don't never leave 'a by 'aself. That's been over year now, so, like I told 'a then, don't nobody but God know.

I'm here the most, cause it's my second home. Plus, I'm the only woman my age ain't got no man, kids or home to look after. Iain been in the fields much. I cleans up round here, cooks 'a meals. I even sleep here when other women come stay, case something happen. Somebody be here while I go get help.

"Woncho stick?" I offer her cane. My heart beating so fast, I'm nervous she gone fall. I think of all the ways she could hurt something if she fall between the bed and the wall. Every step she take closer to me, and out of that trap the betta I feel.

Iain never been 'lowd to watch nobody die. I knowed people that have, but this new to me. Everybody say I'm too young to be here, walking 'a home, but she say she wont me here.

It's tons of children she got to do this; she had thirteen when slavery ended. Had three more by Grandpa Jim, but he died from the fever fore I was born. Miemay always say proudly, "Iain had another man since." And when ain't nobody round she say, she was tied of the married business too, and having to hold 'a tongue cause she a woman.

I help Miemay out to the front porch.

She the only woman in all of Zion ever lived alone. People tried to stay with 'a, and force folks on 'a, but she always make it a point to tell 'em they visiting. Sooner or later, she tell 'em they got to git. I'm the only one she ever let sleep under 'a roof without raising sand all the time.

Miemay definitely something else, and I love 'a for it. She the only one ain't asking me when I'm getting married, or who I'm sweet on all the time. Now that I'm 20 almost 21, seem that's all folks talk to me about. By the time most girls get 22, they got 4 or 5 children. Guess that's cause that's all it is to do here in Zion, get married, raise a house and fill it with children. Iain got no desire to lay with no man or carry his kids.

After we sitting on the porch for a minute she use 'a cane to get up. I catch all the weight she gimme then walk with 'a. I help 'a down the three steps in the front of 'a house. We walk round, look at the other house they spose to be building. The frame up, and the floors laid but it's naked. Lumber and stuff in the barn, but nobody come to work on it no more.

When David and Zachariah first came back from Tuskegee, they got assigned projects to do since they know bout farming and building things better than anybody else. Zion a town of about two thousand niggers that stayed after slavery. Some of us are artisans, draymen, carpenters, seamstress, blacksmiths, mechanics, builders and field hands. So everybody and everything we need right here. Everybody can do a little bit of everything.

All the women learn to sew and cook enough to take care of they families. Miemay joke, say the women of Zion done made enough dresses to bury and marry half the world. All the men show up to raise houses for new families, I go too. All the other women meet for quilting circles to make drapes, sheets and all the other linen needed. Sometimes, I do quilting circles too.

Zion ain't the kind of town you can move to, you either born here or marry into it. I could name everybody here, and tell how we related cause all of Zion made up of seven plantations; Neville, Remington, Belanger, Atwell, Beaumont, Kendall, and Harper. I won't though, that would take all day. We our own world, don't need much from outside, got our own livestock and grow almost anything you could think to eat.

With the railroad coming through, we ship to the other towns and cities round us. Niggas working in neighboring towns or travelling on the railroad come to our little town for supplies and to stay at our hotel. This the only place niggas can stay for miles.

We live pretty good our parents keep telling us, compared to other niggas, compared to old times. We got our own store, school, church, paper mill, post office, cotton gin, hotel, barbershop and a little paper the church put out. Plus we own the land we living on. Doing better than a lot of poor whites, too.

It's a town called Dewey bout 15 miles southwest pass Kendall, it's all poor whites. Folks say they got hit the hardest by the war, cause they was overseers and workers when it broke out. More of them went to fight, and got killed, or maimed. So they hate us here in Zion.

They say we take all the jobs cause white folks hire us over them. But white folks won't pay us like they do other white folks. And for the little they pay, we work harder without complaining. Then, white women think it's nigga work to be wet nurses, cooks and maids. Sometimes I think them folks in Dewey gone stay poor. That's why they always looking for a reason to hang one of us, or set fire to something here in Zion. So Miemay taught us to always let on like we ain doing so good, specially when we selling our goods in Dewey.

Since we surrounded by the seven plantations, and our grandparents were owned by they owners, that keeps them folks from Dewey and the Klan out of Zion. Been a few years since they hung somebody out of Zion, but they always hanging somebody. Some of the women still working in the houses round here for a lil nothing as wet nurses, maids and such. The men fix things, work the land and do what they can, otherwise we stay to ourselves. Don't travel at odd times of the night, less folks sneaking to Uncle Lucius place, he make it a shine house some nights. We don't allow no trouble makers to rile us up, don't get into no politics and just work hard on our little town.

Everything in Zion shared in a way. We share the work and the profit from the land. We all help each other out with meeting the crop deadlines. Specially when it rains a lot and folks get behind. It's a Planter's Calendar at church and that's how we know who growing what and if they need help.

Miemay ain't tied into Zion like most folks. Grandpa Jim bought some land before the Freedmen Bureau parceled out land. So she own tenant properties with sharecroppers on 'em and Zion's town store. Since she own so much land, and the store—her voice just as important as all the business men's voices in Zion, so she have to have a say in everything.

For Miemay not to know how to read, she sho know how to add and run 'a business. Them sharecroppers ain't making enough money to pay 'a nothing really, so she stock the store with some of they crop and buy whatever they don't grow from Zion. Iain never seen 'a work in that store. One of 'a children always there, usually one of the boys. For the last few years she been having me do the books and order things. She sell special stuff there too, roots and herb medicine.

They lynch strangers, what they call trouble makers. Only stranger ever come to Zion white folks like was this man Booker T. Washington. Niggas say he spoke for niggas to the president, so it was an honor when he came to speak at the church. Folks was beaming when he said, "Zion is a shining example of what Negroes could be if we use our resources." He's the reason when we can, Zion send some of the boys to Tuskegee to learn how to make the town better. In fact, he just died last November. Some of the men went up to a ceremony dedicated to him at Tuskegee to pay they respects. When they came back, all they talked about is how nice the niggas' houses were on campus and in the area.

We'd already built a new hotel, church, school, and store fore they left, cause those is the center of Zion. Then we built David and Zachariah nem's family a house, they mama was so happy. Then David got married, so we built him a house. Then Zachariah build him a house even though he ain't got no family. They been teaching us how to lay wiring and install plumbing.

All the houses got to be rebuilt here in Zion, cause these log cabins ain't made for plumbing. We use to fix up the cabins, til we got new tasks and schedules what we work round the crop schedule. The new schedule say, we spose to build at least three new houses a year.

Miemay ask for a new house next, and they grumble bout it cause she older and don't let nobody live with 'a, and 'a kids grown. All they could think about is how much they needed electricity, or how tied they is of using outhouses. Still they started 'a new house but something else always seem more important.

After Washington's memorial, the men came back with a new wind, and we got back on building Miemay house for a while. Then she sick again.

And ever since spring, when Germany sunk the Lusitania, there's been talk of war. President Wilson is up for re-election next year. He built a whole platform on the fact that he kept us out of war. Still, there are rumors about arms factories hiring groves of niggas. We don't know if America preparing for war, or just supporting the side she wont to win with supplies. Another rumor going round say, the Lusitania was carrying ammunition. So Zion's men been getting they own affairs in order, in case they have to go overseas and fight.

I work on Miemay house all the time, what I know how to do by myself. My brother Isaiah come help when he mad, and need space from his wife. Most of the men come help like that too, to get away in the middle of the week.

Spose to have five bedrooms, two bathrooms, look like any white person's house. Raised up high off the ground so when it rain a lot, it don't flood. Miemay ordered the pieces for the house out of a Sears catalog. Then a kit came on the railroad with all the parts.

Miemay say she want two floors like the houses they showed 'a in the picture. It's a beautiful sound house too, specially since we made all the mistakes on the first buildings, and this one came with instructions. Once we get started everybody pleased; it's the biggest and best house in Zion now.

The day is nice, a cool breeze chasing all the heat away.

Uncle Joseph and Auntie Eartha, David and Zachariah's folks, told Miemay to come stay with them cause they got ceiling fans. Say it's too hot to be in 'a cabin. She tell them to hurry up and finish 'a house, and she won't need to stay with nobody else. Miemay love 'a cabin, I cain't imagine 'a ever leaving it, even when this house done, but she say she will.

Finally, we get in front of her new house. Miemay just stand in front of it, with 'a face sour. Then look up at the sky, like she specting rain.

I don't say nothing, just marvel at how big and beautiful her house is.

What culla youa paint dis house?" she ask, looking down all sad, and I'm thinking she might be scared she gone die fore she sleep a night in it.

"Want to sneak over here and sleep a night?" I smile, goosing 'a.

She jump and slap my hand away. She hate being tickled.

I look at the house for a long time, think about paint colors. All the other new houses in Zion white. I think about that picture of a house, it's all black and white, so any light color would look white. Then I realize Ion know what color that house

14

is. Then I think about some of the houses I done seen when I go with Daddy to sell our crops. "A nice soft tan. Keep some of the white and get you some dark brown shudders, or maybe even dark red, match that brick round the bottom. Be real nice." I smile, proud of my suggestions, knowing it'll be nice, like this house I seen in Greenville.

"Humph!" She look at it, with a twinkle in 'a eye and I know she can see it too. Us just stand there and think about how nice it's gone be. Then 'a face fall.

So I say, "But what I know, Iain never had no house, and Iain never gone have one neither, less I get married." I'm getting grounded by the thought of being with Mama and Daddy for the rest of my life. I'm running from my thoughts, so I say, "Ion wont no husband."

"Gittin marred ain't nothin," Miemay huffs, seeming to catch my sadness and dispute it.

After we standing there a while, I look around for somewhere for 'a to sit. I get nervous, cause folks been talking bout how she going any day now. She look tired to me, but I don't know nothing bout dying cept what I hear. My aunts say one day was a good day or another day was bad for 'a. They all seem the same to me. She almost ninety-six, so Ion spect she gone get along like she use to, but it don't mean she won't live to be a hundred.

"They ain fix dis house," Miemay comment bitterly, then look around. "Wait'n fa me ta die, I spect," she spit, then raise a cane pointing at the truck. "Tek me round ta dat chuch."

Since Miemay sick, they leave a truck here with me most times, case something happen. I'm the only woman know how to drive. That's why I'm always here, too, cause if not, when other women come to visit, they husbands would have to stay, too.

The church the center of Zion, everything happens there and somebody always there. Use to be a school, Monday through Friday. We have all our town meetings and things there. Use to have dances there, too, til somebody said it ain't right dancing in the Lord's house. Then they stopped doing the monthly

15

dances and just do formals at the hotel. Don't matter much, Uncle Lucius jug joint take up the slack.

*　　*　　*

When we get to the church, it's quiet. Then I see my cousin off in the distance with his shirt off, wiping his forehead. When he look down, he jump, then disappear in the ground.

"Tek me ova thur," Miemay say, looking in the same direction.

We take slow steps, and my heart beating again. When my cousins tell everybody I had 'a out here in this heat, and she spose to be dying, Lord knows what they gone say to me.

I hear scraping and see dirt coming up from the ground. The closer I get the more I see the hole.

"Who grave ya diggin?" Miemay ask right smartly, leaning on 'a cane glaring at 'em in the hole. You'da thought Abner, Joseph and Thomas seent a ghost way they face fall. I turn my head, to keep from laughing in they face. "What wrong witcha, boy? Aincha hear me talk'n ta yah?"

"Uh . . . um . . . see . . . we," Abner stutters, looking round at his brothers, like they holding some words for 'im to collect. Miemay stare at 'im, in the eyes, and he swallow whatever lie he bout to tell. Now, I'm feeling nosey and wont to know too.

"We . . . um . . . doing what Reverend Patrick say, Miemay."

"Is ya fool? Oh! Ya thank Miemay fool! Dat ain't what I ax chu, boy."

We all stand in silence then it hit me, they digging her grave. I'm sad, and it ain't funny no more. First, I thought we spooked 'em cause they in a graveyard grave and here we come, but now I know why the cat got they tongue.

"Yall dig mah grave, but ain't fix mah house. Gone see bout dis Sunday. Betcha won't be dead by den," she fuss, pointing 'a cane at 'em.

"Wont me to take you round to his house," I offer mad, too.

"Nah, I wont's ta git 'im Sunday in front of dat chuch! He prolly ain eben at 'is house," she thinking. "Dig my damn grave an Iain dead," she say under 'a breath. She so hot she don't even need no help back to the truck, she walking good. Miemay fuss all the way home bout them not fixing 'a house, but digging 'a grave.

I don't say nothing, I hardly ever say anything just think a lot.

*   *   *

Cause Miemay say she don't want to sit there all day with folks rather see 'a dead than in 'a new house, I take 'a to church when service almost over. When we walk in, the church get quiet, all eyes is on us. We both wearing pants. Women wear dresses everywhere here, even in the fields, so us wearing pants to church ain't really welcome.

Miemay been wearing pants since I can remember. When I started staying at 'a house all the time, she fixed me a pair. Mama and Daddy protested, but it don't make no never mind. She told 'em she got work for me to do cain't be done in a dress. I love wearing pants. Like all the women in Zion I sew too, so I'm always making me and Miemay a pair of pants. Now, we all washed up and greased for service in our nice pants.

Reverend Patrick lifts his hand to welcome us. Miemay don't come to church for nothing but weddings, funerals and town meetings. Since I been taking care of 'a, I don't come much neither. Til Mama realize I ain't been in a while, so she send one of my sisters to care for Miemay. They always complain Miemay too much to handle. So I cain't even remember the last time I was here on a Sunday.

"Come have a seat down front," Reverend Patrick offer, his face lighting up, while using his hand as a signal for some of the women sitting on the front row to move, and make room. This is a good day for him, he been praying for Miemay's soul long as I can remember. Even more lately, since he think she dying.

"Ain come ta sat, bout ta die and I got some thangs ta say foe I go. Foe ya push me in dat hole ya dug." She point at 'im then start stepping lively, we moving on up to the pulpit.

I hear people making noises of shock, whispering and moving they weight round on them wood benches. I ain't never seen a woman in the pulpit, don't know if anybody has, but Miemay ain't just a woman, she our mama. When we get up there and turn to face the church, all of Zion looking at us and I feel shy.

Reverend Patrick offer us the mike, but Miemay turn 'a head to it and tug my arm saying, "Ya say what I say so's dey can hear me."

My heart drop but I don't flinch, I just say, "Yes, ma'am." Then I say it almost like her: "The other day, I came to the church after I looked at my house. Had Linny take me round, tied of laying down, I can sleep when I'm dead." She pause and laugh a lil mean, looking round for anybody got the nerve to laugh, too. They don't.

We go on, "Then I see one of my grandsons over here with his shirt off in the graveyard. After I talk to him, I find they digging MY grave. But as you can see, I ain't dead yet, and my house ain't fixed neither. So much as you wont me to crawl in that hole you digging, it ain't time yet. So if you gone send yah children to do something for me, you send them to fix my house and help get it in order. Send them today, cause we ain't promised tomorrow and everybody know, specially Reverend Patrick, I sho ain't."

*   *   *

When the roosters crow, I wake up. I'm starting me and Miemay's breakfast when I hear folks moving round outside. Looking out the window, I see what looks like most of the men of Zion. I run to tell Miemay but stop dead in my tracks when I see 'a laying the way she is, with 'a arms up and fingers together on a chest like she in a coffin. I cain't tell from here if she breathing, but she look peaceful.

18

Sometimes when she sleep, I put my hands over 'a mouth to see if I can feel 'a breath. I worry all the time she ain't gone wake up, even though I know one day she gone die. We all is really. A little sadness come over me and my heart feel heavy.

"Ain dead yet," she say, moving and scaring the bejesus out of me.

"They out there," I announce, pleased and relieved and happy she still alive.

"Bout time," she push 'aself up. It's ironic, this morning she stronger than she been in a long while. She even fanning me away, look at 'a nah.

A smile escapes me.

She getting 'a own cane.

I stand close to 'a, to catch 'a if she fall.

"Gone nah chile," she fuss, walking at me with 'a cane. Walk so good look like she don't need it. "Let's git some ta eat."

"Yes, ma'am!" I smile and follow 'a to the kitchen.

When we sit down, I serve 'a grits, eggs and toast. She point to the jarred apples. I open it and put some on 'a plate, and some on mine.

"I wont ya ta stay with me, so's I can tell ya some thangs." Soon as she start to talk, the front door open on us.

"Yall up?" Reverend Patrick ask and we both nod yes. "These boys gone work on that house and paint it like ya say."

Miemay nod 'a head like he ain't said nothing special. Turn 'a nose up, let 'im know she still mad bout that grave digging business.

He just stare at 'a for a while, then go back out. I hear him give 'em orders. He kinda like run the town, since everything happen at the church.

"See if Zachariah and David out thur, Patrick don't know nothin bout no 'letricity," Miemay order.

So I get up and run outside to make sure they here.

Chapter Four

I'm sitting on the front porch separating tabacca leaves for curing, when I see the dust gathering on the road, way a car do, not a wagon. It's Reverend Patrick, as always, but he got a white man in the backseat with 'im. When he stop, he jump out and get to strutting like the only rooster in a hen house to get the white man's door. Make me laugh a little bit.

"Where Miemay at?" he ask, like he ain never been to 'a house.

I just nod towards the front door, cause whatever he up to, I ain into putting on with 'im.

"You ain gone tell 'a we here? This the lawyer, Mr. Prescott, *she*, ask for," he order me more than ask.

I don't say nothing else cause folks round Zion just knock, they don't go round announcing they comings and goings. Not even for white folks. I know this white man from Beaumontville, it's just one town over. Done seen 'im a thousand times, and he sure to know us all. Plus Reverend Patrick done brought 'im, and he say Miemay know he coming, so cain't be no harm. On top of that, Miemay ain't the type of woman need warning. Shoot, folks need to be warned bout her.

"Well what she doing? Don't want to go in there if she laying down," he looking round trying to get me to go back and forth with 'im.

I still don't speak, cause now he insulting Miemay. Ain't no nigga worth nothing can sleep through them roosters crowing, and it's the middle of the day, too. Sick or not, I got to fight Miemay to rest. Since he talking crazy, he really can ask that white man to wait and go check on 'a hisself.

Acting like he ain been over here every other day since we was told she gone die. He come to pray for 'a soul, and to beg 'a to come back to church, and get 'a heart right with the lord. He talk to 'a while she laying down some of them times. He usually come and go without even knocking on the door, much less being announced. Now I think I know one reason why Miemay don't go to church, after seeing all this putting on.

Finally, when I'm tied of him looking at me I say, "She cooking some kinda stew."

"What chu here for if she cook'n 'a own meals? Spect you got 'a doing 'a own laundry, too. Aincha?"

"If she wont," I say, feeling like I got to explain, or else my mama be over here fore the day end. "Say she tied a being fussed over. So I wait til she get tied then I finish whatever she done got started. Always just let 'a do much as she can, try to stay out 'a way, and never get more than a ear shot way from 'a."

"She wouldn't have no choice if somebody older was walkin 'a home. You over here letting 'a do whatever she wont," he chastises me, gripping his belt buckle and fronting like he making a real statement.

"I's jus doin what I been told, Reverend." I speak in a slow drag, so my silence don't look like insolence to the white man. Make 'im think I'm slow and dumb and Reverend Pat even dumber for arguing with me, or a big bully. Then I bite my lip hard, to keep from laughing.

"That's enough, Patrick. Iain got all day, boy. Get on in there, and let Miemay know I'm here." Mr. Prescott settles it.

I feel Reverend Patrick looking down at me separating this tabacca. I'm holding my "good nigga" pose, while he being a trouble maker. I stare humbly at the ground. A tear escapes me, I want to laugh so bad. Look like I done out foxed 'im, and he got to quit showing out and do what he shoulda done from the beginning, leave Mr. Prescott on this porch and check on 'a hisself.

"Hot day ain't it?" Mr. Prescott finally say after staring at me for what feel like a long time. So long I get a little nervous.

I don't say nothing or look up at 'im either, just nod my head yes like Miemay told me. Miemay say just nod your head, and they leave you alone, think you dumb and no threat. Iain really figured out how to talk to white folks no way. My daddy or Reverend Patrick always speak for me. Reverend Patrick usually speak to 'em for all of Zion.

Here in Zion, we serious bout our relationship with the white folks in neighboring towns. We keep our eyes to the ground like I'm doing, and try not to say much. Shoot, with the Black Codes, any kinda response could be taken as disrespect, and a reason to be jailed or worse, hung.

Shoot, it's a law called Reckless Eyeballing. Reckless Eyeballing get you hung. We so afraid of being accused of doing something to somebody white, we get off the sidewalk if a white person passing, if we even use the sidewalks. Ain't as bad for nigga women as it is for our men. If men strangers, they automatically vagrants. A man could be in prison for years on a vagrancy charge.

Ever since the Union pulled out and Reconstruction ended, the old Confederates been mad they lost the war. So they made up all these crazy laws trying to keep niggas slaves. The rest of the country done turned they back on us niggas in the south. We wont to work in our own fields and stay in our own town, but they make laws forcing us to work in they homes and fields. We scared to be round 'em, and wont to be left alone, but they always needing niggas for something.

Some of our men, arrested after Reconstruction, who survived prison said it was worse than being a slave. If a man goes to prison here, they work him for long hours without pay. If he get tired, they use the whip on him just like during slavery, but they beat 'im worse than they woulda in the old days. The difference is, niggas don't belong to nobody now. Ain't nobody paid for 'im. So the white man beating him don't care if he die or not. A white man's dog got more value than jailed niggas.

Then they get all kinds of diseases in jail. Soon as a man get convicted, his mama start mourning cause folks don't spect he'll make it home. I heard one of the men say, they fed him so little, every day he had to fight for food. They say, the strongest men treat the weakest like women at night. Ain never heard nothing that crazy.

Reverend Patrick come back out, hold the door open. "Mr. Prescott, sir, she ready forya." They both disappear in the house. I start looking out at the corn growing, and missing the fields.

The fields gimme time to think, and stay out folks' way. When you round the house, people expect you to talk too much about nothing. I rather work or read.

The door open again, Reverend Patrick come sit down next to me, done got his self some cold lemonade. He looking at me all crazy again, til he get some corn I got waiting in baskets, and start shucking.

"Most folks just tell me what they last wishes is. What Miemay need a lawyer fa?"

"Why you ain stay in there and find out?" I ask, jabbing him a little bit. He always in somebody business. We sitting in silence, and I'm thinking. The more I think the more I realize, everybody in Zion in everybody business, guess he ain't no different. So I say, "Iain know nothing bout no lawyer til yall showed up."

"You know I woulda stayed," he say and smile a little looking over at me, "but she told me to 'git'." He roll his eyes like a child do, and I smile at him being told to git.

I don't say nothing else.

We work in silence til the white man come out. Reverend Patrick jump to his feet, and Miemay come behind the white man, no cane, her hand on the door way. I jump up to help, but the way she look at me, I know she okay and don't want no help.

"I'll draw it up. Just send word to Beaumontville when you get two witnesses."

"We right here," Reverend Patrick offer smiling, thumbing his suspenders and poking his chest back out.

"Nah ya ain't," Miemay fuss at Reverend Patrick. "Linny, go show Mr. Prescott dah house back there."

"I could show 'im." Reverend Patrick beams proudly, still showing out.

"Nall, you can shuck dat corn why she gone," Miemay order, before dropping the screen door on any disputing he might do, disappearing in the house.

Chapter Five

I love mornings before the rest of the world wakes up, before the roosters' start crowing, and before you expected to do anything, or be anyone, or go anywhere. It's just you and God, and the sun, and the dew on the grass. It's you alone with your thoughts, and the early birds. The smell of morning has no word or sound to push into dreams so you can sort things out.

Mornings are better than the end of the day quiet moments before sleep. In the morning, you are not tired from the day, or worried bout tomorrow. In the morning, feels like the night has washed away the footsteps of yesterday, and you could do anything, go anywhere. If you get up before everyone else, the morning is slow, patient and you enter the world peaceful. Getting up fore everyone, it's like you got control of the day, and you go into the world only after you ready.

Yesterday was wash day, so today all is silent cept the wind whipping through the clothes outside on the line. The fog done settled on the earth, leave it cool for when the sun finally get up.

After I start the stove, cook me and Miemay breakfast and we eat, I leave Miemay to 'a cooking. Go looking for some pants she don't wear that much to cut. I don't want to get none she gone miss. Reverend Patrick say Miemay house be done in bout two weeks. So today the women coming to Miemay's for quilting. We gone make curtains, a table cloth, pillows, sheets and whatever else Miemay say she need, so it'll all be ready when the house done.

Quilting is one of the biggest social events for women along with Spring Promenade, getting married and baby showers. It's house raising for men. I quilt and go to house raisings, too.

They both feel the same in some respects. We all working hard towards something, and learning from each other. Whoever got a good idea, they share it, and we all better for it. Great grandmothers, grandmothers, mothers and daughters learn from each other, get to know each other better. Great grandfathers on down do the same for they boys when we building houses.

The men don't like to talk around me, so when I go Iain really welcome. I still like house raisings though, cause I get to work side by side with my brothers and Daddy. I like working with all new things and the idea of putting something together a family can grow in.

Was a time when me and Daddy was real close. He use to say proudly, I was his favorite child cause I didn't whine like my brothers, or strut around like some kinda princess the way my sisters do. He said I learned quick and was a hard worker. So I was the only girl he took with him when he went to work on things, or sell crop in neighboring towns.

Way I am, use to be a relief to him. I what'n never sweet on no boy, but now I think he wondering when I'm gone be sweet on somebody and get married. Now he always after me to act like a lady, saying I cain't be no tomboy forever.

I love quilting cause it's the one place women don't seem to be at odds with each other, or themselves. Whoever makes the best cornbread dressing, roast, string beans, macaroni or whatever is appreciated and praised. Nobody in competition like they usually is round here. It's the one place I feel free being all parts of me, cause you gotta bring every part of yourself to quilting.

This the only time other women, and my mama, appreciate me being different, stronger. Here, I'm helpful. They tell me to move things, lift things, and do things they'd usually ask a man, but cain't since they ain allowed here while we quilt.

Women seem to reconnect with each other and find parts of themselves they gave up for love, children, family and God. We laugh, sometimes they cry, but we all eat good. Quilting is a sacred space where victories, battles, dreams, fears and sorrows are shared, then weaved in blankets.

A good quilt has the signature of almost every woman in Zion. Not just in the making and planning it, but the pieces come from our lives. Quilting different from house building, cause it take a whole bunch of old stuff, scraps of time and become something new.

Most quilts got little pieces of suits, shirts, wedding dresses, christening blankets, even baby blankets of babies held in them too short a time. We keep friends and family done went on to glory, or just left Zion close with quilts.

I'm going to take some of the first pants Miemay gave me, and a few pieces from one of 'a pants as my part. I keep some of 'a pants for myself, for later, for other quilts. I think, whenever she go, I won't be allowed to wear no more pants, and I want to remember these days, I want to remember Miemay. I want to wrap 'a stubbornness round me and other folks when the world telling us who and what to be. I'm gone keep so much of 'a clothes every time I quilt a little piece of 'a be in it.

I'm helping Miemay cook, lost in my thoughts. Miemay making 'a famous pies and cobblers. It already smell good in here, the sweet potato pies is done. I'm thinking bout how Miemay make things just right, and even though folks say I'm a good cook and my food taste like her's, I cain't seem to get it just right.

I'm trying to be here now, and not start missing 'a before she gone. She been real tired lately, and I can see the fight in 'a to stay. I don't like to think about it, cause now, I'm wondering bout 'a soul too.

"Gone spit it out, chile, been wontin ta ax fa ever," Miemay order, pushing in my head, cutting the silence. She been reading my mind like all the time. It work out most times, cause I don't talk a lot, but right now it's hard, I don't want to ask 'a this.

"You ain't gone have no peace les ya know," she encourage me more.

I search for the words, not to be disrespectful.

"Jus ax me. Iain gone hold it ginst ya." Miemay smile.

For a long while I'm kneading dough silently, waiting on the words. Miemay cooking pie fillings on the stove. I knead the dough harder, trying to find the words in it. Feeling like I might cry, I breathe slow, and work through it, I don't cry. Finally, I feel strong enough to hear the answer, so I ask the question, "You think you going to heaven?"

Miemay don't answer right away, but that's how we is, ain't no rush. Sometimes a question or some words linger in the air for days.

I feel a little ashamed like me asking is like letting 'a down. Everybody got something bad to say bout 'a. I don't wont 'a to think I think she the devil, too. I'm just so use to Jesus being our lord and savior, and she ain't never said nothing make me believe she "saved." Until recently, I didn't realize I was worried about Miemay's soul. I mean, with all this talk of 'a dying.

She don't seem to have the same relationship with God other folks do. When something bad happen, or they worried, people always say I will pray for you, or they ask each other for prayer. Miemay just say she hope things work out. Sometimes she tell them how to work it out, or how to bare it.

"Don't know nothin bout no hebin. Jus know itsa God. Been baptized. Know Jesus real. Know bout light an dawknis. Done led plenty lost souls ta light. I know the way ta light, and the light feel peaceful. Hard ta stay way from it waitin on dis house ta git fix. Some folk full a light, others fulla dawknis. You got lotsa light, Linny." She smile, and I smile back at 'a, as I press the crust down in the tins for the pie.

I think about 'a waiting to go til 'a house get fixed. After while, I press for certainty, "So, you ain't scared of hell?"

"Iain scurda hell, already been there." Miemay twist 'a mouth solemnly, and she get lost in 'a own thoughts while turning them apples in one pan, and peaches in another.

"Yall ain't ready yet?" Eileen ask, opening the front door, her and Anita carrying big pots of chitlins. I can tell by the smell. Cain't nobody cook chitlins better than Anita and Eileen. I don't eat 'em myself, but if I did this would be a good day for 'em.

I look up to acknowledge them, Miemay in 'a own world now don't even seem to see them. Maybe Miemay worried bout 'a own soul and hell, too.

Eileen go kiss Miemay on the forehead, run 'a hands over 'a hair. Take a real good look at 'a. We all worried bout Miemay.

Anita go hug 'a, put 'a hip next to Miemay's and sway a little for a minute til Miemay smile a bit. We should be in good spirits.

Then Miemay look over at me, and I know our conversation ain't over, and they know they done interrupted something.

"Good afternoon! Good afternoon!" Matilda and Ondrea cheer, stepping in the front door. They bring red beans, white beans, corn bread, rice and oxtails.

Everybody hug and laugh like they don't see each other every Sunday. The house get louder and louder as the men bring they wives and daughters on wagons with food, and chairs and they materials.

After Miemay fill the pies, I go on the steps and watch as Uncle Jethro pull off, sadly smelling all the good food gathering in Miemay house.

"Miemay, you already got all this stuff a few times over," cousin Yolanda accuses playfully, but is seriously trying to divvy out the work among us. Miemay moving round the kitchen looking under foil and examining things while Yolanda waiting for some clarity, I guess.

"New house, new thangs! A new woman gone be moving in dat house!" Miemay smile stepping round the table lively like she dancing a bit. We all laugh at this and are much obliged.

Chapter Six

"Cain't right nah!" Miemay growl low, arguing with somebody. The kerosene lamp burning low on 'a night stand next to me, and for a moment I think I see a man at the foot of 'a bed. Then I look at 'a, she wide awake.

"Who you talkin to, Miemay?" I ask, standing up from my corner seat, where I fall asleep sometimes reading. We both looking in the same direction but I don't see nothing now and she look like she still do.

Her fists balled up and she holding 'a arm to 'a body like she been snatching it away from somebody.

I'm scared some, but I don't let on. Miemay told me when people bout to die they talk to dead people. I figure she been visited by spirits all 'a life, so I don't know if they here cause she bout to die.

Ever since I was old enough to understand, white folks been coming to 'a to hear bout they future and to find the meaning of they dreams. She speak to people kinfolk that already crossed over. That's another reason, I think she don't go to church. Everybody pretty much done said she ain't right. I don't know bout that, but she spooking me right now. Still, I'm more use to it than I use to be when I first started staying here. Miemay always know things bout things, it's her way.

"Linay, come 'ere, lay down witcho Miemay."

I see the tears in 'a eyes welling and I try to remember to breathe, and be strong. I ain't the one dying soon. I think, I wouldn't want to go alone. And I think, who will be there for me? I'm worried that in the morning, only one of us will open our eyes. I want to light that candle in the corner where I saw the man, or turn up the light on the lamp, but I don't.

"Was just a gull when Massa Belanga buy me. Use ta be a curse ta be a pretty gull like you is. He say, I gone wuck in 'is house fah 'is wife. I was eleben the first time. He kep comin most nights fah bout thurdy years. Got thirteen chirun by 'im, well, what survive. Anyhow, the Missus beat me, bun me, cut ma hair and everthang she can thank of. I pray she make me ugly, make 'im stop. No matter what, he kep comin.

"Den war break out, dis two diffrent countries, Norf an Souf. Massa pay poe white mens ta tek 'is turn in the war. The rich massas talk bout suppotin the soljuhs, cause dey ain't neva wont ta fight. Den all the poe mens kilt an maimed so, ain eben no man no moe what come home. All the massas go den, ain nobuddy else ta send foe 'em. Last time he come ta me, was the night foe he went ta war. I pray the Union kill 'im.

"Massa gone. Word was, the Union comin, an our days as slaves was numbered. Ain nobody here ta make us stay neitha. Ever nigga wit two good legs an eyes see ta runnin. Folks say niggas fightin in the Union ginst the Souf. Den, all the white men at home gone put a stop ta dat.

"Git a posse togetha of mad white mens missin dey arms, an legs, an wounded. Dey hunt niggas. Niggas gittin hung lef an righ, starvin ta def in the woods.

"Thought bout runnin, Iain neva been scurd ta die, just cain't git mahself hung wit small bebbies. Else dey do ta mah gulls wut dey done ta me, an hang mah sons.

"Den I wont massa ta live, ta protect our chirun. Ain neva had no man I wont. Afta slavery ain wont nan nother one neitha. But chu need a man in the world, women's ain safe. Thank I gone wuck fah Massa Belanga, when ee come back, thank wrong. He treat me lak any otha nigga.

"Ain't give 'is own chirun nothin. Let the confedrets hang our son, his own son Woodrow. Look just lak 'im. Afta dat, I thank, I slit my own throat foe I ever let 'im touch me gin.

"Den, Papa Jim, been savin ta buy 'is freedom foe slavery end, when it look lak we gone be free, he kep dat money, kep on wuckin. Him an some moe skill wuckers what been savin git tagetha, buy the first pieces of Zion.

"Den, white folk done loss ever thang in the war, ain got nothin ta pay niggas ta wuck. Dey sellin land ta niggas, thangs what chu need ta farm, tryna scrape tagetha enough ta make it dey self. Land was dut cheap.

"Jim say, if I marry 'im, he'll tek care me and my chirun. So use ta Massa Belanga, when Jim come reachin foe me at night, it all the same by den. 'Cep I got ta act lak I lak it," she cries, and cover 'a face like she shame.

I pull 'a close to me, and wipe 'a tears. Ain never got this close to nobody since I was a child. Now I feel like Miemay a child who belongs to me. Her tears make me hate folks. Make me angry enough to kill. I hate ain't nothin I coulda done to spare 'a this. When my hands full of 'a tears, I smear them on my face like paint the way I hear Indians do fore they go to war.

We just lay there for a while, then she whisper, "Had three moe bebbies wit Jim."

When I think she sleep, she move 'a face way from me, breathing deep. I know she got something else to say. She move around in my arms til she laying a way she comfortable. The lamp burning so low, it's completely dark now. I'm laying here waiting til she start again.

"Felt bad, but Iain shed no tears when dat fever got Jim an kilt 'im. Mah boys men den, I feel safe. Ain got ta be touched no more, ain got ta be bothered no moe. Ain nothing like goin ta bed in ya own house knowin ain nobody gone be reachin fa yah, breafin on yah.

"Mah chirun done built houses and got family round me den, Zion a town. Ain feel by mahsef. People thank I got money, cause of the store, Jim's bidness and all us wuckin the fields. Ever man from here ta Luseana come ta prune mah garden. I tell 'em, 'mah boss dead an mah massa done set me free.' Ain wont nobody else, do what I wont in mah house. Ain got ta worry bout Massa whupin me, Missus burnin me, an ain no Jim full of dat oil beatin me fa ever lil thang. I's really free an Iain wont ta be no man's slave.

"Folks ain undastand why ain wont no nother man. Iain neva undastand why yung gulls so ready ta be 'a man's slave. Dey wont ta be held down by chirun. So what, folk ain undastand me, folk still don't undastand Jesus, ain gone undastand you. Everthan ain't fa ta be undastood.

"Jus know dis, ya daddy loves ya, and you was always 'is favorite. No matter what folk say, you a good gull. Smart, head strong, stubbun lak ya ol Miemay. Gotcho own mind an ya betta folla it, won't neva lead cha wrong. Got a good heart an a strong will. Don't be fraid a who ya is, what chu is.

"Live yo life, gull, cause cain't nobody live it foe ya. Just like you cry yo own tears, laugh yo laugh, enjoy yo famly, but don't let dem change ya. If ya cry, dig a hole an bury dem tears, an dat hurt so ya won't carry it whichu. And make sho what you cryin fa worf cryin bout. Dis don't mean nothin ta ya now, but one day you gone know what I mean. Long as Zion here, it be home.

"You ain got ta worry neitha. I tell ya all dis cause, if you don't wont no man, ain't got ta git one. You got famly, an ya safe hur.

"I prayed fa ya, Linny, but you ain like otha womens. Ain gone git married. Gone be a hard life fo ya when ya fus git goin. Den it git better. You gone have a good life, a good life," she say, sounding relieved.

"Jus rememba dis what I'm tellin ya when it git hard. I seent it maself. Um hmm. I seen you in pants. Thank on dis, I seent you in pants dancin wit a lady, like you was a man."

Chapter Seven

"Cain't let you do this." Reverend Patrick pleads with 'a, taking his hat off. I get up and start out the doe so he can sit down.

"Linay?" Miemay stop me in my tracks.

Apprehensive, I answer, "Ma'am?"

She look over at my reading chair, to let me know to go sit back down.

Reverend Patrick look at me annoyed. He want me to leave like what he saying private, and Iain seen 'im beg 'a to get right with the Lord.

Honestly, I want to leave so I don't have to hear this, again. Miemay told me don't leave 'a with folks less she say she wont to be left alone. I feel like her knight in shining armor. I git to tell folks things I couldn't never say myself, and when they getting ready to jump sharp, I say, "Miemay said."

Today is what I would say a bad day, too. Usually I don't agree with people, but I see Miemay getting weary. She say most folks know when it's they time. She promise to tell me when it's her's. Miemay say I'll be able to tell, too, cause when she ain't got to go no more and stop eating it won't be long. She ate a big breakfast this morning: bacon, eggs, biscuits and oatmeal. So cain't be today, shoot, or tomorrow.

Reverend Patrick disappear out the bedroom, then come back with a kitchen chair and sit next to 'a bed. Put his hat in his lap and really look at Miemay, for what look like the first time I done seen.

"Ever red the Bible, Patrick?" Miemay stir, her breathing ain't easy. I rise to help, but she fan me away. Push 'aself up in the bed, when the cover fall, her pale skin look thin. She look more fragile. Wonder how she put so much fear in folks.

"Kinda question is that? Read it all the time. I'm a man of-"

"The whole thang. Turn ever page." Miemay cut 'im off.

"Not straight through, but I spose I done turned bout every page. I mean, I reads it all the time," he finally say looking at 'a seriously. I realize he what'n never mad, but scared she going to hell.

"When I was a slave, all slaves go ta chuch wit dey massas. We set in the gallry fa niggas. The white preacha red in dat Bible how we 'pose ta be good slaves. Now niggas can read, yall say it say we pose ta be free. I cain't read, but I know the word in dat book ain't change, and what you say at dat chuch ain't what it say in dat Bible."

"Miemay, Jesus died for everybody."

"Who dey lynch niggas fa? Jesus ain't the only one got crucified."

"Miemay?" Reverend Patrick shake his head in disbelief, moving round in his chair. Like God might hear this and get them both right now, then he say, "You got to stop this kinda talk fore you die. I ain't never read bout no slavery in the Bible."

"You ain't red it all neither. Dat's what dat is."

"President Lincoln said the Civil War bloodshed was God's punishment for slavery."

"Dey shot Lincoln in the head on Good Friday."

"Oh, Miemay! Come on now!"

"It's true. Massas red scripture to missus make 'a turn 'a head, or blame us fa bein rape. 'Be glad o barren woman, who bear no chirun. Cry loud, you who ain't got no labor pains, cause moe is the chirun a the desolate woman than huh who got a husban.' Ever red that in Galatians?" Miemay quote, speaking kinda proper like and I smile cause Iain never heard 'a speak proper.

Reverend Patrick look at 'a blank, like he don't want to be disrespectful, but he cain't believe them no scriptures in the Bible.

Miemay look over at me, to show 'im. These some of her favorite ones, I know where they at easy. I find the scriptures, grip the Bible so I don't lose either page, then I put the book in his hands and point them out.

He read 'em carefully. Look like somebody done turned a light on in a dark room, then he slam the book close, like he turning it back out. "Thank ya," he say leaning away from the

Bible, then passing it back to me. I wonder what it mean for him to accept slavery is The Bible God's way.

"You ain gone neva red the Bible den?" Miemay stare at him; he just look at the ground. Then she say, "Ever hearda Hagar?"

"Yes, ma'am," Reverend Patrick say, stirring in his seat like he wish she would get to the point or get off of this one.

I'm sitting on the edge of my seat, my spirit leaning in to hear better, cause Iain neva heard nobody talk bout the Bible like Miemay.

"She a slave, that ran away. God told 'a ta go back an submit ta the missus that gave 'a ta 'a husband Abraham ta be raped. And ya know she a slave, cause Sarah give 'a ta Abraham. Cain't give nobody but slaves away. You know she been rape cause she mad at 'a missus when she wit chile.

"So Hagar go back, but den Sarah have 'a own son. Sarah don't wont 'a son ta share 'is inheritance wit 'is own slave brotha. Sarah make Abraham git ridda his own son, Ishmael, what 'is name is. Abraham give Hagar one bottle a water an a loaf a bread, den sent 'em out in the wild. Some place call Buhsheeba."

"Cain't say I recall the story going like that." Reverend Patrick frown in disbelief.

"Miemay eleben when 'a own daddy, and massa, sell huh way from 'a ma and home, cause his wife don't like lookin at 'is nigga chirun. I so white, look just like dem otha Jefford's chirun. New massa, say I be 'is house nigga. I eleben first time massa come at night. Eleben. Where dat Bible God at den? Cussin us fa bein niggas.

"Ever seen a man whup'd in front of 'is own chirun, cause 'ee wuckin slow, cause 'ee tied? Ever seent a young gull stripped in front of the whole plantation, beat cuz she wont give 'aself ta the overseer? Ever see a man waiting outside 'is cabin, cause massa in there wit 'is wife? Cain't protect 'a, cain't save 'a.

"Know whut it like ta see folk ya love lynched, while white folk an dey white chirun you done wet nursed cheer? Ever seent a man burned alive? Hear 'im beg fo 'is life? How 'ee scream in the fire? That's what white Christians do ta us on Satday night, den be in chuch Sunday monin. Fa years, got ta sit in chuch gallry fa niggas and lissen ta how bein good slaves what God want."

"But Miemay, the Bible talks about freedom. Ain't that why yall name this town Zion, cause it's the land God promised his people?"

"Boy, Iain neva heard this no promise land. And ain't no woman had no hand in naming no town. Feel like Hagar, got cast out wit thurteen chirun. Massa Belanga wife ain't got but three, an he say ain't enough ta pay us and take care his famly. My chirun his famly too."

She laugh, then say, "Iain wont money, wont food foe our chirun. Folks dyin lef an righ from starvin. Lef me ta die, like any other nigga. Treat his chirun like regla niggas, afta he been comin ta me thurdy years. Least Hagar got water and bread.

"Dem white confederates mad at us fa being niggas. Mad at the world cause they lost the war. Dey lynchin us lef and righ. Nobody stand up fo us, not even Massa Belanga fa 'is own son. If I named dis town, woulda named it Buhsheeba cause we was wanderin round the wild when slavery end.

"God told Hagar, man hand gone be ginst huh son. White man hand ginst all my chirun, ginst the nigga. Ain neva heard bout no freedom in dat Bible. Hear bout being a good slave.

"Watch dem Bible readers hang my boy. Dey hung lots a young boys an gulls. Even pregnant gulls. We couldn't do nothing ta save 'em, nobody hep us. We begged dem, call Jesus and everbody else. Even prayin ain hep. Iain sayin ain no god, just sayin we on' know god plans, how he wuck.

"Sometime I ax mahself, who Paul? Who Daniel? I wonder bout Lot, offerin 'is virgin daughters ta all the town's men, to save strangers. I wonder bout a world where women don't have no say and women ain't protected. I wonder bout what we teachin our gulls, our womens. Den you gone come here, tell me repent foe I go ta hell." She laugh a little fore she go on. "Well, way I see it, I already been there."

Chapter Eight

"We done!" I hear Reverend Patrick bust into Miemay's front door announcing proudly. "Miemay? We done," he keep saying coming down the hall. I wait for him to reach 'a bedroom. I look at 'a; she don't budge.

When he knock, I say, "Come on." Soon as he see 'a laying in the bed, his demeanor change. He like a star losing its light as it falls. He still smiling proudly though, but she too tired to match his enthusiasm. It hurt 'im, when she don't immediately respond. I put down Zion's newspaper, we both waiting. I'm looking at him, having a silent conversation, while leaning into the wind listening for Miemay voice.

"Want me to take you over there to see it?" he offers, looking down at 'a like a kid on Christmas, sincerely happy.

I think he be honored to show 'a round. Tell 'a how he did this or that. They got such a strange love-hate relationship. Yeah, she don't like what he say in church, but he the one person come see about 'a the most. He one of the few people tell 'a how he really feel. And he be calling hisself doing something bout it. Cain't say the same for other folks.

These days she in and out of sleep, but she hear you. If you repeat yourself, it'll make 'a mad. I don't know how much time pass, when she finally stir and mumble, "Ia look in the monin."

Reverend Patrick look at me, grim, then step back gesturing for me to come look at 'a close.

I get up to go check on 'a, and she look back at me like a bright-eyed baby. This Miemay new, strange and spooky. Look like she don't even know me.

"I'm going git one of 'a daughters to come sit wichall," he offer sadly.

"Nah," I refuse shaking my head "no," too. Then I look down at Miemay. "She promised to tell me when it's 'a time."

Reverend Patrick look at me with disbelief. He got something to say, but he don't want to say it round Miemay. He looking back and forth between us, searching for the words. Finally he say, "I done seen lots a folks die too, and-" he stop when Miemay stir. "I'm gone run home cause I got some thangs to take care of, but I'll be back tonight."

When the sun bout to set, I fix Miemay supper on a tray to eat in bed. When I get back to 'a room, she done sat up, and threw 'a legs over the edge of the bed. Kinda scare me, cause Iain expect 'a to ever get up with the way things been going.

"Tek me ta dat house," she order out of breath like she been running from something or somebody. She got a fist planted on either side of 'aself, looking like she gone get up and go by 'aself if I don't take 'a back there.

We walking so slow, seem like forever before we reach the front porch. Got 'a cane, but she don't use it much as she leaning on me. When I pick 'a up, to carry 'a up the steps, I feel how 'a skin hanging on 'a bones. She don't weigh much at all. Feel like she wasting away, and that break my heart. I'm glad she get to see 'a house. I wonder who gone get it later.

When I climb the stairs carrying 'a, I hear how silent my steps are; they don't whine under our weight. Already this house sturdier than 'a old cabin. I put 'a down to open the door. Then turn to pick 'a up again.

"Ica walk," she protest, leaning away from me. Way she looking and breathing remind me of when Uncle Jimmy got drunk, and couldn't stand. Still, she always want to do for 'aself. I've learned not to force help on 'a. People need to feel they got some control, to test they legs and fall if that's what they wont. So I let 'a go in 'a own house first.

From the front door it open to the living room on the right, got the couches already set up in here. Right up front is the stairs. The floors are even, smooth, and polished cause the wood was imported.

Now Miemay can walk round barefoot, well, she do anyhow. Now Iain got to worry about 'a getting splinters the way she do sometimes on them uneven, rough floors in 'a cabin.

Here, the walls insulated, and I feel like I'm inside of something. Her other house part of outside, the wood on it make it look like it grew up tween the crops. The walls are logs, rough, and the spaces tween 'em let the cold through even though they been covered in newspaper, and mud, and white washed. Them walls she got now don't hardly keep the squirrels and possums out. Here, it ain't even a hole for a mouse to get through.

We walk around looking at the kitchen, with the new stove and electric icebox Miemay ordered from the Sears catalog. The kitchen big enough to eat in, but she made them build a separate dining room. I see the table me and the younger grandkids sanded. The furniture in here some of the best wood work I done seen, I done done.

We look in the first bathroom, it's got a sink, toilet and tub. Miemay just wanted a toilet down here, so she ain got to go up and down the stairs every time she got to go. Reverend Patrick said, "Thata be half a bafroom! Whoever heard of a half bafroom with just a toilet and sink?" So he put everything in this bathroom too, a tub, and it's big.

The house all fixed up, curtains hung and everything. The other women done come and made it a home for Miemay. All she really got to do is move in, put 'a own personal touches round here. They wanted to move 'a things in here, too, but she wouldn't let 'em. Say they go when she go.

"How ya lak dis piano?" Miemay ask weakly, laughing. I'm so gone, Ion even notice it sitting in the front room when we first walk in.

"Very nice. Very, very nice." I smile much as I can considering how down I feel. "What made you get this piano?"

"You," she say, smiling sad. "I always hoped you'd git back ta it. Maybe play yo Miemay a song every now an den."

I push down on a few of the keys, and the sounds seem to fill the house.

"I had dis dream, you was playin all the time," she get lost in 'a thoughts.

"Miemay, Iain played for years."

"It be a blessing ta have some music round here. Something other than what they playin in chuch. Back in the day, slaves sho could throw a party, gull. Ooh, they'd git ta clappin and dancin and sangin. Now since we free, everthang the devil. Folks don't jus sang ta sang, or play fa fun no moe. I miss the harvest festival, everbody jus outside round the fire, dancin, talkin, laughin and clappin." She imagining it, and smiling a little.

I press the keys one by one looking at it again. It seem like too much noise for how I feel. The keys echo through the house. I feel like I might cry. I breathe deep hoping a little air'll dry my tears.

"We ain looked at the study." She smile so we go arm and arm to the back of the house. "You ain got ta be readin ta me at the foot of mah bed no moe," Miemay offer, proud.

I just smile taking it all in, I'm gone miss reading at the foot of 'a bed.

There's a large wooden desk and matching chair in here that makes it look like real official business gone be done. There are bookshelves and two matching arm chairs on either side of a large picture window for readers.

"Miemay, you so funny. You done made them fix this room up like this and cain't even read," I tease 'a.

"I'm gone use yo eyes." She laugh leaning on me good.

I feel 'a getting tired, and I want to take 'a back to 'a cabin but she don't like being told what to do, not even if it's for 'a own good. When she take a seat in one of the arm chairs, I really look around. There are a few books on the shelves. I remember her arguing with Reverend Patrick bout this, too. I wonder now, if he ain't the one probly gone get this house in the end. Then he be glad Miemay got all this stuff.

"Come on." She push 'aself up on 'a cane. When we get to the steps, Miemay sit on the easiest one to get to. Seem like she trying to catch 'a breath. She lean 'a head on 'a cane, and look around when she can. I sit with 'a, waiting.

Now I think I know why she didn't really respond when Reverend Patrick came by. It woulda made it seem like he was right bout not building her a new house. He said she don't need no two story. If I have anything to say about it, I'll set 'a up in that study. It's a bathroom down here.

I turn the light off and on a few times. She smile at me, so I keep doing it til she put 'a head down. I think about how easy it is to turn lights on in here. I done it a dozen times in the building of all the different places, and never grow tired of it. This switch is extra special though cause it's in Miemay's house. Be glad when we get round to building my family a new house, and we don't have to use gas lamps, lanterns and candles. No more out houses either. I inhale the fresh scent of new wood all through the house.

"Let's go." Miemay push up again on 'a cane, then fall into the wall so I rush to catch 'a. Holding 'a up, we stand silent. I know she cussing 'a body for letting 'a down. Helping sometimes make 'a feel worse. So I let go slow, watching how 'a body sway even with the cane and wall supporting 'a. I stand close, waiting. She sturdy 'aself, then fan me away. Finally turning around to face the stairs, she look disappointed, like them stairs are a impossible mountain to climb.

"Hold tight to that cane." I grab 'a up from behind before she can fight me. She wrap 'a arms round my neck and rest 'a head on my shoulder without a word. We climb them steps together. I hear 'a sniff heavy then wipe 'a face with 'a hands. I feel like crying too.

I know she won't be here long. I ain't ready to let go. Now I realize what the years between us really mean. I see how the body break down, and cain't begin to understand how much she suffering. Still, it don't stop me from missing 'a, even as I hold 'a in my arms. I'm realizing she my best friend. The only person in the world that knows me. All this time I been thinking I'm here to keep her company. Now I see she been keeping me company. When she leave, I'm gone truly be alone.

We in and out of the four guest bedrooms cause they mostly empty cept for a bed, and window dressings. I leave 'a room for last. When we step in, I put 'a down on the bench at the foot of the bed. Examining the room, she sit on it like a throne. I'm proud, cause I'm the one made all 'a dressers and nightstands for 'a new electric lamps.

"Whew wee!" She smile, looking round nodding 'a head yes satisfied. "This room look like a real lady sleepin in here. I ain't neva seen nothin dis nice fa no nigga in alla mah days. Iain neva thought I would."

"And it's yours." I'm satisfied that she so pleased. I am so satisfied that she getting a chance to see it, I'm shaking my head "no" for some reason. I'm biting my lips and my heart is swelling up in me.

"Stop it!" Miemay bang 'a cane and stomp at me. "Don't chu cry fa me, gull! Ain no reason. I worried boutchu."

I catch my breath and I fight the tears. My heart hurting. I want to hide 'a from death, but it's coming and I know she bout to tell me. I want time to reverse itself, and start at the moment when she smiled, pleased, and I knew she was moved by this big beautiful master bedroom. Or go back just two years, when she was all bright eyed and sassy.

"Linny . . . you ain't no man," she say, looking back at the bed behind 'a, and running 'a hands over the new mattress.

I don't know why she saying that, what it has to do with anything.

"Ain't neva gone be no man," she exhausts, and I'm exhausted, too.

I want my heart to stop hurting, wont 'a to stop talking crazy. I just want 'a to stop talking, cause I'm afraid she gone say it, she dying.

"Ya ain't gone neva be nothin without no man. They ain gone neva let no woman be nothin fa all I done seent, and know bout this place."

"What?" is all I can muster without breaking into tears. I feel like putting my head in 'a lap and crying like a helpless child. Feel like she know I'm gone be alone without 'a, so she saying what everybody else been saying, I need to get me a husband.

"Ain't no endins, just beginnins. Ever time ya thank somthin ova anotha thang git goin. Pay attention, so you know when ta end a thang, when ta go, and where ta go. I was glad slavry was over, den Reconstruction wurse. Soon as we get use ta Reconstruction, the Union lef an afta dey go, wurse den anythang I ever seent in mah life. Some days it made me wont ta be a slave agin, but we made it through, now we here. Cain't believe we made it this long. Never thought Zion would last dis long," she say, thoughtful.

"Come 'ere, sat next ta ya Miemay." She pat the bench and scoot over.

When I sit down, she wrap 'a arm in mine, interlace our fingers, look into my soul and smile sadly.

"Took mah shoes off the otha day, so Ica put mah feets in the cool grass, keep my spirit settled in dis ol body.

"Maybe, Ia find the famly I was sold away from. Ain seen mah sistas and brothas since dey was sold. Don't even know how many I got. The otha night when you woke up and saw dat man at the foot of mah bed, that was mah son Woodrow comin fa me.

"It's mah time, been mah time. Spirits been coming ta git me almost a year nah. I pose ta died, like the docta say. Been waitin fa dis house ta be fixed, cause I know if Ida died they what'n gone do what I said, what I wont. Iain seen my mama since I was sold, she walkin round waitin on me. I'm tied Linny. This body tied, it hurt. It's been hard stayin hur. When Patrick come back, tell 'im ta git mah gulls, let dem walk me home, don't you do it. They need ta see dis body go, you know mah spirit."

Chapter Nine

I put another piece of wood in the stove, and poke the fire up, to warm the stew I made earlier. Then I go back and check on Miemay again. She in the bed stirring, and scowling like she in so much pain she might cry. I reach to help 'a, but she stop me with 'a eyes. I have to hold my own hands back by putting them together to keep from helping 'a, it's hard watching 'a struggle.

She moving like a small baby learning to use her arms and legs. Seem like comfort be just one leg this way, or a lean that way, but she seem to be moving against it. Cain't imagine how I look staring at 'a, but she say, "Ain nothin youca hep me wit. Been layin down too much is all," then she frown even more painfully than before and it's too much. So I walk back to the front, and realize how dark it is in here. How it ain't never enough light in here sometimes.

Feeling powerless, I walk out on the porch to get myself together. I'm wiping my eyes, sniffing, and thinking bout God, and death, and heaven, and hell, and Jesus. Think about 'a alone in the ground in the middle of the night. Think about all the funerals I done been to, where Iain feel nothing, and I was looking at folks cry wondering, but now I understand.

Disappointed, I cain't make myself stronger. I feel heavy, exhausted and my legs weak. Some weight pull my butt down hard and fast on the front steps. Seem like my spirit being eaten alive, so I lean and rock to stop the hurt. Heaving, I try to hold my head up on the banister. I'm ashamed. I bury my head in my lap to hide my face from the night. The night seem to know, and it be louder than me and quiet at the same time. The buzzing locusts and the passing wind in the trees take my sorrow with it.

After I wipe my face, and look up, the sky grayish blue and the earth wet, but solid. Moon behind so many clouds, seem like it ain't no moon. I feel how dark it is round Miemay house, and see how the light from 'a bedroom window spill into the night. I inhale the scent of too many cooked meals to count, soaked into 'a cabin walls and seeping out to mix with the night air. I breathe in the night, slow, and give it back the heat of hurt til I'm still. I breathe out the hurt, til I'm a tree and the wind just passing through my branches.

That's when I hear the bubbling of boiling stew. My footsteps in these work boots so loud it echo all through the house. I always wear these, but today, they disturb my peace as I go back in to check on the stew. I feel alone.

I grab a bowl, use a big spoon, try to get mostly the thick broth out the pot. Take some of the potatoes and carrots then squash 'im into a mushy soup. Start another pot, put more of the potage in there, then I take a lil beef and break it up. Miemay ain been able to eat nothing too heavy. When I get a thick broth with meat pieces, I make Miemay a bowl. She ain't ate all day. Not even breakfast, just a little water maybe and she almost choked on that.

I am a tree. I grab 'a tray and go back to 'a room. "Hungry?" I ask just above a whisper. She look like she going in and out of sleep. Her breathing loud. I put the tray on the dresser, then prop 'a up. She go along better this time. Her breathing ease, and it feel like this moment threatening to swallow me whole. I try to think about something else, and be here now. Putting the tray in front of 'a, I stir the soup.

She stare back at me hard, like she want me to stop, but I don't. She look too tired to speak, and I cain't accept what it mean if she don't eat this soup. Moving 'a head round, she seem to be tasting 'a own words, and trying to push 'em out. Finally she say, "Where Patrick?"

"He be back," I promise, hoping she will eat. Taking a spoon of the stew, I put it to 'a mouth. Put a little on 'a lips like I been doing. I don't know if it's the heat or the scent of it make 'a open 'a mouth, but she usually do once I do that. She don't open up, she turn 'a head to me, and my heart drop. I try again, pushing the spoon at 'a, then she turn 'a head toward the window and away from me, the spoon and life. Defeated, I drop the spoon back in the bowl, and she turn back facing forward. I wipe the stew from 'a lips.

Look like she sweating, her skin got a beautiful glow. It's a ring round the dark part of 'a eye look blue, and it's bright. The grey of 'a eyes is the moon. I can hear the fire dancing in the lantern on the dresser, and the silence threatening to swallow us whole.

"When Patrick git back, tell 'im ta git ma gulls. Ya hear?" Her voice going up and down, seem like she digging in 'aself for some more sound. "Member what I say, ya already done what I wont chu ta do. Don't be like otha folk puttin off livin waitin ta die and fraid ta go."

Grabbing my wrist in a firm grip, Miemay stare in my eyes like she bout to say something, but she waiting for the words to come. Then 'a breathing go all over the place, sound like a tornado in 'a chest.

I get scared, want to help 'a calm down but cain't figure out how. Maybe I do need somebody else here.

Then she say, heaving and holding on to me, "Don't give nothing away." She heave, and I wipe my eyes trying not to scare 'a by getting upset. "Do ya hear me talkin ta ya, gull?"

"Yes, ma'am," I cry.

"Don't chu neva do nothing you 'on wont. You ain't wont ta git marred," she breath pacing aself, waiting for the words. "Don't chu let nobody foce yo hand. You strong. You be strong. Don't let them break you. You ain't got ta be broke. You free, gull," she cry, trying to get the words out, so I put my hand on hers.

"Please, Miemay," I cry too, wonting 'a to calm down.

"I was born ta be broke," she cry. "You ain got ta let nobody break you," she say, out of breath. "You free, gull." She sip air nodding 'a head looking at the ceiling.

"Miemay!"

She lay back easy, looking at the ceiling, but a grip still tight.

I look in 'a eyes. When she silent, I get silent, and breathe easy. She take deep breaths and settle 'aself.

I wipe my face with my free hand and sit down next to 'a bed.

"Linny?"

"Yes, ma'am?" I lean over her.

"Promise ya Miemay," she say breathing like the words trying to go to sleep forever. "Promise ya Miemay, you won't neva ever let folks tek what's yorn."

I cain't move, I feel like she bout to die in front of me and that rattles me. I want to be here for 'a and I want to be strong. I'm a tree and the wrist she clinging to a branch.

"Promise!" Her scream scare me back to feeling, thinking, to speaking.

"Yes, ma'am," I say softly, to calm 'a down.

"Say it," she order, sounding almost normal.

"Say what, Miemay?" I whisper stroking 'a hair, trying to keep 'a calm. I hold 'a hand, and kiss the back of it.

"Say you gone always folla yo heart. Say you won't let nobody tek what's yorn."

"I'm gone always follow my heart," I repeat, sadly, "and I won't never let nobody take what's mine."

She squeeze my hand, and shake it relieved. "You was like my own baby," she whisper.

Again, I kiss 'a hand and look at 'a. I hold 'a hand to my cheek.

"No matta what yo daddy Cash say, or how he act, know yo daddy love you, gull. He loves you."

"I wish you could live forever," I speak clear, as the tears fall heavy. I wipe my face on my apron.

"Den I wouldn't neva know what's pass this." She speak like 'aself now. "Ain't no endings, somethin always beginnin." She get silent and 'a grip get weak.

I'm so glad when I hear the front door close, and Reverend Patrick's heavy footsteps coming back to 'a room. Soon as he close, I say, "Come on."

He come in, stand behind me, and I'm glad somebody else here to share this moment.

"She don't wont me here. Said she wont 'a girls to walk 'a home," I mumble almost like somebody else talking. I'm disappointed and relieved, she don't wont me there to see 'a die.

He put his hand on my shoulders, like he understand. Then Miemay look up at him gasping.

"Hurry," I whisper to Reverend Patrick. "Want me to read you something?" I offer Miemay.

She nods yes, her eyes fixed on 'a lap now. Her whole body seem to be winding out each breath, and she got to remember to breath.

I get the Bible. When I go to sit back down beside 'a, her eyes stop me, then she throw 'a hand motioning towards my reading chair. I obey. I'm a tree. I come sit down over here and start reading.

I don't know how long I'm reading when I hear Miemay stirring in the bed again. When I look up from the Bible, Miemay sitting up. This time with 'a back to me and she facing the bedroom door. She sitting up straight, and done threw 'a legs over the edge but 'a breathing still ragged. She ain moving like it sound, she solid. I wonder if she finally gotta use it, or maybe she want that stew.

Then she push 'aself off the bed on 'a feet. I jump up to help, but she give me that look that stop me dead in my tracks and let me know, she don't wont no help. I start to get close in case she fall. She put 'a hand up fanning me away. Then she walk out in the hall, like it ain't nothing. When I follow, one of them, Ondrea or Matilda standing in the hall too. Since they here, and I know she might have to use it, I go back cause she gone need 'a cane.

When I reach to get 'a cane from the side of the bed, I see Miemay still laying in the bed with 'a long white hair spread all over the pillows. I panic, turn back round, run out in the hallway again. Miemay and the woman gone. I go back in the bedroom, and look down at Miemay in the bed, confused. She blinking and breathing like a new baby again.

I look over in the corner where I was reading, and I'm still sitting there, sleep. I walk over to myself and examine how my chest rise and fall. I look back at Miemay's body on the bed, how 'a chest labor to rise and fall, then at the bedroom door, realize it's closed.

All of a sudden something grab my arm, and I jerk away all out of sorts cause I don't see nothing. The more I pull the tighter its grip on my arm. That's when I see Miemay's face, as I focus, she looking browner, younger.

My heart racing so fast it's hurting my throat. Then I realize, Iain looking at Miemay, it's Matilda's face. Don't know when I sat back down, but Matilda is shaking me awake. The way she shaking me, feel like she been doing it a while and trying to do it gently. When I come to, she put 'a finger to 'a lips for me to be quiet. I can hear Miemay's breathing deep and loud.

Ondrea examining Miemay, when 'a other daughters walk in, Catherine and Nessa. Nessa look at Ondrea for a report. "Dat's the rattle, won't be long now," Ondrea whisper sadly, wrapping a shawl tighter round 'aself, like it's strength in it.

Matilda gives Ondrea a look of warning, not to speak so openly with Miemay laying right there. Then she usher me on.

"Wait," I whisper, looking down at Miemay. I get close to 'a face, almost nose to nose.

She pull the cover up to 'a own face digging a body in the bed like she trying to get away, like I'm scaring 'a. She don't know who I am or where she at, and I realize, I don't know who laying there neither. It's a relief. I don't feel like I'm leaving 'a now, I know she already gone.

Chapter Ten

"It's okay to cry." Ella wrap 'a arm in mine, tears streaming down 'a face. I feel like a tree. I don't even look at 'a. "I know yall was close," she go on, wiping 'a eyes.

I don't feel sad, I feel numb. I try to understand all this. Miemay the first person close to me to die. I sit quiet, and watch as one person after another say what they gone miss. Half these folks didn't even come see 'a, knowing she was dying.

They thought she was crazy, possessed or they didn't want to see 'a dying. After Miemay asked after folks, why she hadn't seen 'em, word came back, this grandchild or that one wanted to remember her the way she was last time they seen 'a. I remember how 'a face fell, receiving that kinda news.

I start to feel something growing in me, but it ain't no sadness or no tears coming. It's rage. I hate the ugliness people showed 'a after all she been through, after all she done for us.

All the reasons Miemay was alienated while she was living, make funny stories now, make 'a endearing. Now folks want to remember how she saved them or their children from yellow fever. Now they want to put 'a up on a pedestal when she ain't here. People talking like they was out at the stream fishing with Miemay a week fore she died.

Humph! I just cain't understand this, them, and how it all works. We don't tell people we love 'em when they here, but we go on and on bout how wonderful they is when they gone. Feel like they using 'a death as a way to get they own attention, and it ain't about saying good bye. Everybody putting on they best show, see who can play the saddest.

Reverend Patrick lift his hand to me. "Want to say a few words?"

I respond shaking my head no, but I want to shout, "NO!" as I'm realizing funerals ain't for the dead, they for the living.

I wish I could've played "This Little Light of Mine" for Miemay. She loved that song. She liked to see me play the piano too, specially since she paid this white lady to give me piano lessons. Then forced Daddy nem to carry me to them lessons every Saturday. Use to come to church whenever she knew I was playing. Hearing this slow funeral drudge, I'm starting to miss the piano and I think about the one in 'a house.

Finally, the pallbearers carry 'a body out. Then we all surround the hole dug too soon. I just keep shaking my head "no" as I feel the anger coming up. Grit rub my back cause she think I'm feeling down, but 'a hand making the anger so hot, I jerk away.

"Let 'a go," Ella tell Grit, as I wrap my arms round myself. Then I go settle on the other side of 'a grave. They think I'm taking 'a death hard. It's the way she was treated in life that's bothering me. I watch as they lower Miemay body in the ground.

Reverend Patrick says, "Ashes to ashes and dust to dust." Then we all throw flowers on 'a coffin.

I plan to take some of the flowers from Miemay's garden, and plant them at home. Wonder if Mama would mind having them in 'a garden.

Somehow, I know when Reverend Patrick came earlier last night fore she died, she was probly slow to respond cause she been getting in and out of 'a body. I'm remembering how she looked like a new baby sometimes, just like she did right before she left for good.

Now I'm sure, I what'n dreaming. Wonder if I done been dead too, since I seen Miemay and 'a mama in the hall. I know if folks knew what I'm thinking, they'd say I was crazy, too.

Part of me soothed knowing she ain in that box and 'a spirit free. Some part of me finds comfort knowing, I'm gone see Miemay again when it's my time. Iain afraid of death no more. Feel like I know what to expect. Since in a way, I already been there.

* * *

54

"Alright now." Mr. Prescott, the lawyer from Beaumontville, stands to read Miemay's will. All the immediate family back in the church, waiting for something. Uncle Victor and his wife already say they gone take the house. Everybody agree, Uncle Victor is the oldest living male in Miemay line.

I'm thinking bout how Miemay put off dying til 'a house was finished, but ain't never get to sleep a single night in it. I try to swallow the hurt. Miemay told me what to do with my pain and tears. But what to do with rage?

I'm so many generations down, Ion even know why I got to be here. I need some time to myself, to think, to breath. It feels bad being here. Her girls already raided 'a house, and divided 'a things up. Her sons seem to be celebrating 'a passing thinking bout what they gone get, more than what we all lost. But the lawyer say we all got to be here. It was one of Miemay's last wishes.

Wish just once I'da told 'a how much I loved 'a, even though folks don't go round talking bout that. Folks brag on they kids to each other, but don't never tell they children how proud of them they is. They fuss over 'em, and give 'em a hard time to prove it. I tried to give Miemay space and peace in 'a last days, did whatever I could to let 'a live how she wonted. I know she know, but I still wish Ida told 'a, just once.

From now on, I'm gone say how I feel more. Gone do what I feel more, and stop being scared. I'm not gone be quiet no more less it's what I wont. Iain gone let nobody else tell me who to be or how to be. I'm gone be happy with my little time in this here body.

"She a gull! Cain't live by 'aself!" Daddy break my train of thought, save me from tears and I realize everybody eyes on me.

Mr. Prescott continues, and I'm hearing what he saying for the first time since he began speaking. "It was the wish of Madelyn Belanger to leave all of her material property to Madelyn Remington. As an executive of the court, I hereby award Madelyn Remington the land with the house and cabin on it, the tenant properties, and the store."

Now I feel like I'm dreaming, anchored, I sit silent. I try to wrap my mind round the moment and the idea of owning anything especially that big house. I look around again, and they ain't just looking, they glaring. If looks could kill.

Uncle Victor's wife stand up sharply staring at me like I challenged 'a, then turns to walk out, but passes out in the isle. Everybody run to 'a aid.

Feel like I just did something wrong. I think this is too much for me. What I know bout running a store or some properties? I shake my head "no" as it all comes to me. Now I know why Miemay introduced me to the tenants three years ago. I think about how she had me going to pick up the rent, or sent me to fix things.

Miemay pushed me to read everything, and learn everything I could. She said because she couldn't read, she needed my eyes to keep 'a from getting cheated. She asked me to give 'a updates, especially when things ain match up. On my word she'd confront Ernest about shortages. I been balancing the books, running the store sometimes, and making orders for years.

"Ain even no man got that much property here in Zion," one of my uncles complain.

"Give a gull all that, and now she got a say in thangs," an older male cousin cosigns, looking at me angrily. You would think I wrote the will myself.

"I'm Miemay's oldest male child!" Uncle Victor pound out on his chest. "It should be a law against this," he protests looking at me like I swindled him out of his inheritance.

I agree, I don't deserve all this. I just breathe and look at the white lawyer.

"It's gone be done." Reverend Patrick look over at me seriously. "It's Miemay's dying wish, and if this what she wonted to do with 'a own thangs, we got to respect that." He look at me for a long time. Then walk over and hand me the keys to 'a house.

For a moment, I wish Iain never go back to get Miemay's cane. For a moment, I wish I'd gone with 'a, but I keep my head up. I listen as Mr. Prescott speaks for 'a, and lists the things as they are to be given to each of her living children.

I realize she was buying gifts for folks, and ordering things preparing for this moment. She make sure some folks got things they'd been working towards, saying they needed or wanted. I listen as she gives away dishes and jewelry to 'a daughters, and granddaughters. She left one of my cousins enough money to go away to college, and paid his first year's tuition, cause he been talking bout leaving Zion since we was kids. She don't leave nothing for Uncle Victor or Ernest, but they already got a lot of they own land, and ain't never really wanted for nothing.

Her daughters scoff at what she left them. Not because it ain't what they wanted, or because they expected more or something else, they just don't think it's right what I got. I stop looking around, but I still feel their eyes on me, in my back, in my face.

I'm ready to give everything away, to somebody, anybody, when I hear Miemay say, "Promise you won't let nobody take what's yorn." I'm thinking she was out of sorts cause she dying, so I agreed only to calm 'a down. She on 'a death bed, I done promised 'a on death bed. This too much, she always getting me in trouble.

Then I know what she meant by me not being no man, and not being anything without one. She gave me all this stuff so I'd have a voice, and ain't got to live with folks my whole life. They wouldn't never let no woman live by 'aself in Zion. I think about Miemay waiting for the house to get built so I'd have somewhere to live, and my heart ache.

Soon as the reading of 'a will over I start out the church doors.

Daddy hot on my trail.

"Git 'a, Cash," Uncle Victor order my daddy following behind me hisself.

"It ain't no problem. She gone do the right thing. Ain't chu, Linny?" Daddy call after me.

I cain't say a word, just keep going til the sun hit my face. I step down the steps, breathing in deep, trying to wrap my mind round it all, and getting ready for trouble.

"Madelyn!"

"Yes, Daddy." I meet his eyes and he know before I even speak.

"You ain't got no right to that inheritance."

"Sho ain't," Uncle Vick cosign.

"Do the right thing. Give them keys over to ya uncle."

"I cain't," I speak just above a whisper, my heart breaking. "I promised Miemay on 'a death bed, I wouldn't never give away or let nobody take what's mine."

"IT AIN'T YORN!" Ernest yell, trying to rush me like a bull, but my brothers hold him back.

"Cash, you got to fix this," Uncle Victor insist.

"I'm sorry, Daddy," I'm telling him this how it's gone be.

"You know this ain't right." He look away from me accepting it, hurt.

"I made a promise."

"You tricked a ol woman, that's what you did. You cheat!" Ernest yell at my face before my brothers pull him back again.

"You know what this mean?" Daddy done already made his judgment, he thinking of the sentence. "That's your final word?" Daddy looking in my spirit.

Ion say nothing else, I just raise my chin and brace myself for the sentence.

"Don't speak to me no more, or nobody else in the family til you fix this. Don't even think about coming to that repast. You ain't welcome in my house no more. That mean Ion even wont to break bread with you. Not even when you come on family field days.

"Come git all yo thangs from my house this evening, they gone be outside. If anything still there in the morning, you gone have to dig it out the trash." Then he walk pass me hard, pushing me a little. "And you can git home the best way you know how."

"That's it, Cash?" Uncle Victor call after my daddy.

Daddy don't answer him, he just get up on his carriage where Mama waiting and start off.

One by one my family climb in they automobiles or carriages. Nobody say a word to me, nobody offer me a ride. Before the last of them come out, before Ella, Grit or Zay come and feel forced to choose, I start walking. I cut through the fields so I don't have to see who all passing me by on the road. I cain't take that, don't feel like I can take much more.

Daddy angry with me, cause folks angry with him. They think he should have done something to keep what happened from happening. I don't know how he could have, Miemay ain't tell nobody what she was doing cept 'a lawyer. Iain never spect to get nothing from 'a, Iain wont nothing. I don't know what to say to them or nobody else. I don't know what to say for myself.

I wish Miemay was here, walking beside me on the road. Some part of me feel like I done buried my own mama in lots a ways. I think about the story she told me bout when she first arrived at 'a master's plantation. The missus had sold the last girl away from 'a whole family, and he'd used the money to buy Miemay. His family hated Miemay, mistreated 'a.

His plantation was a old one, with generations of slaves and family ties. He'd set 'a up, a child in 'a own cabin. Other slaves saw it as a unearned reward. They was crowded in they own quarters, and there were other women with children by 'im. They wondered what made Miemay so special. They assumed cause she looked white, he thought she was better, so naturally Miemay must've believed that, too. It didn't help that Miemay wore 'a fear of being a child in a new place, and the sadness of missing her mama as silence.

Miemay said she didn't know how to be or how to talk to other slaves. Then Mistress Belanger beat and burned 'a so much, she was always hiding, trying to make 'aself small, praying she'd go unnoticed. Other slaves took 'a behavior as evidence that she was being uppity. They didn't know she thought 'a skin was a curse, even as a child, cause how she looked is what got 'a sold away from 'a mama.

Miemay say she felt like a turkey being fattened up for the killing. She felt alone and desperate to be close to other slaves, other children, and their mothers. She missed her mother, but no other woman would mother her. The other slaves set themselves apart, put 'a up on a pedestal. They didn't trust 'a, which left 'a at Master Belanger's mercy.

He was always buying 'a things, and bringing 'a things to ease his guilt. Sometimes she went to him without tears. Sometimes she completely disappeared before he came, and sometimes she was someone else for him.

Marriage something like that she'd say sometimes. Cept it's yo own mama teaching you how to serve yo husband with a smile, no matter if you hurt, scared or tired. All my life she warned me, don't disappear.

There were all these talks we'd had over the years. Now Miemay words coming to me in bits:

"Whatever ya do, keep alla you."

"Life short, and Fatha Time ain't gone stop foe ya ta cetch ya breaf."

"Time don't stop, it jus git goin moe and moe the olda ya git."

"You be the first woman in my line strong enough ta keep alla yahself."

"Men, they git ta grow up, but us women, they try ta keep like chirun," she'd say, frowning like she got a bad taste in 'a mouth at that last part.

"Folks teach they boys ta be strong and smart. Then teach they girls ta marry a strong and smart man."

"Don't never give yahself ta nobody. And don't chu let nobody give you away ta nobody, you ain't no slave," she said one time after hearing a girl just turned 13 was marrying a man over 30 years old. She was so upset, she even yelled at me like I was gone get married to some old man the next day.

"You stay in them books. You gitcho lesson. You ain't no slave what git bought and sold. You ain't worthless, cain't nobody just give you away."

"You share yahself, and if a nigga don't know how ta act or treat cha, you stop sharin. Ain't lost nothing, cain't lose nothing when you ain't never gave nothing away."

I hear wagons passing, all family, everybody else already gone to the hotel for the repast. I'm a long way from the church, fore I'm relieved I got keys to my own house. Iain got to go nowhere and answer or explain nothing. I smile a little, feel like Miemay walking home with me.

Then I remember I got that piano, so I say, "I'm gone play you a song." Wiping my eyes, I feel she gone be waiting there to hear it, too. "Thank you for what you done," I say. When the wind pick up, I say, "I love you."

Chapter Eleven

"Ruthann say she gone leave me if things don't change," my brother Isaiah we call Zay, tell me. "Say she tired of working and not having nothing. Say she could be broke by 'aself.'"

I don't say nothing, just keep picking and moving through the cotton trying to see what I can salvage. He looking too, talking more. Normally, we all on top of each other, working the fields from one end to the next. Lately, we be spread out cause the boll weevil done ruined so much of the crop. We just trying to pick and salvage whatever lil bit we can, ain much of nothing. Under these circumstances, one hand can work two or three times the land they use to could.

Money getting tight and we all feeling the pinch. I even see how the store barely making a profit, when it use to be doing so good. I mean even if folks mad at me, they ain gone waste a whole day riding to another town for the store, specially not since the other store in a white town. We been trying to stay away from them since its election year. My second cousin, Ernest who been running the store since he was a boy, say the hotel barely covering its own expenses. Everybody getting hit hard.

Then again, ain't just the crop got me and Zay over here by ourselves. Daddy still mad at me, that's why he way over there picking with my brothers. Me and Zay was always close. Even though Daddy being mean to me and the rest of 'em following his lead, I can always count on Zay to stand by me. Seem me and Zay got similar spirits and hearts. Sides Ella, he be the next one in the house I use to always be under, when I what'n watching Grit, before there was a Grit.

We silent for a long time when Zay start again. "I know you need some help round yo place, and I'll be glad to help for free. But it sho help if you would pay me a lil something. I'd be willing to do whatever you need, anything?" he plead.

I hear him, but I know our Daddy more. "Daddy would kill you if you help me," I say resolved, and not wanting to pull him in the middle of all this.

"Man cain't worry bout his daddy all the time, specially when he got a family of his own. My wife saying I'm weak willed, and everybody told 'a I what'n no good field hand, and 'a own daddy called me queer. Said I use to fall out from the heat and shit. What is that to say bout another man?"

"Zay, you ain no field nigga, and you did use to fall out from the heat," I remind 'im smiling.

"So what! I know it's true, but what is that to say?" he fuss smiling then keep on talking. "I'm thinking I could come down to the store, you know watch yo back, help out round there and git out this heat. Help you on yo land, since yo crop ain been affected like this, since you ain growing cotton or nothing. I could help you hire people, all that."

"I don't hardly go in that store myself. If I put you in that store that be another bad thing waiting to happen. I try not to say nothing bout what's going on in that store."

"You need to," he say too fast looking at me, and I feel like he telling me something else.

"Why? Something going on?" I stop and stare at him, and the way he move, and avoid my eyes, worry me. "If you know something I need to know tell me."

"Ion know nothing you 'on already know," he say firm, frowning in a way like he holding his tongue.

"Well, in that case, I'm gone leave things the way they is."

"They already bad, cain't git no worse."

"It could get worse."

"Well shoot, Linny, I'm gone git myself hired out either way. I rather come help you over some stranger. I rather you hire family over some strangers."

"Iain hired nobody," I say sadly.

"You got to hire a few hands, you cain't run all them acres by yahself, and the store too."

64

"I know, but I been worried bout doing it. You know I'm already on everybody list, then Zion ain never been too kindly to strangers."

"Well, that's even more reason for you to hire me then, don't you think?"

"I got to think about that," I say looking over at Daddy, and feeling like a stranger in these fields I been working and helping in since I was born.

"Ain't nothing against you, I just don't want to put you in the middle of nothing."

"It's a lot going on you don't know about, and I cain't keep coming here working and ain't got nothing to show for it. My chillen need clothes and shoes. My wife need to feel like she can buy a little extra here and there without it being no hardship. Only so long a man can live like that."

"How much you need?" I look at him, waiting for a number.

His whole body start to stir, his head shake "no" fore his mouth finally say, "I'm a man, cain't take no handouts. I wonna work for it. Iain asking no woman to take care of my family."

"Iain no woman, I'm ya sister, remember that."

"I'll work for my sister, but I won't be taking no handouts from 'a. You hear?"

"I hear you, Zay," I say, looking him in the eyes and seeing he don't understand that taking a job with me be like declaring war on the family.

Nobody talk to me and I don't talk to nobody. Nobody come out to the house, and I don't go to church. I don't even speak when I get to the field on these family days. I just get to work, and Daddy give work orders to everybody but me. I usually just follow Zay, and help him with whatever he assigned. Seem like Daddy be giving him more to do, in an offhanded way to keep from talking to me.

Zay here every day, but he what'n never no field hand. I mostly do his work. Still, it would help to have another pair of hands round the house.

*　　*　　*

"Linny?" Mama whisper loudly, tiptoeing outside they cabin backdoor, where I'm sitting, after cutting 'a eyes round to make sure Daddy ain't round fore she give me a plate. I smell 'a red beans, with smoked neck bones and buttermilk cornbread. "Take this plate and go in the barn somewhere to eat."

"No, thankya," I say painfully, trying not to look at the plate knowing if Daddy find out he might get after 'a.

"Go on now, fore he come back in," she insists pushing the plate at me.

"He coming," Isaiah announce, then disappear, probly to go sit down.

I hear the front door open.

Mama say, "Why you got to be so stubborn, just like ya Daddy? This so silly!" Then she drop the plate so hard and loud beside me on the porch I jump up, grab it and start towards the barn.

When I get there, my first thought is to clean it off in the garbage and rinse the plate off at the pump. Feel like if Iain been eating lunch here for the last few months since Miemay died, why should I start today? Been bringing my own lunch pail this long, and I don't want to go against what he say. On the other hand, I didn't make no promise not to eat at his house, and Mama done gave it to me, and Iain never been one to throw no food away.

Sitting down, I start to eat. I taste everything Mama done put in here. Umm umph! It's been a while since I tasted anybody cooking other than mine. I didn't even go to the dinner after her funeral. Since I'm some kind of outsider now.

"Good, ain't it?" Daddy startle me, making it feel like too much oil in my stomach. I swallow hard then put the plate down. "I asked ya not to eat here til you fixed this, didn't I?"

I stand, feeling ashamed I'm eating at his house. Mad at myself that I keep coming round here, waiting for him to understand. Didn't realize how bad it would hurt me to watch them eat together, and not invite me in. But Daddy's word his law, and so is mine.

I take off my field sack and hang it on the barn wall silently.

"Why you so stubborn? Just give Uncle Victa back his inheritance. So ya Pa will speak to ya, and we can stop all this foolishness. Ain't yorn to keep in the first place." Mama come from behind him. "Miemay was Victa's grandma."

I just stare off out at the wheat fields, I done already explained myself, a thousand times.

"Ramona!" Daddy growl, make Mama jump and get silent. "Stop talking to 'a. Ain gone mind you if she ain gone mind me." Then turning to me he say, "I'm shamed of ya. You a thief, a liar and a cheat. And ya deserve to be treated like one. I done told you don't eat at my house til you fix what ya done." Daddy glares at me slapping the back of his hand in the palm of the other, pounding out each syllable.

Feel like he hitting me with them words. I'm a statue, looking at the ground, any eye contact be a challenge to 'im and a reason to hit me. Isaiah done came out the house now too, and he watching us both sadly. I cain't believe I was Daddy's favorite.

Daddy kick the plate at me, and the beans go all over my skirt. I don't wear pants when I come over here. The he start towards me.

Mama run to grab his arm, and I brace myself for the lick. "Don't do this Cassius," Mama wrap 'a arms round the one he bout to raise.

Daddy snatch away throwing Mama back in the dirt.

Me and Isaiah both move towards 'a. We older now, ain't gone be no more hitting our Mama.

Crying, Mama snatch away from me and Zay, sitting up and pouting, she yell in my face, "I been beggin ya, just give Victa back his inheritance." Screaming and pushing 'a own self up, Mama shout out, "Why Miemay do this? Make 'a promise this? She always gittin Linny in trouble, now all Zion mad at our family. Like we got a whole lotta money."

"Don't speak ill of the dead." Daddy leer at us like he might whup us all.

"Ion mind helping however I can," I offer, not really understanding what she talking bout.

"I'm the man round here, and I don't wont no money from ya. Don't even want ya help round here! Matter fact, don't come round here no more. This house ain't cho family house, and we ain cho family til you fix this."

"I made Miemay a promise on 'a death bed. I'd be a liar if I parcel out 'a things."

"You already look like one."

"I don't care what I look like, when I know how things is."

"Ain't chu something! Gone stand here and sass me. The only one take care of you and watch out for you. The whole damn town know what you done. It's hard walking round here with my head up. Knowing you done tricked a ol woman." Beating on his chest, he scream, "What you do don't just affect you. They thank we was all in on it."

"Who is they?" I ask, and he step to me close. Isaiah jump in front of me like a shield. I don't move, I keep my eyes to the ground, cause he waiting for a reason. I'm afraid we all be fighting round here. Iain gone let 'im beat me the way he beat my mama when I was young. Ain gone run from 'im neither.

"Git 'a thieving self off my property!" Daddy spit snuff on the ground like I'm a stranger, then look at me scowling. Isaiah lean back against me, staring Daddy in the eyes, and pushing me out the barn behind 'im.

"Don't push me, Zay," I lean into him, feeling like a rooster behind chicken wire. Turning around I find my lunch pail. Then I lift my head and look Daddy right in the eyes and resolve sadly, "That's how you wont it, that's how it's gone be."

"Ah nah, Cash," Mama start to moan and cry. "She a girl, cain't disown 'a bout this."

"She don't need no daddy she ain't gone listen to," Daddy turn his back on me and start towards the house. Mama look at me sadly, like it's the last time she gone see me, then turn around and follow him.

"He just upset right now." Zay try to make me feel better. "He just talking."

"Nah, Iain never knowed him to just talk." I stop watching after Daddy and get on the road to my house. Zay don't follow, less he be disowned, too.

I walk towards the sky, between neat rows of crops and feel the Georgia heat soaking in my skin. Wish I had rode Anastasia cause this a long walk. Miss my pants. Wind get where it need to be better than it do in these skirts. Cain't wait to get home, in the tub, then eat a lil stew. Maybe I'll play a little piano to soothe these blues. Or read and try to figure out how to keep my crops up by myself.

After a long while, I come up on Miemay cabin and notice the worn path to 'a house starting to fill in. I see how her house be part of Zion. The wood come from these trees, and was cut by our men. But my house different, the wood come on the railroad, its treated and smoother. Her house airy, the wind pass through the walls. It's better than the old slave houses sharecroppers in now, but not much better. Miemay house wood so dark, and old, it look like it could have grown up from the ground. While the other house she built, stand proud, the walls sound, and smooth against the sunshine.

I'm spose to have her old house torn down, but I don't plan to ever do it. I'd never allow it, long as I own this land. I still come down here sometimes, to walk around in it, tend 'a garden and talk to 'a. Now, I'm staring on the porch like I spect to see 'a there nodding back at me. This usually the time she be sitting out, chewing tabacca and taking in the wind. I swallow her absence hard, push on to my house. Soon as I see my porch, I see him, "The Gravedigger."

"Good evening," Reverend Patrick say, standing up from the porch bench, taking off his hat and walking to meet me at the top of my steps.

Feel like he blocking me from my own front door. I eye the door behind 'im, and feel how uncomfortable his position making us. Still, Iain got no words for 'im.

"Kinda late for you to be out here walking by yahself."

"Well, I guess it's a good thing you always round watching me," I say, putting my lunch pail down, and looking at 'im. Iain gone be forced to keep company with 'im.

He look around like he taking in the evening, like we got all the time in the world, or like he part of the wind.

Iain decided how long I'm gone stand for this. I'm tired and got a early morning tomorrow. So I say, "All the times you been round here the last few months, why you speaking today?"

"I want to see you in chuch Sunday." He speak these words slow, testing the water. See if they light enough to ease the tension, or build a bridge.

I don't say nothing to that. I step up on the porch, sit on the railing and look down feeling his words, and him in them. I'm looking for something, needing something more than a invitation to make me go back.

I'm starting to feel God ain't gone be nowhere lies taught. Where white folks can hate us, hang us, and still get the same salvation as "turning the other cheek" folks. I'm starting to think God ain't found no where you got to bribe people to do right. I'm starting to think, maybe saying serve me or burn in hell ain't loving at all. I'm starting to think being afraid to live, and living for dying don't make sense. I wont to talk to somebody bout that. Start missing Miemay. Now I seen what death is, I wont to know bout life. Feel like Iain living here, just breathing and going through the motions.

"What happened ain't nobody fault. Nobody blame you for Miemay giving you all them thangs. I did think, to be fair, you shoulda gave it over to Victor nem but Ion know nobody else woulda done that neither."

I shift my weight on my feet offended, and tired of this conversation. Always feels like I got to defend myself these days, coming and going. So I say annoyed, "I promised 'a on 'a death bed, I wouldn't never give away or let nobody take what's mine. Iain have nothing then. Iain never wont nothing from 'a, and Iain never thought this was what she was making me promise to keep."

"Miemay was good for seeing to it thangs go 'a way, even in death. Made me promise 'a some thangs, too." He laugh a little, and I smile a little too. It is kinda funny when you think about it, her getting me in trouble and ain't even here. Then I get sad, she ain here to protect me, when he start again, "Miemay the only one treat me like something when nobody else would. Folks been calling me black this and black that all my life. Always been just Patrick to Miemay."

Leaning his back against the house, still between me and my front door, he say, "When I was a young man, she told me one day, I was a handsome boy. Ain't nobody never said nothing good about me, not even my own mama.

"My mama told me to marry light, and, I hate to speak ill of the dead, but she ain never could see 'a own beauty. Was always looking at the other women round Zion with hazel, gray, green and sometime blue eyes. Then she'd say, 'I got regla nigga eyes and regla nigga skin.' Ask my daddy, 'why you ain marry one a dem gulls wit long hair, instead of a nappy headed pickananny?' He'd frown, tell 'a how beautiful she was, but she ain never believe him, it was still hard. She even felt like she was marrying up by gittin him, but soon as 'a babies could cry, we be dark like her. She hated us.

"Then Miemay started coming by to git us and let us play. She loved on us, every part of us. She whup dem kids what called us black all the time. She the main reason I'm reverend here. Her vote here count for a lot. She always go against the grain. Otherwise ain nobody gone let no darky lead nothing. Humph! Maybe it's good you got 'a votes now, so ita be fair."

I take a deep breath, study him.

Then he say, "You was always her favorite, so I understand why she done this, gave you all 'a thangs."

First time I ever hear anybody half way sincerely say how much they love Miemay, what they need 'a for, maybe why they think she done this for me. Still, I don't know bout Reverend Patrick, so I say, "Why you dig 'a grave fore she died?"

"Cause she told me to."

Fore I know it, I'm on my feet, cause I know that's a lie. I'll be alright in my spirit slamming the door in his face now. When I go to get my lunch pail, he follow my movements speaking fast as he can, holding his hat to his chest like it's a lifeline.

"She told me whenever I cry to dig a hole and bury my tears."

His words, Miemay's words, in his mouth do stop me, dead in my tracks, so I look at 'im, in his eyes, at his spirit.

He staring back, clinching his hat, biting his lip and frowning like he gone cry right there. Then he go on and say, "I buried 'a on top of my tears. I dug that hole so I could wrap my mind round 'a dying. For some reason, don't feel like I buried some distant relative five months ago, feel like I buried my own mama.

"Use to come every day cause I love to hear 'a fuss. And I knew she wouldn't be round long. I was just, yah know, giving Miemay a hard time bout the Bible cause I didn't know how else to say . . ." his voice break and he sniffing and wiping his eyes.

"Broke my heart when I found out she knew I done it. I tried to lay dat to rest with 'a, but I'll probly carry that to my grave. Iain do it to harm 'a. I dug the first parts of that grave with my bare hands." He speaking to God more than me, more than to be heard, but because he got to say it out loud.

I stare off into the sky, up over the crops to give him privacy to compose himself. The sun almost gone now, and the sky turning dark blue mixed with a muddy brown. When his breathing easy, and the silence waiting, calmly I ask, "Why you ain just tell 'a that?"

"Cause she the one dying. Ain't my place to tell the person dying, I dug they grave cause I cain't deal with them dying." He ease back to the bench, feeling for it with one hand in a trance, staring at 'a cabin cross the yard.

"It's over nah," I exhaust, looking at Miemay's cabin, too, for a while. Wishing he'da just told 'a fore she went. Knowing she ain never been one to hold a grudge. Knowing she woulda understood. Still, I know she ain' nowhere mad or upset with 'im either. "Wont some tea?" I offer, getting my keys outta my skirt pocket and opening the front door.

When he come in behind me, I say, "She ain gimme all this cause I'm her favorite. She gave it to me so I won't be no slave." I keep on to the kitchen to make us some hot tea. He don't respond; it's quiet in the living room. I see the lamp by the couch come on from the kitchen. I get the milk from the electric icebox, then pour him and me some in the bottom of our tea cups.

When I go in to give him the tea, I ask, "What you ate?"

"Iain hungry. What you mean so you won't be no slave?"

"A woman always a slave to somebody, her parents, her husband and her children. She always got to do what somebody else say, or base all her decisions on the welfare of 'a children. Now, Iain got to be in my father's house forever."

"You ain gone never git married?" he ask, sitting up in his chair in disbelief.

"Cain't imagine it."

"Wait a minute." He move his lips like he tasting the truth as its registering. "That ain't natural, less you . . . what they call them women?" He talking to hisself now, then he say to me, "A nun or something?"

"Iain no nun neither." I laugh a little, first time I done told anybody cept Miemay. He take it better than I spect my daddy would. Hunching my shoulders, I admit plainly, "Ain't got no desire to be married."

"That's what all this about," he say more to himself than me.

Sipping my tea, I say looking at him, "What?"

"She make me promise to watch after you. I cain't think why yo daddy cain't, or yo man won't one day."

We both sit in silence for a minute, let that marinate. Then he say, "You ever tell Miemay you ain wont to git married?"

"Yes. And one time she told me I would never get married," I answer looking at 'im to gage how he taking all of this. I won't never tell him what else she say, cause I don't know what she talking bout. Then again, I never do.

73

I don't know how long we sitting in silence when he say, "You know, I started reading the Bible with Miemay when I was a boy."

Cause he offering another subject taking a sip of his tea, I think he satisfied with me never getting married. I'm glad he don't wont to mill it into dust. So I sip my tea some too, waiting and welcoming the change of tune.

He go on, "Soon as you read it, make you wont to ask questions." Then he laugh a little by hisself, recounting the memory. "Did me that way anyhow. My mama, and daddy nem could barely read. So they told Miemay she couldn't have me readin it til I could understand it for myself. We hadn't got to it too good then. I expect she always wanted me to come back to it, but I never did, just always had a fascination with it. Guess that's another way she made me be Zion's reverend.

"Sometimes I thank, maybe I let 'a down cause Iain never read it all the way. Sometimes I use to be jealous of you being able to read it to 'a, and learn bout it. Sometimes the thangs she tell me, Ion know if she crazy, or if she cain't understand the Bible, or maybe I don't," he say thoughtfully, then seem to get lost in his own thoughts.

"Maybe she was right, maybe I do need to read it all. I think when she was dying, I was trying to git 'a to come back to church, not even to save 'a soul, but, cause Iain sure bout how to save mine, I guess." His voice trail off, and he looking in the tea like it's in there. "Wish, I could, ya know, talk with 'a bout thangs. I done started reading it, and, ain nobody else knows it like she did, cept maybe you now." He look at me like that last statement more of a proposition.

"We could talk about it," I smile, accepting, cause I been wanting to discuss it with somebody, too.

"Be nice if you'd come for dinner sometimes, too. You know Mrs. Harper would love to see you, and fuss over you. She always wanted a daughter, and you was always the closest thing to one." He smile, and I soften at the idea of sitting with her, fussing over me, feeding me.

Specially since Miemay gone now, and I been feeling so lonely. It'd be nice to have anybody fuss at me or over me, don't even matter bout what. I'd even entertain more lessons from Mrs. Harper on how to be a lady for the company.

We sit in silence, listening to the night come. The crickets singing and the wind making the trees harps. I think about Uncle Lucius and wonder when he gone have another party. I want to get out more. I think about how the piano done saved me from the silence. I'm lost in my thoughts when Reverend Patrick sip the last bit of his tea, then stand. Part of me sad to see 'im go, but I don't let on.

I start to put on like I got more important things to do, standing too, then walking over to the front door. I'm moving so fast, it's like, I'm kinda rushing him out. "Well, it was good of you to stop by." Feel like I should hug him, or shake his hand fore he leave.

"I need to tell you something fore I go." He look at the ground like he done something wrong.

"What is that?" I breathe deep and easy.

"I need a favor. Iain wont to do it like this, but it's the only way it happen."

Now I'm folding my arms for the news and really looking at 'im. He finna make me wish Iain never invite 'im in.

"New teacher coming to town. She a woman, no family and I thought," he stop, closing his eyes, like he searching for strength, and I'm already knowing where this going, but I wait. "Let me start again, cause we not gone do this no more. I promised Miemay I'd look after you, and I'm gone do that. And you ain gone make it easy if ya don't trust me."

He clear his throat, straightening up his posture and looking me in my eyes. Then he says, "I want the teacher to stay here. Ain never thought to put 'a nowhere else. I come round here every night to check on you, fore I go home. I know you can handle anything, got ya rifles and all, but I'll just sleep better knowing you ain't out here by yahself."

I lean on the back of the door, unfolding my arms. For the first time I think, I respect him. Feels like I'm seeing who he really is. The quiet of the night, and the silence of this house still overwhelming sometimes, but I'm too proud to ever ask somebody to stay.

Truth is, I be glad he be checking on me. I don't go to sleep til I hear his automobile go by every night. So, I take a deep breath then let it out and say, "That a be fine."

"Fine." He smile, nod his head "good night," then put his hat on and go.

Chapter Twelve

———•✦•———

"Granger still outside?" Mama ask anybody who hear or know the answer, while she heavy hoofing down the stairs with purpose.

"I'm sure he left, cause he said to send word when the baby come," Mozelle answers, Mozelle is my baby sister's best friend.

Having a baby in Zion a community event. All the women in the immediate family, sisters, aunts, cousins and maybe best friends, get involved to welcome the new baby and to help the new mother. It's like a little party that ends when the guest of honor arrives. I have a full house of women moving round.

Two days ago, you couldn't pay nobody to come out to my house. Cain't help but think Grit planned it like this. Even though she say she just wanted to be in a house where there was running water, and where she didn't have to use no outhouse while she was giving birth.

"Linny!" Mama yell like I'm outside.

"Ma'am," I answer softly, hoping to bring Mama voice down.

"Start gittin ya thangs tagetha. You gone have to go out after the midwife."

"It's middle of the night. She a woman. Cain't go by 'aself," Ella protest.

"I'll go with 'a," Mozelle offer, coming in the hall.

"Still ain safe," Ella stand firm on 'a word.

"She thank she a man anyhow," Jenny spit, going up the steps.

"Iain goin no how." I'm shaking my head 'no,' ending the debate reaching for the barn lantern. "Come on, Mozelle." I start towards the front door. Mozelle follow me out into the night.

"Well, where you going then?" Mama call after me.

"Miemay's, to get 'a midwife tools."

"I'm scared." Mozelle stop dead in our tracks, staring down at the old cabin, whose dark windows look like the closed eyes of a sleeping person that don't wanna be roused.

I don't care bout waking the dead. All I can think about is Grit laying upstairs getting ready to push a baby out, and Iain got no good scissors to cut the cord, or no orange stick to scrub under our nails. In case we got to reach in there and pull that baby out. I take long strides, my heart kinda racing from the idea of it all.

"I'm coming too!" I hear Ella call after me, each word tell me she getting closer.

I never look back. When I open the front door of Miemay's cabin the light disturb the quiet darkness. I ignore the coolness, that's more than the night breeze passing through. It's the absence of Miemay, and almost a year of no hot meals or fires in the fire place. The cold done settled in 'a cabin.

I step in the patient room. "Ella, come hold this light."

She don't speak as she takes it and follows me quietly around. We moving so fast. I'm stacking things on the vestibule. I grab Miemay's bag and put it up there. Ella put the things I put out inside the bag, while I get extra wash cloths, newspaper for more padding and extra linens. Miemay patient room stocked like somebody coming any day now to have a baby.

I take the midwife bag back from Ella, and she lift the light while I go through it, to make sure it's got medicine for wiping the baby's eyes, and the other medicine that goes on the cord after you cut it. I make sure it's some cord ties in there, too.

When we get back, I go to put on some hot water to clean the tools, but Ella fan me away to go check on our baby sister Ingrid, who we call Grit.

Easing down on the bed, I look Grit in the eyes and speak slow, gentle, even and firm. "The midwife on another delivery, ain no tellin when she be back, if she be back. So, if that baby decide to come fore she do, we gone have to do this ourselves."

"You crazy!" Virginia, who we call Jenny, the sister tween me and Ella, jump to 'a feet protesting. "Linny 'on know nothing bout birthin no babies! Ain't even got no kids of 'a own." She fold 'a arms like a soldier ready to go to war. Iain never paid Jenny no attention, so I won't start now.

"You had a enema yet?" I ask staring in Grit eyes, trying to keep 'a mind off Jenny.

"Midwife give me one fore she left."

"Shouldn't've never left," Jenny add.

"I'm gone shave you and get you cleaned up, and ready to bring this baby in the world." I smile, trying to appear calm, and make 'a feel assured.

Grit nod 'a head yes, smiling, but 'a eyes full of worry. Then she pull the cover back and open 'a legs trustingly. We both know Mama ain had 'a say yet.

"I'm sorry for this," Grit say when I start examining 'a. I don't touch 'a yet, waiting til Ella come with that water so I can get washed up first.

"Don't be sorry, you ain' did nothing wrong. Baby acted like it was coming and then got cold feet." We both grin a little at this.

"Been here for two days," she say all sorry.

"Be that way sometimes. You ain't the first woman to have pain days before it's time. Matter fact, Miemay use to say them the easiest births. Seeing as how that baby been getting ready since the other day, should shoot right on out." I smile.

Then I hear Jenny pacing like a yard dog behind a fence, and watch Grit watching 'a. I know Grit feel it's something she shoulda done different. I know she always worried bout how she affecting other people, she considerate like that. So I say, "This God's work in God's time, and ain't nobody blaming you for how God work."

Grit eyes stop moving like the pendulum in a grandfather clock, and she stare right through me when she say, "Seem like a woman ain't got no say when it come to 'a own body. Ain't got no say on who she marry. Ain't got no say on when she git pregnant, when the baby come, how many babies come, or how much 'a man touch 'a." She start to heave, working 'aself up, and the tears fall. "Linny you knew, you always knew and understood didn't you? You the smart one."

"How she the smart one?" Jenny jump right on that. "Twenty-two and ain't got no man or children of 'a own. Shoot, Grit, seem like you oughta know when ya baby coming, it's only the third one," Jenny fuss at us both, looking over my shoulders at Grit.

I turn around and look at Jenny crazy.

"I'm just sayin, I be glad when she push it on out so I can git back to my own house and bed. We been here almost two days now. What'n even close to 'a time when she called us. Shoot, I got six of my own, maybe one on the way, and ain trying to have this one waiting on-"

"Why don't you shut up and sit down somewhere. Stop runnin ya mouth. You wouldn't wont nobody to be on yo nerves while you goin through it." Our eldest sister Mariella, we call Ella, chastise Jenny when she come in with the hot water. Mozelle behind Ella with some wash bowls, and Mama hot on they heels.

"You best go git that midwife, gull. This a life you playing wit," Mama fuss, hitting me on the arm to get moving.

"This women's work," Jenny spit at me, annoyed.

"It's bout twenty chillen tween us all. If we cain't figger how to git this baby outta Grit, it ain't Linny fault," Ella reason.

"Linny ain't even got none! What she know bout birthin babies?" Jenny making a case, and starting the war of words. And I expect Mama to back 'a up the way she always do, but I don't stop moving. Ella pouring water over my hands while I'm washing up, cleaning under my nails with the orange stick and rinsing the razors. Then I get another bowl and soap Grit up.

"Need more light?" Ella offer as we both concentrate on shaving Grit.

"Please," I accept, pushing Grit gown back and moving the cover out the way, and putting another thinner pad beneath 'a tail to catch the mess I'm bout to make. The oil lamp better than the electric one but its pushing off more heat. Feel like the heat making me tired, I'm so tired, we all tired.

We ain slept much since the midwife went home yesterday, saying Grit's pain was false. Said she would be back, but then again she'd just come from delivering another baby, so she mighta said anything to get outta here and home to 'a own bed.

Then Grit husband, Granger, went to get the midwife again but she send word she already with another expecting mother in 'a house. Said she be here soon as that baby come. Granger done left fore the midwife come back. It's a mess, but we gone make due cause we have to.

Grit pains ain't coming close enough together no how, and she ain open enough to have no baby, but I can tell she opening. She just in the first part of labor, so I go down stairs and contemplate taking a little nap while waiting for the baby.

I try to be invisible, as I move the coffee beans I done peeled from over the fire in the fireplace where I was roasting 'em. Then I go in the kitchen, where I done started some milk boiling in one pot, and water in another. Drop a little nutmeg, and vanilla flavor, and sugar in the milk. Put the coffee beans in a big flower sifter that kinda fit in the pot of hot water. After the beans boil, I fix some mugs of coffee and pour a little hot milk in them. I drops a little coco powder in the bottom of my mug.

"Put a little coco at the bottom of mine, too." Ella come in the kitchen and watch me. "You always did make the best cup of coffee. You make a lot of things really good. You one of the best cooks I know." Kinda laughing to herself she continue, "Ain got no man or chillen to cook for. Gone figger dat out! Miemay taught you a lots of thangs, didn't she?"

"Yeah, she did." I agree thoughtfully, turning round and leaning against the counter watching the fire on the stove.

"How you been gittin along round here by yahself?" She examines me the way Mama should, but never does.

It's common knowledge nobody in the family will make the ride out here to help like they use to, since they feel I done took Uncle Victor's inheritance. Other folks don't help, cause it's easier to be against one than a whole family.

Looking at the ground, biting my bottom lip, I'm feeling my chest heavy and anxious to tell Ella the truth. But my pride won't allow me to admit Iain able to clear enough ground to keep the crop from failing. Or that I'm lonely and sad. Instead of answering what she really ask, I say like it ain't nothing, "Might have to hire a few outside hands to help me round here."

The heaviness of how I really feel become a wall of tension between us. Ella know I'm shrinking from the question, but out of pity she don't challenge me. Still, she worried and that makes 'a uneasy. So she start moving to ease the worry, cleaning clean counters, and pouring out the water from the bath pots, we fixed earlier when we thought the baby was coming. Then taking down some more mugs for others.

"How were we all raised in the same house, but I what'n never in the house even if I was home? I saw Miemay, Reverend's wife, Daddy and you more than I ever did Mama. I remember how you use to comb my hair if Reverend's wife didn't."

With a sad smile Ella say, "Mama just a person, too. She was finding her own way when you were born."

"Seem like Mama left me to find my own way, too."

"Sometimes life is hard on us, and we do our best to love the souls God gives us to protect, but because we working through our own situation we still fall short," Ella defend Mama, like always. Then she step over to the stove and turn the milk so it don't get skin on it. I see she deep in thought. "You're strong. Smart. Guess you'll be alright," she surrendering, and not gone try to dance me round in my feelings.

"I will," I assure her, solemn and relieved. Just above a whisper as the day settles in me and what is going on becomes humbling, I say, "Pour that milk over them coffee beans, that coffee done."

She does, and pours us both a cup. We stir it with our cocoa on the bottom, blow it and drink the rich thick goodness. We drink all of it like some secret pact, then drop more cocoa to the bottom of our cups, make us new mugs of coffee. Then we prepare a tray of mugs so everyone else can have some.

Chapter Thirteen

Folks done had a few babies since Miemay passed, but this the first baby in our immediate family since she been gone. In the past, lots of folks come to Miemay house to have they babies, and that's where my sisters use to coming, too.

I miss it sometimes, taking care of the new mothers while Miemay out delivering babies somewhere else. Til 'a last year alive, Miemay was always on the go. One time she had three new mothers in the cabin with 'a. One went into labor travelling, the others lived in too poor of conditions to safely have they babies at home.

Most midwives here only go for a day, and women usually come back home to they mama's house to have babies. Just depends on where you live when you get married. Like, my Daddy live on his daddy's land, and his daddy on his daddy's land. We like beehives or something, slowly branching out over different parts of the same plots. The kids got tons of children to play with, cause their cousins all over. And working together fun, you know, but I'm getting off on to something else, missing feeling part of the family.

When it's like that, the mother go back to 'a mama's house to have the baby and the in-laws look after 'a house, husband and kids. Usually the woman's sister-in-laws, or the mother-in-law helps until she gets better. When my sisters got married, they moved to their husband's families' land. But we was always so close to Miemay, they use to just come to 'a house to give birth, less Miemay got a full house. Then she would go stay with them.

Anyhow, I explained all this, maybe for myself to understand how my baby sister arrived at my front door, heaving. Iain never been allowed to stick around when they was having they babies.

For some reason, cause Iain married, they always treat me like a child. Like it's things I cain't see or do, or know. Even though living with Miemay all the time, and helping 'a out mean I done seen lots of babies born. Shoot, I done helped deliver lots of babies to tell the truth.

I'm glad Grit here though. Always been protective of Grit, and it broke my heart when I what'n allowed to be there for 'a first baby. That was the first time I wondered, if this what'n how helpless husbands feel when all them women get to swarming round they house, busying they self, barking orders, and telling 'em how much they need 'em to do this and that, and then how they need to get lost, too.

I've boiled water and even chopped wood a few times, but there I was waiting like a husband and not a woman with sisters. With the birth of all they kids, I was sent to do some task, wash laundry, or watch children, or cook, or boil water, but never just to be there, to watch them move into motherhood. Seem like it was sacred, and cause I what'n married I was being punished or condemned.

Sounds dramatic, felt dramatic every time it happened. Being unmarried, I'm like some eternal child, less than a woman, less than a man and always at odds with everybody.

Then again, may not have nothing to do with none of that. Mama was always hovering over my sisters, and I was always running behind Daddy when he what'n pulling me with 'im. They always use to tease that he raised me like a boy, and that I would grow up to think and act like a man. They say that's probly why I'm so stubborn and ain't got no respect for men. I know all they know and can do all they can do, so it ain't no place for one in my life. That bother Daddy, don't bother me. Didn't bother me none til Mama shut me out of the room with Ella, then Jenny and finally Grit, saying, "This women's work."

Mama done said it so much, til Jenny start to say that about anything got to do with having a family, and then anything to do with being grown. Jenny start to treat me like a boy child to be mean. Sometimes I don't care, cause I don't want to hear or talk about what they think is important anyhow.

I was always outside their little circle of womanhood. Miemay or Reverend Patrick's wife, Mrs. Harper, always helped me with things. Mrs. Harper had eight sons and no daughters, so she always doted on me.

When Miemay bought me this big, beautiful, lilac dress for the spring formal, it was Mrs. Harper who sat me down for hours pin rolling my hair. Even then, Mama said my ways were too ugly for me to be pretty. Ella had said it was the prettiest she'd ever seen me. And whenever someone comments on my looks, and they do all the time, if Ella round she always say, "You shoulda seen 'a in that lilac dress."

Honestly, I only wore all that stuff to make Mrs. Harper and Miemay happy. I coulda cared less bout a spring formal. I was already tired of people staring at me all the time. Tired of men's breath shortening and other women going on and on bout my hair, and hating me at the same time.

Folks never talked to me, they always talked at me, or about me. Made me so uncomfortable with all the attention folks was giving me.

Miemay promised she wouldn't ask me to go to nothing else. Seem like she always knew me, understood me. Somehow, she even realized I didn't like dresses and things, so she got me tools, lots of tools. When Daddy noticed, he started telling me to tell Miemay I needed this or that for some project.

Miemay was sharp as a nail. Cause one day when Daddy came to get me, she say, "I got you that tool you said you needed." When Daddy's face lit up, she added, "And I got ya daddy one, too." Which made his smile weaken, but it didn't stop him from asking me to ask 'a for tools.

Now Reverend Patrick's wife, Mrs. Harper, was always after me bout acting like a lady. Mama, on the other hand, was hands off. She was always helping my sisters with things, teaching them things, and combing their hair. If it weren't for Ella and Mrs. Harper, I wouldn't never have got my hair combed.

Shoot, one summer Mama was so tired of my hair she cut it off. Which was fine with me, cause it was probly the best summer I ever had, not having to deal with prying hands pulling you every which-a-way. All that hair use to get in the way, and be hot, too. After that, Daddy ain leave me home with

Mama no more. And Miemay had Ella or Mrs. Harper comb it, whenever it got long enough to catch. Seem like it came back in no time, too soon really.

Now that I think about it, Ella and Grit was always too busy having they babies to say who could be there or not. They probly wouldn't have minded me being around.

That's why I'm so glad Grit chose my house to have this baby. It's hard not to prance around like a race horse finally getting a chance to stretch its legs. After folks been treating it like an old mule and underestimating it. I cain't imagine nothing going wrong, but I don't want to be too green, like Iain watch cows, horses and pigs giving birth all my life. Like Iain helped Miemay deliver too many babies to count now. Still, it's different when it's Grit, and when she in my house. Feel like I got something to prove.

"Linny!" I hear Mama call from upstairs.

Me and Ella both rush up the steps, but when I get to the bedroom door Mama coming out.

"Grit just calling fah ya, ain time or nothing," Mama spit, looking at me, and then at Ella with me.

Ella look in on Grit and go back down stairs with Mama.

"How you doing?" I grab Grit hand and fawn over 'a like she a new baby. This sister of mine I adore and protect, always have. Ella protected me from Mama, I protected Grit. Ella took beatings for me and on account of my protecting Grit, she done took a few for Grit, too. Always felt like Jenny was on 'a own, always in competition with me. She took all the trouble she could find and couldn't blame on me for 'aself. That's another story though, we talkin bout Grit.

Grit, almost five years younger than me, just seventeen years old now. When she was born, Grit was my baby. She the last of the bunch, and I gave 'a all the goodness I could cause she was all good. She was always such a happy baby, laughing and full of light. Mama use to make me watch 'a like it was some kinda punishment, but I use to love holding Grit in my arms. Whatever treasures or treats I got while I was gone with Daddy during the day, I brought back to Grit.

Grit was the most beautiful brown bundle in the world. Like a fresh loaf bread with a little butter to add. She grew to be a lovely woman, who likes seeing 'a loved ones happy. This makes 'a easily led and eager to please. So when Granger came saying he wanted to marry 'a, even though she was in love with a certain Davis Lloyd from outside Neville town, she didn't protest.

Davis had come on the night before she was to wed Granger, asking 'a to run away with 'im. But she knew Daddy and Mama nem woulda never forgiven 'a. Plus Davis' folks was poor sharecroppers, who ain even own the land they was working. Davis ain have no way of taking care of Grit. If she married Davis, they would have said she threw 'a life away.

Now I'm staring down in 'a eyes, looking at the pain of childbirth in disbelief that she just seventeen and already on 'a third child. Then again, that's how it go round here. Soon as you get bout fourteen or fifteen years old, men start wanting to marry you.

One came for me like they came for her, but I refused. I went so far as to run away. Miemay the one stood between me and my spose to be husband. Some man, Iain never looked at twice, decided he wanted to take me away from Zion, my family and everything I ever knew, to some other town where he built hisself a house for a family.

Shaking my head, I take Grit in, thinking. It ain't never one of the boys you mighta liked from school. It have to be somebody older, who done figured out how he gone take care of you and the family yall might have. And Lord please don't be barren, that's a whole nother way to make a woman feel like she ain't nothing. But that's something else Iain gone get into right now.

Anyhow, you lucky if you get a husband bout in his early twenties. Cause usually they late twenties, early thirties, and in the worst cases early forties. Sometimes they done had one wife, who got sense enough to run off. Or the worst done happened, they wife died in childbirth or something else, and they looking for somebody to come in and take up the slack.

By the time Davis came that night, Grit had already gotten over the romantic notion that she wanted to get married for love. Daddy had beat us both. I'd tried to shield Grit from Daddy's rage, and he'd hit me, too. She'd cried beneath me, and he'd cursed me and cursed her, that she didn't want to end up like me.

Me being unmarried seemed like the worst fate a woman could imagine, but it didn't seem so bad to me. Still, my particular predicament and the threat of Daddy nem never speaking to 'a again, convinced Grit she had to marry Granger.

I remember what it felt like, each step as Grit came closer to the end of that isle, closer to the alter, and closer to marrying that old man. I counted inventory in my head. Didn't seem right, that Daddy would turn 'im loose with Grit.

Granger seemed too old to come calling for Grit. Still he and Daddy had laughed and talked. They had taken walks together and went fishing as the wedding day approached. Granger had come to dinner, and sat next to Grit.

Even Mama had pushed Grit to make 'im plates, and wait on 'im. Mama taught Grit to be silent, while Granger and Daddy talked current events and local affairs. One time Mama said it was a woman's job to smooth out 'a man's rough edges. With that, she taught Grit this fake laugh women do when their men tell bad jokes, or say inappropriate things.

Mama barely spoke to me, so she never even tried to teach me to be a lady. I was learning different lessons. I was being raised by the only woman allowed in town meetings. Even women whose husbands had died, sent their eldest sons to represent them. Miemay was the only woman who spoke for 'aself in all matters of business. So she wasn't teaching me silence. In fact, I was being encouraged to find my voice. I was being taught to hold my ground, and to fight.

Sometimes Miemay argued, and caused meetings to go long by refusing to accept one thing or another. She argued facts, and had lived so much longer than many of the other men; often times there were a few older men standing with her. They all stood together against the younger men, who'd assumed their fathers' and grandfathers' businesses and land.

There was some feeling that the younger ones didn't understand what they had inherited, or that they made decisions like the other folks in town didn't exist. Miemay stood for all the people of Zion, and never chose to make a dollar at one soul's expense. Sometimes, she took a favored girl child with 'a to witness and understand. When Miemay got sick, she charged that girl child to attend every meeting, and vote on 'a behalf.

Not wanting to make a mistake, I paid close attention. I read newspapers from all the local cities and towns. Sometimes I knew things, even my own daddy didn't. On top of that, Miemay taught me to hold my head up, and not get small for men, or other people. She told me to always look people in their eyes, at their soul, and not only listen, but feel what they be saying.

I was being taught and trusted to make decisions on behalf of my grandmother. Miemay always asked why I made one decision or another. We'd discuss facts, feelings and consequences. Miemay taught me how to look at a thing from every angle. Then, after listening to my reasoning bout one decision or vote, she'd either agree or say why she would've made a different choice.

Still she wouldn't tear me down or fuss at me. Sometimes she'd even say, "You so smart" or "You sharp as a nail," like she was proud. Then she'd get all excited and start smiling and rocking 'aself looking at me. I learned to decide, not beat myself up, to trust my thoughts and my intuition.

Miemay ain't never talk to me about being no lady, or how to act like one, cause I was a woman and would be, no matter what I did. She respected me, and others respected me cause of her respect, and the way she taught me to act. They came to expect me to be how I was, more than how they expected and wanted all girls to be.

That's why me and Daddy always use to sit on the porch talking bout things after supper. After a long day in the field, we might sit in total silence and just stare off in the night. So when

Granger and Daddy took their coffee on the porch and began to talk, I got me a mug and settled down there to talk as well.

Then Granger said something that didn't make sense. At first Daddy was calm, and I followed his lead. We was gone let it slide, but Granger went on and on like he knew what he was talking bout.

Made me think I was crazy, so I started questioning him, and asking him to explain. He started to stutter like he had some kinda speaking problem, and then he got mad. Iain realize he was mad right then, so I'm recounting facts and comparing 'em to what he said.

Fore I know anything, he done started saying that's why ain no man gone have me, and he ain't never met no woman like me. Then I'd laughed, unmoved by his words. I even told him, "I'd be a better woman if I was more like you. If Iain have no facts, just go off how I feel. Just run my mouth to hear myself talk, and don't give a care to who I might be speaking to."

That set him off. He started speaking only to Daddy, saying I was a handful, and that Daddy what'n gone never get rid of me talking like I do. Then I'd said to anyone who was listening, Daddy might wont to consider who Grit marrying. Considering this man would make such a good woman, seeing as how he ruled by his emotions, and cain't see the point for stating how he feel.

Daddy agreed with me about the matter, but Granger hit a sore spot when he said I'd never get married. Daddy couldn't allow a woman to talk to no man like that, and then side with that woman against a man. I was a woman first, before I was right. I was to remain mute, dumb, docile, and just above a child. So he reminded me, like children, women were to be seen and not heard.

I can hear Daddy indignant with the audacity of me to sit among men, even though he'd raised me in the comfort of them my whole life. "Gitcho ass back in the kitchen wicha Mama nem!" He'd sat up in his chair, scooting to the edge of his seat, and holding his weight ready to attack me. Some of that was about him showing out. Some of it was because he felt I was showing out, even though it was common practice for him and me to talk town business.

I moved, cause even though Daddy hadn't beat Mama since my brothers got grown, and Isaiah threatened to fight 'im one evening when he raised up like he might hit Mama. I what'n under that protection, daughters are always children long as they under they parents' roof. I know women been beat and slap by they mama and daddy well into they thirties and forties. You ain't never too old to be beat, long as you a woman. If you get married, you become a child to yo husband.

I never cared for conversations with other women. They always seem to discussed who liked who, and who was sleeping with who, or who got new this or that. Now when me and Daddy talk, or when I talk with other men, we talk about what it would mean to grow more cotton. How cotton ruined the soil, and the best way to rotate the crop. We talk about the best things to feed horses, cows and mules to keep 'em strong and keep 'em from getting sick. We talk about missing the old days, when we could sell meat to travelers in open markets before the Food and Drug Administration. We talk about how as much as we hate the new laws, they do good things too. Like, they stop swindlers from coming to our town selling us all kinds of elixirs to cure every ailment from exhaustion to broken bones, when the medicine ain't never nothing more than sugar water. We discuss the cost of crops, and what local town's people need from the Zion store, or the rising or lowering cost of different imported and exported goods.

Men talk money, going places, laws, and building things. Which seems to matter more to me, than who sweet on who. They never sit around talking bout women, or maybe they do and because I'm a woman they just don't around me. I cain't imagine it though, cause a man saying he like some woman is like asking to be janked. All the married men seem to go on about needing a break from they wives. They always saying, "I wish more women was like you."

Then again, the way they talk about women when I ain't around probly ain have no love in it, and no reason to get them janked. Shoot, now that I think about it, maybe I'm the woman they be talking bout. Cause I sho feels it, the change.

When I was a girl and I knew things, my daddy was proud and other men would be amazed by what I knew. I could show they sons something, and learn from 'em too. They liked teaching and learning things with me.

Now that them same boys men, it's different. Some rather do something wrong, and pretend to know over letting a woman tell 'em. Some go ask another man. Daddy or one of my brothers always have to cosign on what I be saying now. Men go back and forth, from wanting me, fearing me and hating me. The more I think about it, I feels it all the time. Them thinking I should be broken, and sometimes wishing they could break me.

So I got right on up without another word. I remember now, how embarrassed I was Daddy let Granger speak to me like that, and then how Daddy spoke to me in front of Granger.

I remember what Daddy said to Granger as I walked away, "I tried to marry 'a off, but she just too damned willful, and that's my fault. As God as my witness, Iain try to spoil that girl. I always knew my girls would one day have to leave, but the others was different, they had one foot out the door soon as they could walk. Linny the only one listened to me and I'm shame to say, I taught 'a almost everything I knew. I was proud of 'a, and prayed she wouldn't never be like 'a sisters.

"No man wants a woman who know more, or think she know more than him. Now she gone be a burden to me the rest of my life, and then one to 'a brothers after I die. That's why they say be careful what you ask for, cause I swear Iain never seen a man turn 'a head."

I don't care if a man never looks at me. But something bout Daddy saying I was a burden on him, and would be one on my brothers, too, weighed heavy on me.

When I got in the kitchen, Mama was waiting to pick up where Daddy left off. Snatching the cup of coffee from my hands, she told me, "They always said you was the prettiest of my girls, but look at you now. An old maid!

"Let ya youngest sister beat chu out the house, and you still ain't got a lick a sense. Cain't blame ya daddy for everythang wrong wicha. He mighta raised you like a boy, but you still a woman. Some of your natural instincts ought to take over. But it don't do you no good do it?" She stood staring at me for a while, before turning back to Grit, who she was giving another one of 'a classes on how to be a good wife.

"Come stand next to me, hopefully one day you'll need to know this, too." Then she told my sister, my baby sister, "Give him more milk than coffee. Just enough to give it the coffee taste. Otherwise, you'll never get no sleep. He'll be after you all night. Less that's what you like."

I remember feeling like I would cry. Thinking bout coffee and its potency making him more potent or not. I remember feeling like she was selling my sister, and thinking my sister felt sold. I remember my sister being considerate and attentive to details, while tears rolled silently down 'a face, feeling trapped, I assumed. Felt like I was screaming inside and I wanted to cry, too.

I stood next to Grit, interlaced my fingers with hers. When Mama was away, getting more things for 'a perfect wife lessons, I'd said to Grit, "You don't have to do this."

But Grit was there to see how cruel our parents had treated me after I refused to marry. Considering that, she'd probly felt it better to go kicking and screaming into marriage, with a man she had no love for, over being here. Where every day she woke up under they roof, she'd be reminded of how much of a disappointment she was to them.

"I am not strong like you," Grit broke into loud audible sobs snatching 'a hands away from mine, bracing herself against the counter like she would fall.

Then Mama came back in the kitchen. For a moment, she ain say a word, just looked at me and Grit. Like she could read our hearts. Then she slapped me, and blamed me for Grit being upset.

Chapter Fourteen

"I should have listened to you, you know." Grit grabs my hand, smiling sadly, pulling me back to this moment.

I don't take much heed to 'a words. Pregnant women always talk crazy when they wrapped up in the fear of they baby coming, and the pain of it arriving. Mothers with twelve kids say birth never is easy, though it gets easier. The pain is never anything you get use to.

"Are you tired?" I ask Grit, looking in 'a eyes, concerned about 'a laying down.

Miemay use to always say she didn't know where women learned to have babies on they back. I guess it's harder on their body to do it that way. And folks who had babies on they back and then had babies with Miemay, always said Miemay knew best, and walking round and squatting worked best.

Miemay would curse organized medicine, and doctors, and men who never had children telling women how to have babies. Cain't even imagine a man telling me how to do something with my body, but they do in some places. I've heard of women going to hospitals and letting men cut them open to take the baby out.

"Mama told me to lay down but my backs hurting," Grit whines like a baby, and I baby 'a too.

"Get up." I pull Grit up with me as I stand, "Let's walk around up here."

"You always do everything like Miemay, don't you?" Grit laughs and follows my lead.

I wonder if she really wanted to lie down, and if she isn't just doing this to please me, so I say, "This moment bout you right now. Don't let me push you if this ain't what you want. You having the baby, whatever you want be fine with me. You wanna walk around or lay down?"

"Linny," Grit smiles, "You always looking out for me, I feel alright telling you how I really feel."

I take a few deep breaths, accepting what she say. The way Grit looks at me warms me, eases me.

"It's what I want. I had my last baby over a pad on the floor. Mama was so mad, but I spose it be better than having one on my back. And I felt good afterwards. Shoot, I coulda cooked Thanksgiving dinner after that baby came. What'n a whole lot of soreness like with the first one. I think cause Iain have the second one on my back like Mama insisted, and cause I listened to Miemay.

"Miemay told me not to lay around, and walk while I was pregnant. She said fat lazy women have the hardest times. But Mama say it was easier cause I done it before. She say it get easier every time. Maybe it's all that and then nothing at all."

I smile at Miemay's words, cause I done heard 'a give that advice a thousand times. Then I go start a fire in the fireplace, so when it's time, I can heat some water upstairs, too. "Think you want to rest in the tub again?"

"That bath did help earlier. I don't know what happened. Felt like the baby was ready to come. I mean, I had low back pains and no matter how I turned, they kept getting worse. Then I git to yo house, and for some reason my body just stop opening."

"It happens like that some times. Cain't be too worried. Too much noise, or fussing, or you just get all upset, and fore you know it, the baby done went on back in there to wait for a better time."

"Ha ha ha," Grit laughs and slaps my arm. "Linny, you such a mess. Sound like Miemay. I'm so glad you here this time. Want you to be here with me when I have this one, and the next one."

I nod smiling, moved and a little emotional cause I really want to be here. "All the way," I say, grabbing 'a hand, and we walk.

Then she drop in a squat, bear over, and moan. The contractions are back and I know these the real ones.

"Boil me some water!" I yell down stairs. Then I fill the bath pot in the bathroom, and put it over the fireplace in 'a room. I get some padding and place it on the dresser. I already know she ain trying to have this one in the bed either. I hear feet stomping heavy up the steps coming to help.

"Linny, git out of here," Mama say soon as she walk in.

"Yeah this ain't no place for you," Jenny agree.

"Linny, stay!" Grit scream, looking up, one hand on the edge of the bed, the other on 'a knee squatting.

"Move, move, move," Ella come from behind them with a pot of hot water she musta just knew to be boiling. Then Mozelle behind 'a with empty bowls to wash hands. Everyone starts to move.

I get Miemay's bag and start setting things out on the dresser again. I go get the chair because Grit is dead set against laying down, she walking this one out. Whenever she's not bearing down to ride the contractions, she holding on to the wall, and taking steps while breathing. Miemay woulda been so proud.

I wash my hands, and get the orange stick to scrub my nails. I roll my sleeves up and soap my hands several times, as Ella runs water so hot over my hands I have to shake them a bit. We lay out the towels and the old t-shirt. I get the basin for 'a to squat over.

"Can I see," I ask standing a good distance away, cause new mothers like quiet and they don't like feeling attacked. Putting 'a leg up on the chair and hiking up her gown she show me 'a openness. I've helped deliver babies a few times, but this time is different. It's my baby sister having a baby. "You doing good, Grit."

Frowning and nodding 'a head thanks, Grit bears down again on the chair. I put my hands between 'a legs and feel the warm wetness. I push my hand up inside of 'a to see how open she is, and I can feel the baby making its way down out of 'a.

"Come on now." I sit down in the chair and let 'a lean back on me while she squat over the little tub we done filled with material and newspaper to catch the baby, and all the stuff it be wrapped in sometimes when it come out.

The sound of hands being washed with orange sticks sooths the silence. Until Mozelle pours water over their hands to rinse away the soap.

Putting 'a armpits on my thighs, Grit leans back against me. I'm glad I'm in pants so my dress won't be getting all in the way. She quiet as she riding them pains.

"Breathe," Ella remind Grit, when we don't hear nothing. Then Ella hit my arm, pull me up from behind Grit.

I hesitate, looking at Mama and Jenny. This ain the time to be trying to show out or nothing. I just want to be here. I feel like if I come from behind Grit they gone find a reason to throw me out.

When I pull back from Ella too many times she say warmly, "Ita be okay."

Then Jenny start fussing. "I cain't hardly stand to watch this! Ain got no midwife, got a girl ain't got child to the dang first doing women's work. And Grit shouldn't be having no baby over no pail. She need to git in the-"

"GIT OUT!" Grit manages, screaming and interrupting Jenny.

"Well, least we know she breathing," Ella jokes, laughing.

"Go on, Jenny! Git out! Git down stairs! I don't want to hear no moe shit tonight."

"Alright nah, I know you in pain but ain no cause to talk like that." Mama stands waiting to help, watching and taking steps in and back trying to find a place.

"You can git, too," Grit spit, looking up at Mama like she possessed.

"Gone now, Jenny. She need 'a Mama here," Mama cosigns and surrenders to my surprise. Some part of me feels bad that Jenny is being kicked out. I know what it feels like to be left out.

I don't know if Jenny ever leave or not. I'm guiding the baby out, and telling Grit how to push to keep from tearing. Ella holding Grit in 'a arms and riding the pains with 'a.

When I hear Mama call out the door, "Send that midwife up soon as she git here."

"Baby be here fore the midwife," Ella warn.

"I'm gone go downstairs and brang some more towels up," Mozelle offer.

"It's coming!" Grit scream, gritting 'a teeth, balling 'a fist up and throwing 'a head back.

"Easy, push slow," I say, guiding the baby's head, turning its body so the shoulders don't rip 'a down to 'a tail. The urge to push too much for 'a tho, and she push hard, then it do spill out in my arms.

Soon as I catch the baby, I'm a little scared to slap 'im on the tail cause he so small. Grit bigger than she was with the other two, and them two was much bigger than this one. We been saying this one gone be 'a biggest baby yet.

Some folks say, this one gone be a big boy, cause she already got two girls. It is a boy, but he tiny, just a lil bigger than my hand. I already know he gone be called Granger, Jr. after his daddy.

I hold 'im while tying two ties on the cord. I feel warm tears fall from my eyes as I wait, for the heart beat in the cord closest to 'im to stop, so I can cut him away from his mama. I hold him close, keep 'im warm. Seem like the whole world moving round me, and I see how God work. I see how life and death so close.

Most dangerous thing a woman can do round here is work for a white man ain got no wife, and having a baby. Be a blessing when mama and baby both come out alright. Be another blessing when a baby makes it to five round here. There are so many things we pray pleading for, because so many people are lost to things, but this moment God be showing out.

Finally, the cord closest die and I ask my new nephew, "Are you ready to be on your own in the world," as I happily cut the cord. Then I wait for 'im to take a breath, but he silent. He so small and still in my hands, it make me nervous to do what I'm spose to if he don't breath. Still, I give 'im a good lick and he screams.

"He got a big spirit, ain he." Mama sigh relieved, and it seem like the whole room breathe easier and smile at his crying.

The women smile approving, telling Grit, "You finally done gave Granger a boy."

Their words make me a little sad. We don't marvel at just bringing life into the world. It ain't enough to survive bringing a healthy baby in the world. You got to give yo husband a boy.

I think about what we telling ourselves bout being women. I'm thinking about how we teach our girls bout they value. A man couldn't do this. If it what'n for daughters being born wouldn't be no mothers to have sons.

Once I'm done, Mama take 'im, wash 'im and put 'im on Grit, skin to skin. While Grit holding him, me and Ella push on 'a stomach to help get the sack out. The pressing help the sack get loose from 'a stomach walls. It's a lot in 'a when we stop and leave the cord hanging.

The baby so small and Grit stomach still so big for the baby to be done come. We all notice but don't say nothing. I don't cut the cord; I'm waiting til she get some more labor pains and give birth to the sack. I tie the cord close as I can to 'a opening, so I know when some of it coming out. Some mothers be so caught up in they new baby, they barely notice giving birth to the sack.

While waiting, we clean up the baby bath, as much as we can. We set out a new pad and wash basin to put the sack in, to be examined. If even a lil bit be left inside there, it'll make the new mama sick. It could kill 'a. We clean Grit up some, and put 'a on some clean pads, but we still waiting. I'm glad it's almost over and won't be long til it is.

*   *   *

I hear the roosters start to crow. I smell breakfast. I hear laughter and loud talking, and heavy footsteps down stairs. Then I realize I done fell asleep in the sitting chair, and that sack still ain came.

"Grit," I call, and startle her out of sleep. "You hurting?"

"Nah, I ain't." She sit up, and the baby lay peaceful on 'a chest.

"He did the crawl yet?" Mozelle come in.

"Nah, he ain't." Grit ease back down. "But I'm ready to git up and do something. I feels good."

"She ain gave birth to the sack yet, has she?" Mama come in behind Mozelle with hot water.

I shake my head, "No." We all a lil concerned but we act like it ain't nothing, even though too much time done passed. I get up, wash my hands, then check Grit. Grit hole done closed, and the cord still alive. I can feel the heart beating in the end before the knot. Still, I move like it ain't nothing, and everything is as it should be.

My heart feel like someone got they hand wrapped round it, squeezing. Mama watch close, but she don't say nothing. I don't know if she know something wrong, and just don't want to upset Grit.

I clean Grit up again, cause on top of the heart beating in the cord, she bleeding bad. Since the cord ain't died, every heart beat pushing a lil blood out. I am scared.

I tie another cord in the same place, tight as I can this time. I notice the first one ain moved. Then I tie another two more on there, cause what's already on there slowing the blood but not completely stopping it.

"That's why you shoulda went and got that midwife," Mama fuss.

"She was already delivering another baby," Ella remind Mama, who I can feel is looking for some way to blame this on me.

I blame myself, even though I don't know what I coulda done different. Seem like a normal birth, ain have no problems, 'cept the false start and even that's kinda normal. I feel anchored there, til Ella touch me and say, "Go eat something."

I smile at Grit, but feel sadness creeping up on me. When I turn to walk out, I see where somebody done brought Grit a tray upstairs with a lil of everything.

When I get down stairs, the house full of women. I put on some water for cleaning. Then I wash my hands, eat a few bites of food, speak to cousins and auntees. I wonder where they got all this meat from, cause I don't never have this much meat in my smoke house.

I step out on the back porch and see the home garden been weeded. I can tell by looking in the coup the chickens been fed. I'm bout to walk round and do the other morning chores, when I hear Jenny call down to us, "He crawling! He crawling!"

We all go running up to watch the new baby crawl up Grit body, and find 'a nipple. Cain't just put yo nipple in a new baby's mouth, gotta let the baby's instincts kick in and let 'em find they way to they mama to nurse. Otherwise feeding be painful to the mama, and it be hard to ever get the baby to nurse. Least that's what people say.

When he latch on to Grit's breast and start nursing, we all laugh and slap each others' arms. Then we know he gone be alright even though he ain but this big.

"Alright! Alright! I'm here now!" the midwife, Mrs. Jessamine, shout, coming in smiling and cheerful. The sun done start spilling in the room, and here come Ella with more water. The midwife a heavy set older woman, with grandchildren of 'a own. Her hair pulled back and she look tired. I know she done had a long night, and probly ain't been to sleep.

"She ain't had the cord yet," Ella tell 'a.

"How long its been since she had the baby?" Mrs. Jessamine ask over 'a shoulder.

"Been a long while," Mama answer.

"I need some space to look afta 'a," Mrs. Jessamine command, turning round and looking at everybody in the room.

Women start to leave, and here come Mozelle with more towels. The midwife clean 'a hands without ever looking at 'em. She looking at Grit, frowning. "Alright honey," she say, shaking off 'a hands and walking over to the bed.

Easing down on the bed, Mrs. Jessamine moan, tired and then pull the covers back. "Umph," she say, leaning one way, and then another, moving 'a hands around Grit.

I take slow long breaths.

"Why it's so many ties on here, and all this blood?" She examining my work and I'm feeling like I need to explain. I'm afraid ain do something right.

Clearing my throat, I step up closer. "I put another one, ma'am. She was bleeding something awful. The heart was still beating when I checked."

"I see dat," she say, frowning at the space tween Grits legs. Everybody else done went back downstairs. It's just me, Mama and Ella in the room. "The hole done closed tight like she done, and the cord ain't die or nothing." The midwife announce shaking 'a head worried.

Grit starts to cry, cupping 'a baby head and kissing him like she protecting him from hearing the news.

Ella grab my hand as she walk closer to the bed. Ella swallow hard, and I feel like stone.

"I don't know how we gone git it out. We cain't pull it, don't wont the sack to tare. And I'm gone haveta put another tie on here, cause she bleeding through these ones on here," Mrs. Jessamine say, more to aself than to us.

"Say it plain," Mama sit down on the bed and look at Grit with 'a.

"Well, we see what happen. I done heard they cut women open in the hospital when this happen."

Grit cry out. Then say, "I rather die than be cut open!"

"Don't speak death over yo life, girl. Need to be praying for help and time. Ain't no hospital seeing niggas for miles."

Ella legs fail 'a and I catch 'a, then pull 'a up next to me. Hold 'a close til she solid. We look at Grit, sorry, silent, sad.

"She cain't have this up in 'a." Mama reach like she might snatch the cord. Mrs. Jessamine close Grit's legs and guard it, looking at Mama like she crazy.

"You cain't cut it no moe, til the heart stop beating in it. It ain even stop bleeding. Iain never seen this much blood this long after the baby come. Then she ain even got a piece of the sack, she got the whole thang in 'nere. All we can do is wait. I cain't even git my hand in there."

"I wish you hadn't left," Mama say just above a whisper, staring at Grit like it's the last time she gone see 'a, tears streaming down 'a face.

Chapter Fifteen

Ella ain't asleep. Even though it's been years since all us was sleeping under the same roof, and even longer since me and Ella shared a bed, I still know her. Funny how so much change, and then so much stay the same. The rhythm of 'a breathing the same as when we was kids. I still know the difference between 'a being quiet, and being sound asleep. Maybe if she went to sleep, I woulda got tired of listening to 'a deep breathing and fell off myself.

That's the way it always was when we was kids, I'd fall asleep to 'a breathing. Wake up when the bed got cold, after she'd gone to help Mama with morning chores. If she stayed til the roosters' crowed, I wouldn't even wake up for them.

Been years since Ella got married, left me behind, to save myself from Mama. Soon as she left things changed. I don't know how long she had been gone when she pulled me aside at church one Sunday, smiling and hopeful, asking how was everything at the house. What she was really asking was, how I was getting along with Mama since she left.

What'n nothing to say to 'a. What could she do then, living with 'a husband and expecting they first child? I couldn't bring myself to tell Ella, how Mama ain speak to me less she had something bad to say.

So I answered, "Same ol same," smiling. While the place under both my arms hurt something awful whenever I laughed, or even breathed too deep. I didn't scream or cry when Ella hugged me tight, even though it took all of me to keep quiet, and force a smile. I didn't tell 'a how much I missed 'a, or how lonely I was now that she was gone.

Ella what'n like a lot of other women. Ella made sure she married who she wanted to. She told any man thinking bout coming for 'a hand and anybody else listening, she was waiting for Prentice to make them a way. Mama worried she'd never marry. Some folks still say she married old, but Ella married 'a sweetheart. So she was really happy, and pregnant.

Ella was a worrier, and Iain wont to upset 'a. Plus I was ashamed, I felt like I had to be doing something wrong or something was wrong with me. I didn't want the only person that loved me to think I was bad, too. Specially since I knew, soon as Grit got old enough to know the difference between right and wrong she probly be with Mama and Jenny nem, against me.

So Iain tell Ella, Mama told Daddy I was getting too old to be trailing him all over town. Said I was becoming a woman, and she needed to teach me how to be a wife. Guess that's why Mama had me watching Grit all the time. Iain mind Grit. I just couldn't never do nothing right according to Mama.

When Ella was around, she would show me how Mama liked things. Ella would take the blame for things, watch me, and would be patient while I learned.

Mama never taught me nothing, but held me accountable for knowing. That's how Jenny came to be the smart one, while I was pegged the stupid one always working Mama's nerves.

There was a time, when Iain go two days without Mama slapping me, and not a week without her or Daddy beating me for something. It was like she hated looking at me. She'd frown as she watched me walk in and out of a rooms, like I what'n even hers. Wouldn't comb my hair, or keep my clothes up.

Whenever I got a good licking, Mama would keep me in the house. She be telling people, I think I'm a boy and always getting myself hurt some kinda way. She told people I was wild, whenever they asked how come I was always bruised, or what happened to my lip and eye.

Mama made so many excuses bout my bruises, even Daddy believed. Daddy started to feel like it was his fault I was always getting myself hurt. He felt so guilty bout my wild-boy ways, soon as he'd get home he'd be on me.

Then Mama ain beat me with no belt or switch like she did everybody else, even the boys. When she whup me, she used 'a hands, she used 'a fists. Sometimes I would walk around the house, just waiting for it.

No matter what I did, how I did, I was still wrong. If I tried to explain, it be like I'm talking back. My words be used against me, turned around, and I be thinking I'm crazy. Cause I be done thought about what I'm saying a hundred times fore I say it. Especially after my words been turned around so many times.

So, one day, after too many "stupid cows, slow mules, or worthless cusses," I just stopped, just stopped trying to please Mama. Started doing the best I could, whatever I know how and just waited. Didn't matter no how, one way or the other, I was wrong.

I would never say anything. Wouldn't never sass Mama, and then that behavior give them reason to say I'm bad, wild. Start Daddy to do more than yell at me all night, he start beating me, too.

Fore Ella left, Mama was on me so much he didn't never bother me much. Plus, I be with him all day, so whatever trouble everybody else done found, Iain in. After Ella left, and I stopped trying to please Mama, it be like I had gone crazy or something. Mama have a bad day, or for any reason she be on me. Then for some reason, Jenny be always telling 'a things, and pointing out my mistakes.

Miemay ain go to church, so I don't know how long it was fore she seen me. When she finally did, I musta look something awful, cause it took 'a breath away. Made 'a eyes so thick with tears, she grabbed the back of Mama's kitchen chair, and buried 'a head in the bend of 'a arm to hide 'a face from me.

It was the first time, I'd seen 'a cry since a hanging years before, she say, "Lawd Jesus!" Every time she look at me, her voice crack, and she cry like a child, "Jesus!" Then she say, "Gitcho thangs." Then she walked round our house shouting at Mama saying, "You oughta be shame!" Then to me, "Gitcho thangs!" No one protested, and it seemed like Miemay was looking for a fight but Mama watched silently as Jenny helped me pack.

Since I couldn't hardly lift my arms an my sides was hurting, Miemay took me to see a real doctor. That's when we found out my ribs was cracked. After that, I what'n at home much no more. It be like I'm staying with Miemay most times.

Miemay be asking where I'm at all the time when I start spending the night at 'a house. She say, "Come sit out here on dis poche wit me."

I had got so use to hiding, and being invisible at home, I be afraid of the sun it seem.

But Miemay be telling me how smart I am, and letting me help 'a with things grown women do. And Miemay ain never hit me. She always talk to me, ask me why I did a thing, and tell me why I shouldn't. She expected me to know things, and treated me like I had already been here before. Cause she expected me, I arrived.

Then one day Miemay say, "You relly tryin ta keep up, ainchu?"

Another day she say smiling, "Guess ya ain't dat wild and crazy afta all." Then she explained how people always call crazy what they don't understand, and wild what they cain't control. I think about how they called 'a crazy, but she was one of the most rational folks I knew. Didn't mince 'a words, but she'd give you the shirt off 'a back.

Miemay. When I think about Miemay, coming back to get Grit, I know Grit be okay. I know death ain the worse thing, I already been there. Thinking bout Miemay, I go from being overwhelmed with sadness, to worrying if Miemay can get Grit out of 'a body fore the pain start, and 'a body start to shut down.

Some other part of me, I'm ashamed to say, is content having all my sisters at my house under one roof, and Ella laying next to me. I wont to tell Ella bout Miemay, cause I know she up, but I know better than to say that out loud. People don't see death the way I do, the way Miemay did, and the way Miemay showed me.

Ella wouldn't understand if I told 'a how even though Grit may die, these last few days of Grit life been some of the best days of my life. Being able to be with them all, bringing Grit's baby in the world make me think God hear me sometimes. I feel guilty Iain sadder. I'm worried but Grit ain gone yet. I wont to enjoy these last days if they be 'a last days.

Smell of sausage, bacon and biscuits make it safe to move, stirring Ella in the darkness. Maybe she know Iain sleep either. I lay silent looking at the ceiling thinking bout Grit dying.

Don't seem right, or fair, or possible. Think about other mothers who died as I was growing up. I remember the faces of children I met at church and played with who ain make it to five. Too many to name, too many to remember. Death seem to be just a thing that happen.

I'm remembering going with Miemay to deliver herbs to folks with fevers, and flus, and aches. I'm thinking bout folks being quarantined, and whole houses dying from one thing or another. I'm thinking bout the midwife curse, and people blaming midwives for they babies dying. Or being afraid cause a baby died, that the midwife bad luck. I'm thinking bout folks fasting and praying for people to be saved, and still burying them.

Mostly, I'm thinking bout after all these years, how much I missed my sister. Being in this house alone and having Ella here, now, laying next to me make everything feel like it's gone be alright. A peace come over me, and something tell me Grit ain gone die at all.

"What you thinking bout?" Ella ask and I realize, I done interlaced my fingers with hers. The ceiling is a blur, my eyes sting, so I hide my face in the bend of my arm to keep from letting the tears escape. I'm ashamed to tell 'a Iain crying cause of Grit.

I find myself when I think about what Grit must be going through in the other room, thinking bout dying 'aself, then with Mama and Jenny nem treating 'a like she already dead.

"Nobody I ever seen fore they died was ever ready, but Miemay," I say for some reason.

"Miemay lived a long life. She was round bout ninety-five or ninety-six. Probly was ready to go cause everybody she knowed done went on."

"Nah, what'n that." I put my hand on my stomach, trying to touch and soothe the uneasiness that's a feeling of obligation to deny Miemay was ready to die, cause everybody else she know dead. We lay silent for a while. Ella looking off in 'a own direction, when I add, "We still here, she know us, and loved us. Miemay liked taking care of us, and helping us have our babies."

"Why you think she was ready then?"

"I don't know if anybody ever ready to go. It was just 'a time. She use to tell me, 'Death a natural part of life, we all dyin.' Miemay what'n scared, she knew where she was going." My voice trails off, as I think about 'a jumping in and out of 'a body. As I think about 'a leading folks to the light.

"She what'n scared of nothing." Ella smile agreeing, feeling Miemay spirit, and it's like she walking in the room. All her strength be here, with us.

"On top that, she had a chance to live how she wanted. What'n always trying to please people way other folks do. She ain't let fear rule 'a. The threat of burning in hell what'n enough to break 'a, or make 'a mind."

Ella laugh at that. "Sho what'n. I member Reverend kept tellin 'a, 'You betta come to chuch or you gone burn.'"

Then we both laugh, mocking Miemay saying to Reverend Patrick, "Gawd everwhur, boy!" We elbow each other in bed and laugh. Tears streaming down our eyes, we recount the story, line for line.

"Oh, ya thank Gawd only come ta yo chuch, boy?" I say.

"Thank you, John DaBaptiss or somebody?" Ella say.

"You savin folk nah?" I say.

"Let me find out Jesus done come back, and walkin mongst the poe-ass niggas of Zion," Ella shout, tickled.

"Nah dat's, blaspheme'n, Miemay," Reverend say. I puff my chest out and sit up even more ridiculous than Ella.

"Betcha cain eeben spell dat big word," Ella moan low way Miemay did when she said it to Reverend, or how she did when she get going on somebody.

"Why I'm gone spell a word for somebody cain't even read? You ain't got no way of checkin whether I can or cain't spell it no how," I answer all smart, high and mighty way Reverend did; looking down my nose and playfully fixing my collar.

"Readin ain't hep chu none, cause you sho ain red dat Bible. And I might cain't read but I bet chu I know moe of it den you, Patrick. How ya lak dat nah?"

"Oh lord," Ella finish. "'Any day nah, come see bout me any day nah, and I know it betta den you. Any day. How you lak dat nah?' That was 'a favorite sayin, what'n it? That's when she really be gittin on you. 'How you like that nah?' Ima have to start sayin that when Prentice gittin on my nerves, and I want to git back on his. How you like that nah?"

Knocking on the door tells us we're too loud, and I just know it's gone be Mama or Jenny fussing and telling us to hush our mouths. When the door open, it's Grit, so me and Ella hop to our feet.

"What's so funny? I wont to laugh, too. All this sadness round here, you think I be already dead," Grit say, holding 'a new baby and still walking like she pregnant.

"Come over here and sit down," Ella say and try to help 'a to the bench at the foot of my bed, but she hold still.

"I'm tired of laying down, and sitting. Been two days since I had the baby, and I feel fine."

"Good," I say, running my finger along the baby arm, and kissing his little hand. Inhaling him, I try to release the heaviness of the moment when I exhale. Still it lingers and make the morning stale.

"I'm going downstairs," Grit announce defiant. "And maybe even out on the porch when the sun finally come up."

"Not with Mama and Jenny nem down there. Honey, you be lucky you can use the toilet by yo self," Ella tease.

"I'm going down stairs," Grit say in a way don't leave room for arguments. "I'm tired of living for everyone else. Tired of doing what I'm told, and trying to make everybody else happy." Putting 'a baby's mouth to 'a nipple, Grit look at him like he some kinda revelation.

"Thought I'd be tired, and old when my time come. Thought my kids would be grown, married, might even have some grandbabies. Everybody say my time is now. Truth is though, I'm feeling more like myself than anything. My pregnant self anyway. Anyhow, I don't want to lay around no more. Think I want to take a walk or something."

Chapter Sixteen

It's been four days, and Grit still ain't gave birth to that sack. Everybody gone to church, just me, her and the baby sitting upstairs. I moves to help 'a up, but she fan me away.

Getting up, she move like it ain nothing. Opening the curtains and windows, letting sun and cool air in. She say, "Sure is nice outside."

We go out walking, and it's silent. It's like we the only ones alive on earth. Me, her and the baby. I listen to the wind stirring, not enough to feel, just enough to hear.

"I don't know when the last time I was off like this. Iain never missed a Sunday from church. Now I see how it could be good to stay home some times. Its nice, ain it?"

I'm holding 'a baby and we going pass the barn. I'm just looking at all the work folks done done since Grit got here. They done filled my smoke house with meat. Somebody done cleaned out my little garden, and left some vegetables for the house.

Shoot, every since my sisters got here, folks been bringing food. They always do when a baby come, like they always do when somebody die or bout to die. They said Grit wouldn't last another day, and here it is the fourth day. Show you what folks know.

I looks over at Grit, and wonder if it's her will keeping 'a here. I think about how Miemay fought death all them days and months, waiting for this house to get done. Then I think about what Grit got to live for, and I'm thinking on 'a kids, and husband. It be something awful if she gone. But we'll make a way, we always do. I don't want to think about Grit dying. The thought of it breaks my heart.

If anybody should go, probly should be me. I got the least amount of folks depending on me. I won't be missed let Daddy nem tell it. Then things go back to being right, I guess. Everybody be getting what they think they spose to have, I expect.

"Linny, you hear me talking to you? You always in yo head." Grit touch my arm.

"What you said?"

"I said something is wrong, I don't know, I feel funny. Like I need to git on back to the house or something."

I give 'a my arm and we start moving, quick, and she gittin it. Soon as we get to the stairs she bow down, hold on to the banister. "Oh Lawd!"

"What's wrong?" I ask, concerned and looking at 'a trying to gauge what it is. She don't say nothing, she just bite 'a lips, and I see she hot. Then right there on my front porch I see it come gushing out, down 'a legs into 'a boots.

"Oh Jesus!" she cries, as we climb the steps, and then the steps inside the house. I don't know what to do, I think about getting somebody, but know I cain't leave 'a here by 'a self.

"Lay down," I order her, putting the baby in the bed beside 'a so we can watch him, too. I open 'a legs, and look, and sure as a summer day can be long that hole done opened back up.

I run down stairs to get some water, and get Miemay midwife tools. I'm so worried my hands won't be steady. Fore I go back in the room, I get myself together. Ain no use to us both worrying or being upset.

When I know I can act like I got everything under control, I bust back in the room. I move quickly, silently. If I don't think about it, it won't hit me that she might die right here, right now.

Oh lord, let 'a make it, let 'a live. Don't let 'a die on my watch, Lord. I what'n never the kinda person ask you for much. Fact is, I don't even know the last time I came to you for nothing, but, Lord, please guide my hands. Lord, guide my mind, and lead me.

After I wash my hands, I reach up in 'a. "Feels like-" I stop, and I must be frowning cause Grit frowning, too, like she mocking me. I feel like our faces the same, and we both feeling round in 'a, but it's just me.

"What's wrong?" Grit say, after I don't speak for a while and we just looking at each other.

"Feel like . . ." I don't want to say it and sound crazy. I don't know what's going on with her. Maybe it's the cord and the bag all bald up in 'a, I'm feeling.

"What is it, Luhnay?" She call my name the way Miemay do, or the way Mama use to when I was in trouble.

"Feels like," I start again, and look at 'a ashamed I don't really know what it is. Worried, that no matter what I say it's gone get Grit all upset and hysterical. "Feels like . . . another baby in here. Feel like a baby head do."

"Oh," she say all calm, suddenly letting go all the air like she relieved.

How calm she be make me uneasy. I wonder if this ain't the calm before the storm.

"Yesterday, I was trying to fall off to sleep, but my stomach was so busy, I kept thinking how it felt like I was still expecting."

"Iain never heard of no babies being born days apart," I say.

"Me neither," Grit say, reaching for my arm and pulling herself up.

"Ima go boil some water."

"Ain't no time for that." She laugh a little like the pain a relief.

Soon as she stand, she grab holt to the bed like she might go down on the ground. I hold her, and wish there was more than just me here. She start to walk holding on to the wall. When I can move, I put out all the pads I got near a chair, where she can hold on and squat. Every so often I check and the hole giving way, and that cord coming on out slowly.

"Oh, oh," she moans and leans into the pain. Holding on to the chair she gets a good grip and starts to push.

I reach in to see where the baby is, and turn his shoulders so it don't rip 'a. I'm trying to get a good grip, but the space so tight and whenever she breathe and stop pushing, it's like he go on back up in there some. I try to hold tight to his head, but it's hard cause he wet and slippery. I don't want to hurt him, or break his neck.

"Easy now, you almost done," I say, looking in Grit eyes trying to see how she doing. She seem better than she did with the first one, and this one coming fast. When I get him out the way of 'a tail, I say, "Come on, give me all you got."

When she push, the baby getting free.

"One more!"

Then she grit 'a teeth, and make this loud noise Iain never heard from 'a, and fore I know it there be another little one in my arms.

"This one a girl," I say smiling and reaching for the scissors to cut the cord.

Grit laugh, relieved. I don't think it's a real laugh. She been told she gone die and now she gone live.

I feel like crying too, I'm so happy. We both looking at 'a beautiful baby girl. When the heart beat stop in the cord, I cut it and wrap the baby in blankets.

"All folks been talkin bout is if I have a boy we got to name him Granger. You know, I hadn't thought about names for a girl really. I had been wanting to give Granger a boy myself. So, you already know what I'm gone name this one."

"Do I?"

"Ima name 'a after you. Gone name 'a Madelyn, just like 'a auntie."

Breathing deep, I look at the small little bundle and it feels like she mine. When I caught Granger, Jr., felt like I couldn't be more relieved or more happy, and now, there is something pass that. I cain't believe how beautiful lil Madelyn is. And some part of me wonders if this ain't how Miemay felt when I was born, and they named me after her.

Then I think about how Grit naming this baby after me, cause she hadn't been thinking of a name for 'a girl. Then I think about how all Grit wanted was a boy. Then I wonder if Mama ain have no name for me cause she wanted another boy. Then I think about how Mama didn't even name me, Miemay did. And I wonder, if Mama ever wanted me at all.

Chapter Seventeen

"Yah!" I command, leaning left, holding the reigns, guiding Anastasia down an old dirt road lined with big oak trees, standing like guards of the past. Use to be a plantation here; it was abandoned after the Civil War. I what'n born then, but Miemay use to tell me stories bout how grand this house use to be.

Seem like ages ago with another war brewing, but we all still be standing in the shadows of its dead. The people ain never come back here after the war. They say the women stayed on while the men went to fight. They say all the men were killed, and the women left before the Union could make it down here. Now, it all be ruins. The house stand like a reminder of what use to be, feel like a lot of what was, still is right here on the edge of Zion.

Every once in a while, at some church function out on the green, people get to talking bout what they could do to make our town better, and this land, the Hilliard House always come up. Folks be going on bout how we should put this land on our town schedule and do something with it. The yard would be so beautiful if somebody would keep it up.

All these beautiful flowers, make you know God still in control. No pruning or watering, and there be more colors and flowers here than any other kept garden in Zion. That's how you can tell it's some good land, cause the grass done got so tall, and the trees so strong, seem like the plants swallowing the house, and eating the memories to survive.

Then again, fixing this house up or taking care of the yard, or using the land is just for talk. Some white people already say we don't deserve the land we on. If Hilliard was somewhere else, it be full of white folks, but they ain trying to live surrounded by no niggas. Still, any nigga take it upon hisself to do something to the Hilliard House, be good as dead. This the house where the Klan meet before riding through Zion. When they come to remind us they still here and that they like God, still in control.

One time when me and Miemay was coming from town, cause you got to go pass the Hilliard House to get anywhere in Zion, she told me they hung a whole family. It wasn't enough to hang the men, they hung babies, a grandmother, two pregnant women and raped the young girls before killing them. The worst part of it all, was they was known niggas. The grandmother was owned by the Harpers, and raised some of the men who put 'a neck in the noose.

It's the story we remember and tell each other whenever we forget our place. They hung they own mammy, maid, cook, and field hands for moving into a empty house. Miemay said the police ain never come. Nobody talked about it, and it what'n put in no papers. The Klan even gave a speech to Zion right in the middle of the town. They warned all niggas, we were never to sleep in that house where white folks once laid they heads.

Ain much land left to the Hilliard House. The house set off far from the road. Years before I was born, a man and his woman were out here naking, when the Klan caught them behind the house. Before that day, lovers use to sneak here, and get to know each other.

The Klan tied the man to a tree, and beat him almost to death. The woman was raped. They say the man asked them to kill him so he could stop hearing the woman begging them to stop. As for that woman, they say she was strong cause she ain never talk about what happened, except to say she glad they didn't kill 'a man. These beautiful tall strong trees, be the same trees they hang strangers from, or niggas they catch out too late by theyself.

The sound of Anastasia's hooves hitting the red earth hypnotize me. Pass the Hilliard place, I'm taking in clean rows of one crop or another. I dream, and try to breathe in the sky. Seem like the sky inviting me to ride to the end of the horizon, and away from Zion. Every time we riding, feel like I make a decision to stay here. Now Miemay gone, feel like the question being posed more often. Feel a hankering to be somewhere else, see something else. Want to know what else under the sky sides this town.

It take all morning to go round Zion. When Anastasia feeling up to it, we go the whole way round, and through the worn roads. Feel like I'm flying when I'm riding her. Feel like I own the earth and ain't nothing impossible.

Anastasia a proud horse, seem like she be happy when I'm pleased. I try to pay attention so I ain't too hard on 'a, but she fast, beautiful, got strong legs and like to show me what she can do. When I think I'm doing too much, I can feel 'a wanting to give me more in 'a trot. She hop a little, like "Let's go!" So we do. We'd ride all over the world if we could.

We back to riding every Saturday morning, like we use to before Miemay got sick. Ain't normal for a woman to ride horses way I do. We all get taught how to ride when we young, but I ride for fun. Most women could probly still remember how to harness horses if need be, or get a buggy together. Still, mostly men do it cause women don't travel by themselves no how. Ain lady like to be out on no horse like this either. That's the reason I get up and out so early in the morning. Specially now, I'm back to wearing dresses. So this the only time I get to be free in my pants.

Anastasia's mane, and my hair flapping in the wind like flags of freedom. Feels like me and Stasia one, chills rush over me when it feel like we racing together against time. Then I see the family's buggy. Almost wont to turn around and go another way, since I got these pants on. But I don't want to break my stride, plus I know they hear me coming. And besides all that, it's time to get on back so Stasia can get some water, we been riding since first light.

I ride up long side the buggy. Buggies always slower than riding, cause the horses pulling more weight. This one got so much stuff on back, it's gone be all day getting somewhere. Daddy and Isaiah up front. Zay smile, and tilt his hat good morning and I nod back. Daddy just look at me, then my pants, frown and shake his head. He hate I don't live with 'im no more, so he can watch me, and make me do what he wont.

"Morning!" I say smugly, knowing Daddy wish he could whup me now.

"Git on back round to ya house, with them pants on," he order. "You already making a bad impression on yah guest, and yall ain't even met." He shakes his head frowning sourly and sits up.

Curious, I get closer to the buggy, watching the wheels making sure to keep Anastasia's legs from 'em. I look inside. First I see Mama's disapproving face, then her, the stranger looking back just as curious as I am.

"Morning," she smile scooting closer to the window and leaning out.

Mama push 'a back way from the window and poke 'a lips out at me.

I don't say nothing back, I cain't. For a moment I just stare at 'a. Then I look at all the stuff on the back of the carriage, again. Look at 'a again, think about how long she gone stay, and what room she gone sleep in. She so different looking, so beautiful it stir something in me. I cain't take no more. I tap Anastasia on the tail and we take off.

When I get round to the house, Reverend Patrick waiting on the front porch with his wife, Alice, or Mrs. Harper I call 'a. They dressed in their Sunday best. I can tell how they standing Mrs. Harper wearing a corset, cause of how stiff she moving. She wearing a dark green dress look like it should have a wedding train, and matching hat. They standing so strange, look like they bout to take a photograph. I feel like they gone be after me bout being underdressed.

When I ride up, I don't know what possess me to do it, but I tilt my hat at Mrs. Harper the way a man would.

"Ain't that some mess!" she fuss, stepping to the edge of the porch like she coming to get me. "You been over here by yoself too long! And why you riding round in pants?"

"Iain spect nobody to be round here but me," I explain, getting down off Anastasia, leading 'a to the post and tying 'a there. Reverend Patrick and Ms. Harper looking at me crazy, like they waiting on something.

"Your garden needs weeding. You couldn't have started planting, cause it doesn't even look like you finished harvesting the last crop. Your smoke house empty, and I didn't even look in the cellar. What are you doing over here?" Mrs. Harper fold 'a arms, and Reverend Patrick look like he uncomfortable.

"Iain but one person," I say defending myself.

"Well hire some hands to help. You can afford to pay somebody. And folks need jobs round here," Mrs. Harper push.

"I don't feel right hiring nobody, being nobody's boss and we all know ain nobody in Zion wont to work for me. Not after all this mess with me getting Miemay's money and land. I cain't just hire strangers, they always bring trouble."

"Well, you gone have to do something. You sure are Cassius Remington's daughter, with yo stubborn self.

"I'm gone tell you what. This week, before it's out or the first of next week, I'm sending one of my boys over here to help you git this place in order. You pay 'im whatever you think is fair.

"Lord knows they could use the money to help with they taxes, specially with all this boll weevil business. The crop ain't hardly yielding nothing. I don't know how nobody gone make ends meet. I don't know why yo Daddy won't just ask you for the money to pay his taxes."

Soon as Mrs. Harper finish, I understand why Daddy so mad. "They got a family trust everybody pay into for all the Remington land. He don't pay for taxes by hisself."

"Oh," Mrs. Harper look at Reverend Patrick, he turning his hat like she done stepped in it. "I'm sorry, I didn't know you didn't know."

"Know what?"

"Ya daddy been moved out the trust cause you got Victor's inheritance. They say since he rich now he don't need to be in it."

"Miemay woulda paid for them all to keep they land."

"It ain't over yet, the time to pay the taxes on his land ain't completely passed. Then, it take a few years fore they take your house for being behind. But they usually be done paid that money already and be on to making other plans. This year it ain't so."

"I'll just pay their taxes."

"Yo daddy ain't gone accept yo money. He a man and they pigheaded, got to have thangs they way." Mrs. Harper nudge Reverend Patrick.

"That's enough." Reverend Patrick puff out his chest, but Mrs. Harper don't hardly pay 'im no mind. She keep right on saying what she gone say.

"Oh Patrick, it's true. Men always got to have things a certain way or it cain't go. Ain't like this girl don't love 'a daddy and don't want to help. Ain't like it's her fault Miemay left 'a everything, what can she do?"

I realize why Daddy say I cain't come around no more. "You keep the land books, I'll pay his taxes directly to you," I tell Reverend Patrick.

Inhaling deep, he look over at me, and then at his wife. "Fine, but yo daddy gone be mad."

"He'll still have his house." I dismiss that, he can be mad.

"Back to you," Mrs. Harper go on. "You being stubborn and not liking to ask for help, you got that honest from ya daddy. You want one of my boys to go with you to help find some hands to work in these fields? You could git a crew and let them stay in Miemay's old place during the week. Then they could go home on the weekend. Maybe you could even charge them a little room and board. You could cook them meals, and then you could just tend to the wife duties."

"Even if I hire help, I'm still gone work my land, and work the big fields with everybody else."

"The town land ain't what's going to ruins. Worry bout your own back porch fore you sweep off your neighbors," Reverend jump in.

I get silent, and try to contain myself. "I don't want to be in my house like some queen. Miemay what'n never in no house, she was in the fields, at 'a store, on 'a properties and visiting folks. That's how she always knew what was going on."

Reverend breathe heavy, frustrated with me. "You hire people when you have as much responsibility and money as you do. It's impossible to do everything and be everywhere. You don't work in your own store, you hire someone. What you do is check the books, make sure the money is right. You do the ordering so the store stocked. How you think Miemay was able to be midwife and root woman, seeing bout the sick and tending to 'em?"

Mrs. Harper start, "Then, you ain't Miemay. Miemay whole family was helping 'a cause they all had they eyes on getting a piece of land or money, whenever she died. She gone now, and she done left it to you. Now ain't no reason for them to show up no more. I wouldn't be surprised if that uncle and cousin you got working in that store ain't stealing from you right today. They all feel they entitled to what you got, and to take a little ain nothing."

"Uncle Victor and Ernest wouldn't steal from me."

"It ain't stealing if Earnest feel like what you got his. If he feel like you're the thief who stole from his father Victor, why wouldn't he? In his mind them things rightfully his anyhow. You better git yo head out the dirt, girl, and come out that fantasy you living in. Truth be told, they stole from Miemay when she was living."

"Alice." Reverend Patrick look at 'a stern, as if his look could stop 'a mouth, when we all know it never could. "You better be checking them books and hiring some more workers," Mrs. Harper point at me, like she wish she could pinch me they way she use to when I was a child.

"We don't know they stealing," Reverend add.

"Victor living better than he ever did, him and his son Ernest. All while Linny ain't paying no attention, he probly robbing 'a blind. She a woman by 'aself, she got to live, too. So she best be gitting on down there, and staying on top of them books."

Turning back to me, she say, "If you ain't gone do wife duties, don't be in no fields. You best git down to that store and find out bout how much your part is for that hotel. The traffic been picking up, the train bringing way more Coloreds here, and the hotel always pay the store. I bet Ernest collecting on some of that, too."

I feel too ashamed to look up. I feel like a fish on a hook, waiting to be pulled in and gutted.

"Hurry up and git changed out of them pants," Mrs. Harper order, like she my mama.

"You got company coming today." Reverend Patrick face sour taking in what I'm wearing again. "I wished we'da got word sooner. I just got the notice in the mail this morning, so Iain even have time to prepare, or git the town ready." Reverend Patrick look concerned.

"And you ain't gone have 'a over here with you acting like no heathen. You bring 'a to church. I don't understand why you ain't there every Sunday no how. But you better have yourself in service this Sunday. I'm cooking dinner too, and I expect you to be there." Mrs. Harper finish fussing. Then stand wit' 'a hands on 'a hips like she expecting some back talk.

Reverend Patrick don't say nothing, he stand mute like she the law round here.

I just smile at 'a, realize how much I miss having her around. She kinda be like my mama, too. "Yes, ma'am." I hug 'a.

"That's all she got to do is tell you she expect you to come and you gone show up? You sass me when I talk to you," Reverend Patrick say annoyed, staring at me like he ain never seen this side of me.

Then Mrs. Harper start pulling me close and hugging me the way ain't nobody done in a long time, saying, "That's cause she my baby," like she got one leg up on 'im. When he roll his eyes, she say, "Run on in the house and git yo self cleaned up. Cain't be meeting folks looking any kinda way. First impressions are important, and you representing this town. So you behave over here, and act like a lady. You hear?"

"Yes, ma'am," I agree, pleased I can make 'a smile the way she smiling. Been a while since somebody looked at me like I could do anything right.

"You always was a hard working easy child," Reverend Patrick add looking over at me.

"Grew to be such a beautiful woman, and you so humble. I like that you 'a hard worker, and that you ain rule by ya looks. Ain stuck on ya self like some folks."

"Alice, don't talk about ya son's wife," Reverend remind 'a.

"Anyway, I was just telling Patrick the other day how strong and smart you are. I couldn't imagine being out here by myself. Didn't I say that Patrick?" She lifting 'a head proud of 'aself, and me too.

For some reason, I start smiling and I'm glad Mrs. Harper think so much of me.

"You know, I always wished I had a daughter. And if I did, I hoped she'd be-" she breathe out hard, smiling and doting on me. She don't finish, cause she done said it to me a hundred times. Mama don't like Mrs. Harper, cause once she told Mama I shoulda been her own daughter.

"Wish we'da had more warning," Reverend Patrick say, still looking off in the distance. "The mail come here so slow."

"Probly cause white folks going through it, making sure don't body send no newspapers or nothing," Mrs. Harper put in.

"The letter just got to the church, almost a month old saying she was gone be here today. Then Iain even open it til this morning. It was real short notice."

"Go on in the house, and git yourself cleaned up," Mrs. Harper picks up a box from the bench. "And take these dresses I done brought you from Atlanta." So I take the dresses and start in the house.

"Never mind that, it's too late," Reverend Patrick stop me, stepping off the porch and taking his hat off his head. The dust rising on the road can be seen pass the tabacca fields, getting closer. "Wonder what she thought of our school?"

"What's 'a name?" I grab the brim of my hat, use to be one of Miemay's straw field hats, and pull it down over my eyes.

Seem like Reverend Patrick in shock, he act like he don't hear me, and nobody move. We all stand silent watching Daddy's carriage pass Miemay cabin, getting closer. Putting the box down with the dresses in it, I get down off the porch and pump the trough full of water for Anastasia.

All while we waiting, I'm thinking bout how Miemay told me I needed to make two dressers and four lamps. She said there was gone be a house guest coming to live for a while. Then for some reason, I thought she was talking bout me living with 'a. Now I see what Miemay talking bout, this school teacher coming. Then I think on other things Iain pay no attention Miemay say, and I know I got to pay attention for when things change and it's time to leave.

Closer they get the more I remember how mad Miemay use to get, when they try to put somebody in 'a house. Gone have to wear dresses even at home maybe, and talk. Iain much of a talker.

Soon as they reach the front of my house, folks start moving like a king or queen bout to grace us with they presence. When the door of the carriage open, Isaiah put his hand in to help 'a down, and I know she a lady. I stand in awe watching all them, expecting to see a white lady even though I done seen 'a and know she Colored.

Then the small brown woman, or girl, eases down from the carriage moving like she appreciates, and needs all the assistance and attention afforded her. Wearing a dark grey dress, and belt, with what looks like matching shoes and hat. She is the first woman I ever seen this sharp. Her hair pulled so tight you can see the brush strokes. She steps on the dirt like it's the first time she ever seen some, holding 'a dress up like it might soil 'a shoes.

"Zay! Jermy! Let's git these bags," Daddy order my brothers.

Mama jump out the carriage by 'aself. Seem like Isaiah forgot Mama was even in there. Mama in 'a Sunday best, too. I feel like I should speak proper English. First time I ever felt underdressed, and dirty. Especially since I been in the stables all morning. I can feel everybody else trying to be they best.

Then again, she gone be living with me. She gone have to get use to this. I got to work in my fields, and I sho ain't gone be working in no dress.

"Good afternoon, I'm Reverend Patrick Harper," he takes the woman's hand. For a moment, look like he cain't decide what to do, kiss or shake it. He shake it rough, and I cain't hide I'm smiling at all the putting on. "Most folks just call me Reverend Patrick."

"I'm Coletta Graham, please to meet you Reverend Patrick." She smile and do this little curtsy.

"And this my wife, The First Lady of Zion Southern Baptist Church, Mrs. Alice Harper." He turns towards Mrs. Harper.

"Most young people call me Mrs. Harper," she shakes the woman's hand gentler. "Now what do people call you? Is that Miss or Misses Graham?"

"Alice?" Reverend Patrick try to hush his wife, but Miss or Misses Graham, however she gone be addressed, is getting 'a first introduction to Zion. People here gone ask questions. Whatever on they heart usually said and asked, and they feel entitled to have they questions answered.

"Well?" Mrs. Harper insists, ignoring him and holding the woman's hand too long. "Is there a Mr. Graham?"

"Don't be silly, Alice. Of course she isn't married." Reverend Patrick takes the woman's hands from his wife. "No man would allow his young wife to be travelling alone, and you don't see no ring on 'a finger. You don't have to answer that question, Ms. Graham. What did you think of our school?"

"I don't mind answering." The woman smiles at Mrs. Harper. "There are two Mr. Grahams, my father Coleman Graham and my brother Coleman Graham, Jr."

"See Patrick, no harm's done. A single woman wants that known. How else will eligible men know?" Mrs. Harper gives Reverend a sly grin, then he roll his eyes in response.

"Bum!"

We all turn to look at the carriage, and they've dropped 'a trunk on the ground. The teacher seems worried and I'm tickled cause I know Daddy embarrassed.

"See! That's why I told you to let me git a good grip fore you moved it," Daddy fuss to save face.

When I see it's more suitcases, I wonder what all she done brung and how long she staying. I remember how mad Miemay use to get when they use to try and put somebody in 'a house. She use to say new folks change the spirit of a place, even babies can bring a family together or push folks apart. I'm wondering if she gone make the spirit of my place better or worse.

"Ms. Graham it is, so we can address you properly." Mrs. Harper smile, too pleased.

"Oh, you don't have to call me Miss, ma'am. I-"

"We insist," Mrs. Harper cut 'a off.

"We cain't call our new school teacher, from _____?" Reverend leave it open for Ms. Graham to answer.

"Atlanta." She smile uncomfortably.

"By 'a first name," he finish, and Mrs. Harper pick up where he left off.

"We need to call you something formal for the children. Not to mention, you gone be a role model for our girls and young women. We don't want them calling you by your first name."

"Yes, ma'am," Ms. Graham shrink under the flattery. "I'm just honored I can serve Zion."

"Not as honored as we are to have you, sweetie." Mrs. Harper beams.

There is a long uncomfortable silence where you can feel the three of them fishing for words. The Reverend stare at me, like I'm spose to say something but Iain got no words for 'a neither. Mama don't even try to speak, it's always been like The Reverend nem above everybody else. This conversation ain't for us common folk.

"Madelyn! Pay attention and stop being rude. I swear," Daddy complain as they lifting trunks up off the back of the carriage.

"Forgive my rude daughter, Ms. Graham." Mama bury me the way she always do, and I feel 'a looking at me.

"She ain't rude, Madelyn has always been shy," Mrs. Harper correct what dirt Mama trying to throw.

"Who's Madelyn?" Zay laugh from the carriage, and Jeremiah punch 'im in the arm.

"Ms. Graham," Mama poke 'a chest out looking at Mrs. Harper. "This here one of my middle daughters, Madelyn Remington. She gone be your host while you here in Zion," Mama say all official and proud of me for the first time I can remember. Zay raise his eyebrows at me like he ain't never seen this neither.

Ms. Graham offer 'a hand nervously, and say, "Good afternoon" with another little curtsy.

I'm looking at everyone round, and her. Iain never seen no nigga bow like that cept for when serving white folks. I accept 'a hand, but I don't smile, all I can do is nod hello and stare. Ms. Graham a small girl, slim, brown with sharp features and beautiful eyes. She has the longest most beautiful lashes I done seen on a woman and 'a lips is full, and she smell good, too.

"Ain't chu gone show 'a round?" Mama push me a little, maybe I'm lost, maybe I stare too long. "Make me thank I raised ya wrong. Where dey treat people like dis?" Mama fuss, then take the small bag Ms. Graham holding. "Excuse 'a, honey, she ain't neva seen a lady. That's why we wont you to stay wit 'a. Maybe she'll stop wearing pants," Mama fussing at me more than saying it to her, "when she thank ain't nobody round!"

I just stand there watching them going in and out my house, moving 'a in the bedroom across the hall from mine. Everybody else do the talking. Iain shy most times cause I know everybody round here, but new people and white folks make me hold my tongue.

"You never did say what you thought of our school," Reverend Patrick ask again.

"Honestly, I . . ." Ms. Graham searches for words. "I didn't know what to think."

Her words received cold, Reverend and his wife looking at each other having they own eye conversation. "No, not like that," she try to clean it up. "I didn't have any expectations. I don't have anything to compare it to. I mean, this is my first assignment."

Reverend Patrick relaxes and starts skinning and grinning again. Mrs. Harper stare at Ms. Graham like she still waiting on something.

"Well, Reverend Patrick, there were a few things I'd appreciate if . . . I wondered if someone could take a look at, and some things would need to be fixed before school begins." She finishes politely, avoiding Mrs. Harper's eyes.

Reverend don't pick up on it, the way me, Mama and Mrs. Harper do. Me, Mama and Mrs. Harper know immediately Ms. Graham is disappointed, and there is more wrong than she willing to admit.

"Linny will come see about it first thing in the morning, or over the next couple of days depending on what else going on," he say, looking over at me.

Before Daddy and nem leave, Zay tease, "Now Madelyn, you be nice, and you might learn a thang or two bout the world and being a lady."

"A lady," Mama put in wryly.

"Yall gone need a man round here to help you git settled." Zay go on staring at Ms. Graham. "Think Ima be stopping by here more often." He take off his hat, smiling all big teefed and then put it over his chest like he bout to sing a song to the lord.

"Make sure ya brang ya wife witcha, Zay," I remind 'im teasing back.

Chapter Eighteen

When I get back in the house and close the door, I don't look at 'a or say nothing. I just go back to the kitchen and see what I can make us for supper. Then I look out the window at Anastasia, Ms. Graham follow.

"Would it be alright if I go get cleaned up? I've been traveling all day and night it seems," she say, laughing fake.

I just nod yes mutely.

"This is a beautiful house."

"Thank yah," I'm sure I say just above a whisper. She walk away slow, then ease back.

"What happened to your husband?"

"What make you think I was married?"

"This house, I guess. I don't know any other women living alone, except widows. Back home, a girl doesn't move out until she's married."

"You married?"

"I always wanted to be," she say all dreamy, like all the young girls in Zion do when they talk about marriage. Then I know it cain't be that different where she from. Then again, here she is travelling way from 'a family.

"How much should I pay you for letting me stay here?"

"What do you usually pay?"

"I've never lived away from home, except for when I attended college, and then room and board was part of the tuition."

"Well, Iain never had a guest. So I'll let you know when I figga it out."

"You own this house, and all the land round it?"

"Yes."

"What did you do to get this house? I mean, how did you get this house? I mean, your folks didn't seem rich."

Holding the poker and some wood, I stop lighting the stove and stare directly at 'a. "You ask a lot of questions."

Turning 'a hat in 'a hands, squirming under my gaze, she smiles fake and apologetically, the way women do when they ain got the gall to stick to they guns. Or they find they done over stepped they boundaries. "How else do you get to know someone, if you don't ask them questions?"

"That another question?" I decide to leave 'a and take Anastasia to the stables. Then I can come on back here and tend to her.

"Where you going, Madelyn?"

"To put Anastasia away," I answer absent minded; I'm wondering if this is how it's gone be. She gone be talking at me and asking questions all the time. I like the quiet of being here alone, now that I done got use to it. Still, guess it won't be so bad having somebody else here with me.

"Mind if I go?"

I don't say nothing, just go out the back door and leave it open for 'a to follow. And she do. I go look at Anastasia, see if she tired, too tired to carry two folks. Maybe I'll walk and lead them to the stables. Once I start rubbing on Stasia, seem to make me feel better, calmer, and I find the will to ask, "Ever ride?"

"No, I've never been out in the wilderness like this. I'm a city girl. I've ridden trains, carriages, cars, and walked, but nothing like being on my own horse."

After I untie Anastasia, I decide it ain't a good idea to put 'a up there by 'aself. So I climb up first, then move my foot out the stirrup. I grab hold of Anastasia's reigns so she be solid like a wall.

Then I tell Coletta, "Put yo foot in that stirrup and gimme ya hand. When I pull yah up throw ya leg over." I pull 'a up on the horse. Then she scoot in close, wrapping 'a arms round me to hold on. How nervous she is makes me feel protective. Ms. Graham trusting me make me feel proud and strong.

I rub Stasia to calm 'a down when she starts to dance trot, meaning she ready to go, go, go. "Hold on." I lean back guiding Stasia back and away from the trough. We start slowly.

I feel Ms. Graham tense against me, holding 'a breath. "I've got you," I promise. She feel so scared I forget I'm shy. First me and Stasia do a little trot. I ride gentle, then when I feel Ms. Graham breathing easy, and she rest 'a head against me, I trot a little faster. When I feel she know Iain gone hurt 'a, I take off.

"This is soo much fun!" Ms. Graham yells. I decide to take 'a for a lil ride. When we hit the main road, Daddy nem ahead of us.

"Madelyn!" Daddy holla at me standing up in his coach when I pass. I just speed up and laugh.

"You sure like to pull your father's chain," she say, holding on to me and 'a hat.

"I couldn't pull it if he ain't leave it out there." I turn my head to smile back at 'a. She holds on tighter, and I feel better, more relaxed.

"So what they call you, Ms. Graham? Coletta?"

"Coley."

*　　*　　*

"Guess, since you here, Iain gone eat leftovers," I think out loud, just accepting it, I guess. When I see I'm making 'a feel like a burden, I remember my manners and explain. "I just hate cooking late in the day like this cause it's so hot, and cooking make the house hot. Not to mention, I had planned on doing other things today. Now I got to make a whole nother meal."

"It is hot," she agree, using a hand to shield 'a face from the sun and squinting at the red road ahead. What I done said seem to ease 'a mind. "It's not the heat that bothers me so much though. I don't like being out in the sun. If I keep on, I'll be black as a piece of coal."

"You ever seen a piece a coal?" I look at 'a good. She don't entertain the question, just keep on stepping.

"You're so light." She stare at me like she in a daze. "You don't have anything to worry about. So I don't expect you to understand how the blacker you are, the harder your life is," she add after it's silent for a while.

"You got a real sensitive nature. Cain't stand the scent of the stables. You making all kinds of faces, and they was clean. This gone be a hard transition for you."

"Transition?" she repeat like I'm stupid or something. Like she cain't believe niggas read round here. I don't even entertain 'a now. I just feel how different we is, as I walk with my hair blowing in the wind and hers all pinned up. I have to keep slowing down cause she walking in that dress like she ain never done no work in a dress.

Since we back here, I decide to go head and stop at the chicken coop. Shoulda asked Reverend Patrick if he had some extra meat in his smoke house, fore he left. Then I coulda went and got that. Since I'm by myself, and got so much work to do, I don't be having time to fill my smoke house. Mostly I'm eating from the garden, and I like that. Whenever I do eat meat, it seem to wear me down.

In the silence I start to feel Coley's uneasiness, but I don't address holes without clear questions. And the questions, I may not have the right to ask. So I just stare at 'a curiously. Most folks cain't stand to be looked at. Usually they start talking to calm they self.

"You know how to make fried chicken, or baked chicken, or chicken stew?" Coley ask, her face lighting up.

I respond by smiling at 'a.

Then she smile back and say, "I miss my mama's chicken. Then again I miss all of her cooking. She don't cook much now." Her arms swinging a mile a minute, like I'm walking too fast. So I slow down and find she catch 'a breath. She slow down and stay in step with me. She a short thang.

I'm going through the back gate on to the chicken coop, Coley gums still a flapping.

"This is my first time away from my family and Daddy's friends. It's also the first time, I've been out of contact with them regularly," she saying more to 'aself than to me, thinking, she getting sad. "W. E. B Du Bois is a close family friend. You ever heard of him?" She pull 'a spirits up.

"Cain't say I have," I answer absent mindedly. I'm looking for a bucket. Coley hot on my heels, her mouth just going. For the first time since I met Coley, I'm glad I ain go riding in nothing nice.

"How don't you know who WEB Du Bois is? Every Negro in America should know him. But I bet you know who Booker T. Washington is?"

"Yeah, cause he came here a few times. Use to put stuff in our newspaper fore he died."

I've found a bucket, now I'm looking for a apron so I don't get nothing on me. I've already decided not to cut the head off til it's dead, keep from getting mess everywhere. I'd rather cut his head off, but Coley a lady and the blood be everywhere if I do that. I get a knife off the wall in the barn, and sharpen it out of habit, cause it's already clean and sharp. Just a couple times on the sharpening leather to get a feel for the knife.

"Washington kept Du Bois out of most southern Negro papers. They didn't really like each other. Washington was a back woods Uncle Tom."

"You ought to know who you talking to fore you start talking bout folk," I say, tying the apron on and looking at 'a. I walk to the chicken coop.

Coley following. Then she stop outside the gate surrounding it, like she scared of chickens. "Are you some kin to Washington or something?"

"No. But you ain't know that fore you started dragging the dead through the mud. He did a lot a good for us niggas."

I go in the coop, and Coley keep on talking, but I cain't hear what she saying, it's loud in here. The chickens going wild cause I'm in here. When I see the one I want, I snatch it up by the feet and hold it away from me to keep from getting pecked.

When I come back out whatever Coley was saying she freeze. The chicken flapping it's wings and trying to get loose. I close the door on the coop, walking as far away from it as I can inside the gate so the chicken will calm down. Soon as it relaxes, in one smooth firm move, I grab it's neck tight, snatch down, jerk up til I feel it snap and drop it.

"Aaaaaaaah!" Coley scream like a crazy person when the broken-neck thing run at the gate.

I just stare at 'a, she real emotional. I lean on the inside of the gate and wait for the life to run out of it. When the chicken finally fall, I grab the bucket, the knife and cut the head off.

"Oh god!" Coley cry out.

Iain paying 'a no more attention, cause she running out. The chicken jerk a bit, but that's normal. Then I turn it over in the bucket to let the blood drain out. When I look up, Coley throwing up.

Knowing she got a sensitive nature, I think it be best if I can get this off 'a mind. Best way to make folks feel better is to make 'em mad. Standing up, I put my hands on my hips and look at 'a for a while. When she pull a handkerchief from 'a dress and clean 'a lips I say, "Now what was the name of that uppity nigga you was tellin me bout?"

"I beg your pardon?" She stands poking 'a chest out like a rooster, and matching my stance. She done forgot she sick.

I try not to laugh at 'a lil biddy self getting all worked up, and prepare to get my head tore off.

Then she gets going, "I'll have you know Mr. Du Bois isn't an uppity nigger. In fact, I'm appalled by the word 'Nigger,' and you should be ashamed you don't know who Du Bois is. He has earned the right to be referred to with honor and respect. He is the first Negro to ever attend Harvard. He got his Bachelors and PHD from there. He has travelled all over the world, and is a credit to the Negro race. Where have you ever been except here in cotton-picking country ass Zion?! What schools have you attended outside of that broke down back woods cabin?"

"That's where you gone be teaching," I egg 'a own, while taking off the feathers.

Now she ignoring what I'm doing, she so upset.

* * *

"This is very good. I was starving when I got here."

"Ain nothing." I suck on the chicken bone, tasting the gravy made from its broth and spices, taking 'a in.

She don't eat like she starving. She taking small bites, and cutting everything into small pieces. A bit of this and a bit of that. Then she got all this silverware laid out beside 'a, stuff she ain even using. Done asked me for a towel for 'a lap, and now she dapping the corner of 'a mouth after every other bite. It seem harder for 'a to eat dinner than it was for me to make it.

"Oh don't be modest, I haven't tasted cooking this good since my grandma lived with us."

"What'n that hard, it practically cooked itself." Compliments always make me feel uncomfortable. For some reason, her's don't make me feel as uncomfortable but I'm so use to responding like that. Folks round here don't say you smelling good or beautiful unless they want something. On the other hand, if somebody say I'm strong or smart, it's easier to take, but I wouldn't let them know I appreciate that neither. Plus, Iain did nothing big, ain't nothing but some boiled chicken, gravy, cabbage and rice. Supper did pretty much cook itself.

She smile while she eats. That's more pleasing than compliments. What be more pleasing if she eat like my brothers do, like somebody got a clock ticking and all they don't get down somebody gone take from 'em. Still, I'm glad for the company, and wanting to ease 'a, I don't want 'a to think she no trouble.

"How do you get by out here? Working on the farm? Are you a sharecropper?"

"You must not know any sharecroppers."

"Does a man stay here?"

"There you go with that again." I watch 'a looking round like she expecting somebody to come. "Not unless you a man."

Cracking up, she slaps my hand, "Your mother told me you come across hard like your daddy, folks think you're mean, but you're really sweet. I must admit, I didn't expect a young woman to be so ornery. Then again, yellow women usually are."

"I don't like being called none of them names, redbone, yellow, high yellow, mulatto, octoroon or light skinned. We all niggas round here. Field niggas at that."

Clearing 'a throat she gets serious and antsy again. Away from 'a familiars, she takes another bite. "You just aren't what I expected when I met your mother and father is all."

"How you got expectations for a stranger?"

After a moment or two, she say, "It does sound foolish." Then she do that little laugh for comfort, not because anything funny. "You feel safe living here by yourself?"

"Why wouldn't I?"

"I mean, doesn't there need to be a man here, too." She stops to reconsider 'a train of thought and the direction of the conversation. "You know, to protect you? Us?"

"Who after you?" Curious I'm trying to understand 'a reasoning. Worse thing could happen to a nigga round here, Klan catch 'im out somewhere by hisself. Matter fact, when I think about it, be a woman come to beg the Klan for 'a husband, or son life all the time. So we ain really the ones got to worry. It's just lonely, and a little scary being in this big old house by myself. Then when I think about what I'm scared of, I'm alright.

"Nobody is after me! I'm just concerned. No man is going to be here with us at night?"

"Not unless you done brung one with you."

Clearing 'a throat she starts again, "Well, what do you do for fun round here?"

"Kill chickens and skin rabbits." I clean up around my plate and put all my dishes together.

"My mother bought a piano when I was a girl. We all learned to play some. I don't remember anything now. I think she made us take lessons to justify getting it. It was just for show. As soon as one of us protested about taking lessons, we were allowed to stop. I didn't expect to find a piano in this house." She looks over at the piano in the living room. "Mama says you always know a family has money if they have a piano, and you can tell how much money by what kind of piano."

I don't say nothing, just look at 'a hard, hoping it make 'a uncomfortable enough to keep talking. She don't disappoint.

"Who are you trying to impress with that piano?" She looks at me expecting an answer.

I don't say nothing.

"I mean, you don't play do you? I mean, there isn't anyone to entertain. I'm just thinking, why you would have a piano out here?" She finally settle on what she saying or asking, but I still don't say nothing. "Aren't you going to answer me?"

"Have you gotten an answer?"

"No," she pushes 'a food around on 'a plate, staring at me like she's trying to convict my spirit, or like 'a feelings hurt.

"Silence is an answer. Specially when you sitting here like you know everything, and coming to your own conclusions."

"You're not saying you play the piano, are you?"

"Are you asking me or telling me?"

"I'm just making conversation."

"With yourself?"

"What?" She stop eating like that answer done turned 'a stomach.

I get up to clean up and put the food away.

"Wait a minute. Where are you going?" She stands with me, grabbing 'a plate, too.

"I'm finished. Want anything else fore I put this food up?"

"But . . ." she say, holding 'a plate and looking at mine, "I haven't finished."

"And you ain never gone finish between running ya mouth, cutting and eating them tiny bites and wiping ya mouth." Getting the silverware off the table she ain using and dropping it on my plate, I say, "Now do you want any more of this food fore I put it up?"

"We don't get up until everyone is done eating at home."

"Are you at home?"

Slamming herself back down at the table, she stabs 'a fork into the cabbage and eats hungrily now. Annoyed.

Lost, I say, "Good evening," then go on into the kitchen and clean up. Now that somebody here, I can go out on the porch, enjoy the last of evening light and read. Before she came, I never felt comfortable letting night catch me outside.

Chapter Nineteen

"Morning." I knock on Coley's door after I walk out in the hall and don't hear 'a stirring. "Want me to take you around to the school, so you can get it in order?" I think I better give 'a Anastasia, cause I just broke Teddy in and don't think he ready to be rode by a lady. When she don't say nothing, "Coletta?"

"Coley," she moan, like she correcting me from under the cover. I wonder how she sleeping through them roosters' crowing. Once one get started, they all get to going. This my first time ever meeting a nigga who can sleep through it, or anybody for that matter.

"You hear me bout that ride?"

"No, thank you. Reverend Patrick and his wife are coming to pick me up in their automobile." She sound annoyed.

"Alright then." I start towards the steps.

"What time is it?"

I stop. "Maybe 4:30 or 5."

"In the morning?"

"Unless you use to sleeping all day."

"Who gets up this early?"

"We do."

"Who is 'we'?"

"You, me and the whole town, I expect."

"Oh my! What the? Is that a chicken howling like that, at this time of morning?"

"Roosters crowing." I'm tickled.

"I knew that. What time does school start?"

"Bout 8:00 or 8:30. But you need to be there round bout 6 to get the fireplace started and get the chill out fore the kids start coming at around 7. Cause some folks gone be dropping 'em off early, so they can catch work trucks to other towns, or to be in the fields early."

"Why are you up so early?"

"We gotta feed the animals, and milk the cows fore breakfast. Get supper started, too. Plus, I think I'm gone bake us some bread for later on."

"You're making breakfast and dinner, now?"

"Well, we ain't gone be home all day. So who else gone fix us something to eat?"

"I had a maid at home."

"Well, that's too bad you ain't bring 'a. Come nah, get on up and get dressed."

I leave 'a door and go on down to start the day. I put some wood in the stove. Put a few pieces in the fireplace, too, to chase the draft out since I got company. I'm gone have to make sure there's more wood in the house now, so she can have some in her room for that fireplace.

I put some butter in the skillet for pancakes. Turn the bacon over again and stir the grits. Been awhile since I cooked a big breakfast. Iain cooked like this since Miemay could eat. She loved her some apple or grape jam or syrup and biscuits.

All while I'm thinking bout Miemay, I hear Coley's slippered feet whisk overhead. Then I hear 'a boots fall heavy in front of the bed bench. As I'm scrambling eggs, I hear 'a stand solid, them boots on, then 'a footsteps going cross the floor to the door. I like the sound of somebody else in the house.

"Breakfast smells good. What? No, who's on your mind got you smiling?" She is seemingly dancing as she asks.

Straightening my face, I order, pointing with the fork, "The plates are over there." She follows direction, rinses them under the sink and walks over to me placing them in arms reach.

*   *   *

Look like all the lights off cept for the ones in the back office when I reach the school. With all the trees and few windows, it's kinda dark. Plus, the sun ain't got all the way up. I don't see The Reverend's auto.

Opening the door I look around for Coley but don't see 'a. So I go back to the office, to find out where she wont me to start.

All of a sudden the cleaning closet door bust wide open slamming against the wall, and I see a bat coming for my head. I use my tool box to shield my face. I keep moving the tool box round to guard me out the way of that bat.

Coley screaming, "Get out! Get out!"

When she get close enough, I push the tool box into 'a, forcing 'a to the wall where she cain't move or swing that bat no more, but she fight and kick, and knee me hard where it would've really hurt if I was a man. Finally, I think to say, "That's enough, Woman!" Then I hear the bat hit the ground and realize we both breathing hard.

"I think you bruised my ribs with that tool box." She hold 'a side.

"Better that, than what you was trying to do to my head with that bat." I step back from 'a, still feeling my heart racing, and then I laugh. "You got a lot of heart."

"Why didn't you say something when you came in here? And why are you here?"

"Came to fix the things you say need fixing. Reverend Patrick told you I was coming."

"He said a man named Lenny."

"Did you even wait to see who was in here before you started swinging that bat?"

She don't answer, just look at me sorry for trying to take my head off.

So I go on, "Well, the only man in Zion could go by Lenny, is Leonard, but we call him Leo or Bug. And Bug wife ain't gone let him come fix nothing for the new young school teacher, when it's all these single men round here to do it."

"Well, why didn't one of them come?"

"Cause Reverend Patrick asked me. Or maybe cause they know you hiding and jumping out of closets with bats," I tease, getting my bearing and looking around.

Coley walk away from the wall where she was pinned, then goes and turns on the lights. "You can see what lights need to be replaced. And I put the desk and chairs over there that need to be tightened up." Holding 'a side she walks like a wounded dog.

"I'm sorry bout ya ribs." I watch how she moving worried I might've really hurt 'a. I remember how bad I was hurt when Mama broke my ribs. "Want to go let a doctor look at you?"

"I'll be alright, I'm sure." She disappears in the back again. I get the bat off the ground and put it in the cleaning closet with the other supplies, then come out and get started.

It's been a long while, when Coley come back in the classroom. I'm on my knees working. She slide back on 'a desk and watch me. I tilt my hat down, so I can stop thinking bout 'a watching me. I look through my tools, for a few screws for this last chair, I'm gone have to replace them all. This my last lil project, and I'm glad so I can get on to the store, and make my orders fore the postman come.

"You're the only woman I've ever seen in overalls."

"Maybe you need to get out more."

Laughing, "Says the country bumpkin who has never left her podunk town. Why do you like wearing pants so much?"

"Same reason you like to ask so many questions."

"And why is that do you presume?"

"Cause we wont to." I smile, standing up from the chair and closing my tool box. "Have a good afternoon, Ms. Graham."

"Coley, please," she insists following behind me. "Why do you have a man's nickname?"

"Why you ask impossible questions?"

"How's that impossible?"

"Am I a man?"

"Oh, Madelyn! You are impossible as your father said you are. Now I see why you will never be a lady."

"Who wonts to be a lady?"

"Madelyn, why must you answer every question with a question?"

"Linny," I correct her, and wait silently, until she calls me by the name I asked to be addressed by.

"It's a man's name," she refuses.

So I start out to my horse. I touch Anastasia gently. Then I start to put my tools in the saddle bag closest to me.

"Linny?" She trying me more than accepting my wishes.

I hesitate a little, before looking back and acknowledging her.

"Why do you answer every question with a question?"

"You don't like questions?" I tease, smiling and untying Stasia.

"Seriously," she pouts, folding 'a arms.

"You seem to like questions," I jank 'a more, mounting Stasia. We stand firm, blocking the sun from 'a face. Now I can see she really upset so I add, "Sometimes a question is the answer."

"Well, I have a few statements to make, too." She put 'a hands on 'a hips.

"That's one right there." I smile, me and Anastasia stepping back away from the hitching post.

"Just because you're out here in the country, doesn't mean you've got to be stuck in the past. You've got that house, all that land and a store, so I know you're not broke. You need to get yourself an automobile."

Moving closer to the school, I look at her, take 'a in. I've never heard what anybody outside of Zion think of me. It's interesting to say the least. Feeling that maybe she upset me, she drops 'a hands and starts fingering 'a skirt nervously. I just stare at 'a, not speaking, just feeling 'a out.

"It's probably because you're a woman you don't have an auto. I don't know how to drive either. I don't even know any women who do, but you live alone. Suppose something happens. Are you going to ride your horse in the middle of the night to get help?"

Seeing she really concerned, and this something she giving real thought to I tell 'a, "I can drive. I like my horse. And she likes me." I rub Stasia lovingly and she lean into my hand. "Plus, getting petro to run a automobile ain't easy. Keep you going in white towns, and the nearest filling station bout 10 miles. So most folks doing both, using wagons to lug all the petro they gone need to get around here."

"Somebody should open a filling station here."

"You should learn to ride."

"I've never considered learning to ride a horse, by myself," she say staring at Anastasia distrustful, like she spect 'a to run up to 'a and bite.

"Well you out in the country now, so you gone have to learn to ride. And something else-"

"What?" She smiles friendly.

"You smell nice."

"Thank you. What does that have to do with learning about the country?"

"What happens when the bees and wasps think so, too?" I sniggle, turning Anastasia round and start trotting off.

As Coley starts screaming and swatting, realizing she surrounded. Well, not really surrounded. It's just a couple bees, but you'd swear she was fighting a whole hive way she cutting up and hollering.

Chapter Twenty

There is a gentle tap on the door, so I say, "Come in."

"You going to bed?" Coley ask from the doorway, wearing a big robe and a gown with 'a hair all over 'a head, holding a brush.

I'm scared to answer, cause I've been even more busy these last few days with Coley here, and I still got my own hair to do. Not to mention, this upcoming Sunday gone be the first time I been back to church since Miemay's funeral.

Still for some reason I admit, "I'm gone be up awhile."

Now I'm parting my hair into sections so I can make four big braids. Gone comb the curl out of it, and braid it tight. Hopefully I don't get sick going to bed with a wet head. I done lit the fire place to keep warm.

She sit next to me in front of the vanity, blocking the light, looking at my hair like she under some spell. I move the light in front of us, so I can see again. Reaching for my hair, she stop just before touching me and ask, "May I?"

I nod yes and breathe out, realizing I'd completely stopped breathing when she reached. Nobody but Mrs. Harper or my sisters ever really touched me.

She hold up a handful of hair, staring at it, then run 'a fingers through it.

I got my eyes closed, feeling the chills on my scalp, neck, over my arms and down my back.

Stretching out some of the curls, she put it to my waistline measuring the length. "Your hair is so long, and beautiful." Then she sit up and put my hair to 'a own waist. "I've never had hair pass my shoulders." Looking at our reflections in the looking glass, she take a deep breath, and kinda shrink, smiling at me. "You're just a beautiful girl," she adds, and it sounds almost sad.

"You're beautiful, too." I feel like I'm consoling 'a, but what I'm saying true.

"There's no harm in admitting the truth, Linny. I'm not saying I'm the ugliest girl in the world. I'm just saying you are one of the most beautiful women I've met. Probably the most beautiful woman I've actually had an opportunity to build a friendship with, and I think friends should encourage each other."

"We friends?" I tease rather than say thank you, cause I cain't be serious in moments like these, when folks going on and on by how I look. Makes me feel strange to have 'a saying all this.

"Did you know that where I'm from, just being seen with certain women raises your status?" She ignores my uneasiness, and keeps on. "Did you know, that in almost any room you walk in with other Colored women, you would be the most desired? That's all I'm trying to say. Your beauty can't be denied."

"I don't know about that." I look at 'a seriously, taking my hair back. "You the most beautiful woman I ever seen round here. Everybody round here looking something like me, Iain special or different. Feel like you the special one, the different one, the beautiful one. You got your own look, and what we here in Zion call a disposition. You sharp, cultured and know how to make men jump to your aid. When I think about how Daddy nem was unloading your things, they had a little pep in their step."

"Men help women out of obligation. That's what they've been taught they're suppose to do." She challenging what I'm saying.

"Yeah, ain't no arguing that round here. But when they was helping you they was honored. Honestly, I'm honored you staying here." I stare in 'a eyes, and it make me feel some kind of way.

To change the subject or lighten the mood, I say, "My hair so heavy when it's wet, I hate washing and braiding it. I think about cutting it every time I do it. I don't never really wear it out no way. Then it'll be easier to manage, but Mama nem say it's a sin for a woman to cut 'a hair. They say a woman's hair her glory. Feels like her headache, too."

"You're so lucky, and don't even know it. I'd kill to be light skinned, with green eyes and hair growing all down my back like you. Even if you don't notice it, you even move like a queen."

"I don't feel like no queen," I'm almost whispering, getting lost in my thoughts. Then I get back to combing my hair.

"Mind if I comb your hair?"

Fore I know anything my heart drop, and I'm feeling all uneasy and uncomfortable. Then I look in 'a eyes, and up at 'a hair standing on ends and say, "Nah, I'm tender headed. And you got to do yo own hair. But that's awfully nice of you to offer."

"But, I really want to," she insist, putting some of my hair in 'a hands, and staring back. "I'll be gentle."

I breathe deep and easy, taking it all in. Feeling something new. Getting up, I go get a pillow and sit it on the floor between 'a legs, the way I use to when Ella use to comb it.

When 'a hands brush my neck, or my hair move, I get covered in goose bumps. I put my knees up and rest my head on 'em to brace myself, cause it feel like Iain never been touched. She gentle like she promise, gentler than I expect, and gentler than I am with my own head. She being so gentle, I think we gone be at this all night, and Iain upset bout that neither.

The wind coming in my window, breathing on my skin as she parts my hair, then 'a warm finger tips rub oil on the skin bared. I try to think of a way to repay 'a for this moment. I am thankful to God for 'a being here, since I been so scared some nights I couldn't sleep.

"If I looked like you," she say solemnly speaking to my scalp, parting hair and sweeping it against my neck, forehead and soothing me. "I would have passed the paper bag test. Then I'd be an A. K. A."

"What's a A. K. A.?"

"It's this Colored women's sorority called Alpha Kappa Alpha. I didn't have a good name, and most of them don't just have a good name, they are blue blooded too. My family has new money, and our great-grands were freed just before the war because they moved north.

"My mother's family continued working for white people in menial positions. My mother's family had been servants so long, they were given some land. Some of the next generation found different ways to support the family. Some people might say we didn't own what we have on that side, but we did build on the gift. You almost can't tell Mama has that background.

"Many of the women in the sorority were blue bloods. Their families actually held slaves at some point. They came from old money and land. They have names."

"What's blue blooded?" I hear the question before I realize I'm speaking. I'm so tired, and 'a hands so soothing.

"Blue blood means a lot of different things. For white people, it means they have old money, or they'll have money for every generation that follows. They're like royalty and everyone recognizes their last names, like Vanderbilt, Carnegie or the Rockefellers.

"For Negroes, it could mean different things. Blue blood could mean you worked for a family of old money, and they took care of you. Usually that means you're some relation, but it's improper to talk about that part. Blue blood is also when a person is so light you can see the veins in their wrist. Or it's like what you are, Linny, when you're so light you could pass for white.

"I can see the veins in your wrists." She breathes deep and dreamy. "Light as you are, you could do anything you wanted, and you wouldn't even need a good name. They'd accept you. They'd marry you, and teach you their culture to preserve their skin. Do you know how well you could marry?"

I don't say nothing to that, and she silent for a while.

Then she start again. "The AKA's don't accept any brownies, not even with good names, you have to be light skinned, or 'fair' they say. I didn't want to believe it. I worked so hard in college. Not a lot of women even go to college, and I graduated at the top of my class. I did all kinds of community service, got professor recommendations, and recommendations from my field work. They still wouldn't let me in." She finishes with a bitter laugh.

I don't realize I'm falling asleep, til I feel the emptiness where my words should be, so I mumble, "Well, you better for it."

"How you figure?" Her voice louder than my mood can take, and I hear the disbelief. So I clear my throat and wake up so I can talk.

"Cause who want to be part of a group that pick folks based on things they ain got no control over. You working hard, going to college, and earning people's respect so they'll give you recommendations, is something you yoself done. Whether you dark or light, nigga or white, ain't got nothing to do with nothing. Ain't no merit in things we cain't control."

"What about people who can sing? Or people raised playing the piano, or dancers?"

"That's different. They still got to sing to be heard. Or learn and practice the piano, or the dance steps. Ain't no way to learn to be a nigga or white, ya just is what chu is."

"Such a beautiful girl. Wish you wouldn't use such an ugly word. Say Colored, or Negro," she say, then snicker. "That's not a proper word for a lady, and it's an insult to the whole race."

"Niggas thinking they better than other niggas is an insult to the whole race," I say firmly. Then my eyes get heavy, I feel chills, I hear the wind singing a lullaby, and when she part my hair, I wait for 'a warm fingertips. Surrendering to 'a hands, massaging oil in my scalp, I lean on my knees and drift back off.

*　　*　　*

When I come back in from feeding the animals, I smell something ain never smelt before, burning or cooking coming from the kitchen. Nervous I start to move quick, wondering what Coley could be making. I know she don't know nothing bout cooking, and it don't smell like nothing I done ever smelt.

I find Coley standing in the kitchen wearing a long white nightgown, looking like an angel with 'a brown skin, and dark hair. Me and my sisters slept in old clean clothes we couldn't wear out the house no more. Iain never seen a woman wear a real gown, and it's beautiful. She almost too pretty to be just waking up, and the gown too beautiful to be slept in. I don't realize it, til she turn around that I'm staring.

"What chu doing?" I take off my work gloves looking at Coley, and looking around as the thick smoke fills the kitchen. There are two iron combs in the fire on the stove. Her hair up in pins all over the place. She done braided 'a hair into thick black ropes of cotton hanging down, to between 'a shoulders.

Coley stand stiff, looking away from me pulling 'a hair out with something, like she cain't talk and do what she doing. Then I see 'a hair smoking, so I get closer to look at what she doing. Iain never seen nothing like this. She turn around frowning at me, looking all serious. Maybe that's why I start frowning too, when I ask again, "What chu doing?"

"Hot combing my hair," she answer, like I'm on 'a nerves, and like I should know.

"Do it hurt?" I'm studying her, watching as she put grease round a section of hair, then rake the hot iron comb through it. Her hair sizzle like water boiling over on a fire, or the last of the water burning into a forgotten pot on the stove. She rakes the black cotton til its quiet, flat, straight and shiny like black silk. Its other things I should be doing but I cain't move.

"Madelyn, you mean to tell me, you've never seen anyone else press her hair?" Before I can answer she say, "I guess not. And no, it doesn't hurt, cause I combed it out and braided it after I washed it last night. All your sisters must have good hair like you." She parts out more hair to burn, and that last statement seem like she trying to be funny acting.

"I don't know if they hair good or bad, but they ain never 'pressing' it neither." I say it just like her, tasting the word. Once I sit down, I'm going over hot combs and pressing hair. Then I lean to the right, watching how she lean with that comb, then the steam come up from 'a hair sizzling like bacon on a hot skillet. "You ain't scared you gone burn yo self?"

"No, I'm not. And being burned isn't the worst thing in the world. I've been burned a lot of times. Mama always said 'beauty hurts.' And I sure don't want to be nappy headed.

"Shoot, my mama use to light me and my sisters up when we were coming up. I was so glad when we got old enough to go to the beauty shop. Ms. Lena didn't get it bone straight like Mama, but then again, maybe she did, and she just didn't put all that grease in our heads.

"Hair will turn back sooner if you don't put enough grease. Mama use to put so much grease in our hair, even the rain couldn't get through." She laugh to 'aself at the last part then continue, "Here lately, I've been doing it myself. I couldn't get it done when I was at school. Some of the girls would take turns pressing each other's hair. Then sometimes I'd pull it out, and let one of them do the edges. It's hard to get those naps in your kitchen without burning yourself."

"Kitchen?"

"Yeah, the naps on the back of your neck." Then she look over at me, and I can tell she thinking about it til she finally say, "I guess you don't know anything about that either."

"I know about nappy hair, but we usually just comb and braid it down with a little grease and it be all good. I ain never seen nobody do what you doing."

"What do your sisters do about their nappy hair?"

"Comb it and braid it up. Seem like it be too hot round here to be doing that all the time. Specially when the summer come. It take bout all a woman got to come in here and cook a little something, or warm some food up. I'm sure they ain gone be getting they self all hot and sweaty for the sake of having hair like white folks."

"It's not hair like white folks. Lots of Colored women have straight hair, too. Haven't you ever heard of Madame CJ Walker?"

"No, I cain't say I have. Maybe my sisters have. She be with Du Bois?"

"Ha ha ha. She's a millionaire, who made all of her money making women beautiful." She smiles impressed. "Whenever I go home I like to go to her salon. I read somewhere Madam Walker has found a way to get our hair straight without pressing it. I can't wait to find out how when I get back home, I am so tired of doing all this to be pretty."

"Iain never heard of Madame. In fact, I don't know any ladies who go around calling themselves Madame at all." I tease 'a, and she grunt like a pig. "That ain lady like either," I tease leaning back watching 'a press 'a hair.

We in silence for a long time, while the smell of 'a hair burning, the comb on the stove, the morning's bacon and syrup mingle. It's amazing to watch what she doing. I cain't believe she doing this all the time. Then she jump, and say, "Oooh this hair is so hot."

I worry, looking at how she lean to keep the hot hair from touching 'a neck. "So you could burn yourself, but you ain scared, cause you got to be pretty?"

"I just put too much grease that time. Unless I put too much grease in my hair, or on my scalp I should be fine."

"How does the grease burn you?"

"The comb heats the grease up and moves it around. It can roll down to my scalp or get on my neck or shoulders. Still those burns aren't as bad as when the comb touches your ear or scalp. Umph, now that's real painful."

"Why you do this again if it burns you?"

"To get my hair straight."

"I guess I just don't understand why you would go through all this trouble, especially when it hurts." I'm thinking out loud.

"I've got to get my hair straight so I look presentable. I'm a lady, and no man wants a nappy-headed woman for his wife."

"One's round Zion ain found that out then, cause they love our nappy-headed selves. Iain never knew to be a lady you got to burn yourself."

"I'm not burning myself, I don't burn myself on purpose. It's what you have to do to get your hair straight and presentable if you don't have good hair."

I see she getting defensive, and Iain trying to fight with 'a, so I just watch quietly. She got three combs, one on the fire, the other on a wash rag look like it done seen better days and one in 'a hand. She turn the comb over on the rag, and wait to see how it scorch the towel. When it don't burn no new spot, she grab the comb, and put it in 'a hair, then pull 'a hair between the comb and the rag. Coley hair start off a dark dusty brown. Then she put some grease and rake it with the comb til its shiny, black and straight.

I get up and open the windows, let the smoke out the house. I want to cook, but I don't feel comfortable cooking in the kitchen with 'a hair everywhere. I think I better get our dinner on soon so we have something to eat when we get back from the fields.

So I say, "How long you gone be?"

"I don't know. I don't usually do it all by myself without a mirror. One of the girls would help," she say calmer, putting the comb on the fire. "No men are coming today are they?"

"No, not that I know of." I open my legs, put my elbows on my knees and lean on my hand.

"Good, so I can get this done."

We in silence for a long while again, and I cain't stop watching 'a doing 'a hair. Til I realize I'm letting the coolness of the morning get away from me. I got a lot of work to do. She need to get out of the kitchen so I can put this food on fore it get too hot. It's miserable cooking when it's hot outside, that's why I usually do all the cooking early in the morning, before the heat pick up.

* * *

"You tired?" I ask, when I find Coley in the bed laying down in the middle of the day. I'm a little disappointed to come back from the fields and ain't nothing cooked. Plus I was waiting to talk to 'a, or show 'a what chores she gone have going forward. She don't even think to try and do nothing round here. She the one walk around like she some kind of queen.

"Doing my hair usually takes all day, especially if I do it all by myself. So I plan to take it easy for the rest of the day." She got 'a arms wrapped round a pillow laying on 'a stomach. Her head wrapped tight in a scarf, and I feel bad saying what I came to say, but it's got to be done and I need 'a help.

"Well, you asked me what I wanted you to pay for staying here."

"Let me get you some money." She start moving and moaning like she exhausted.

"I don't need your money. I need your help round here, doing the wife duties I been thinking. And I'll have to show you how to do them today, and then we gone go over them a few times over the next few days til you get 'em."

"It's Saturday," she whine breathing hard. Then when she see it don't move me, "What are the wife duties?" She sit up like a stick in mud staring at me like I'm working 'a nerves again.

"Well, you would be doing all the house work except the cooking since you don't know how."

"I already work. I have to prepare lesson plans for each of my students. I teach school remember?" Folding 'a arms, "When will I be doing all these wife duties? When will I have time?"

"We both have to work, and somebody got to feed us. Somebody got to tend to the gardens. We ain got no maids round here."

"Fine," she say upset, and I can tell she feel bullied like she ain got no choice. I feel bad bout that, but I got so much to do I cain't let feeling guilty keep me doing everything. "What are the duties?" she asks, poking 'a chest out and lifting 'a head proud.

Never missing a beat, I start to rattle off the chores I expect 'a to do. "Feed the hens in the morning, weed the garden once or twice a week when needed. Pick some vegetables and fruit for the table and our meals. I'll help you do the jarring. I'll stock the smoke house since I know you cain't stand seeing nothing kilt. I know I cain't expect you to butcher no guineas. I need you to sweep out the kitchen since I do the cooking. We can alternate cleaning out the stove, and we both need to be gathering wood."

"You said, garden. You said feed the hens, and they look like they bite. Not to mention, that means I've got to work outside."

"Most of the work you need to do is around the outside of the house. I expect you to help me milk the cows, and feed the livestock in the stables, too. And when the school closed, and it's harvesting or planting time I expect you to work in the fields with me, and to help the town in the big fields."

"I don't want to be outside more than I have to. I was thinking I would just be out enough to get to and from the school." When I look at 'a like she crazy, she whine adding, "I'm not trying to be a tar baby. I just don't want to get black from the sun."

Chapter Twenty-One

"Ain my grandbaby darling?" Mrs. Harper coo at Esmeralda, showing Coley their newest granddaughter. I feel out of place standing there on the Harper's porch. "You ain seen this one have you, Linny?"

"No, ma'am, I ain't." Feeling obligated, I get closer and take a look. I don't know what it is I'm feeling looking down at this child. She beautiful, all babies beautiful, but I'm feeling some kind of way.

"Way you spoil these babies, and then send them home to us to raise is a shame." Patrick Jr.'s wife take the impatient baby, and put 'a head under a small blanket, then start moving to nurse.

"I use to take care of you, Linny, and spoil you as much as ya mama would let me." Mrs. Harper smile at me, reminding me of all she done for me, again. "Look, Cynthia, look at this dress Linny wearing. It's one of the ones I bought 'a when I was up in Atlanta. Ain't she beautiful? Wish she would dress like a lady more often. She's such a beautiful girl."

Me and Coley been invited to dinner, they welcoming Coley to town. I'm wearing a dress so fancy Coley had to help me get it on. I'm even wearing a double-skirted slip and stockings. It's been a while since I been to a formal family dinner. In my family we don't do formal dinners less somebody getting married. Seem like the Harpers be doing this a few times a week.

I watch all their sons sit down. Each one looking like they daddy with none of they mother's color.

I'm nervous. All the women are so proper acting. Seem like them and Coley cut from a similar cloth. All but three of the pastor's sons married light-skinned educated women. The other three still married light, like their father, but they married Zion girls. To see all their brown, sharp-dressed children running round, I feel like I'm squeezing into a tight space meant for somebody else.

When the food comes I try to remember what Mrs. Harper told me. I don't think I eat like no animal or nothing, still I'm careful, to eat slow, chew my food and not talk with a full mouth. I don't say much anyhow, Iain never been no big talker and my family ain nothing like this. So I don't know what to say no how. What my mama taught my sisters bout being wives wouldn't be enough to serve round here.

One of the women here in town helps Mrs. Harper for money, and they have folks working in they fields. Iain never seen one nigga hire another one to work in their own kitchen. It's something folks round here sometimes complain about, that The Reverend living beyond his means. Then again, when you think about all the places they go in a week, visiting the sick, entertaining town guests, and having to see bout town business, may not leave any time for working on they own house and land.

I'm so use to working, soon as I got here I went straight to the kitchen and put a apron on. I was pleasantly surprised to find everything cooked and laid out ready to be served. It was interesting to see Sadie, this older woman from round here, working in they kitchen like she would any white folk's house.

All while Sadie serving us it feel wrong. Me and the Harpers kids half her age. I have to keep reminding myself the Harpers are very busy. Still, I cain't imagine hiring nobody to help me round my own house.

"I've been reading your local newspaper. It's really wonderful for such a small town. You don't talk about much going on in the world though. I mean, we are on the brink of war. Then there are so many things going on with Coloreds all over the country. It would be nice to read some of that, you know, for uplifting," Coley offer while we standing on the porch.

"White folks check our paper. They don't like that," Reverend Patrick inform 'a.

"Well, now that Washington is dead, it would be nice if you'd print articles by other noteworthy Coloreds on the race matter."

"We git letters and articles from people writing on the race matter, but what does Booker T Washington's death have to do with who putting columns in the paper?" Mrs. Harper ask.

"I'm thinking of articles by Du Bois. He is the leading voice now that Washington is gone, and when Washington was alive, Du Bois couldn't get in your paper."

"Sho couldn't and still cain't," Reverend step in shaking his head 'no.'

"Why not?" Coley demand to know.

"He's a trouble maker. He don't live down here, and he ain't got to deal with all the problems us printing his crazy ideas gone stir up." Reverend fold his arms.

"Crazy ideas? That Coloreds should be allowed to vote? How is it crazy to expect to exercise the same rights as every other American? You're paying taxes like everyone else."

"Girl, we in the middle of an election year. They already hanging niggas as warnings for us not to git no good ideas," Reverend Patrick warn her. "Then President Wilson, working on passing laws to separate blacks in government offices. Shoot, he even said "Birth of a Nation" is one of the best and most accurate depictions of what's going on in the South. We cain't git into no voting drives here. Zion ain't one of the few Colored towns still standing, and probly the most successful because we fighting for our rights. We keep to ourselves, and worry bout our own.

"That paper is to help this town do better. It got crop schedules, birth announcements, church bulletins and jobs. We advertise if some fair is coming. But we ain't gone git in no politics with this paper that goes before the committee on every printing."

"Why do you have to give them all the parts of your paper?" Coley make faces at him like she cain't believe what he saying. "Why would whites want to read what we're writing anyway?"

"See you ain never been to the South."

"I lived in Atlanta for two years while I was doing my Masters."

"Did you ever gitcho head out of them books?" Mrs. Harper tease 'a. "White folks want to know everything going on round here in Zion. They want to know every Negro they don't know, and every Negro want to make sure they known."

"And now we got this moving picture, "Birth of a Nation," they say making the Klan numbers grow bigger than ever. They say it's the reason folks been gittin hung left and right. The Klan back to night riding real tough, burning crosses in people's yards and killing niggas' livestock. I said I was gone have to talk about it this Sunday."

"And for yall boys, think you gittin over going to that jug house in the middle of the night, if the Klan catch you on the road ain nobody but Jesus gone be able to save you," Mrs. Harper warn.

"In the afterlife," Annette, one of the wives, add.

"Please tell ya mama, yall gone be in yah house after the sun go down." Mrs. Harper eyeball 'a boys.

"Yes, ma'am," they answer 'a, while she staring at them one by one.

"Speaking of that, Linny, we also brought you here so we could take you to the council meeting to stand with Coley," Ms. Harper announce.

"Why me?" I look around at everyone stirring in their seats like there's something I don't know.

"You was requested," Reverend answer.

Chapter Twenty-Two

"Round here, theya hang you for sport. They been known to let a nigga accused of something outta jail so the Klan can hunt 'im down." Reverend Patrick look back in the rearview mirror at Coley, to make sure she understand how serious this all is.

Coley don't say a word.

"My boy tell me in the city, white folks don't out right call you a nigga. Don't out right let you know they don't like you. So I'm thinking where you from they ain hanging folks way they is down here."

Reverend Patrick holding the steering wheel and looking back at Coley to see if she following. Coley still quiet, planted like a tree looking right back at 'im. Guess that mean she understand how serious it is, cause he go on and say, "It's gone take you a while to git all the rules, so I'm gone speak fah yah, much as I can. But I'm still gone tell yah the rules and we gone have to be working on you learnin 'em. Else you be done got the whole town burnt down."

"How could I get the town burned down, when my only intention is to help? All my instructors, mentors and Alumni impressed upon me a responsibility to the Negro race. Which means I have to set positive examples by striving for a quiet Christian life and following the laws of the land. I always thought white's just hung Negroes who raped white women."

"Who told you that?" we all say almost together, and Mrs. Harper turn around like she got to look at Coley face to see if she lying or crazy.

Our attention seem to scare 'a. "I," she stumble, looking at us hanging on for 'a next words. "Well, I heard about lynching in New York, and when I was in school in DC. People were always saying, you know, that it happened because of some crime the Negro committed."

"Ain knowed none of them men they done hung raped nobody, specially not no white woman. Niggas ain even making eye contact with no white folks, so they definitely ain got the nerve to go round raping they women," Reverend Patrick challenge.

"You don't have to be do nothing at all," Mrs. Harper add. "They just think they can treat us any kinda way."

"They think it cause they can," Reverend Patrick go on. "And while we talking bout this, you make sure you don't accept no work in they house or be out walking on the roads by yahself. They always worried bout somebody wonting one of them skinny misses, but they the ones always raping our women."

"That's enough," Mrs. Harper says, stopping The Reverend and looking back at me like it's the first time I done heard this warning.

"Well, why don't you all just move?" Coley ask, like we all stupid for being here.

"Where?" Reverend ask.

"Up North? West?" Coley offer.

"Our family here. Parents too old to just up and go. Who gone take care of them? We own our land. Been had it in the family since slavery ended. How you think we gone git by somewhere else?" Reverend Patrick ask. "Whole town have to go. Ain't that easy. This all we know."

"When Ida B. Wells wrote about lynching in Tennessee, almost the entire town left. It's possible. Then there are tons of jobs in Michigan, New York, Chicago, St. Louis and E. St. Louis. A lot of Coloreds are moving out of the South. Employers are always looking for Negroes to hire. They are tired of all the politics and strikes with the white labor groups in New York," Coley explain.

"We've heard about your jobs up North and in the Midwest. Klan round here harassing and hanging anybody they think got 'Northern Fever,'" Reverend say.

"Um hmm," Mrs. Harper cosign, nodding 'a head yes, and adding, "You have to be seeing how you can git out of Zion. Every agent ever came looking for labor to break strikes in Chicago and New York, giving out free tickets and making promises to families of a better life, first had to figure out how to keep that workers neck out the noose. The Klan be waiting at the train station."

"Speaking of the train station," Reverend Patrick jump back in, "Linny's daddy, Cassius, told me you was looking white folks in the eyes and walking on the sidewalk. He said white folks started coming out they businesses and stopped what they was doing when you got off the train."

"What's wrong with the sidewalks? And my father taught me to always look a man in the eyes."

"I don't know where yo daddy from, but down here that's stepping out cho place to the white man. Surprised he got you out of there safe. Then again, you was at the train station, and you ain from round here. Looking at you, they probly knew you ain know no better."

"Don't stop 'em from teaching folks a lesson," Mrs. Harper put in.

"Sho don't," Reverend Patrick pick up.

Coley, take a deep breath, looking lost now.

We on our way to introduce 'a to the counsel. Every new nigga come to Zion the counsel at some point have to be told about. Coley must be special, they don't actually wont to meet every stranger, just to know who in the town gone be here awhile. Usually, The Reverend have to make a note of them being here. Otherwise that nigga be walking round on borrowed time.

The Klan ain killed nobody from Zion in a while, but they still whupping grown folks. Lately, they been really hanging niggas in other towns. All they need is to see some stranger round here, late at night or dust. Ask 'im who's boy they is, and if he cain't say no name they know, he be lynched. I done watched a few strangers get cut down out of the trees round here, been getting worse lately.

Reverend go on, "First off, you don't look 'em in they eyes. You answer every question with 'Yes, sir,' or 'No, sir.' You say 'Yes, ma'am' or 'misses,' 'No, ma'am' or 'No misses.' Some of the white ladies will tell you what they prefer. I calls 'em all 'Misses.' Iain never been corrected, so maybe you should just call 'em that, too."

"Stop fidgeting!" Mrs. Harper fuss, looking back at me digging in the neckline of this stuffy dress. I hate these things.

When we finally get to the place where they say the counsel gone be, we ride on round to the back of the house. It's a big white house with columns and balconies up front overlooking the land. Reverend say the family older than he is. Say this land been in this family since the 1700's. He say they restored it after the war, and a lot of the Confederates and The Daughters of the Confederacy consider it to be a special place, something of a landmark.

Mrs. Harper and Reverend Patrick get out first, and I get in line behind Mrs. Harper, wondering what they brought me along for. I mean, Mrs. Harper be better for this, but I guess it be my age. Me and Coley are closer in age.

Old man Grover meet us at the back door. "The Master been waiting for yall to arrive." He look at me for a long time, then say, "Uh, Reverend, they just want to see the school teacher and Linny."

"They know I'm coming?" I ask surprised.

"They know everything." Grover raise his eyebrows.

"I don't want to go without you." I wind my arm in Mrs. Harper's. "I thought you said I was just coming along to stand with Coley."

"Hush, girl," Reverend Patrick say, staring worried at the door, then looking at me like it's the first time he ever seen me. "You'll be fine."

"Go on in there with 'im, Pat." She press 'im, but Grover looking like he don't think that's a good idea.

*　　*　　*

Soon as we walk in the room, Douglas Belanger lean over saying, "Patrick, you can excuse yo self boy."

Feel like somebody done took my coat off or something. I'm feeling more alone and nervous cause of Coley not knowing what to do. And when I think about it, Iain never really spoke to no white men neither.

"So you're the new school teacher?" Wyatt Neville, start in, nobody introduce they self.

Still I know them all, at some point in your life here in Zion you run into these white men. They are the richest men this side of Georgia, and the last of the old plantations still standing. They run the Klan, the police, and they be the ones deciding what niggas 'llowed to do. They wont to know everything going on in our town, and they wont to know everybody coming and going in Zion. They make the laws round here, and break the laws round here.

From left to right, there is Orson Harper, Titan Kendall, Stanton Atwell, Wyatt Neville, Douglas Belanger, Alton Remington, then Lowell and his eldest brother, Hunter Beaumont. All of them fifty years old or better.

Stanton Atwell got a piece of paper, and he writing little notes on it, looking us both over. "Girl, don't you hear this man speaking to you?" he ask, tilting his glasses at Coley.

"I'm nervous, sir." Coley hold tight to the edges of 'a dress, looking round. She scared, and she need to be.

"I said, 'Are you the new school teacher round here?'" Mr. Neville repeat hisself.

"Yes." Coley look up, then I step closer to 'a and grab 'a hand, and she look down gulping for air, then add, "Sir." It don't even sound right coming out 'a mouth.

"You're definitely something. Don't look like none of the niggas round here." Alton Remington comment, leaning back in his chair and folding his arms. "You come to start trouble?"

"No, sir." She breathing heavy and 'a eyes wild like maybe she been caught, or what she saying ain quite the truth.

"You sure you didn't come down here to rile our niggas up?" Hunter Beaumont, the eldest of the men, and the one who has been on the counsel the longest ask in disbelief.

"No, sir." Coley shaking 'a head 'no' nervously too.

"You ain't gone be encouraging them to vote or nothing like that? Talking bout nigga rights and being equal to white men?" Lowell, his younger brother, dig into 'a answers, sifting.

"No, sir."

"Ever heard of Booker T. Washington?" Hunter Beaumont ask.

"Yes, sir."

"What you think of him, girl?"

Looking over at me, Coley grab my hand tighter. "Well, I've never had the pleasure of meeting him, sir, but I hear he's done a great deal for Zion."

"That was a fine nigga. A fine nigga." Hunter Beaumont nod his head, and then all they attention turn to me.

I'm trying to look around, and I'm surprised it ain what I done thought. Whenever I hear about the counsel, I be thinking bout a big judge bench, and men sitting behind it like the drawings I seen in school books when they talk about the president. I spect they be wearing wigs and sitting up above us. They ain't. Just a big house, and they all in the study surrounded by books. Ain't but eight men, but the room is full of their own self-importance.

"What's your name, girl?"

"Coletta Graham sir," she answer, and I realize she don't do that curtsy for white folks.

"I know your name, girl. I'm asking the girl standing next to you."

"Madelyn Remington, suh." All they eyes on me. Then I wonder what I done did to deserve to be brought before them. Then again, I know they know every nigga round these parts, so it's got to be a reason for me to be here.

"Speak up, girl."

I say louder, "Madelyn Remington, suh," and don't swish all my words together way I been taught to do when speaking to white folks.

"Well now, ain't you a jewel," Lowell Beaumont say, and I don't know how he saying what he saying, cause it don't feel sexual, it feel strange. The way he looking at me got a different interest, than the way men in Zion look at me. What he want from me? Want me to work in his house cause I'm so light? Since Ion know what has earned me a place before them, I'm scared. I don't wont no white man to ever take no interest in me, specially since I'm living out by myself.

"Step forward girl, and let us get a good look at you," Hunter Beaumont order, his face hard.

"She almost white," Lowell Beaumont add.

"Been a long time since I seen one look that much like us," Wyatt Neville seem to be joking.

"Lift yah head up, gal," Lowell Beaumont order, and I look him in his eyes then down at the ground. "Keep yah head up gal," he demand louder, like I'm getting on his nerves. Then he do something ain no white person ever done, he look right in my eyes. For a moment, I feel connected to him and that send chills down my spine and scare me even more.

His brother Hunter, next to 'im staring at me, too, then he say, "She looking just like a black diamond," all dreamy.

My heart drop, and I remember what Miemay always told me. Stay away from white men. Don't talk to 'em and if they take any interest in you, don't never be too far from home. Always tell 'em you too busy, and go looking for work at some old white lady house, so you ain't available to be forced to take no work in they house.

White women look down on their men chasing us. If you tell 'em you're afraid of a white man, they'll shame 'im, and other white women'll be weary bout dealing with 'im. I drop my head.

"Keep ya head up," Hunter Beaumont warn.

I lift my chin up, and look at 'im, and then at the other men at the table.

"What you doing with yourself, gall?" Hunter Beaumont ask.

"Working in the fields, sir." I speak clear, proper.

"Ain got no man, or children," Hunter dig.

I don't know if he saying or asking, but I don't answer. I'm afraid what he asking is do I live alone. Maybe so they can come later on to see about me. For a while no one speaks, then I know they waiting for an answer, but I don't say nothing. I just stand there rocking back and forth, holding Coley hand, looking right in Hunter Beaumont eyes.

All of a sudden, Lowell Beaumont touch his brother's arm, then shuffle the papers in front of him, and I drop my head. "We know you done inherited most of Miemay's property and money. You gone have a say in the committee now. We know you the only woman on Zion's committee. Git on out of here, gal. We know who you is, you ain got no man or no children. We know you live over there by yourself on all that land, too. We done with yall. Yall can go," he finish.

Iain looking at 'im but I can feel his eyes.

"You make sure you ain stirring our niggas up round here, or it'll be you be stirred up. You hear me, girl?" Douglas Belanger warn Coley, as we make our way out the door.

"Yes, sir," Coley answer.

"Yall can git on back over to Zion, too."

"Don't dawdle," Hunter Beaumont, who been staring at me all this time, say like he real concerned. "It's getting late, and you know the Klan been riding. Don't want nothing to happen to you."

* * *

When we get back out to the car, Reverend Patrick ask what they said, and Coley say, "They called us niggers, to our face. Told me not to stir yall up or they'll stir me up," she speak, like she in a daze.

"Did they say anything to you?" Reverend ask me, then him and Mrs. Harper seem to almost stop breathing for my answer.

"They just looked at me mostly." I feel kinda dazed myself, and weird cause of how they acting. Then I'm worried.

All while we silent riding back to town, I be thinking bout how I got to start sleeping with my rifle. Be worried if, no, when and what night they be coming for me. I think to ask Reverend Patrick if I can stay with him, but Iain wont to let on I'm afraid. I what'n going out running, or begging. I decided fore we left out that house, I would fight.

Chapter Twenty-Three

Walking up the steps, I smell the soap, aftershave and some perfume, or the oil babies are greased up in just on Sundays. Clothes fresh with starch and laundry soap make the house feel more inviting for God, maybe. Then again, God everywhere— whether you preparing for 'im or not. Everybody I see, I remember a song, and I hear their pitch. I know what field song is their favorite and what they good with.

Sunny could carve anything out of wood, and Etta good with hand stitching. Sally always fixed good hair, and Mrs. Clara can cook.

I watch Mrs. Clara find 'a way round the people, smiling and easing in and out of hugs, back pats, kisses, and people asking 'a to come sit with 'em. I see how much she got in common with Miemay, and me now. She a woman owning 'a own business, too, but she well respected. Her husband ran off with another woman fore I was born, and she ain accepted a serious man calling for 'a since. Folks say, she got visitors, but folks always speculating on how a woman getting by when they ain got no husband.

Still, Mrs. Clara done found a way to be accepted round here. Iain never seen 'a at no meetings, and the way I remember it, it be Miemay that use to speak for 'a. Then again, what'n much never come up bout the hotel. She don't say much, just smile all the time, and work hard. It's just her way, that she make people feel at ease and feel at home. Maybe that's why she own the hotel, and live there. Every day she get up and fix breakfast, lunch and dinner. She even use to clean the rooms by 'aself fore she got older and had to hire help.

"Well, if it ain't the devil himself," Martha teases soon as she notices me coming in the door.

But I don't find 'a funny, so I don't smile, or look on 'a easy. Just gone keep staring at 'a til she shrink and look away, or til something better catch my eye.

Something better does. My sisters off to they selves with they own families. Fore I seen them, I just knew it'd be awkward coming back. Thought whenever everybody was finding their places with they family, I'd be realizing Iain got one, a place, a family.

Now I see how a woman, who live alone got 'a own place, she 'a own family. I see how Mrs. Clara find 'a own seat. Then look forward at the pulpit like she waiting for 'a own personal word, and it make it easier being here.

I use to love church, Sunday school, and days on the green. Then I see her, Norma Jean, standing tall, anchored and black as a coffee bean. Her hair all gathered to the top of 'a head and sprouting out in one big puff of black cotton. She wear that ribbon in 'a hair like a crown. Chin high, and 'a nose all pointy and up like she stuck up, but she ain't. One of the most down to earth people you ever want to meet. One of the most beautiful spirits I ever had the pleasure of knowing. It's been a while since I seen 'a.

"Linny, why don't you go on over there and speak to 'a," Grit whisper in my ear, resting both 'a hands on my shoulders shaking me, when she notices me staring. "She use to be yah best friend."

I don't even entertain the notion. Last time me and Norma Jean were alone, she told me we couldn't keep meeting like this. She had a husband now and children. They had a home.

She seemed sad when she said it, but what else could she be, having to choose between what everyone tells you to want, and they expectations, versus what you want and need. I think she needed me. Then again, maybe she just wanted me and I needed her. What she chose, is what she needed.

I don't know how long I'm looking at Norma Jean fore she must feel it, then turn and look at me. Our eyes speak. I feel heavy on my feet. So many things have happened since we last talked, kissed, held hands. I try not to stare at 'a, but I cain't look away.

Then she smile, warm and guarded. The space between us and her smile hurt me. I breathe easy to forget 'a, who she is, how she is.

She the first person I think I ever wanted to help, hold, support or take care of outside my family. First person I feel protective about, other then Grit. I use to get mad when Dexter be coming over here from Hardingtown to see Norma Jean. She use to promise she ain like 'im when I'd get mad and jealous.

I knew Dexter was a good kid, and he came from a good family. I knew Norma Jean was a child from 'a mother's first marriage, her daddy ran off. I knew she felt like a burden on 'a family. Her step daddy treated 'a different from the others. Then she be like the house maid, it was the thing we had in common. Cept it was different. My daddy seem to treat me different from my sisters and brothers, not better though, just different. It was Mama treating me like a step child. Me and Norma Jean was our families' maid.

We use to go walking at the end of the day if we could get away and talk about our days. Between helping Miemay and staying on top of my chores at the house, I be something tired. Still, I was looking forward to when I could unwind from the day with 'a. She use to let me hold 'a hand sometimes when we'd walk and talk. If we made it down to the creek, to lay in the grass, we be laying there watching the sun disappear, kissing. One day we kissed so much I thought my heart would break. Ever wanted something so much to hold it made you sad?

Use to lay awake at night thinking bout Norma Jean. What she doing? Was she sleep? Use to hate for school to be over every day, or out in the summer. Use to always be too much time between seeing 'a again. Now it's been forever.

We was out at Sumter's Creek, swimming in our skivvies at dawn when she told me she was pregnant. Then she told me she was gone marry Dexter. I didn't know what to say, or how to feel. Felt like I was a volcano, with all these feelings welling up Iain know what to do with. My body was on fire, my skin was too tight or heavy on my bones.

I knew what she was saying, things was gone change and we was gone change. I what'n gone be walking 'a home no more or seeing 'a in the fields. She what'n gone be spending the night with me and Miemay, and I what'n going over there neither. She wouldn't be here anymore.

We were just 15-years-old then, but then again most women were getting married bout that time. So I guess we were women, too. I always knew we couldn't be together forever, but I hadn't imagined when it would end. Then it was too soon. Fifty years from now would have been too soon.

"Come on sit up here with us, Linny," Mrs. Harper insists, touching me, breaking the spell. I watch Mrs. Harper go on to 'a seat.

"You looking mighty pretty and lady like in that dress. School teacher musta already started rubbing off on yah," Zay tease.

I give 'im that look so he'll know to shut up. Iain in the mood to be playing, or going back and forth with 'im, bout this dress Mrs. Harper done bought me. My heart heavy, my spirit swollen, and I'm holding on to the back of the pew just to keep myself grounded in the moment.

"Oh, don't be mad. And don't come in the Lord's house being evil." Zay go on, laughing, and I think, showing out a lil for the new school teacher. Zay always played too much. Sometimes he get on my nerves, even though me and him the closest between me and my brothers.

"Where you git this lovely thang from?" Jenny come pinching the material and holding one of the twins.

"Mrs. Harper got it for her, and made her promise to wear it today," Coley fall right on in, grinning and what not.

"Heard you had supper with the Harpers. We ain't all able. Iain never had dinner at they house, Iain never even been invited to they house. Must be nice," Jenny digging into me, making that face like I done something to 'a just by being here.

"Whatever, I can still outride you, Zay, any day and any time," I challenge 'im.

"Not in that dress," he add, laughing. I'm bout to tell him bout hisself when she touch me.

"You look beautiful. Never thought I'd see the day you'd turn in your pants for something so lovely," Norma Jean add smiling, and then it ain so bad if she think I'm beautiful.

Shyly, I say, "Thank you," staring in 'a eyes. Our eyes stay fixed for just a moment, but it's long enough to stir my spirit. Then I know, she still love me, maybe, I don't know. The way she turn, and walk away remind me of how she use to tell me to meet 'a.

I watch Norma Jean float away to find 'a husband and their children. I wonder what made 'a come all the way back to Zion from Hardingtown.

Then I remember what I use to love about church. Sometimes it be the most excitement for anybody ain old enough to go to the jug house. Between folks catching the spirit, the testimonies, all the music and songs, and hearing the town news ain being wrote in Zion's paper. Since white folks be reading it. This all the excitement this town see, right here.

Then when folks come to visit they always make sure they get a Sunday in so they can see everybody. You never know who gone come through, never know what to expect, and then again, sometimes it be the same o' thing every Sunday. Maybe I always missed it, but something bout seeing Norma Jean, her saying I'm beautiful, and seeing my sisters, make it okay to admit how I feel.

"Morning, young lady?" Lydia leans in Coley's face forcing a handshake and introduction more than offering, soon as we sit down.

Then I remember what I don't miss, questions, and people prying in your business. I don't miss people making judgments bout each other.

"I'm Lydia Atwell and this my husband Paul Atwell."

Paul just nod his head and smile, like he been dragged over here. He looking every way but at Coley.

They is older though, so maybe he ain't trying to be disrespectful. Coley dress ain't small or nothing, but it ain't got as much material as we use to seeing on women round here. All our dresses drag on the ground, Coley's higher then 'a ankles. Her hat different—small, fitted, with all these bright pinks and yellow flowers on it. Iain seen a bouquet that colorful in a wedding or a funeral.

Here in Zion all the women wear lots of dark colors; navy blue, black, grey, and brown. If it's a formal meeting, might be a white blouse. If it's some kinda promenade or spring formal, may be some color.

Coley got this pink dress on with 'a arms all out. No matter what time of year, we don't never come to church with our arms out. She sticking out like a sore thumb. If I'da known she was gone wear this, I mighta wore me some pants so we coulda both gotta talking to, and believe me, she getting a talking to.

Lydia got Coley cornered so she cain't get up, so sitting, Coley nods 'a head in a way that reminds me of the curtsy she did when we first met. "I'm Coletta Graham," Coley smiles warmly. Now a crowd of women gathering as people notice they don't know 'a. People looking at me to explain who she is, I just sit mutely and watch.

"I'm Anita Atwell." She forces 'a hand.

"I'm Precilla Beaumont." She forces 'a hand.

They all stand around me and Coley waiting for some more information, until the piano starts playing the music for us to get in order. People start to find their places.

Then I realize, Iain the only one ain know Coley was in town. The whole church is in motion, looking over in our direction and talking among themselves trying to find a solution to 'a. The Atwells and Precilla done spreaded out, so they telling what lil they know of course. Then Coley here by 'aself, and women don't travel without a husband or family so they really lost.

"How do they get their hair all wavy like that?" Coley ask as the choir coming in.

"What do you mean?" I say, following 'a eyes to the back of the woman's head in front of us.

"How'd she get it to lay down like that? She must be mixed." She answer 'a own question, then say, "I've never seen anybody that dark with hair like that."

When people stand to receive the choir and it ain't so quiet I say, "She bout the same color as you if not darker. And we all mixed, cause we all come from slaves. And she got just regular nigga hair. That's how yorn would be if you let it alone and stop pulling it out with that hot comb."

"My hair would never lay down like that."

"How you know, you ever tried? Them ain nothing but braids she put in 'a head after washing it. You tie it up at night, and it'll be fine."

"Is everybody's hair braided? Don't women want their husbands to run their hands through their hair and brush it at night?"

"What man you think coming in from the fields brushing some woman's hair?" I laugh, and too loud cause people look back at us. That's why I put it off on Coley by telling 'a, "Be quiet, pay attention and stop talking in church."

Then she look at me like I done threw 'a on the train tracks, and 'a face so funny I laugh at that, too.

Soon as the women start to hum along with the piano, I recognize the church favorite that always bothered me. It's called "On Our Knees." Anybody sitting down stand up too, to receive the choir. Fore Eudora belt out the first note, folks start two step foot tapping, clapping and keeping time. The whole church house moving to the beat. Them tambourines get to ringing and going.

Eudora sing lead:

> Once we was slaves
> Now we's freed
> Cause we stayed
> On our knees
> Closed our eyes
> And believed
> Just like Moses
> Split the sea

The Lord done came
And set us free.
What a day
Of jubilee
I praise yah
On my knees.

Chorus:

Lead sing: "So I!"
Then the choir follows:
I keeps on
Praying
On my knees

Lead: So I
Choir: Keeps on
Waiting
On my knees

Eudora sing lead:

The Lord is
In control
He makes the
Wounded whole
And gives rest
To weary souls
The Lord is
Keepin names
So our work
Ain't in vain
That's why I
Praise his name
And cain't wait
Til he rise again

The song moving but the words troubling. Coley up clapping and going, and I'm trying to stomach the words. The Klan coming here every other week now, bothering people. The other night they was outside of Uncle Lucius place. They didn't kill nobody, this time. Was a stranger had made it out there looking for a drink, and they done cut his privates off. Then they shot all round in the woods, folks was sleeping in the woods, and laying in dirt. Remind me of the stories Miemay use to tell me, bout how they was killing niggas on the run, right before the war ended when they was officially declared free.

We free now, they say, but we waiting on our knees for somebody to come and save us. It always bother me, way they do things round here. I be thinking it's enough folks in Zion that we could fight back, or at least keep them from coming in our town. But we don't never try to help ourselves, we just stand around while they hang our sons and rape our daughters.

Then Reverend Patrick, even though he good to me, he don't never open the Bible. He might say anything. Most of the things he be saying don't even come out the Bible. Now I understand why Miemay didn't never think it was important to come here. This could be a whole nother kind of church if he would stop saying what he heard or think, and teach what's in the book.

People got Bibles in their house, and they be keeping them up high on pedestals and marking who born and who died. It say who married who. Some Bibles got a family's whole history since they could read and write. They be putting new names and words in the Bible but don't never open it up and just read it.

One day when me and Ella was alone, I had worked up the nerve to ask 'a if she ever read the entire Bible. She got all defensive like Reverend Patrick did when Miemay asked him, which kinda surprised me, and then it didn't.

She started telling me how the Bible is a spiritual book, and that I cain't just read it. You got to read it from your spirit, and you got to pray to get understanding. When I tell 'a it be saying it's okay to be a slave, she say, "Too much of Miemay done rubbed off on you." Then she don't want to talk with me about the Bible. Tell me she gone pray for me, and I'm thinking, I'm praying for us all. We be the blind leading the blind.

"You paying attention?" Coley nudge me.

I come out my head hearing The Reverend breathing and heaving and singing the way he do while coming to the pulpit. We good and ready to receive the word. There is a commotion, and folks is talking where usually they be quiet or cosigning. I look around and everybody looking at Coley, who sitting oblivious looking at The Reverend.

Reverend Patrick seem like he feel 'a eyes on him, cause he look over at 'a and smile. He need to say something bout 'a presence or Coley be the devil this Sunday, by distracting folks from hearing the word.

"Before I git started I need to make an introduction and announcement. We have a visitor in church today," he say, extending his hand in Coley's direction. "Please stand, Ms. Graham." When Coley comply, he continue. "This here is Ms. Coletta Graham. She earned 'a bachelors from Howard University and is a recent graduate of Clark University, with a masters in education. The Freedmen's Bureau has assigned 'a to teach the children of Zion."

A few folks meet the news with applause, but you can tell the whole church ain't receiving it well.

"You may have a seat, Ms. Graham." Reverend Patrick turn to face the congregation sternly, and you know he ain't pleased with his job, but he go on.

"This ain't no attack on the skills of Zion's on Prudence Beaumont. She been doing a fine job for the past fifteen years. There are just rules and regulations we have to follow cause we protected by the Freedmen's Bureau. We need that state money.

"Yall know the Freedmen's Bureau, the ones what parceled out most of the land that we now call Zion. They the reason we only pay taxes on the land. Well in order for us to keep our town, and receive state funding, git roads and other thangs, we have to follow some rules. So they decided they wont Niggra children to have educated teachers, not just other Niggras who can read. Times are changing and they believe it's better for the children."

Prudence stand. "When somebody was gone tell me ya gave mah job away? I be countin on that money, even if it ain't much."

A woman's voice shout, "It ain't right! Nobody cain't just come to our town and tell us who gone teach our chillen!"

"I just got word a few days fore Ms. Graham arrived. I believed I was gone have more time, cause school ain't startin for another two weeks but now she here."

"She don't look like no teacha I ever seent!" Another woman starts.

"Alright nah, alright," Reverend Patrick pleads, raising his hands like he leading a choir but he trying to get hold of the congregation. "I understand we all upset, but Ms. Graham our sister in Christ, too. Let's not attack 'a, she just doing what she told and following the assignment she was given and-"

"What about my pay? What I'm pose to do nah?" Prudence cut in.

"If you let me finish, I'll tell ya." He stop to see if she got something else to say fore he start. "Now we ain't even the ones paying 'a, the Freedmen's Bureau is paying 'a salary. So we can keep paying you to do other thangs, or til you find different work."

Prudence slam 'a body back down in the seat on hearing this, folding 'a arms, snatching and refusing to be consoled. Then she look over at Coley, if looks could kill, lawd.

"I said there is peace in heaven. I ain't looking for no riches here on earth. This is man's world, Iiiii'm not of the world. I'm of the Father, the Son, and the Holy Ghost," Reverend Patrick get started. Almost like he talking right to Prudence, and she make a face at him to suit.

Then he look over at me, and then down at the ground like he thinking. I'm nervous he bout to say something to me like he said to Prudence.

Then he say, "I think what I shoulda done was talked about this sooner. Should have told yall what was going on, but I'm just a man dealing with my own earthly concerns. I was afraid to talk about it cause so many folks was upset, but God said that no weapon stands against his children shall prosper! Today it was laid on my heart to talk about what happened after Miemay died."

"Mmmm," some of the women hum and "Aarghnnn" some of the men.

"When you die, don't you want me to uphold your last wishes? What Linny got, no kids, no husband and no family now, since all this done happened. Loss Miemay, who practically raised 'a.

"Our Linny needs help on 'a land. Me and Mrs. Harper been telling 'a to hire some hands. She thinking yall don't wont to work for 'a cause yall think she stole from Miemay, from 'a family. Yall thinking, she tricked an old lady into giving 'a the eldest son's inheritance. We don't have no law here and that's how we teach people and help them stay in line, by stepping away from them. But if anybody knew Miemay, they know she couldn't be tricked. She died with a sound mind. And what'n a trick she hadn't seen."

"I know that's right," people start to laugh and cosign.

"Linny faithful to our town and don't want to start no trouble. She been trying to work the land 'aself rather than go out and hire strangers."

"Come on now!" I hear Ella shout.

"She got the money to pay workers, but she trying to do it 'aself. I'm proud of 'a because she could have said, so what to 'a daddy, and mama, and family. She could have said so what to this town. Or she could have made everybody happy, and went back on the promise she made to 'a grandmother on 'a deathbed. But she is a woman of 'a word, like Miemay raised 'a to be. She is a fighter like Miemay. She loves Zion like Miemay. The way Linny has handled all this should prove 'a righteousness.

"In 'a last days, Miemay told me to stand with Linny cause she was gone need somebody. Miemay told me to check on Linny. I asked what about 'a own daddy and mama. Miemay asked me to promise 'a while she was dying. Then I didn't know why she kept saying this, anytime Linny would leave the room. She told me to watch after 'a like she was my own. I agreed.

"Then she made Linny promise to never let nobody take what's hers. She made 'a promise not to give it away. She wanted Linny to have a home, where she wouldn't be in 'a mother's way. Yall know what I'm talking bout. She wanted Linny to have something when all the dust settle I'm thinking.

"Truth is Miemay got one over on both of us, if you really wont to know the truth. I don't mean to speak ill of the dead, but I thought I was gittin that house she was building. I know saying this ain gone make me too popular but the Lord done put it on my spirit to say it. But I hold 'a word like I would any of yours.

Miemay told me she waited to die for the house to be finished. One of the reasons I took so long building it. I was trying to keep 'a here. Then I see how she suffering. I wanted 'a to see it finished. What a will, that she waited til the last nail was hammered, and the paint had dried fore she took 'a final rest.

"Then she left 'a grandchild, named for 'a, in our hands the way we always was in 'a hands. How many times did Miemey come see about you? How many times did she pay for something for you? How many times was she helping when people in 'a own family was saying, 'What about us? We should live better.'"

"At every turn, people shouting "Amen!" "Hallelujah," "Alright now!" "Tell it," and some people just laughing like what he saying done touched a part of them too sweet or good to speak. The fans going and the heat rising.

I'm willing myself not to cry, I'm trying to disappear, I'm missing Miemay. I'm looking out the window, smelling the morning disappear and the heat of the sun taking over. I look at the red dirt surrounding the church, and the wagons, and then the trees.

I miss quiet Sundays, where me and Miemay talked about the Bible, or nothing at all. Some Sundays, we use to get up early, feed the animals, make a big breakfast and supper. Then me and her be laying round all day, not speaking just being. Let the breeze catch us whenever it come.

When Reverend Patrick winds down, I am barely there. I am barely anywhere. I'm thinking how I never told Miemay I loved her, again. I'm deciding to tell people I love what they mean to me.

When we all stand to say the closing prayer, Reverend Patrick says, "Yall who working in "other" folks' fields gone have to be careful. There is a movie out, called "Birth of a Nation," that's got the Klan all riled up. There was a hanging in Hardingtown. Anybody working in Dewey got to stay away from there. Last week, they whupped Selma's boys for no good reason."

Then Reverend ask that we bow our heads, and he prayed for families to mend bridges, and for people not to hold they children accountable for what they parents have done. He prayed for us as a community, church, and town to take care of and look after each other.

When he done, Mrs. Harper his wife hug me. Then she say, "You got another mother, you ain't alone."

Soon as she let go, people start coming to hug me, and pat me on my back. And I am so glad I came back this Sunday. I missed the people and I missed the babies. I missed being smiled at, and acknowledged. I missed being loved. Even Martha apologizes for calling me the devil.

Iain never really been hugged, and even though it feels good it starts making me feel strange. Mrs. Clara hugs me, and says she wasn't never mad at me. She give me the longest, warmest hug of 'em all. I could feel 'a genuine sincerity and I start to cry in 'a arms. She old enough to be my grandmother, and it mean a lot to have 'a say that to me. She say I need to get out more, and I'll find everybody doesn't dance to the same beat.

Ain wont nobody to see me crying, so I make my way to the wagon fast as I can. I'm using the handkerchief from the stupid purse Mrs. Harper and Coley talk me into carrying, when I hear him say proud, "You tried to work all that land by yah self?"

"Yeah I did Daddy." I don't turn and look at 'im, I keep looking in the way of the wagon. Women crying make him uncomfortable. Plus, I don't ever want him to see me cry. I've always been proud that he doesn't consider me like other women. I want him to still think I'm strong.

"Well," I can almost hear 'im smiling and poking his chest out a little. "I still expect to see you in my fields some days, too, after you hire all them hands."

Clearing my throat so I will answer strong, I say, "Yeah, Daddy, I'll be over there." Then I start walking again towards the wagon. All I wanted was for Daddy to speak to me, and know Iain never want to hurt our family. Him saying I can come back and work with him and my brothers make me smile in my spirit.

I already knew he what'n never gone say he sorry, men don't apologize, they come to agreements. Ain no hard feelings between them neither, least that's how it is between my brother nem.

Now I'm missing Miemay, and 'a cobbler. People always be saying I make mine just like hers, but I taste the difference. I miss the little differences.

*   *   *

"Ay dur! Don't believe I done had the pleasure of makin yo acquaintance." My cousin Thomas bows, taking his hat off in a grand display of chivalry.

Hard to believe we just 50 feet from the steps of the church, and not even five minutes out of service. Nothing like a new hen to get these roosters struttin. All the young single men of Zion start to introduce themselves.

Zachariah, the boldest, he take Coley hand and kiss it. Seem like Zion done gone and got itself a new automobile and parked it under this tree, way all these men catchin shade over here. I wont to tell Coley, she better be mean to 'em if she wont any women friends. Believe it or not, these men can take it. Matter fact, if she mean to 'em, they'll put a better foot forward.

Not to mention, the women here might have they rivalries but when it come to an outsider they gone stick together, and against Coley. They gone be sour for a minute bout Prudence's job being given to Coley. Zion already ain't welcoming to strangers, then Coley gone be educated and pretty, too. It's enough to be a scandal for weeks out.

One thing I can say, I understand these roosters. Coley is beautiful. She dress different, smell different, talk different, and walk different. She's a real lady, cain't even imagine 'a throwing 'a body like old Prudence did, Coley too proper for all that.

Then these men always trying to one up each other. Always battling bout who the strongest, meanest, smartest or best dancer. Whichever one of them land Coley, be a respected man. Ain't more than a handful of women been to school outside of Zion's school house, and when you look at how Mrs. Prudence Beaumont act, you already know what she teaching us women.

We all read, but we ain't seen nothing but these fields and creeks and springs. Coley a travelling woman. Don't even make sense for a woman to leave Zion, got 'a family, and once she get married they build 'a new family a place to live. She gone always have work, if it ain't here in Zion there's always some white family needing us to do something. We don't pay nothing but taxes on the land. Why leave? But when I look at Coley, I think, why stay? She be like a princess here, just gracing us all with 'a presence.

"Ms. Graham?" Reverend Patrick come out the church, moving through all the people like he trying to catch us fore we get away. Me and Coley on our carriage, getting ready to go home and I know its coming.

"Yes, Sir?" Coley smile, waiting, and not picking up on what's bout to happen.

"Um." Reverend Patrick seem to be searching his mind for the words.

After a while, I'm tired of waiting. So I say, "Yo dress too short, and you need to cover ya arms for church."

"Yes." Reverend Patrick nod his head yes, too, looking at me thankfully then add, "And the color is really bright. It's a nice color, nice dress, but something not so flashy. Please?"

"Yes, sir." Coley accepts solemnly, looking around at all the men, and I can tell she shame, and all that's happened is settling in on 'a spirit. We ride to the house silently.

Chapter Twenty-Four

"I can't keep doing all this," Coley pout like a uppity child. "I can't keep up with this and my work, too. All these chores are too much, Linny. I'd rather just pay you for the room, or go stay in the hotel."

"Cain't keep doing what?" I examine Coley dragging 'a body, and throwing 'a legs like 'a arms too heavy for 'a to carry 'em, and 'a legs too heavy to walk.

"Look at my hair? I've got to hot comb my hair every other day, and I'm touching up my edges daily just to look decent. I'm dog tired. My clothes are all sweaty and I feel so dirty. Feels like I'm not ever clean, because of all the sweating. I'm tired of the sun. I'm getting so black. I've never worked this hard. I don't do hard labor. I'm not a field hand.

"Mama said go to school, marry well and I wouldn't ever have to do all this. I went to school, I'm a school teacher, not some sharecropper, or farmer, or a maid." She slam 'a body down at the kitchen table and look at me like a little white child with money, or one whose daddy on the board of the counsel. Like she ain some common nigga, too.

"Want me to set the table, too?" I ask 'a while she sitting at the empty table, while I'm warming up our supper.

"Don't you see me? Don't you hear me talking to you? Does anything move you? Don't you listen? I'm not the maid."

"Well, where the maid at?" I ask 'a, not letting 'a being upset stir me. One thing I learned, let people have they ways and they words. I just try to see the best in 'em. She be complaining bout what she got to do round here, but she do it. I don't care if she run 'a mouth every day and complain from sun up to sun down. She ain doing nothing but making it harder on 'aself.

"I am not the maid!"

"Well, where she at?" I ask again, starting to laugh. I love to see Coley really get going. This be our appetizer before dinner every other night.

Then she fold 'a arms and look off at the wall, refusing to move. I start to fix the table. Then I say, "You wouldn't have to do so much to your hair if you just wore it the way it grows, like everybody else round here."

"You are going to tell me to do something like other people?" She laughs mean. "When was the last time you did anything like the other women in town? As you stand here with those pants on, other respected women have asked you specifically not to wear. I've heard them talking about how you refuse to marry. Well, I'll take the same thing you're having, I'm not everybody else either!"

"Yeah but you the only one mad about who you is. Seem like to me, if somebody found something work better than what I'm doing I would be smart enough to try something different. Steada sitting round whining like a small white child, crying bout how you ain't this and you ain't that."

"Don't insult me!"

"You insult yourself acting how you act. Want me to rock you? Want me to tell you I'll do all the work round here? I'm one person who owns a house by 'aself. I cain't get to all the things I got to do in a day, and when I wake up yesterday's work waiting with the work of today. Do I come in here and cry? What that's gone do?" I don't even look at 'a when I'm' done speaking. I hear 'a weight shifting round in the chair, and feel 'a looking at me. "Need to fix yo face, and stop acting, and help fix this table. It's the least you could do."

"You don't know what I've been through."

"You think you the only person ever been through something?"

"I didn't say that."

"Well, you acting like you the only one got problems. Like you the only one got to work. You talking bout you not the maid, but Iain asked you to clean up after other folks or cook for them, or grow food for nobody but cho hungry self. You always hungry, and thirsty, but don't want to tend the garden, or make the tea and lemonade. You cain't cook to feed yourself, and you ought to be working on that while you talking bout getting a husband. But you ain't. You sitting round here whining bout being asked to help take care of you."

"I didn't think about it like that," she pout, sitting up in 'a chair and lifting 'a chin. Looks like she saying humph to nobody at all. She keep turning 'a head looking round, must be fighting the truth.

I just look at 'a til she get up and get the silverware. I always be surprised by how open she is to change, most folks keep on when they wrong. But if you straight with Coley, and at least tell 'a you don't want to hear it, she'll spare you the nonsense sometimes.

She start to help me put the food out on the table. Then she say, "I did lose weight," like some crazy person ain just had a fit.

I don't even look at 'a. I know that's a bad subject for women, to say anything bout how they looking. I usually say what my daddy would say, "You always look the same to me." Then folks say to me, something like what they say to him. "You such a man, don't notice nothing." Mama and my sisters would always tell 'im, and for me they'd say, "You just like yo daddy, don't notice nothing."

"Did you know they built a Carnegie library in Beaumont, five miles away from Zion?"

"I heard about it." I keep eating. I'm looking forward to getting out on the front porch and watching the sunset.

"Did you know that when I told Reverend Patrick about it the other day, he said it didn't make Zion a bit of difference, because Negroes wouldn't be allowed in there. It got me to thinking about what we need around here. Our books are outdated and I need help.

"I'm teaching all the children in town. I can't focus on one grade. It takes me about two hours and a half to get them all started on their work. Now they're cutting the day down to four hours. Then at lunch time they'll go to the fields to eat with their own families. I only have four hours with them, which means they'll only be working two hours, and that's on the days they come. Reverend Patrick said some people won't even bring their children during the planting or harvesting season."

"You got a hard fight ahead of you. Some people don't see the purpose in school once they kids learn to count and read. They don't see the value in teaching them about the world, when they gone be right here in Zion."

"That's crazy. You can't know where a man is going to end up by where, or how he's born."

"I'm living proof of that. I wouldn't have ever thought I'd be where I'm at." I think about the house and the store.

"I just can't believe they're cutting into their learning and studies for harvest and planting."

"I can't believe they gone have school during planting and harvesting now."

"Are you saying they usually don't?"

"Things change so much since I was in school, what I know. When I was a girl, we didn't have school during harvesting and planting. Prudence Beaumont got 'a own farm to tend. She have to help 'a own husband and family."

"That's horrible! How do you people learn? The books are outdated, and pages are missing. Then when I finally teach a child something or get one caught up on something, before they get enough practice to move forward, their folks are keeping them out of school to work. You know some of the boys barely come, if at all. How am I suppose to teach them anything under these circumstances?"

"I don't know what to do about that. They folks need 'em to help out on they farms. They got to eat and make a living. It's always been like that, I was raised helping my daddy nem on our land." I hear the real reason she throwing fits. I hear how the way things run round Zion weighing heavy on 'a soul.

"I think it's crazy how people here put their children to work so young."

"I don't. It's been that way long as I can remember."

"Linny, you have to allow children to be children. You ever read about the coal miners children? They started working as young as five, and ended up dying from breathing in the air from the mines. There are child labor laws now, and I'm pretty sure they say children are to be in school learning. School should be a child's first priority. They have their whole lives to work."

"Kids learn everywhere they are. And ain't no mines out here. Here they need to know bout crop schedules, moon tables for planting, and how to take care of animals. And kids gone be kids no matter what you want them to be, cause its they time to be what they is.

"Shoot, me and my sisters and brothers, and all our cousins was glad to be working in the fields together. Them was some of the best days. Usually it be some big kids kinda watching us, and we be running together singing songs and working. Didn't never feel like work.

"All us kids liked to make our parents proud. We be working to see who can get the most cotton, strawberries, berries, plums, pecans or whatever we was picking. Most of our bags be light cause we been eating more than we packing. Then our arms be all scraped up and ashy, but we be toting our lil loads of cotton. Our parents be making a big deal bout who got the most." All while I'm talking, I'm smiling and remembering, and Coley she smiling, too.

"I can't imagine my whole family working on anything together," she say amazed. "Did you ever work with your father?"

"Of course, as far back as I can remember." Then I'm there again, in the fields with my cousins as me and Coley talk, and my spirit smiling, too. "When I was real small, my daddy use to take me on his horse with 'im. Or I'd be out there in the fields behind 'im while he was running mules, plowing the fields.

"Every day I'd wake up, get dressed, and be gone with 'im all day. Use to watch 'im make things, fix things, feed and take care of the animals. When I was small, it what'n nothing like spreading some feed and having the chickens jump up all round you squawking. Or to give a horse some carrots or a apple, and feel like you done made a new friend."

"My family and I barely speak when we're all together," Coley share sadly, frowning, look like she somewhere, too. "My daddy has a big job, we couldn't work with him. When he's on speaking tours Mama doesn't even go.

"I mean, Daddy loves us all, but he doesn't really talk to us. He just provides for us. Sometimes he might ask about something if Mama put him up to it, but mostly he spends his time with my brother, Coleman Jr. He was always grooming his Jr. how to be just like him."

"That might be a man thing. My daddy didn't really talk to my sisters neither. He more like watched out for 'em. He left the talking and teaching them up to Mama."

"Your mama didn't teach you, too?"

"She did, but I was with my daddy more for some reason. Seem like he was teaching me to be more like him. I was right there with him and all my brothers. As far back as I can remember. Iain never get no dolls or nothing like that, I was always getting tools.

"Then one day when I was about 9 or 10 years old he got me my own horse. A filly named Anastasia. She was mine to take care of and feed. Ain't none of my sisters never had or wanted they own horse.

"You should have seen me. I was so happy, I could barely sleep them first few nights. Shoot, I couldn't sleep them first few weeks I was so worried bout Anastasia and the rest of the yearlings. I wanted to sleep out there with my horse. I was always wondering what Anastasia was doing, if she was warm, if she had enough to eat. Use to get up fore the rooster crow to take care of the colts and fillies."

"Colts and fillies?"

"Most folks say yearlings. We talking bout baby horses, colts are boys and fillies are girls. Our horses must have had a busy winter cause that summer they was pushing 'em out. I had to take the yearlings out and walk them around, cause they needed to be exercised, and they was too weak to be rode or worked. I loved it. Didn't seem like no chore at all."

*   *   *

"Linny? How does it feel being different?" Coley ask thoughtfully, while we walking back to the stables to get us a horse to ride to the big fields. This 'a first day working outside with other people, and I can tell she nervous.

I'm full as a tic, cause I done got up early and made us a big breakfast. I hate to eat heavy fore I go to work, it wears you down and make you feel something awful. Then we gone be late getting there this morning, not that I even got to go. But everybody do what they can do, cause it's a few who cain't do much. It's the way Zion works.

Finally I say, "Ion know, I ain never been under the impression everybody the same, I guess."

"Humph." She smile at me and make a face I don't quite recognize. I'm too tired to pry or get too deep so I ask something else.

"How chicken yo favorite food but you ain't never seen one kilt?"

"Where I'm from we buy our food from markets. Meat is just meat, I've never thought about how it use to be a living thing. Except, when I was younger, my father sometimes would tell stories about when he was a boy, and how Granddaddy use to kill a turkey for Thanksgiving."

I walk on curious about being from a place where they don't kill they own food. "So you ain't never picked ya own fruit or vegetables? Don't know what the ground look like it growed out of?"

"Well," she smiles looking a little embarrassed, "there was this family that use to live next door to us before we moved in the city. They had plum and berry trees, but other than that, no."

We keep on for a while, then she say, "You know it's a good thing you know where your food comes from. Lots of folks use to die of food poisoning. Before they passed all these laws on how they have to treat and store food. My family never had that problem. My mother use to have my father take her to open market, where she'd buy most of our food from the Amish."

"The Amish? Who they is? That's a family name?"

"No." She laughs like everybody knows who they is and then she say, "They're white people, but different from other whites. They're hard to explain. All the men look like Abraham Lincoln. They seem to like doing things the hard way. They're some kind of religious cult, or something."

"Cult?" I repeat the new word for clarity, to feel it in my mouth, see if saying it give it any meaning. When nothing comes to me, I look at 'a to explain.

"Cult. It's like any group of people with extreme beliefs. You know, people who are not Christian."

I laugh at 'a answer, and wonder what she woulda thought about Miemay. I think about what she say, and how folks in Zion probly think the same way. Then again, the Klan claim to be Christian, but I think they pretty extreme. So I say, "Like the Klan?"

"No, they don't hate anybody. As a matter of fact, they're pacifist," Coley say thoughtfully, then continue, "In fact, they never held slaves. I think Mama said they were even against it, and helped slaves escape."

I choose my words carefully trying to get at what makes their views extreme if they ain't like the Klan, cause not being Christian don't seem extreme to me. And not having slaves seem to be the most right thing I can think of. Fact is, I'm starting to think being Christian kinda extreme, but I know better than to say that out loud. So I say, "What make them like a cult then, cause a cult sound bad?"

"Well, they just have their own communities away from everybody else. They don't vote, by choice, or participate in America. You can't just go there and live. You've got to be born Amish and maybe . . ." she stop like she considering what else she bout to say, "You could marry into it."

"Niggas can?"

"I've never seen an Amish Negro, but they aren't racist like other whites. They just don't like anyone except their own."

"Well, that don't make them a cult. Sound like Zion to me."

Chapter Twenty-Five

I'm glad for Coley arms round me, when we on Anastasia to the big fields. Folks done already started getting into they task groups. You can hear the low talking, and the pace of they feet over the earth. I look for Jasper, the man who usually separate us and give us our tasks, before tying Anastasia up.

I'm feeling some kind of way, cause it's been a while since I been to the big fields, since I been around everybody. This common for me to be here, but I'm feeling like things done changed. I feel like a stranger.

Iain got to be here, Mrs. Clara ain't here, Reverend Patrick and his wife ain't here neither. Ain't no other business owners here, cept for Amos from the Barber shop. Zion got a way of deciding who people spose to be and how they spose to act. People got a way of acting like some folks better than others, and even if them folks feel the same they treating them different. They putting them on a pedestal, bowing down and acting like they cain't be they selves. Sometimes I feel like Iain myself cause of how different I'm treated, and how they acting.

Folks been treating me different every since I moved out of Daddy's house. Them knowing Iain tricked Miemay ain't changed nothing, or maybe they still feeling like I did. All I know is, when I go in town they ain calling me Linny no more, its Ms. Remington, or Misses, or Ms. Linny.

The first time Mr. Dallas, this man over twice my age, called me Misses, I bout laughed before correcting him. Then I realized he was serious, and that made me sad. Zay say it's cause I hired people to work for me, and that change things.

Things really changed, when word got around I'd submitted a proposal to the counsel for my own filling station. After it got approved, and the white man who specialized in building petro stations came to see the store and draw up plans for the addition, even Uncle Victor and Ernest were different.

Before they were standoffish, but they pretended to be kind. Once I hired more men to have it built on, they stopped speaking. Whenever I'd go to check on it's progress, they started to make little smart comments in the place where there had been silence, or fake conversation.

People started to treat me like Iain grow up right here in Zion. They started to treat me like I was more than I feel I am. It started to feel wrong doing what I would normally do, work in my fields, and help out round town. It's nice to have Coley to worry about, to speak for, and to introduce to folks so Ion have to think about how out of place I feel.

Soon as we get down off the horse people stop to look at us. A little bit of me mad at Coley, cause I feel like she making me look bad. Coley ain't done none of what I asked 'a to do this morning. She the main reason we late. She went back to sleep after I woke 'a up. Then she took all morning getting dressed, and then we had to fight about what she was wearing. I told 'a to get some work boots from the store, I even offered to give 'em to 'a, cause I knew she was gone need 'em.

This morning when we started towards the front door I could hear them heels, and how she was planting 'a foot was all wrong. So I pulled 'a dress up to see the boots she put on for work. When I grabbed 'a dress I felt all that extra stuff she had on under. I almost had to beg 'a to take some of it off, it's gone be too hot for all that I explained. Then she threw a fit, but she changed. Then she came back down stairs saying she took some of it off, and she did put on a different dress, one where the material wasn't so heavy, and what'n gone be soaking up all heat.

Still, she had that little dress hat pinned on 'a head, like she was going visiting. I offered her a straw field hat, but she turned 'a nose up at it like it stank, said it was dirty, ugly and didn't match. Then she folded 'a arms and refused to put it on 'a head.

It was already too late to be going back and forth. Now she looking like she don't belong, and I'm feeling like somehow it's saying I don't neither.

"What she is?" Jasper tilt his head in Coley direction then take 'a in from head to toe, looking at 'a shiny black boots.

Coley ain't paying him no attention, she looking around, cupping 'a eyes, and looking off into the sky like we ain even talking bout 'a. Wouldn't need to cup 'a eyes if she took the field hat I offered. Now she be the only one out here with a dress hat pinned on 'a head that ain't blocking no sun. The way Jasper looking at 'a make me feel some kind of way, like maybe Iain prepare her.

"She a quarter hand, if that," I answer Jasper honestly.

He grin at Coley like he waiting for 'a to get mad, and say or do something. Coley don't challenge what I'm saying, she don't even realize she being insulted, even though that ain't what I'm trying to do. I just don't wont 'im to assign 'a to nothing over 'a head.

See, a man be a whole hand, and women cain't be but 75 to 90 percent of a hand at best, cause it's some things they won't allow women to do. Still some women be saying, they 100 if need be. Mostly children be a quarter hand, and teenagers be between 50 and 75. Every boy working to get everyone to acknowledge he a full hand.

My daddy use to say I was a whole hand. Funny how things change. Now he wishing I was more lady like, and he hate how strong willed I am.

I spect Coley will do better tomorrow after the sun get 'a real hot, and the sweat start running down a face, and all that grease she been putting in 'a head get to frying 'a like bacon. I spect when all that oil be in 'a eyes stinging 'em, she'll be glad to get a hat, and maybe even a scarf, too. Shoot, she'll probly be dressed like one of them olden time slave mammies, like the ones be cooking food for the white folks at the fair. I can tell it's gone be a hot day, by the way the heat already kissing my spine, promising this shirt be soaked, and sticking to me fore noon.

"What's so funny," Coley turn 'a nose up at me making this face like something stink.

That's when I realize I'm smiling, thinking bout how she bout to learn a real good lesson. Cause Coley mad she acting stubborn, she wont everybody to know how upset she is about working out here, or anywhere else outside, even if it's 'a own home. So she doing 'a own self a disservice by not coming out here dressed to work.

"Ms. Graham! Ms. Graham!" some of Coley's big students call excited. The people start to gather round, everything done stopped. It's something for 'a to be out here, but Coley don't really notice how folks taking 'a in.

Most of the women looking at 'a and comparing 'a to they own selves. Some of them touching the material of they own dresses and finding it better for the field, but still wishing they was better dressed. Coley too dressed up for the field, even though she thinking she dressed down. Still, this the worse she would leave the house, and what she wearing some women would wear to church. They judging 'a, but Coley smile like a candidate on the back of a automobile passing through, full of herself.

"I want to work with my students!" she insists, walking towards them.

Jasper look at me crazy, like I can stop 'a. "Them kids picking cotton. That ain no easy task, even with the boll weevil problem. You said she what'n hardly a quarter hand. I was gone put 'a with the little children or something."

"You better take this hat," Harlene, one of the moms, offers Coley, taking it from 'a own head and I think feeling sorry for Coley.

Burning bridges she ain't never thought she might need to cross, Coley stop in 'a tracks and stare at the hat, frowning like it stink.

"No, thank you," she dismiss Harlene, and all the other women take it personal. Prudence Beaumont look around at the other women, like what Coley done is proof of something.

"I guess I'll have to watch 'a," I say, going to get a sack and follow.

Once we in the fields Coley ain't complaining the way I was expecting. Having 'a students around making 'a act right. She working and not thinking bout how much she doing. She talking bout they schooling, they family and trying to learn who everybody is they've told 'a about, I guess.

The older girls introduce 'a to the boys they courting. Then some of the boys that don't come to school no more, telling 'a bout the past fore she came. Some of them boys men now and they crushing on Coley, but she don't seem to notice, or she ignoring 'em. The rest of the field is singing, but we moving in words.

When we first got over here, I missed the songs; they make the time go by. Then after I started to hear what 'a students was talking bout, words were a welcomed change. Something bout Coley make them feel open enough to talk about they dreams, love and maybe even leaving Zion. Other folks don't talk about dreams, love or ever leaving Zion. Zion is the dream.

All my life I had to hear about how blessed I was to be born after slavery, to have my family, and not have to worry where my next meal was coming from. All my life everybody here been stressing how important it is to have our own land, and how we need to preserve it so we have something to pass on to the next generation. Somebody was always talking bout Reconstruction, and how niggas was being hung left and right. How white people grew to see how much they needed us, and if we stay in our place we can make something of our life, and have something.

Coley must not of had to listen to that all 'a life. She don't seem to be tied to nothing, no dreams or ideas. Everything open for discussion. All she serious about is us all being equal, and earning our rights. Still what she believe don't seem to anchor her, and stop 'a from growing. Some part of me wish there was a Coley when I was in school, to push me, share my dreams with, and maybe give me some other choices outside of Zion.

My parents always been practical people. My brothers worked the land and my sisters learned to be wives. We all were taught and understood one day we'd all have our own homes, so we needed to be ready. Outside of learning to read, write and count, they ain never see the importance of school.

Coley all about 'a students learning, what's in them books but mostly what's inside them. Iain never really heard nobody talk about that. I see how the boys who already done been out of school too long to go back, wishing they could have met 'a before they made that decision.

I remember being the oldest girl still in school, I remember the boys waiting for the day they parents said they ain have to come back. I remember some of them thinking it was an honor, to be told they was needed more in the fields than school. I remember Prudence Beaumont cheering 'em on, saying they was whole hands, they was men.

Now I see how they questioning everything we been taught. I see how they questioning what's inside of them, and getting to see different sides of themselves through how Coley teaching the ones that still come. I can tell by what they saying, they trying to figure out if they can be all they is or find everything they need here, in these fields. Then I understand why the Freedman's Bureau sent Coley here. I see how she get them to stay, learn, and how she make them want to come to class.

"My feet hurt," Coley moan when she think cain't nobody but me hear 'a. I don't say nothing, I just keep picking. She not even working as much as others and she had to go pass a whole area to come complain. "Linny? Can we please take a break?" She whining, "My feet hurt, and I don't feel so good."

"I told you to wear those work boots at the house. I told you those shoes were going to be too hot for the field, and they got that heel on 'em, too," I fuss at 'a shaking my head.

"Ain't that high!"

"What kind of word is "ain't" for a teacher to be using?" I tease.

"'Ain't is the perfect word for a teacher toting a bag of cotton in the hot sun."

"You ain even got that much in yo bag." I take a deep breath. "Ion wont to stop cause they gone call us in, in a little. We came late and now we gone stop working early, it won't look right,"

"Please?"

I just look at 'a tired, and then I think about everybody else. Iain never been one to think about what other people think, as much as I have been lately. Living with Miemay kept me out of most of that, now it seems all I think about is how I'm being seen. Then Coley making this sad face, floating from side to side pleading silently with 'a face.

I decide they'd probly expect this from a city girl, and make an exception for her. "I spect we can take a little break," I say looking at the water pump.

I go over to the pump and don't rinse the pail that good cause somebody else been using it, and it's already clean. I rinse the cup off and start pumping us up some water in the pail. I take a few chugs and give it over to Coley.

"That's nasty! I am not drinking out of that! There's no telling whose mouth has been on it."

When we look up, folks is looking our way. "Suit yourself," I say, drinking all the water I done pumped up. "But it's hot, and you eat more than you drink. I been telling you, you probly thirsty more than hungry."

Then we go back out to our part of the field. Now I'm the only one really working at all. Coley just walking behind me, dreaming. "I sure could use a cold glass of lemonade, or some tea, ooh I'm not picky. I'd be glad to get a cold glass of water. I don't even need the water to be cold, just clean. I think I'm hungry or something, too. I can't even breathe in without my stomach cramping."

Then we quiet except for the sound of them singing off in the distance. I'm thinking that it's hard picking in silence. The singing help you keep a steady rhythm and work faster. Truth is, even though I picked more than Coley, Iain done so good today either.

"You ain't tied is you, Ms. Graham," Caleb, one of 'a students, ask.

"Feel like I'm gone swalla my tongue," Coley say, exhausted, and before I know it, she hit the ground.

"Get your hands off of me!" Coley wake up swatting when they put the smelling salt under a nose. Then Delilah douse 'a with a pail of cold water, that's when Coley scream like somebody killing 'a. Trying to push 'aself up and pushing Delilah away, she throws a fit when 'a legs won't work.

The women done surrounded 'a and made a shield so they could take some of them clothes off of 'a, so she can get some air. Now she wet, and indecent, but she keep on trying, on 'a knees crawling trying to get to 'a feet.

"You fainted," one of the women tell 'a thinking its gone calm 'a down. It don't, she still pushing this way and that.

"You need to drink some of this water," Delilah offer, but Coley slap the cup from 'a hand.

"I'm not drinking that."

One of the older women Caroline force the cup to Coley mouth. She fight some til she get a long gulp. Then Coley hold on to the cup like she ain't never had water before in 'a life and drink it good. When she get it all down, Caroline dip it in the pitcher and give 'a another cup. Coley keep on drinking, til she relax. The other women start to go on back to the fields when they see she gone be alright. Some still standing round frowning, I think they cain't believe how Coley acting.

"I'm so embarrassed," Coley say, finally seeming to find 'aself. We help 'a to a feet and I can tell she still a little light headed the way she wavering.

"You should take 'a on home," the women still around say almost together, so I do.

*   *   *

This morning Coley got up on time. She put on some work boots and didn't wear all them underclothes. I can tell by how loose 'a clothes fitting and how 'a body look. She took the hat off the wall, and put it on top of a scarf, she done wrapped 'a head. I try not to look at 'a, not even looking like 'aself. Still she look out of place, she make them field clothes look different the way they hanging off of 'a.

going on our first long drive. She wanted to know if we were gone go visiting that day, so we could show it off. She wanted to know if I would teach 'a how to drive. It was bittersweet.

Last thing on my mind was showing off. So Coley was real mad the next morning when she came outside, and saw I'd saddled up that horse for 'a to ride to school. I still take 'a on a horse most times, unless it's raining, because I'm so ashamed. I guess I am hiding it. And I don't even know why, cause they all know I got a Cadillac.

"I don't understand, you don't even drive it when it would be practical. Everyone who has a car drives to church on Sunday. Why don't you?"

"Just don't seem right."

"Feel like I got something to prove," she tell me thoughtfully when we almost to the field. "I always say I want to help my people. I say I want to be a credit to my race, but then I was so upset about a little hard work. It wasn't even that bad, and I liked being able to be with my students. I feel like I understood a lot more by working with them yesterday. We don't have that kind of time in school.

"I like how what we're doing changes things immediately. One of the girls told me how the community fields pay for all the upkeep of the town buildings. Another student told me how the money will be used to get plumbing all through Zion, electricity and school supplies.

"Not to mention it's just a few days, then we all go back to our own concerns. I've been supporting Negro equality for years, and I haven't seen change come this fast if at all. Working in the fields brings immediate change. It's inspiring to be a part of something where you can actually see how your hard work is paying off.

"I am going to drink more water, and I guess I'm gone have to drink some from that pump," she say, laughing at the last part, mocking us country folk.

When we get there, I ask Jasper if Coley could help the elderly in the shade, snapping peas or the kids in the orchard, but Coley refuse. She say she fine, and she just needed a little rest. Then we go pick up our sacks and get started. I'm kind of proud of how Coley comes back, and I'm not sure what's gotten into 'a.

Jasper do the call and we all sing the answer:

If I Was

Call: If I was a scarecrow
Ans: Then I'd stand around
Call: If I was a scarecrow
Ans: Then who'd tend the ground
Call: I don't see no scarecrows
Ans: Ain no standin round
Call: We got so much work to do
Ans: Foe the sun go down

Call: If I was a sparrow
Ans: Then I'd fly around
Call: If I was a sparrow
Ans: Then who'd tend the ground
Call: I don't see no sparrows
Ans: Ain no flyin round
Call: We got so much work to do
Ans: Foe the sun go down

Call: If I was an overseer
Ans: Then I'd look around
Call: If I was an overseer
Ans: Then who'd tend the ground
Call: I don't see no overseers
Ans: Ain no lookin round
Call: We got so much work to do
Ans: Foe the sun go down

Call: If I was a King or Queen
Ans: Then I'd look on proud
Call: If I was a King or Queen

Ans: Then who'd tend the ground
Call: I don't see no Kings or Queens
Ans: Ain no lookin proud
Call: We got so much work to do
Ans: Foe the sun go down

Coley working steady, she don't even try to talk to nobody, she just doing 'a own thing. I'm surprised, she done stopped complaining bout the heat, her feet, being tired and she singing along, too.

Chapter Twenty-Six

"Mammy Pancakes?" Coley reading the box out loud frowning.

We all just getting to the fair. We walking down to the nigga section to set up our stands. It's a big black woman in slave clothes with 'a head wrapped in a red scarf tied to the front, wearing a big old timey dress and apron. She working behind a table, under a tint, with an open fire and cast iron skillets cooking up pancakes to order. Three young girls dressed like lil picannanies, probly 12 or 13 years old, back there helping 'a. They making bacon and eggs to order and the white folks is lining up.

"You ought to be ashamed!" Coley say loud enough for everyone to hear 'a, with all them white folks standing round. The mammy-looking woman just look at Coley lost.

"Come on." I wrap my arm in Coley's and pull 'a on with me. I see a white man looking at us, adjusting his belt buckle and rattling it. I'm afraid he looking for trouble.

"These niggas sho charging a lot for a lil breakfast," another white man comment. "But my wife cain't cook 'em like this Mammy can. I come every year just for this."

"The missus sho could suh, iffin she git this here box of pancake mix," the Mammy say.

Then the boxes start to travel through the line, and I see how things change and then stay the same. Always be some big black woman cooking something for some white people, but this the first time I've seen 'em selling something other than the breakfast.

The fairs done changed so much over the years. When I was a little girl, use to be somebody here selling us all kinds of ointments and medicines. One thing make you sleep better, another thing give you energy, and another thing make you live longer. Folks be buying all them elixirs, and when they don't work they go on back to they own gardens and remedies. Now it's laws, the government keeping people from selling us sugar water and saying its miracle medicine.

Use to be a time, when I couldn't go to the fair less I was working in it. Niggas what'n welcome; now we got our own day. Guess white folks figure all our money the same color.

It's early, and the folk here now mostly working the fair. Most of the men in line Iain recognize probly came from the other towns to see the fair. This year be a good turnout cause it's election year, and Wilson probly gone come through here fore the fair over.

We pass a stand where a man putting up pictures of gorillas and naked niggas he say live in Africa. Coley get all mad, say she cain't believe it.

I laugh cause walking to the back with 'a like going to the fair for the first time. She get to see how the whites don't make eye contact with 'a, cause they don't want 'a trying to buy nothing from 'em. Or they looking right at all of us, daring us to do or say anything so they can make trouble. Some of the vendors here don't want niggas here, but the council voted and they allowed a few of ours.

I'm gone be selling tabacca, candy, pickles, candy apples, stuffed animals, rag dolls and wooden toys. Sometimes I be taking orders for things too, for when I get back to the store. Another family selling barbeque plates, with baked beans, macaroni and cheese, greens and sweet tea. Food probly the best thing going down here.

Then another family selling all kinds of seafood. They got gumbo, ettoufee', fried or grilled fish, with cabbage, grilled potatoes or corn, maybe all that together in a corn and potato mash, some cornbread, spaghetti and lemonade. I'll be trading for the whole week. Iain gone cook supper one day while I'm coming down here.

"Why do they have those pictures up like that?" Coley point at the gorilla and African pictures.

"Every year, it be some scientist at the fair talking bout how niggas came from gorillas. How we ain smart as white folks and all."

"Oh Linny! That's horrible." She say staring over at the white man organizing his area, and lining up chairs. "How do you feel about that?"

"I don't care."

"How don't you care? I mean, he is talking about you."

"He ain talkin bout me. That man don't even know me."

"You're a Negro, aren't you?"

"You is too," I say, laughing. "What I care what white folks say about me?"

"And what about that woman, who is up there dressed like a slave? She ought to be ashamed of herself. She's embarrassing the whole race."

"That woman make more in a day on tips than you probly earn from a whole month teaching."

"Everything isn't about money. We have to do things for the uplifting of our race. No one could pay me enough to wrap my head, then act like some old slave mammy and serve them."

"They sho could pay me, honey. I be done got my whole house fixed up." A woman call from behind us and I laugh. "Hard as things been round here with harvesting a good crop and actually making a profit, whole lotta folk be willing to act like a slave to make ends meet."

Whispering, Coley complain, "Some people . . . I just can't believe that Colored woman is up there acting like a slave. I think her behavior is ignorant and selfish. To pretend to be a slave, when all these other Negroes are out here risking their lives, and fighting for our rights."

"You know what I think, white people will fall for anything. They all farmers, too. Most folks round here land owners who need to make a living off of what they grow. Then they gone pay some nigga for a box of pancake mix, when they got all the things in the box on they farm. No, white folks ignorant, and any other farmer buying into box pancake mix."

"Sho is," an old man agree with me, snickering.

"Niggers," Coley reads out loud, as we entering the area where we can set up.

I don't say nothing. I'm use to the word nigger being posted to tell us where it's safe to go. Cause if you find yourself on the wrong side of that line, it could be the last time you cross one. I try not to pay 'a no attention, cause I can tell the word done wore 'a spirit down. But she got to learn or else she might get us all in nooses.

It's different though, seeing how she respond to the word. Iain never knew us to be nothing else. 'Negro,' a word we use amongst ourselves sometimes, when we feeling proud, but we call each other 'niggas' too, or 'hands.' Say, "A nigga got to work to eat." Or "You know where they hiring hands," another word for niggas.

White folks, men mostly, call us niggers. If they low class, even the women call us niggers. We answer too. If they high class, and some white women, mostly the older ones, call us something between the two, 'niggra.'

'Colored,' a word you learn later on in life. Negro a word, when you first hear it, seem like they talking bout somebody else, some other race, you been so use to being called a nigga.

I don't wont no soft word like 'Colored.' 'Colored,' like lines drawn in sand, or too hard to see. 'Colored,' make it seem like maybe white folks care about you. 'Colored,' sound like maybe they gone listen to you explain, or take mercy on you if you cry, scream or beg, but ain't none of that true. White folks don't listen to niggas. Fact is, they like when they scream and cry.

One of the things we all try to do, or tell ourselves we gone do if we can, is go proud, silent. We gone pray, and try to keep our mind on something else if we ever get caught by a mob. Less they put that fire to you, then you may not be able to help screaming. Not to mention, they cutting fingers off and stabbing all in men's guts. Then again, folks say they done seen someone burn proud.

Please don't be no woman caught by a mob. Lord, the things I done heard they done done to a woman. It's been a while since they actually killed a woman round here, but they'll rape a nigga girl child, or woman, if they find 'a on a road by 'aself.

One time they rape two sisters walking together from school, thinking they was safe together, but they was both too small to be any help to the other. Then again niggas cain't hardly fight back. They be saying you attacked them when you was just trying to keep them off you.

Anyhow, I just think using the word 'nigga' keep everything clear, and time you hear the word, or see it wrote somewhere you reminded that they don't care nothing bout you. When they call you a nigga you understand they like to hear you scream, and beg for yo life while they putting you in that noose. You remember, they cut fingers and toes off of you for good luck like you a rabbit. Or keep pieces of us, like they would stuff a deer head, or bear, like it's a game or sport to kill us.

Sometimes they burns, and shoot all through some ol' woman's son. So when they call you a nigger you know who you is and you understand who they is. I don't even take offense when somebody call me a nigger, I'm thinking that's what I'm is anyhow.

Every time Coley hear the word, or see it, she get like this, get to acting and poking 'a lip out. Walking round with this sad, pitiful look. Then she go round pouting and looking at other niggas like they owe 'a something.

She always talking bout uplifting the race and pushing books about who we should be, and how we should want more. She always saying how this about more than us, we fighting for our whole race. She ain never seen a man lynched, or had to watch 'a own daddy, or brother, or cousin drug out in the middle of the night. Ain gone even talk about all the folks right here been strapped to trees and beat for some white man feeling they wronged him. She ain never seen a man or young boy be cut down out a tree.

Other times she be talking down to us, like we all children and she the only one know anything. When it seem to me like she's the one don't pay attention, don't understand who she is or where she at. This a different world then where she come from. Don't seem like 'a folks got the same concerns as us. Where she from, folks got time to get groups together, organize and picket.

Here, staying alive hard enough. Then she start asking me, "Don't it make you mad the way they treat you? Don't it make you sad that they talk to you like this, or yall like this?" Like she ain no nigga too. I usually tell her, Iain never know no other way to be treated or nothing else to be called. Being called a nigger ain no insult, it's just what we is. 'Colored' some word they use up north somewhere.

She always going on and on about how we need to fight back, or how we need to protest so we can get the same rights as white folks, so we can vote. I don't care about voting, if it mean it's gone be night riders, rapes, hangings, and we ain't gone be safe in our own house. I definitely ain't yearning for what whites got, if what they got ain't enough to keep them from bothering us.

Niggas could be happy if white folks would be happy with what they got. But they always trying to find ways to get more, and make you work for what they want. They don't never want to be fair and pay you what you worth. Just give you what they feel.

What I want and wish, is that they would leave us niggas alone. Stop coming through our town and picking anybody out and asking them to wash they laundry, or cook them some meals. I wish they'd stop coming to our land and telling us to be at they house at some time in the morning to work they land.

And you cain't never hardly say no, that be like sassing 'em. They make it like you taking care of you and yours is a sin, and refusing to take care of them cause they cain't or won't take care of themselves is yo problem. They be saying you too proud to work.

They hung a man for saying he got his own field to plow and hoe. Then they burned that man's barn down, and killed some of his cattle. All I want is to live on my land without them bothering me. Which here lately it's been good, but this movie done got the Klan started again, and they done got started good.

"Hey girl, what time yall niggas gone be set up?" one of the local white men ask anybody who hear and know the answer.

But he looking at Coley cause she the one stop moving and stare 'im in the face like she got the answer. Standing there all strong like she running something. They both anchored awhile, looking at each other fore I realize ain't nobody gone speak for us. So I go on, for the first time speaking out of turn, and I take up for Coley.

"She touched," I'm excusing 'a behavior while I'm trying to get to 'a fore she can dispute what I'm saying. Then I push 'a towards some work, but she still moving stiff like she mute and dumb. A boy come with me to help give 'a something to do.

An idle nigger be a dead one round here, and Coley looking this white man in his face like she know 'im.

I keep my eyes to the ground when I say, "We should be up in less than an hour, suh."

"You betta watch that retard you got! Don't look like nothing wrong with 'a to me. Cept she might be done got that Yankee fever, and need to be broke," he say, challenged to hold the reigns on his restless horse.

I hope he ain't restless. We be surrounded by Klan, and they growing in such large numbers. Even the police Klan now. Hate to see a hanging at this fair, way they did over in Louisville.

"Best looking retard I done ever seen." He stare at Coley in disbelief.

I'm scared cause Coley looking back as bold as if she was a white man herself. "Yes suh!" I say, nervous. "Church folk keep 'a up."

"Got me fooled." He staring at 'a half way trying to figure out what else he gone do, cause she cain't keep looking at 'im like that. I don't know how to make Coley stop without letting on she just high strung, and ain't never been in the south. I'm praying he go on, but he don't.

Fore I know anything, Prudence jump up and come running towards Coley. Then she slap Coley to the ground. I clinch my dress to keep from stopping 'a. I know what Prudence doing ain't half as bad as what he would do to Coley. Truth is, Prudence might be saving 'a life, saving all of us some heart ache.

When Coley look up shocked, Prudence slap 'a again, and again looking over at him waiting for him to tell 'a it's enough, but he don't, he just sitting there waiting and expecting.

Coley lost, keep poking 'a head up, and Prudence keep on knocking it back down.

Fore I know it, I done closed my eyes, hunched my shoulders and I'm flinching with every lick she putting on 'a.

Finally the hitting stop. When I peak out, the white man done rode away, on his restless horse. All the other women done surrounded us, watching Coley wallowing in the dirt. Her hair and dress caked with the red-clay dirt. She moaning and crying audibly. Her whine start off small, then grow big. Many of the women hold their chins up as if this is some kind of initiation. Like this humiliation had to happen.

"Shut up!" the women start to shout in whispers at 'a, looking round like they scared of they own voice. Looking like they expecting somebody to come down here after us, to shut Coley up. The men look away. Coley cry into the ground, use 'a arm to muffle the sobs. The women circle round 'a, like they might beat 'a.

After a while, we all go back to working as if it ain even happen, but we remember and every once in a while they glance at Coley on the ground, then at each other. I don't offer her a hand, or try to help 'a up cause I think if somebody white see this, then they be sure I was telling the truth. Way Coley acting got to be cause she crazy.

Then again, I keep searching my mind and cain't find nothing I can say to 'a to make this better. I wait til she ready to get up first. I work around 'a, let 'a lie there flapping round, crying and moving like a fish on dry land feeling for the stream.

It's a long while fore Coley stop whining like a small child, kicking and screaming, and she start to get up. I reach to help 'a but she swat at me, like I'm a stranger she don't recognize. She get up holding 'a face, backing away from me like I'm gone hurt 'a, then she take in everybody else. It's some mix of anger, shame, betrayal, loneliness and confusion.

They all meet 'a eyes, hard and unflinching. Most of the women give 'a stiff faces, and even stand proud. The men look on with a mix of pity and fear. She a loose cannon, and outsiders been known to invite trouble. And when the Klan come they don't come for the women, even if the woman be the one started it. They come for the men.

We all stand silently as she gets 'a footing. She spits blood from 'a mouth and you can already see how 'a face gone bruise. She moving slowly, convicting and condemning each of us with 'a eyes. Then she start to move fast, like she going somewhere.

"Coley?" I follow behind 'a, cause I know she ready to leave. But I cain't take 'a back right now, not by myself. That's why we all met in town on our horses, wagons and cars so we could be together, in case there be trouble. Me and her cain't get on the road by ourselves. Specially since she done did what she did. Maybe he see us and try something. Not that there is safety in numbers or nothing. Our whole town done watched people beat and hung. But they won't usually start nothing with a lot of niggas.

When I catch up and grab 'a arm, she swing again, and I grab 'a tight. Then hold 'a in my arms to keep 'a from hitting me. She jerk, but she weak, and I hold 'a tight.

"She a crazy heffa!" Sisera say, shaking 'a head.

I don't say nothing. Coley jerk and fight in my embrace.

"Get your damn hands off of me," she scream, pushing free, then stumble off again, like she drunk.

"You cain't just leave," I reason with 'a. "It ain't safe." I follow 'a deeper into the nigga section, while folks watching 'a nervously.

"Leave me, the hell, alone!"

"You got to calm down fore-"

"Fore you be done got us all lynched, you selfish cow," Mitylene bark, interrupting us.

"Somebody else need to smack 'a, and bring 'a down another notch," Priscilla add.

"Or two," Mitylene put in.

"Yall ain't helping." I look 'em in they eyes as I'm chasing 'a. I'm trying to think of what to say, how to make this right, or at least to smooth it out. She cain't keep screaming down here, drawing attention.

Then again, it ain't just about that. I do want to say something to comfort 'a, cause I know what it feel to have the whole town turn on you.

She walking fast, frantic, hysterical, crying. I'm keeping a good stride just keeping 'a in sight. Ain't no changing what done happened.

When we get down to the last tent, she go behind it and put 'a face to the side of it and cry. She cry loud, then scream at the top of 'a lungs and jump up and down like a small child having a fit.

"Aaaaah!" She show a face to me. Her eyes are red with hurt, and it makes me sad to see 'a broken.

I don't know what come over me, but I grab 'a, and hold 'a tighter. This time when she kick, and punch and scream, I don't let go.

"Let me go! Let me go! I want to go home to my mama!" She scream into me. "Aaaaaaaah!"

"Shhhh," I whisper. "It's going to be okay. Shhhh." I rock 'a, and hold 'a.

Iain hugged nobody since I don't know when. Iain felt no emotion at all, no sadness or happiness. Been trying to forget to feel, and just keep moving. Ain't no point in tears, don't nobody care if you hurt. Pain part of life. We all got our ailments.

I don't realize I'm crying til I have to sniff to breath. Where she was hitting, she clinging to me, and I'm holding 'a tight in my arms. We both crumble to the ground, and I rock her. I start to feel all the pain of losing Miemay, and not having nobody to talk to. I start to feel the pain of going to a empty house and not feeling welcome in my own town. I think about working in my fields, and not being able to cover enough ground, and how much crop been lost.

I think about how I always planned to go back to church after Miemay passed. Then I feel how I done become like Miemay.

Chapter Twenty-Seven

"Jesus," Ella whisper, staring down the lane of vendors as a tall lean dark-haired white woman comes. She got an umbrella shading 'a from the Georgia sun, and so I cain't see 'a face. I look at my sister trying to read 'a mind, but she don't say a word. Just stand stiff, swallow hard, look at me, then at the woman.

I feel like it's something I should know, but I don't press Ella for details. Maybe she cain't tell me now cause Grit here. After what happened with Coley, I just take every day as it is cause you never know.

Me and Coley ain't spoke much since the first day of the fair. Today I'm here at my stand with my sisters, Ella and Grit. They sitting with me behind the counter, helping pick pickles and apples out of barrels. I'm glad to have 'em with me, I'm feeling so different.

When the woman finally gets in front of us, she stops too, staring at me. I look down at the ground, and over at Grit. I ain't sure what's going on, but I cain't be in no trouble, I mean, I ain't never seen this lady.

"Hold your head up, girl," she speak firm. I do and try to find something to look at, avoiding 'a eyes.

"Diamond! Why is your head hard as a rock! Your father told you this what'n a good idea." A white man I ain't never seen before come storming down the lane after 'a.

"I want to meet her, Clayton. I haven't got any other sisters or brothers. My mama is dead. I don't care if she is Colored, I want to see her. Family is family, and I'm curious. They say there is a striking resemblance."

When she say that, I look at 'a, in 'a eyes, and it's like looking at myself in a mirror. Cept it's more detailed than that blurry-looking glass I got at home. Only real difference between us is, her eyes are bright blue and mine green. Both of our faces have sharp features, high cheekbones, sharp jawlines, long necks, pink lips and hair bout the same length. Her waves relaxed, like she had to braid it to make it bend that way. Mine braided too, into two thick braids and tucked under a hat.

"How old are you, girl?"

"Twenty-two." I'm still in shock, trying to understand what's happening, how we looking like twins. I'm remembering Hunter Beaumont telling me to turn around. I am remembering his brother Lowell Beaumont saying, "she looks just like a black diamond." Then I didn't know there was a woman named Diamond. I actually do look like her.

I look more like her than I look like my own sister Ella standing next to me. I glance over at Ella just to check and make sure Iain forgot who she is, what she look like. Her hands different, her fingers larger, the tips of 'a fingers stubby, mine flat like boxes. Her features are rounder, softer, and when I look back at Grit, she looking like a younger Ella. Then I look at the woman's hands.

"Guess it ain't no harm in it; Mama was long dead fore you were born, or conceived. I'll be twenty-eight my next birthday, and she died in child birth. I was the first and the last. From what I understand your mama worked in the house for our family."

Ella come stand behind me close, looking at the woman in front of us. Ella don't seem as shocked, and I'm wrapping my mind round it all.

"So what do you do, girl?"

"Work," I say short. Way she looking at me remind me I'm a nigga and she white so I add, "ma'am." Shrinking in myself, I start to feel shy.

"You married? Got any children?"

"No, ma'am." I look at 'a hands and the ground.

"You're a lil old to be without a man. Then again, I'm even older and I'm not married either. I think being high strung run in the family. I'm thinking about getting married, but Clay works my last nerve."

"Yes'um," I say, staring at the table, comparing 'a hands to mine. I'm thinking bout whether anybody else look like 'a. I'm running my mind over my brothers and sisters. I'm looking for another mirror. I think about my oldest brothers, Jeremy, Noah and then Zay. I try to see myself reflected in Jenny, and Grit and then Ella. Ella and Noah look so much alike folks use to think they was twins, but it's eleven months between 'em. Then I think, Ella and Noah brown like Daddy, got his . . . I swallow hard.

"Daddy ain my daddy?" The tears fall, and I lean on Ella. Breathing, I hold my lip tight, it tremble, and my eyes do what they want.

"I was gone tell you, but it just what'n never the right time. Then all this happen with Miemay, and Daddy, and you and Mama ain never got a long no how." Ella speaking to me firm, like she trying to calm me down.

I don't remember breathing in but I feel all the air escape.

"Take it easy," Ella warn.

"Ma'am?" I breath slow, putting my hand firmly on the counter between us trying to brace myself. "Is you saying?"

"Yes, she is," Ella say gently, but firm. She standing so close to me, half 'a body against half mine. I realize she bracing herself for me to fall.

My brains swimming in the muck of all this. Iain got no daddy. Then I think about why Mama hate me. I look at my skin.

"Oh." I cup my mouth to catch the sound and I try to swallow it. It's too much hurt, it get out. "Oh." I shake my head to try and stop the feelings from coming, but they come hard as I realize, "Oh, oh." Is all I can say as the pain ooze out of me, as I remember how Mama looks at me, and I know.

"I'm sorry, I thought you knew." The white woman, a stranger reaches out to me and touches my arm like she know me and rubs my shoulder. "I thought you were proud like most niggers are about their white daddies. All I been hearing is how there's a girl walking around here, who looks just like me. The other day even my own daddy said so."

"Your daddy?" I get out just above a whisper, and I challenge 'a with my eyes for crushing my world.

"Our daddy, Hunter Beaumont," she say like I should be honored.

Shaking my head I step back, slowly. I look at Ella, and feel betrayed she ain never tell me and I find out like this. I look at Grit and can tell 'a heart heavy, too. Iain got no room in my mind or heart to think about nobody else's feelings.

I don't know how many steps I take back before I almost stumble over a chair. Then Ella catch me by the arm and hold me up. I feel Ella's strength, and think, maybe I got my strength from Mama. Iain small as this woman standing in front of me, but I'm seeing myself for the first time and understanding.

When Ella let my arm go, I start out of the stand, and then out of the fair. Ella hot on my trail.

"Linny? You cain't walk back to Zion. They be done done something to you. You light, and you know how they like nigga women." Then she pull me and I snatch away from 'a.

I ball my fists up, open my arms and punch all round me like one of them wooden toys. Like my arms only got so much motion. I punch and punch. It's a tightness in my arms, and I swing, and fight, and cry. Finally I hear my own voice, "Nobody wanted me! Miemay ain't even my great grandmother! Mama hate me!"

Ella cry, looking at me. I snatch off my hat, and grab my braids and cling to 'em like a rope over a cliff.

"That's why you use to comb my hair. That's why Mama said it was hard to comb my head. Every time Mama looked at me, she frowned. I tried to figure out what I done to make 'a not love me. She be hitting me, and I be trying to figure out how to make 'a love me. And now I know why, she don't wont me."

"How it happen?" I ask, looking at Ella and she upset, too. Her chest heaving, she shaking 'a head no, like she got a choice on whether she can tell me bout how I came to be. Her eyes pouring. "How did it happen?" I demand to know, wiping my eyes and staring at 'a.

"You already know, she ain wont it. What else is it to say? Why you wont to go over every lil detail? Ain't gone change nothing."

"Aaaah!" I cry loud like I'm wounded and get scared of my own voice. "Why me?" I whisper pulling on my own clothes.

Then I remember Miemay telling me how she loved 'a children, even though she didn't love their fathers. I remember her telling me bout wanting to be mothered, but wouldn't nobody mother 'a, cause she was a stranger. She was telling me in 'a own way, why my mama wouldn't mother me. She said if nobody else loved me, she did.

I breathe heavy, I accept, I know and I understand. Things make sense now. Why Mrs. Harper and Ella be combing my hair. Why Daddy, ain't my real Daddy, take me with him to work every day after Mama cut my hair off. They all knew she hated me.

Same reason Miemay charged Reverend Patrick with looking after me, cause she knew this day would come. Same reason Reverend Patrick tell me bout his mother hating him, and his sister and brothers cause they was black.

"People been telling me all my life in they own way." I'm smiling at Ella through tears, wiping my nose with my bare hand, getting up, pulling myself together cause crying don't change nothing.

"Linny, I love you. I'm glad you were born. The situation what'n the best, but you here now, and you cain't take no blame for what happened to Mama. You was a innocent child."

"I remind my mother of being raped," I resolve, dusting myself off.

"You cain't do it like this. You cain't take all that on you." Ella grab me, but I cain't be consoled.

"Iain Madelyn Remington, Cassius Remington's sixth child. I am Madelyn Somebody, who ain't part of nothing." Something bout all this make me laugh, this painful laugh Iain never had before. "Is that the real reason everybody was so upset about the inheritance? They probly saying, 'Linny ain't even our blood.'"

"Blood ain't everything."

"It's all there is."

"Miemay gave you 'a name and raised you like one of 'a own. If anything, you was like a daughter to 'a."

"Like her daughter, not her granddaughter, not even her great granddaughter."

"Oh Linny." Ella hold my face and look in my eyes. "This is why Iain never had the heart to tell you. We all knew, cept maybe Grit. Ain't never been a right time for this. We all knew this would break yah heart."

"How it happen? I wont to know. I wont details."

"You don't wonna know."

"I'm tired of not knowing. I'm tired of secrets. I don't wonna find nothing else out by nobody else. You got to tell me." I breathe deep, tired and angry.

"Mama and Daddy, they," she stop looking off somewhere, maybe for 'aself. "They the Hilliard house couple."

Chapter Twenty-Eight

When the rooster crow, I barely stir. I watch the sun creep up over the hills and into my window, making it hot. I know it's things got to be done, but for what? I think about how my mama look at me, how I came to be, and I think about how Miemay gone now.

I think about Miemay telling me bout just laying there and letting somebody breathe on 'a. I think about Mama and Daddy. Wonder if my real father make it so my mama cain't stand to be touched by my Daddy, but she got to do it. I want to stop thinking bout all this, it disgust me, but the thoughts keep coming til I'm sick.

Then my mind get wild. I start thinking bout women not loving the men touching them, but cause they wives and have some duty, they allow it. I think about Coley wanting a husband, and how all women being groomed for that day they come to bow for some man. I think about Grit and Granger.

I hear Coley moving across the hall. She cain't cook to save 'a life, so I been getting up to fix 'a something. I don't get dressed, just slide on some shoes, and go down in my sleeping clothes. I start some water to boiling, drop a little salt and butter from the cooler. Then I go out to the coup, and get some eggs from the hens. Then I get a little meat from the smoke house.

I don't know how I look but I feel ugly. I feel heavy as this morning, when the day don't seem to have no possibilities. Tomorrow I will be the daughter of the man who raped my mama. Today, I'm a woman with a mother who hates 'a because she reminds 'a of her father. Then I think about how I ain't blood. I think about how Miemay ain't my grandmother. I remember the day before the counsel, and the way those men looked at me. I remember being afraid night riders would come, rape me, maybe kill me. Little did I know one of them had already raped my mama. There was my father looking at his work.

"Are you trying to burn yourself up?" Coley push me back and start hitting my waist with a wet towel.

I didn't even smell my nightshirt catch fire. Ain much when I look down. Done burned a hole, but it's a bigger hole in my spirit. I feel dizzy, tired and barely here.

"When was the last time you ate something?"

I don't say nothing. It's like I can hear 'a talking but I cain't respond. I'm in some kind of fog. I don't even want to play my piano the way I did after Miemay died. It usually get me through hard times, but now I cain't even muster the strength it'd take to sit up on the bench in front of it.

When I look down and see that everything done, but the bacon, I don't even wait. I figure Coley can finish making 'a own bacon.

I climb the stairs, on my hands and knees. I feel like crying but I won't. It's no point, and Iain got no more tears. Some part of me wish I what'n born, so my mama ain't got no living reminder. Some part of me shamed.

All the times somebody said I was the prettiest or most beautiful child, it was cause I got lighter skin than my sisters. And knowing that everybody knew now, makes it seem like they was poking fun, maybe at my mama, maybe at me. What's pretty bout what happened to my mama?

* * *

"We've got to get out of here, or we'll never leave this house," Coley calls through the door.

I don't want to leave this house, don't want nobody to see me. I feel like they looking at what my real father done, and I'm ashamed. I've been looking at my blurry image in the looking glass, and I see how I look more like Hunter Beaumont than anything else. I don't want to look like him.

Today, Iain even weed the garden. All I did was get up this morning and feed the animals. Ain nobody pulled the eggs. I don't know what Coley eating and I don't ask or care.

"Linny? You hear me talking to you?"

When I sit up to talk, words seem to carry tears. Sound got tears in it. All I can do to keep from crying or killing myself is lay here in this bed til this pain get away from me. But it don't go, it's like the night sounds, it's still stirring, but the pain get more peaceful.

Soon as I move, I remember how much I hurt. I remember my mama don't want me with good cause. I remember my daddy ain't my daddy, and my sisters and brothers only half. Then I think about how they wholes and I'm half. I remember things, things I wish to forget. I long for the time before knowing who I really am.

Then again, it seem like I ain't none of the things I'm is. I ain the woman who ain't got no daddy. I'm Miemay's granddaughter, who makes decisions, and dreams, and makes things. I'm the woman with her own land, and world to consider. I'm a woman who didn't marry, and doesn't have children of her own. I'm a woman who could go anywhere or do anything cause I ain tied down. I'm the woman who tends to her own fields, and fixes things in her own barn. I'm this woman who rides horses, and dreams of a world where she can be all the things she is, and it be okay.

Then again, I wish I what'n so many things. Wish I what'n stubborn. Sometimes I wish I was more like my sisters. Wish my whole life be thinking happiness is some man choosing you, and yall having some kids. Then again, maybe I wish that what'n what made other women happy, or that it what'n enough alone to make 'em happy. I wish they were really free, to go searching for what they really want. Then folks wouldn't think I'm so strange.

"I know it's hard to go on, but the world isn't going to stop because you don't go out in it. We've got to make the most of it." I hear the door knob turn, and Coley push the door open slowly.

I keep my eyes on the wall and stay silent. I'm afraid if I think about 'a coming in here, I'm gone cry, or be mad. I'm so mad with the world, with God really.

"I don't really know what to say. I heard what happened at the fair. Maybe-" she say, sitting down easy on the bed, "you know, they say everything happens for a reason, and everything to fulfill God's will."

"What could God's will be? What I done, but be born, to deserve all this? Why my Mama got to hate me? Why my daddy ain't my daddy, and I got another daddy done forced hisself on my mama?"

"I don't know." Coley scoot closer to me.

"Lately I-" I stop myself cause I don't want to talk about the Bible like it's just any other book. Don't want to ask questions bout it, or force nobody to really think about what it say.

Still, it's been burning me up, this whole talk of destiny and will. What's my destiny? What's God's purpose for my life? I certainly ain't trying to be no wife, and I don't fit in here. I think about what Miemay use to say, she say, "You'll know by how it feel if you on the right path." She say, "It come easier."

It be hard sometimes cause life ain easy, but it come easier than all the fighting. Sometimes it be a easy choice to fight, cause the battle be destiny. This fight over my inheritance don't feel right.

"Lately what?" Coley keep prying with 'a questions, and I feel like talking, and not talking.

"Look at Judas. If he hadn't betrayed Jesus, they'da never killed Jesus and mankind wouldn't have been saved. But how you think that made Judas feel? But it was his destiny? Am I cursed? Is it my destiny to suffer? I don't wont that for my life."

"I've never heard anyone talk about the Bible like this. I've never even thought about Judas' destiny. Nobody ever talks about that."

"You know Judas hung himself?" I look at Coley, feeling a tear trail down my face; I hope the pulled curtains and darkness hide it. Not trusting nothing, I wipe my eyes.

"I didn't know that. Where are you reading all this?"

"The Bible."

"I've never read that."

"You ever read the whole Bible?"

"No," she say, like she ashamed.

Maybe to console her, I say, "I don't know nobody other than my great grandmother that has."

"You are really smart," she say, in a way that sound like she surprised, or that she was expecting me to be dumb. "Folks told me you read a lot, but you don't speak like you do."

"You always speak without thinking." I am too tired to be kind, or welcoming.

"I'm sorry." It sound like she crying.

"Don't be sorry, just pay attention. Stop acting like you better than everybody else, or you came here to save us. We don't feel like we lost, or that we need to be saved. You see how they acted when they found out you was replacing Prudence.

"Then again, I guess it ain't all yo fault. Seem like you come from a place where niggas sit around making decisions for other niggas, and thinking they know best for us all."

"It sounds strange when you say it, like it isn't the truth. Especially since I know the truth. I don't know what to do with my own life, and here I was thinking I could tell someone else what to do with their life."

I feel 'a lay down beside me, feel 'a weight pull us down together in the middle of the bed, and I don't fight.

"You know I came here to get away from my mama and daddy, Mama mostly. They always had this dream for me, of who I would be. I was going to marry a light-skinned man who could take care of me and some children. Now I'm just 25, but I'm an old maid.

"Mama takes every opportunity she gets to tear me down, to remind me of my misfortune. Every day I woke up under her roof, she'd pointed out that my sisters were all married, and my brother has his own family. Then she'd ask, what will I do with myself?"

Scooting 'a face under my arm, and making 'aself a place in my mind, she makes my skin feel too heavy for my bones. Prying in my pain she press with 'a own.

"I did everything I could to come home with a husband. Did my work and this young man's work all through college. He married another woman, a blue blood.

"Then I met another man, a better man. I thought I chose him with a woman's eyes and a woman's heart. I even left DC after I graduated, and instead of going home I followed him on to Atlanta. I thought, this is the man I'm going to marry. I couldn't imagine someone who said he loved me could be lying.

"Then one day, there was this big banquet. I had been planning what I was going to wear. I had been saving money so I could get my hair done, and be pretty so he'd be honored to be my escort.

"You know, I couldn't ask Mama or Daddy for money because a woman shouldn't follow a man. Daddy would of said he needed to pay my way, and Mama would have accused me of sleeping with him.

"Me living down there in Atlanta by myself already worried them. Every letter I received from them they wanted to know when I'd be home, when I'd be getting married, and if I was seeing anyone.

"Every letter I sent back in response to theirs was a disappointment. I'd told them I was going to Clark for my masters. I did graduate from the masters program, but that wasn't the reason I was there. He was the reason I was there.

"Anyway, the banquet came. We were all residing on campus. Students had their dorms and staff had their living quarters. I asked him what time should I expect him to be downstairs for me. He told me I'd have to meet him at the banquet because he was at a host house, and would have to bring all the people with him to come get me.

"I felt slighted that he was escorting me but would not come to get me. At the same time, I felt honored he was escorting me, and by some turn I'd have the honor of hosting visiting guests. I didn't want to inconvenience anybody, so I didn't make any noise. I thought it would all be worth it, when I could say I'm Mrs. Dr. Brendon Holcomb."

"He was a doctor?" I ask thinking bout what she saying.

"Yes, he was a doctor of psychology, and he was my professor. When the A.K.A's denied my request to enter their sorority, cause I was too dark, he was the one who held and consoled me as I cried. He had written one of my recommendations.

"Then he started taking me out to dinner all the time. He started walking me home every evening after class. He'd spend hours talking to me, and telling me about his dreams. He even helped me get in Clark's program where I could teach part time, and work on my masters. The teaching paid for school.

"For the first time, someone wanted to know about me, and he asked me about my career and dreams. He was the first man supportive of me having a career and goals, outside of just being a wife or a mother. He was the first man who ever asked me who I was, or what I wanted out of life.

"Everyone else had already decided who I was, or they were trying to force me to be who they wanted me to be. All the other men I met, were weighing me against these standards. How would I look on their arms? How much money my father earned? Who my father was? Could my father get them a job? Where would we live after school?

"Even my own folks, were putting pressure on me to live this certain way. I tried to do what was asked of me, but sometimes I didn't make it, and failing wasn't enough. I had to hear about it from Mama day in and day out.

"She didn't ever say, 'Coletta, you are beautiful, or smart.' She is still always telling me how I don't add up. How she wishes I was taller, or that my hair was straighter and longer. How I should eat to be slimmer and stay out of the sun because I'm already too dark. When it's not that, its how to stand; 'Hold your stomach in, keep your chin up, straighten your back and pull your shoulders back.' She even tells me who to befriend. She is just like them, I went right from trying to fit in for Mama's sake, to trying to fit in because I wanted to make her proud.

"Neither of my sisters went to college, my youngest one didn't even finish high school, but they both married well. Mama didn't even tell me when my youngest sister, Minerva, was pregnant. Even to this day, she won't admit Minerva got pregnant out of wedlock, she says the baby came early.

"Being in Zion, this is the first time I've ever had people think I was smart. This is the first time people actually treated me like I was anything. Then when that woman hit me at the fair, some of them were staring at me like I deserved it. Some of them even yelled at me while I was crying.

"Then you just left me laying there, and when I got up, the men, they wouldn't even look me in the eyes. Here I was coming to this small town thinking I could help, but the people are telling me I don't fit in, again.

"I'm trying to help, but everybody is saying, I could have gotten them killed by my behavior. How can the world be so different and then the same. How is it I don't have a place anywhere. Mama said I wouldn't have a good life because I'm too dark, head strong, and I talk too much. Then the people here say I'm going to get them killed by being here."

"Ain't just cause you here. It's cause you don't follow the rules," I say soft, but it sound hard against 'a hurt.

"Now that I think about it, and I have been thinking about it, I realize I brought all the things with me I was trying to leave behind. I carry all those things Mama has been putting in me for years, wherever I go. I left New York, DC and Atlanta to get somewhere else, and to be someone else, maybe. You can't get out of where you've been if you're carrying the place inside you."

"I sometimes think about leaving this place behind, too."

"Where would you go?"

I hear 'a smiling, and it lightens my load to hear 'a smile. "New York, Chicago, E. St. Louis, and sometimes I think about Atlanta cause it's so close. Just a couple days ride north by wagon from here. Then again, if I leave, I want to get out of Georgia.

Folks who done left always talk about Chicago and New York like they a different world. Even the work they say different. You in buildings. I hear ain't really no trees or fields to work. I cain't even imagine that."

"I think you'd like New York. I think you would be happy there, because you aren't corrupted by the other stuff. The fact that you can be out here in these woods and not go crazy is something to talk about."

"Iain in the woods." I laugh a little. "You ain seen the woods. You should let me take you hunting sometimes."

"Hunt what?" she ask, like the idea is so farfetched she cain't even wrap 'a mind around it.

"Deer."

"What would we do if we found a deer?"

"Shoot and kill it."

"We would shoot it?" she ask loud in disbelief.

I roll over stretching and smiling, and feeling all the time Iain been moving much as I should. She move back, then snuggle in closer to me, when I raise my arms. I don't know what make me do it, but I pull 'a close and put my head on 'a hair. Hold 'a frame close to mine.

"You own a gun, Linny?"

"Yes, ma'am. Wouldn't be out here in 'these woods,' as you say, by myself under no other circumstances. I got a few different rifles." I roll away from her, and she holds on to me going with each of my movements like we joined at the hip.

I'm reaching under the bed, feeling for it, then I pull my rifle from under the bed, where I keep it in arms reach. "This the main one I use, but I got other ones." I'm pointing the barrel at the roof. Then I toss it up a little a few times, so I can get a handle on it where I want.

She sits up, leaving me cold to run 'a hands along the metal.

Showing Coley my gun feels different from when me and my brothers are talking bout our guns. It's like guns are tools we're comparing. We talk about mastering our guns; how one has a better aim, while another is easier to handle. I know every part of all my guns. But for some reason, when Coley ran 'a hands along the barrel, it felt like I was seeing this gun for the first time.

"You ever shot anything?"

237

"Of course."

"Then what did you do with what you killed?"

"Eat it, woman. Yo daddy ain never took you hunting?" I smile, feeling myself, and finding the strength to get up. "I guess not." I think about who she is, and how she is. My daddy ain never took my sisters hunting neither, and they was right there at home when we was leaving all of them times. He ain take me cause he wanted to or nothing either, he just didn't want to leave me with his wife, my mama. "Whatever happen to that man you followed to Atlanta?"

"Oh, I didn't tell you the end of the story. I forgot where I left off."

I remind 'a, "He said he couldn't come get you, and you didn't put up no fuss."

"Yeah, well, he said he couldn't come and get me, and to meet him at the banquet. When I got there, I saw him, and he was so handsome. I went and stood behind him, because he was surrounded by what looked like a lot of important people.

"When he noticed me he turned around and started introducing me to everyone. There I was, you know, bowing and nodding to everyone. Linny, I felt so important that he was introducing me, I was just smiling from ear to ear. For a moment, I knew this was the reason I was on the road with him, and he was the reason I'd taken the job teaching at the local school.

"For a moment, I finally felt like I'd made a good decision and things were going to work out. I was so proud that he was my man. I thought about how proud I would be when I finally introduced him to my father. I was just about to loop my arm in his, when he said, "Coletta Graham, this is Mrs. Dr. Brendon Holcomb, my wife." Then he looped her gloved arm in his.

"Oh Coley," I say, pulling 'a closer.

"I felt so stupid. There I was chasing this married man and he never mentioned he had a wife."

"What did you say after he introduced you two?"

"Nothing. I just excused myself and started back out to my quarters. And you know who came after me, his wife. She was so beautiful and nice. I couldn't even hate her, as much as I wanted to."

"What did she have to say?"

"Nothing really, now that I think about it. She probably knew what he had done. She said she'd heard so many good things about me, that she was looking forward to us meeting. She said she admired her husband's dedication to his profession, and how he takes such a personal interest in his best students. It's one of the things she loves about him. Then she said she met him when she was in school, too."

"How old was he?"

"Thirty-five. They had children and everything. They lived in Philadelphia, where he was from. He travelled for work and lecturing. I travelled with him. Felt like his wife on the road. Dreamed that one day, I'd be married to him, and we would be going back and forth across the country. His wife doesn't work. He doesn't like his wife to work, she said. That's what makes me think she knew then, as I'm thinking about it."

"They always do," I say acting like I know his wife's type. I'm surprised to hear that Coley wanted to keep working after she got married.

"I was his wife on the road."

"How so?"

"I washed his clothes, ironed, cleaned and cooked for him. I made sure he stayed organized for his lectures and classes. We worked so well together. I started to think we were such a good team. That's what I always wanted when I thought about marriage. I didn't want to be in the dark about what was going on around me, or at home somewhere like how it is with my mama and daddy.

"I mean, don't get me wrong, Daddy is good to Mama. She doesn't want for anything, but him. Daddy is always gone on some speaking engagement. When he's home he's working late. There is this whole world Daddy is in, Mama isn't part of. Seems like my father is always growing, going somewhere, meeting new people and learning something. While all Mama knows is New York.

"I want to travel, too. I don't want my life to stop because I'm married. I want to at least be a part of my husband's successes. Especially since it seems, society won't allow me to have my own.

"Mama seems so bitter about all she had to give up for Daddy. Still, for some reason she tells me to find a husband like Daddy. So I can give up my dreams and be unhappy, too."

"Well," I say, at a loss for words and searching for something, to comfort 'a, but I don't know what will. Finally, the words come, "At least you didn't let him get the best of you." I'm rubbing 'a shoulder, and rocking away 'a sorrow.

She scoots into me until there is no way for air to pass between us.

I'm glad she's here, so I hold 'a closer, thankful for this moment. I stroke 'a face and hair.

Then I hear 'a moaning low, sniffing loud and realize she crying.

I'm still, silent.

Her body starts to shake, and I realize she upset. The crying get loud, if it what'n for my body against hers smothering the sound, feel like she be screaming. I don't know how long she crying when she finally start huffing and calm down.

After a while, I'm thinking she sleep when she stir and say, "You know, he had the nerve to ask me if I wanted to stay on the road with him." She kinda laughs like she cain't even believe it now. Then she say, "He never wore a wedding ring, until the night he introduced me to his wife."

Sitting up, she looks around the room like she looking for something and wrapping 'a arms around herself she says, "He did get the best of me. I gave myself to him. I did everything I thought a wife would have done."

Chapter Twenty-Nine

"Anybody, ever tell you that you remind them of a," Coley stop 'aself and look out at the sunset.

I don't press 'a, and sometimes between me and Coley, be like how it use to be tween me and Miemay. We don't press the words, we be waiting for them to find the best route to come.

It's after supper, we out on the porch looking out at the sun setting. Tonight Coley doing some needle work, Ella done taught 'a. Tonight she ain't doing no complaining, bout how I expect 'a to do too much work. Fact is, she don't complain much at all no more. Days been going and coming without a word bout what tomorrow gone bring.

I got a lantern on the edge of the bench I'm gone light when it get too dark. I'm reading, *The Souls of Black Folks*, a book Coley done gave me by W.E.B. Du Bois. She wont me to know who he is, so we can talk about his ideas. So I'm reading slower, thinking bout every word he wrote. Been reading this book for almost a week now. I read about an hour or so a day. Now that Miemay ain round to read to, reading seem wasteful, especially with all I got to get done in a day.

"Sometimes, I just feel like I'm in the house with a man," Coley go on, pressing the needle through the fabric and making a huge show of pulling it out. "I don't feel like I'm living with another woman. I use to try and figure out what it is you're doing, what you are. I mean you cook, but the way you carry yourself is different.

"At first I thought you were so beautiful, sure of yourself and just regal. I still think all that, but it's different. Like, I feel safe with you. I don't feel like you competing with me, or trying to hurt me, the way it is with most women. Even among sisters sometimes it can be downright ugly, with our rivalries."

I hold the book open, reading about Du Bois losing his son and the way he views death. I think about the idea that because his son died, he will never have to experience the veil. I think about the veil, the wearing of different masks, and having to be what people expect or want you to be to survive.

"Did I offend you," she asks sheepishly.

"No," I say immediately, when I realize it's my turn to talk.

"What do you think about what I said?"

"I spect most women be like men to you round here. We work in the fields and you a lady. You use to being inside, reading, teaching, learning and doing paperwork. With all your fancy ways and things, no offense could be taken," I add on the end when I see 'a shifting 'a weight.

I know what she means. I get this all the time. Most women who been round me long enough say I'm different. Longer than a little while, they all be saying I make them feel like they in the presence of a man. Iain ready to admit that to Coley for some reason.

"I know what I feel, and you aren't like other women in Zion. I don't know," she put a piece of thread in 'a mouth and put a loop through it, break it and start again looking off. Her hands concentrating on what they doing, and I see she done got it. Her mind wandering on me.

This another thing about Coley, she wont me to talk about everything. She bring talking to life. Try to make me think and go over how I'm feeling bout every little thing. I'm in my head a lot, because I know better than to say half the things I be thinking. If I did, people be saying I'm like Miemay, be saying I'm crazy or a witch.

I love to hear Coley's stories. She tell everything, the good and the bad. In my family we don't talk about how we feel. We don't talk about what's happening on the inside, cause of what's happening around us.

Coley be so open and honest sometimes you be sitting in silence like you there with 'a. I be happy to listen to anything she got to say, she know a lil bit about everything. She really funny too, and the way she see the world so different than folks round here. Once you get pass 'a thoughts rubbing you the wrong way, they be something to think about.

Half the things she be talking bout Iain never thought about. And when she go on and on bout how country people don't care, I have to remind 'a our worlds are different. Ain't that we don't care, be that we got different concerns on some things, and on other things it be that we ain never thought about it.

We see how the Klan raid Zion, people get whupped, and strangers get hung if anybody even talk about niggas voting. We just trying to survive. Right now, we always worried, afraid of how if someone even hint at letting niggas vote they lives in jeopardy. So we don't talk about how us voting might improve our lives in the long run. Shoot, white folks will kill other whites for talking bout letting niggas vote.

Coley say we don't care cause she don't understand we care too much. One nigga could bring the Klan down on the whole town. One nigga could have our whole town burned to the ground and half us kilt. And ain't no law gone come and protect us or stop it. Ain't nobody gone write nothing bout it.

Coley ain never see a man lynched, or cut down out of a tree. I think if she had she'd understand we do care. I don't wish 'a to witness no lynching, but I know if she did it would be life changing.

"You're not concerned with being pretty. You put a dress on like a hanger, and don't give anything to it, beautiful as you are. The way you talk to people, men, and expect them to respect you is different. You don't bow and they don't seem to expect you to either. You walk in a room like you own it. Even when there are other women around, they respond to you almost the way they would a man. They're always offering you things and waiting on you, like how they did at Reverend's house that Sunday. The way you move around, who you talk to, what you talk about isn't what, you know, other women are concerning themselves with."

"I was raised different," I brush off what she saying. I'm trying to deny it. I'm afraid she might get like Norma Jean. I might scare 'a if I tell 'a the truth. I feel something happening between me and Coley. I don't want to do nothing to stop it.

Don't want to do nothing to undermine how comfortable she feeling with me, and how close we getting.

Some nights she be climbing in the bed with me, talking bout she heard a noise and she scared. Some nights she say she cold. Other nights she come just to talk. One night she knocked, and I told 'a she could come in, but she had to be quiet cause I was tired. She seemed relieved, not to go on making up excuses to get in my bed. Lately she been just crawling in bed with me, wrapping 'a arms round me. On the nights when she don't come, I miss 'a, but I know better than to call for 'a. Been a few days since I slept alone.

"Linny?"

"I'm thinking," I answer. I know what I want to say but I don't know if I can say this. I don't know how the words arrive when they start flowing, but it's starting to seem like if you prepare a reception for anything, they be more than willing to show up. So I say, "I feel different than other women. I feel different when it comes to you. I want to protect you."

Then I'm silent, looking at the page in the book cause it's all I can think to do while I'm waiting for how she gone take that. I'm waiting for 'a to pry into what I mean by 'different.' I'm waiting for 'a to ask me to explain that word, 'different.' What it mean when I say it.

We silent for a long time, so I know she ain gone press me on it, and I don't wont to be pressed no how. That's why I go on, "I don't have a need to compete with nobody, cause all we can be is who we is. I cain't be you better than you, and you cain't be me, better than I'm is."

"I've never thought about it like that."

I'm relieved again, that she don't talk about what I said at first. Maybe she denying it too. I'm okay with 'a not thinking bout what's happening.

"I've been going up against my cousins and sisters for so long in different things. Mama always comparing us girls. Who's the tallest, who's the smallest, who's getting fat, who's the smartest, but mostly who's the prettiest, and the prettiest one is always the lightest. My sisters and I aren't the lightest, but my sisters are all lighter than me. My sisters are all prettier than me," she stop, and I can hear the heaviness of sorrow in 'a throat, threatening to make 'a cry. I watch 'a inhale deep, til she get 'aself together.

"I think you beautiful," I say sincerely, not to console 'a, but I hope it do. I stare at 'a in a way that she can feel, and I feel 'a knowing I'm looking, but she don't look up. She just sniff hard, and keep on sewing like Iain said nothing. Raise 'a eyebrows like something interesting done happen in 'a hands, but she sowing the same as before, then she go on talking.

"Every big holiday, or on some Sundays, they sit around comparing who does what and who married who. I was, am," she stop, breathing to find the strength to tell it like it is, "an embarrassment to my mother you know. Not being married and all."

"I sure know about not being married." I think about Ella telling me I need a man, and Daddy saying I'm a burden. Then I open up my book and look at it, cause Coley proud like me, don't like nobody to see 'a cry. "You done way more than I can hope to in this life, so you sure ain't no embarrassment."

"I'm older than I told you." She breathe deep like a weight lifted off of 'a.

"I know." I look at 'a, but I don't ask 'a how old she is. I don't care, unless she care to tell me.

"Are you ever going to get married, Linny?" Her voice cracking, and she fighting crying, trying to talk like nothing's wrong.

"Cain't imagine it." I'm looking at 'a seriously and the mood change. I feel our spirits shift, and she give me this weird look, don't look like fear, but Ion know what it is.

"I can't imagine you married either, especially not to a man."

Chapter Thirty

I don't realize I'm waiting, til I hear Coley knock on the door and ask, "Is you decent?"

"Come on," I say, but I don't know what to feel until she climb in the bed with me. Words fall from 'a mouth like rose petals to the bed. She cain't just come in here and get in the bed, she got to come in here talking. Still, I'm relieved she here.

Coley come in the room moving like a sneaky cat. Feel like she hiding behind something waiting to see if it's safe. She don't want nothing but to be in here, and I want 'a in here, in my bed.

I don't wanna talk, don't wanna listen, I just wanna close my eyes and feel 'a next to me. I cain't say that though, so I just listen to 'a talk. Seem like for all the talking she be doing, she talking 'aself into things, and out of things.

"Don't you ever go anywhere? Don't you ever want to just get out? Aren't there any shows around? I get antsy, I like to just get out and walk, see some different things. Don't you ever do anything that doesn't need to be done? You ever just go in town to have dinner? Ever just go out to the stream and just you know, sit on the edge of it just to sit on the edge of it?" Coley talking 'aself to sleep like she do sometimes, and talking me awake.

I been so busy with the fields, the tenant properties, and running the store Iain realize I what'n really doing nothing for the sake of just doing it. I mean, I read but by the time I sit down to do that, it be too dark to do anything else. I haven't played my piano since Coley arrived. It seem too loud against the silence. Then it come to me, and I know what I do just for the sake of doing it. "I ride Anastasia for the sake of riding her."

"How do you feel when you ride?" Coley whirl round like a child in the bed waiting. Before I was tired, but when I think about me and Anastasia, I get excited.

"When I'm riding, it's like—I'm flying and I can go anywhere in the world. Feels like I be choosing to be here." I end kind of sad but don't know why.

"You don't feel like you have any choices?"

"Where would I go?" I start to think about how I got all this land and the store. "How would I support myself?"

"There's a whole world out there," she answer, like its easy.

"I figured as much, but what I know about the world out there? This my world here."

"God made the whole world, and it all belongs to us, to you," Coley say thoughtfully, holding my hand and laying beside me. "You ever been to another town to stay, or just to be?"

"Only to work, to sell things, Iain never stayed nowhere overnight."

"We should! Let's get on a train and just go. Maybe we'll go somewhere close first, like Atlanta. Or we could drive down to Savannah or Florida and see the beach." She start getting excited and full of ideas. "You ever had dinner at a restaurant?"

"What restaurant? Ion go nowhere but round here. And I don't go nowhere hungry. I think it's wasteful to pay people for food, when you got a houseful of food, made the way you like."

"See, you aren't just paying for the food, you're paying for service. You're paying for someone else to do the dishes and clean up the kitchen. You're paying to just eat, get up and go."

"You had a maid, what'n it already like that? What was you paying for?"

"Well, then you're paying for different scenery. You're paying for an experience. In New York, they have all these different blocks of people from different places with different cultures. There is Little Italy, where most Italians live. Then there is a place where mostly Germans, Dutch and Irish people live.

"Then you have all these different kinds of Negroes; Haitians, Grenadians, Trinidadians, Jamaicans, Nigerians and they all have their different foods they make, they like. There is China town, and Chinese food is so good, Linny.

"Then you have Spanish Harlem, with the Puerto Ricans, Cubans and Dominicans. Food made by West Indians, Spanish people, Germans, or Italians are all different. We cook different from them, so you get to sit at their mama's table and eat," she say all excited and dreamy. "You know what we should do, we should go into town and eat at Mrs. Clara's."

"The hotel?"

"Yes, it'll be fun. We could go Saturday evening in our Sunday best, and you could drive."

"Why would I want to get all gussied up in some stuffy dress, and give up a Saturday in pants doing whatever I want round my house?"

"Because," she put 'a leg over my thigh, "I'd be really grateful." She put my hands in 'a hair, and look in my eyes in a way stir me. Then I understand how it is a man's wife rule him. Why men be bathing in aftershave and all. If I could figure out a way to make 'a smile at me way she just done, I'd be hop toing to that beat all the time.

"What's your favorite kind of food?" I'm thinking of all the places she must've ate and all the things she just named.

"Your's," she answer smiling. Her answer do something to me.

"Thank you," I say painfully.

"Good." She put 'a face against the back of my hand. "You're doing so good Linny. Look at you accepting compliments. I should just tell you all the wonderful things I think about you." She turn over looking in my eyes laughing.

I don't know why she likes messing with me, but I build myself up for it.

"You're beautiful, and strong, and smart. You have a bright smile and beautiful eyes." She looking in them like she might kiss me.

I feel how awkward it make 'a, I feel 'a pulling away and I don't want to lose 'a so I say, "Thank yah" real country. Then she laugh and relax. We quiet while she deciding whether she should go on. I'm breathing easy trying to take it all in.

"You're such a hard worker. You are the best cook I've ever met. You are the best friend I've ever had."

"We friends?" I ask instead of saying thank you. When she don't answer, I add, looking at 'a in the eyes and watching how she shrink, lie to 'aself, and try to lie to me. "I think we more than friends." I interlace our fingers, and pull 'a hand to my heart.

"Well, I don't know what we are, there are no words for us." She doesn't duck the question this time. Instead, she scoot closer, take 'a hand and wrap 'a arm round me and get quiet. "I know we more than friends," she resolve, and I feel how uncomfortable it make 'a. For some reason, the same thing make 'a uneasy give me peace.

Iain never knowed nobody talk much as Coley do. My daddy use to say, you can tell a man by his actions, so he ain never been one for words. My family nem ain never really said how they felt bout nothing. My daddy ain never said he loved us, or my mama that I can remember. If somebody try to talk about how they feel or what they need, my daddy start speaking over them.

Men don't seem to talk about nothing at all, especially not among they women. They don't want to upset 'em or worry 'em. That's why women don't find out they husbands behind on the taxes for years, after they been round here buying new curtains every other season. Most I've ever heard men say, is they miss their wives cooking or help when they're away or just had a baby.

Ella be the first person in our family, I know, to talk about how she feel. Ella use to sing while she was doing 'a chores, too. She was always singing, always happy. When she left, she took feelings and singing with her.

Sometimes she would talk about how she loved 'a some Prentice. She be saying how his eyes smile, and how he look gentle and kind. She be talking bout how his whole body listen when she talk. Least that's what she use to tell me while she be folding laundry, or cleaning up, and I be following 'a round.

There were church songs she knew she'd sing. Ella has a beautiful deep rich voice. Most times she be making songs up. There was a bread-baking song, a cooking song bout how hot it was, and a song bout how dusty it always was, no matter how much we swept.

Ella was the only person ever told me I was any good. She use to tell me I was a good child. Use to say, she had never seen a person with such an old spirit. She was the one person in the house use to always tell me I was smart. She be combing my hair and talking bout how easy it was, and that she wished she had hair like mine. What'n like Coley wishing she had my hair, it felt different. She didn't want my hair for nobody else but for 'a own life, to get it done easier.

Ella would call me her lil baby. Her arms are the ones I remember more than Mama's. I remember my small hand in hers. I remember her telling people how to treat me, and how to treat her. She knew 'a mind early in life, and has always been a fair one. Even in arguments, upset or hurt Ella can see what's right and do it, too.

When people talk about being Godly, I be thinking Ella who they be talking bout. She be the one who told me I need to think about what I'm saying to people, and to consider what other folks going through. Iain saying she ain never whup my tail, but she be feeling bad any time she had to whup any of us. Ella be eleven years older than me, and she before 'a time, too. Ella got married old some folks say; I was almost nine when she got married.

"Why you don't ever say anything, Linny?" Coley get up on 'a elbows reminding me to talk, trying to force me to talk.

In the dark, the fireplace lighting 'a face makes 'a look like a angel, but when she smile full and big, her lips let me know she's a woman. I just stare at 'a, until she lays down.

Lately, I don't ever respond to 'a prying when it's late like this. All that talking ain never helped nothing. I think about all the people I know, how we be silent for hours and just be together. Words ain always needed. Still I like to hear what Coley got to say.

When it gets late, she be talking crazy, might say anything. One night she told me how she gets fevered and aches inside of 'aself. Even said that's why she wants a husband so he can sooth 'a.

Coley know a little bit about everything. She the only other person I ever met who read all the time, and ain afraid to tell you what she think. She like to discuss ideas and things, that ain't gone change nothing. She like to debate and get 'aself all worked up, like whatever solution we come up with gone mean something. She say we got to change our thinking before we can change our circumstance.

Not if you starving, I once told 'a. Iain never knew a man could think on an empty stomach, much less think hisself up some food. She got so mad, and kept waking me up to explain how that wasn't what she was trying to say. We have very different ways of looking at the world, still it's nice to hear somebody else's thoughts.

She be coming in the room almost every night and laying down with me. We sometimes talk til we fall asleep. Other times she just climb in the bed with me, ball up with a pillow and doze right off. This kind of remind me of how it use to be when me and my sisters use to sleep together, but its different cause we ain't family and the energy ain't the same.

Even though we both women, she ain getting dressed in front of me. And I cain't say I feel comfortable being naked in front of 'a neither. I be feeling shy bout the littlest things now. Iain never had no sister of mine knock on no door neither. Coley be coming to my door asking, "Is you decent?"

Chapter Thirty-One

The soup get heavy in my stomach, so I swallow slow. Iain wont to know it was true, but then again it is, and ain nothing more than what it is. Now I got to do something. I look over at Coley, who always oblivious to everything going on around 'a. She smile at me, and I don't even have the spirit to smile back. Cain't make no kinda face really. My mood changed. I think, I can at least finish my supper fore I get into it.

"Linny," Coley say, grabbing my arm. "You okay?"

"Nah, I ain't," seem to come out too hard, and it's all the breath I got to push out. "I'm tired of fighting, tired of being alone, tired of having to take stands. Tired of having to explain myself, or apologize, or excuse myself. I'm tired of having to beg people to respect me, and treat me with a little human decency. I keep asking myself what I done to deserve all this."

Lost, Coley don't even respond. She just look over at Mrs. Clara across the room, like maybe she can help. After we sitting awhile, and Mrs. Clara walk by, Coley say, "Mrs. Clara? I think something's wrong."

"Ain't got no fever." Mrs. Clara touch my head with the back of 'a hand, and stare in my face and eyes with real concern.

"What do I owe you for the meal?" I ask Mrs. Clara, scooting back from the table and smiling sadly at 'a. "I didn't wont no attention, that's why I was staying in the house in the first place," I remind Coley.

I don't want people looking at me. I think I'm mad everybody knew my daddy what'n my daddy but me. I feel like people owed it to me to tell me, somebody owed it to me to say something. Now I got to deal with all this other family stuff. Now that Cassius Remington ain even my daddy, Iain really even Miemay granddaughter. I shouldn't be receiving none of these things. Then again, Miemay knew she what'n my grandmama, too, and she ain never tell me, and she left me all these things. Making matters worse, I got to deal with this store business, alone.

"I wouldn't never take no money from you. We business partners. I knowed your grandma forever in a day, honey. She asked me to look after yah when she gone."

Mrs. Clara's words push in my thoughts. Knowing Miemay done charged 'a with taking care of me, make me smile. It warms my heart and breaks it at the same time. I miss being taken care of. My spirit is kissed and moved at the thought of Miemay preparing a way, and leaving a place for me even in 'a dying. Clearing my throat, I ask, "You said business been real good?"

"Yes, honey. This railroad, and the cars done changed everything. Shoot, with you opening that filling station round here, I don't know what to do with all the money I been taking in."

Standing, I lean on the back of the chair looking at 'a. Then I look over at Coley. "Coley, you stay here. I'm going over to the store, and I'll be back for you."

"Why can't I go?" she protest, and Mrs. Clara look at me knowing.

"You know Cousin Ernest told me business done dropped off since the boll weevil done ruined so much of the crop." I look in Mrs. Clara's eyes, waiting for 'a to challenge me or confirm him, maybe to tell me anything. The store right down the way from 'a hotel. She could tell if folks going in and out of there or not. She can tell if business slow. Just with coming in town, and seeing all the foot traffic and strangers, I know business should at least be steady.

Tasting 'a words, she look off to the side. Putting the pitcher of lemonade down on the table she rest 'a weight on one foot. "Humph," she say, counting the what for's, what if's, and maybe's.

I'm waiting to see who she is, cause I know she know what I'm asking 'a.

"I wouldn't say business been slow. Matter fact, I'd say it's been better than steady." She look me directly in my eyes, and now something got to happen.

"You been giving Ernest the store share of the hotel money?"

"Every three weeks, like always."

"Have you given him more than you use to give Miemay, or less?"

"A heap more. The store supply all the food and thangs. Then I got to give the store Miemay share. You know she help me git this thang started. Zion ain't friendly to no strangers, so what'n nobody thinking bout no hotel. Then I got the regular folks round here, the workers on the road, and the widowed men all coming to eat a meal a few days a week. I been busy. So busy I had to hire a few somebodies to help out, you know. Ion even cook no more."

I don't say nothing. The food getting sour in my stomach. I just smile as I'm letting go of the back of the chair, and trusting my own legs to hold my weight. "Guess I better get over to the store," I say, knowing I got to say something, do something.

"You can't go over there by yourself. You need a man with you," Coley say, wiping a mouth and getting up with me, like she bout to go find me one or something.

"She have to go alone, honey. It's huh business. Cain't git nobody else to speak for 'a, or they'll never respect 'a voice. She'll never respect 'a own voice. This part of being a woman, and a woman holding 'a own," Mrs. Clara say to my surprise, cause I know Miemay use to speak for her. Then she smile at me. "Go on. I'll be over there later."

Soon as I get in the road my boots seem heavy, holding tight to my calves. I look over at the store and see all the people on the porch, the people walking in and coming out. I see the men sitting outside the barbershop. I never noticed how many people were in town when I came before. Never thought about all the eyes watching what's going on, all the unfamiliar faces taking our stories back to places I don't even know.

When I walk in the store, I'm disappointed to see that Uncle Victor, the one everybody expected to get the inheritance, is here, too. He leaning on the counter picking his teeth with a blade of straw. He smile a knowing smile when he see me. His son Ernest behind the register ringing somebody up. People smile and speak, like I'm visiting somebody else's house. And to tell the truth, it don't feel like my store. Feel like we both been playing this game.

See, when I first inherited this store I shoulda came down here and fired Ernest. Or at least I shoulda worked a few days a week so I would know what was going on. But I was so upset about Miemay dying. I was upset Daddy what'n speaking to me. I was hiding cause folks was saying I had tricked 'a into giving me all 'a things, and I didn't wont to be looking at people. I was ashamed. I didn't even leave off the land cept family days to go help out on Daddy nem plot.

Then, Iain wont nobody saying I was taking over everything and trying to rule over everybody. Iain wont them to say I was full of myself cause I had all this money. I didn't wont my family to think I was trying to take nothing from them, or that I didn't trust them. So I left everything the way it was when Miemay was alive.

When the books wouldn't make sense, I'd ask Ernest bout the counts, and miraculously they started to make more sense. He would find money or stock somewhere I hadn't looked, even though I had looked. I never accused Ernest of stealing, I just balanced the books best I could and did the ordering.

Sometimes Ernest even acted like he couldn't add too well, or didn't understand how to work the weights for dry goods, or that his age was getting the best of him. He'd often say, "Maybe it's time for me to find different work, cause my mind slipping." Or while I was going over the books, he be watching over my shoulders coming back and forth saying, "I don't know why I wrote seven when it should have been a one." Or, "I don't know why I turned that nine upside down like that."

Still, I wanted to believe whatever nonsense he was doing he'd eventually stop. The truth is, he always took a lil from Miemay too, cause there were times when things ain add up for 'a either. Then they blamed it on me being young, or not understanding.

When Miemay was alive to say 'a piece, she be saying, "Linny ain't that young, and she ain't never been dumb neither." That was her way of letting 'im know she what'n completely fooled, and he would, I guess, steal less or do better hiding what was missing.

Iain never get in it. Miemay was big on taking care of family and people. She would say something like, "If you catch a man stealing, if ain nothing unreasonable, and you can do without it, let 'im have it. Specially if it's some food or something like that. People don't steal cause they bad, they steal cause they hungry, cause they need." So Iain been asking bout the books too much.

Now for some reason though, I wish I had been stronger, done something sooner, or said something. Especially cause they stealing way more from me than they ever stole from Miemay. The truth is, they taking so much it ain't even really no way to hide it, but Iain wont to fight with 'em. Plus, I been feeling guilty bout getting all Miemay money. I guess it was kind of my way of making it right in my own mind, not standing up for myself.

Now I think cause of how long I let it go, its finna be a harder fight. Even though I was thinking Ernest would stop stealing, and things would get better, and all this would blow over. I kept thinking his conscience'll get the best of 'im, and our spirits would lead us all through this disagreeable time, back together, cause we family. It's cause we family, what I got to do feel impossible.

"Good evening!" Ernest greet me smiling, but I hear the smart alecky tone, and I know he ain't sincere.

"Evening." I go to the back of the store to get the books. Soon as I look at the log, it confirms what Mrs. Harper and Mrs. Clara say true.

Still, I feel heavy, my mind weighed down by it all. I keep staring down at the books, because I don't know what to say or do. Iain never had this kind of problem with nobody. Looking up, I see Uncle Victor in the doorway. Then he go back out.

I take a pencil with me and start walking up and down the aisles, comparing what's there to what it say been sold, and what it say need to be ordered. Ernest looking uneasy; he keep adjusting his pants, and rattling his belt. I carry the ordering and sales log in my arm like it's a child.

I can already tell by what he say been bought, and how much money he turning in to me something wrong. Store ain't hardly making a profit, but the store full right now. And the money he give me just barely cover his pay, and the restock order.

Ernest greet every person coming in. I look around and the store ain been swept, things ain clean as they was when Miemay was alive. I'm hurt cause I don't expect people to hurt me on purpose. Iain expect family to treat me like this.

Looking at Ernest again I breathe easy, then go back to the store room. It's almost bare. I close the door behind me, and think. I got to fire a man twice my age, he got children with children older than me. Respect go a long way around here, but then what happens when people don't respect you and your things?

I tell myself, I gotta be clear even if he don't agree with me. I tell myself, I gotta be firm. There are no deals, or discussions. There will be no talking me out of running this store myself. I know this mean he and his family gone start going miles out to another store. I figure they gone struggle cause he ain got no job. Then again, Iain fire him, he fired hisself.

I won't feel bad for what I'm bout to do, cause all the times I been checking the books and pointing out the issues, he had chances to do things different. He decided to keep doing this hisself.

I've always been fair with him, no matter how he feel bout what I got, or how I got it. That don't have nothing to do with him being a liar. More I think about it, the more I know, it don't even make sense to try and explain why I'm taking over. He know what he done, and all I'm saying is, he cain't do it no more. I'm gone just send him home, forever, far as I'm concerned. I cain't trust 'im far as I can throw 'im.

Taking a few deep breaths, I push myself from the wooden chair, open the door and walk directly to 'im. "I'm going to take it from here," I say firm as I can without it sounding disrespectful.

"Beg pardon?" Ernest lean into the air like he cain't hear me, or like Iain speaking clear enough for him to make out the words.

"I said, don't worry about the store. I'm gone run it by myself. You can go home."

My words seem to be said from a pulpit the way they received. The whole store get quiet. I feel all eyes fall on me, on us.

"Well, I know you ain never ran nothing before," he spit, coming from round the counter. "So you don't know it's gone be hard running a store by yahself." He laugh, looking over at his father Victor, and then round at the people in the store, like we puppets at a fair being worked for they entertainment. He looking round like he getting ready to show out.

To nip this drama in the bud, I say, "I need everybody to step out of here for a minute, we need to have a little family meeting." With that I start to close the blinds, cause I know how Zion work. People be talking bout what we said to each other for months. I'll be 60 years old and they'll still be saying, "'Remember when you and Ernest was arguing in the store?'"

"What's going on, crazy lady?" Ernest tease me, laughing mean spirited, like he halfway trying to convince the people to stay, like he own the store or something. Then again, maybe he trying to convince hisself. Working at this store is a good job. It's one of the few jobs actually pays round here in cash, not crop, or barter.

"They need to leave," I say, firmer, looking at the people. Then I realize they don't know what's going on, and it ain't no reason to be any way with them. So I say calmly, "I just need a few minutes with Ernest here, then we'll be open in a few minutes." The women look at each other and one man grab his wife and they go out on the porch. This store always been a place where people just be standing round, specially visitors. I don't want to scare business away, then again where else they got to go?

"Oh, now she wont to have a family meeting," Uncle Victor add.

"Need family, to have a family meeting," Ernest say, smiling.

Soon as the last person out of the store, I close both the front doors behind them. The bell above the door dings loud in the silence. My heart is heavy and I feel a greater weight as I avoid the stares of curious eyes, while pulling the shades down behind the doors.

"Gimme yo keys, Ernest," I demand, being considerate of my tone.

"Why?" He pretend to be surprised

"Yall told me business was slow. I understand you think I owe you, and that's why you done this, but it ain't right. Just gimme the keys. Ain't no way around this."

"I'll give 'em to you, soon as you give me what you owe me."

"Ain't got no respect for 'a elders. Ion know what it is with these youngins these days," Uncle Victor say, staring in my face.

"Maybe it's cause she think she white, she can do anything she want. Or is it cause of who huh real Daddy is?" Ernest add, staring me in the eyes.

"What I owe you?" I dismiss the insults, Iain come here to exchange words with 'im.

"I done worked a week and a half. Friday would have been another pay day."

"All you done took outta here, you best get out of here fore I call the law."

"Yeah that's what I heard, you know all about the law," Ernest say.

"And lawyers," Uncle Victor jump in.

"Keys!" I put my hand out and stand firm, looking at him.

Then he drop 'em heavy in my hands with his fist, and push me out the way, going towards the counter, then the register and say, "Iain gone be fired like no thief. Ain gone go nowhere til I gits what I earned. Specially not gone give up what I's entitled to, for some poe-ass nigga done got 'a worth tricking a old woman. You ain't got a inkling what it is to do an honest day's work."

I cain't believe he done pushed me. I don't budge much as he expect, but I go into the shelves, and stuff fall over the floor. I push myself from the shelves. I follow close behind him.

He go round to the front of the register, and open it.

I jump across the counter slamming the cash drawer close.

Then Ernest howl grabbing his hand.

That's when I realize I done slammed his hand in there. When I slide back on my feet off the counter, I hear somebody coming up behind me.

Uncle Victor slap me.

Before I know it, I done hit him back with the hand holding the keys. Blood gush from his face, and he step back, staggering.

Then Ernest come round and hit me again, this time with his fist.

I reach for something to hold me, but don't get nothing and fall hard this time.

"This been a long time coming. Yo Daddy should of been done reckoned with you." Ernest shout down at me. "You ain nothing, walking round here acting like you somebody."

I breathe slow, on the ground, start to think about what I can get to hit him back. Ain't nobody gone hit me, nobody.

"Stay down!" Ernest threaten me.

My head heavy, but Iain gone let nobody take nothing from me, or treat me any kind of way. I hear the change hit the floor behind the counter, and I'm thinking Ernest hand ain't hurting that bad. My body feel heavier than I remember, but I pull my legs under me. Reaching out, I get holt to one of the shovels for sale. Then I stumble, getting it to sit right so I can use it like a cane, and get my bearing so I can stand.

When I get up, and turn around, Ernest smiling. I take that shovel, and swing it round. He think I'm going for his head, so he lean away, but I get them knees good for 'im. And when he down, I hit him on his back and then his shoulder.

"Put my money back on that counter!" I'm breathing heavy. "You ain't leaving til you both empty yah pockets."

Uncle Victor look like it's a fire in his eyes when he go help Ernest up.

"She cain't do that," Ernest argue.

So I lift the shovel and stare at 'em, like I might take they heads off.

Uncle Victor push Ernest on the counter and move at me. His face bleeding, his eye weak, but he still coming. I swing at 'im, and he back up, then I move behind the counter.

Then he pick up a shovel, too.

So I run back to the store room, and close the door behind me, just in time before the full weight of the shovel hit the door. It make a dent in the door where he hit. Field hands strong, and I know he think I'm a child that he can chastise.

I snatch the rifle off the wall, crack it and check the barrel to make sure it's loaded. Then I slide the latch and charge it to shoot. "Bang!" A little dirt fall on my head, and I realize it was one in the chamber. Still I snatch the door open and start after them.

I hear pennies, nickels and dimes hit the wood floor again, the front door bell ring like somebody coming in. When I step back in the shop, the front door is wide open, there's money all over the floor, which I suspect be all he took out the register.

I walk heavy footed to the front door, and see them falling all over each other and pulling each other to stay on they feet as they run.

"She shot at us!" Ernest holler.

I don't aim at 'em, I just hold the rifle by its charging handle, and keep the barrel aimed at the roof. People start laughing at 'em wallowing in the dirt, trying to find they footing. All while, they going on and on bout how I'm the crazy one, or how I tried to kill 'em.

I step out on the porch, and look at all the people waiting, watching, some so shocked they just stare back and the rest look in another direction. I look out at the front of the other businesses, then I shake the rifle again, discharging it.

Then Ernest, limping, start with more shouting, "We gone leave, but this ain't over! This our family business! Not Yorn! You ain't earned this! This my inheritance! This my daddy land, yella gall!"

I stand quietly on the porch and watch 'im scream. Something bout the way I look at 'im take some of his fire. Cause he start to talk lower, as I stare at him, til he silent. Then they waddle on, and I see they ain't coming back anytime soon.

Coley the only one moving towards me. Then she get all in my face, holding it with 'a hands, murmuring, "Oh my God, look at your face."

I don't say nothing, we just exchange glances, mine feel sad. I don't know how I'm seen, but she looking sad. "Mind helping me clean up this mess?" I ask.

"I don't mind," she answer, then dust me off.

"Me neither," Mrs. Clara say from the side of the porch, while pulling 'aself up on the porch where there ain't no steps, then looking out at the men run.

"Thank you." I nod my head, my heart still racing, my mouth dry. "The store is open," I say to no one in particular, then go on back in.

Chapter Thirty-Two

I stop moving to hear better. The drain gargle louder swallowing water in the tub. I think Iain really hearing nothing but Coley feet moving up over me. Then again it don't sound like feet, sound like a knock, and it's getting louder. I pull my shirt over my head quickly, step in my night pants, and wait, hoping, maybe, they'll go away.

It's so late and so much has happened early on, the night don't even seem real. Iain wanting to know who on the other side of the door. I've taken an early bath, my eyes are heavy and my heart heavier. I hear Coley creeping round upstairs. I want to ignore the knocking, don't want no more trouble for today. Somehow I'm always inviting it.

I come out of the bathroom into the darkness of the hall. The front door don't seem to be enough between me and whoever on the other side. I can hear my heart beating inside of me. My mouth dry, my throat remind me I'm breathing cause the air push hard in and out. I grab the rifle from the kitchen, and start towards the door. I expect Uncle Victor or Ernest come to settle the score.

"Linny!" A woman's voice come clear, and familiar.

"Ella?" I put the rifle down on the side of the door, and pull it open. Fore I can say another word, she grab me and hug me, crying. She taking deep breaths like she ain spect to see me at my own house. She hold me for a long time. I feel the cool of the night settle on 'a, while whatever else she be feeling lifting up off of 'a. I see 'a husband Prentice outside on they wagon.

"Oh lord, I just got word what happened at the store. You alright?" Her breath escaping 'a, and she upset, staring at my face. I'm ashamed I done got 'a all worked up like this. I don't wont 'a worried and I don't wont 'a looking at me.

"Don't hurt." I turn my face and chin out of her grip.

Then she hit the light, and cry like she seen a monster. "Oh God, Linny. This ain right, look at cho face."

"It don't hurt," I say again, firmer, and holding the door open to see if Prentice coming in, too. He lean back on the wagon, pull his hat over his eyes. He enjoying the night; he ain't coming in. I close the door not knowing what else to do.

"It's all over. Zay gone help me run the store. I got a plan, everything gone be alright. I'm more worried bout yall being out here this late, and travelling with the Klan riding." I stand between Ella and the rest of the house. I want 'a to leave fore it get too dark. She still got time to make her way back safe. "Ain't safe." I fold my arms.

"Iain the one you need to be worried about. Look at cho face," she repeat, walking around looking me over.

Just then Coley start coming down the steps, and we both look up at 'a. She beautiful, her hair up in drying braids, with hair pins holding them in place. If she had some small buds in 'a hair, it could be 'a wedding day.

"Good evening, Ms. Graham," Ella speak, nodding at Coley with a painful smile.

"Coley," she correct Ella. "Is everything alright?" she ask the question staring at me.

I'm looking at Coley like I'm waiting to take 'a hand.

"No, it ain't." Ella push pass me and go for the kitchen. "Gone make me something. Tea, coffee, something, to rest my nerves. I cain't believe all this happening." I hear Ella opening cabinets, and pots rattling. "What's this I hear bout you shooting at cho uncles, and making nem dance in front of the whole town?"

"She didn't shoot at them," Coley laugh, correcting 'a, again.

Ella don't meet 'a laughter with a smile. This all real serious, and I'm wondering if she know when Daddy coming. If he coming.

While Ella getting the tea ready, Coley telling 'a what happened at the store. I don't say much, just feel peace come over me when I see how my sister own my kitchen. I sit at the table watching Coley tell the story, watching how Ella hear it.

Coley tell a story with way more words, and moving this way and that way. I wouldn't never tell it like her, don't even think

I got it in me. Coley make me feel like she saw the fight. I'm even surprised to hear how I looked when her and Mrs. Clara finally came over.

Coley puff 'a chest up like a rooster when she say, "You should have seen her standing on that porch holding that rifle. She was so fearless, brave and strong. Her face was already showing red where it's bruised now, but everybody was already saying how she did. Linny had won." Coley pats me on my arm like she proud of me.

I don't know how long me and Ella sit in silence staring at each other, or talking bout much of nothing. Feeling like they're things need to be heard and said between us sisters and not Coley.

"Good night, Coley," I say staring in Coley eyes.

"Good night?" she smile back excited, ready to tell another story, leaning over 'a tea one way and then the other, staring back at me blowing.

"Good night," I say firmer, and Ella look down at a spot on the table and you can feel 'a closing 'aself to Coley.

"Good night," Coley accepting we asking 'a to leave more than she saying it to us, wounded, she looks back and forth between us as she gets up. Some part of me hurt how she taking it, and some part of me want to explain. Some part of me worried after Ella leave tonight, Coley won't come to my bed.

I don't realize I'm staring at Coley leaving til Ella say, "I'm still here," leaning into the table. Ella eyes so serious, she don't flinch and I feel like I'm in trouble. "You sure seem different. Yo spirit mighty high, considering." Ella voice heavy, grave.

"I don't feel no difference."

"Yah daddy ain't cho daddy. Miemay ain't cho great grandmama, she done gave you alllll the family money, and land. Which if someone wanted to press it, you ain even 'a great granddaughter so you ain't got no blood claim on nothing. Then, way the story being told, you shot off at them in that store. Iain saying who wrong or right, but I cain't see how you still smiling. How is you smiling?"

"You want me to be sad?"

"Iain saying what I want, I'm saying this ain't the Linny I know. You ain't never been this high spirited. I see it all in yo face. What I wont to know is, who making you all high spirited?" She smile and do this little wiggle over 'a tea.

"What foolishness you talking?" I get up from the table, taking up our tea cups and filling them again.

"Naw, don't run from the question. You got the look of love. What's his name?" She sing the last question.

Shaking my head, dismissing 'a, I fill our cups again. Then I hear Coley feet moving above me in 'a room, that do something to me. I'm looking forward to laying next to 'a, and holding 'a all night. "You best get out of here and get home. Its late and we all gotta early morning."

"First tell me, what you smiling for?" Ella trying to follow my thoughts.

I shake my head no, like it ain't nothing, cause I know I cain't tell 'a this. I want to tell somebody, but it ain't safe. Just then I realize how I cain't hold Coley hand, or take 'a nowhere. I think about how much I want to tell the world how I'm feeling, but I cain't even tell Coley how I feel. It'd scare her, and the thought of 'a leaving scare me.

Ella use to always say I was the only one could keep a secret. She use to tease, I would keep a secret from even myself, and that be dangerous, make life hard. Things don't feel real til you tell somebody. She told me she was in love with Prentice fore she told him. She told me the first time he told 'a he loved 'a, and the first time she felt loved.

I remember where I was when Ella man asked 'a to marry him. Even though she knew he would, it didn't stop 'a from crying—she was so happy. Knowing he loved 'a didn't change how much it moved 'a to walk down that aisle, and let the whole world know she was his wife, and he was her husband. Knowing didn't stop Ella from beaming from 'a soul, the day they turned around at the alter to face all of Zion, and The Reverend introduced them as one.

"I know that look. Ooh, I know that look, I know that look," Ella keep pressing me, taking a deep sip of 'a tea. "Who is it? You gone tell me his name?"

Not a word.

"I can tell your spirits lifted, and you filled with something. You know I can keep a secret."

"I can, too," I smile losing the fight to stay serious. My voice sound harsher than I mean, and what I've said seem to hurt 'a. That hurt me but I cain't spare 'a this time. She wouldn't understand, and I don't know the words to explain. Don't think it can be explained.

"First, I blamed Mama for, not treating you right, I guess. Even if she had her reasons. Then I blamed Miemay, for making you so headstrong. I blamed Miemay for having you wear pants. I blamed Miemay for letting you birth babies with 'a before you had cho own. If Ida seen a baby born fore I had my own, Ida probly been scared of men and gitting married, too. Then again, children part of life. Pain part of life, too. My children make me a different woman. Children are a blessing.

"Then I blamed Daddy, for raising you like your brothers. I even made him feel guilty. I told 'im he needed to start leaving you at home with Mama, to help with Grit. Told 'im you needed to focus on women duties, wife duties."

"I thought Mama told Daddy that." I'm thinking out loud.

"I said it so much, Mama probly did say it a few times 'aself."

"After Miemay told me how bad Mama was beating you, I blamed myself for not taking you with me when I left. Every girl needs a mother, and every woman needs a husband."

"What are you talking about? You cain't blame yourself for nothing that happened here today. You didn't steal from me, or hit me, and you didn't abandon me. I'm not your child. I'm your sister."

"But you needed me, you needed somebody. I thought if I stopped speaking to you when Daddy did, you would stop being so headstrong and git married. Sumner Harper is a good man, and he would take good care of you."

I start to stir, looking at 'a, refusing to accept anything she saying now.

She go on, "He's handsome. A lot of women like him, but he's only got eyes for you. He well mannered, he owns his own land."

"I'm not listening to no more of this."

"If you had a man to speak for you, none of this woulda happened today," she say loud, firm and steady over anything she think I might say back.

"Miemay ain't never needed a man to speak for her. And you don't need one to speak for you, Ella. Seem like to me, you running Prentice."

Grinning, Ella try to explain. "A man who loves his wife lets 'a have 'a way, long as he gitting what he wont."

Frowning at 'a teasing, I grab my cup. "I don't want to hear bout you giving Prentice what he wont."

Laughing harder, Ella touch my arm to hold me there at the table, and keep my attention. "Iain talking bout that. I mean, I recognize and respect him as the head of the house. I git his say on things. Even if I know he ain gone care, I make sure he feel he part of everything, and we a team. I make sure I come to him about everything, sometimes." She bow 'a head smiling, like she don't even believe what she bout to say, "He do say no."

"When was the last time Prentice said no, Ella?"

"That ain't the point. I always ask. He the person who speak to other men on behalf of our family. Men, they speak they own language. You ever seen them haggle over the price of something? They be talking in a tone and saying things be fighting words for women."

"Ella, getting married is the last thing on my mind. In fact, it ain't on my mind at all." I sip the tea, and start thinking I want something tastier. Some coffee with the works would be good, but I don't feel like mixing all that. I just want to get off this conversation, where she telling me I should find me a husband before I get too old. Or where she tell me I need a man to stand up for me.

"You been saying that too long. I thought after Norma Jean got married you would, too, but you still ain't."

Norma Jean's name, here in my house, make me sit up in the chair, and look at Ella intensely for the first time.

"I know about Norma Jean," she say, looking at me firm. "I've known for years. I told Miemay yall didn't need to be spending the night together. Miemay said you were girls, best friends, and everybody needed somebody.

"Norma Jean was running round saying she what'n never gitting married. Cause she's two years older than you, I thought she was putting them thoughts in yo head. I blamed Norma Jean for you not taking Sumner Harper more serious."

"Ella, what are you talking about?"

"Linny, I know." She get sad and the mood change.

My spirit get heavy. It feel like to get a word out you got to pull a wagon out the way.

"I blamed Norma Jean cause she was so wild, and you ain have nobody else to show you the right way. I even thought if she got married to Dexter, you would change. I thought you would see how she became a wife and a mother, then you'd see you have to grow up, too."

"I am grown." I put the tea down and stare in Ella eyes. "And I'm tired of you and Mama acting like having a husband, doing it, and having babies is what makes a woman a woman. That's your dream, ain't mine, ain't never been mine."

Ella take the news hard, and 'a eyes get full of tears. Not enough to fall, but enough it hurt me, that I hurt 'a enough to cry. Still it's the truth, and she got to get use to it, and stop trying to force me to do things I don't wanna do.

"Since I thought Norma Jean was making you how you was, I told 'a I was gone tell 'a mama what yall was doing. Liking each other the way you should be liking men."

"What?" Something make me shake my head no, and I'm already to tell 'a it's a lie.

"Norma Jean was going round saying she loved you. It was just a matter of time fore people started talking."

"She did? Norma Jean and me ain't never talked about loving each other."

"I thought yall was close cause of all yall was going through. Still, something had to change. I told Norma Jean I was gone tell 'a folks that yall ain't need to be friends no more. That's when she told me that 'a step Daddy was touching 'a. You know that boy Dexter loved Norma Jean so much, he married 'a even though that first baby what'n none of his. She thought, whenever you found out she was pregnant you'd be done with 'a anyways."

I'm silent and hurt Norma Jean didn't know me better. I'm sad she didn't trust me more with 'a heart. I must look angry cause when I look up at Ella she start trying to explain.

"I wanted what was best for you Linny. You my sister, and my main concern. So I told 'a ain't nobody gone believe 'a step daddy did that. I told 'a it would ruin 'a family, and make 'a mama look bad. I asked 'a what would happen to 'a other sisters and brothers if 'a step daddy was killed? How would 'a mama take care of them? I told 'a every woman needs a man. I told 'a Dexter was a good man."

We silent for a long while, my mind still trying to make sense of it all. When she say, "I'm the one told Dexter someone raped Norma Jean, I didn't say who, and I asked Dexter to marry 'a fore she started showing. Her and Dexter hadn't even been together when she told you she was pregnant."

Shaking my head no, my head start to feel heavy and I'm angry. "You didn't have no business getting in between me and Norma Jean." I feel a sadness and a new wound opening.

I think about how me and Norma Jean was. I think about Norma Jean not telling me what was really going on. I think about all the nights when I held 'a while she cried 'aself to sleep. I feel bad, Iain recognize she was crying like Miemay cried over being raped at times. And whenever I'd ask Norma Jean why she was so upset, she'd just pull me closer, pull my arms around 'a tight, always saying it what'n nothing.

"What would that have looked like in Zion? Her having a baby for 'a daddy? People would have looked at 'a different. Somehow she would have had to pay for it."

I still don't know what to say, I just keep looking at Ella sitting across the table from me, like this the first time I ever seen 'a before. Then she look back at me, like what she did was right.

"Miemay told me you said you ain't wont no husband. I hoped when Daddy quit speaking to yah you'd break and give all this up. Hoped you'd git married like Norma Jean. You cain't live like this forever." Ella try to excuse what she done.

"Who says?" I'm so angry I'm not afraid to tell the truth.

"Every woman needs a man. Only a fool of a woman thinks different."

"Well, I must be a fool," I admit and stare at 'a, then stand. "Good night, Ella. I want you to leave."

"Norma Jean married now. She got kids, and she got a husband crazy bout 'a. If you just say the word, you and Sumner Harper could be married, too. Then yall would have two houses and all this land between you."

"Stop talking, Ella."

"Hmph," Ella stare at me sliding from under the table, and then leaning on it to help 'aself up.

I realize she getting older, and moving tired. She always was older than 'a age.

"I'm gone leave, cause you right, it is late. But I wont you to know Iain done with this. Something got you going, and I'm gone know what it is. I'm yo sister, I helped raised you and I know when something up. You ain smiled this much since-" she stop and think.

Standing, pulling 'a wrap off the back of the chair, and starting towards the door. Then she say, "I cain't say I ever remember you smiling this much, or seeming to feel this good. You always be walking round quiet, small, like you trying to git around without being noticed. Now, seem you got some other reason to live, and I'm gone figure out what his name is."

"I promise it ain't no 'he' got me acting no kinda way," I say pulling the door open and finding Prentice still on his wagon, with his hat pulled down over his eyes. He probly sleeping.

"Ain't no he," she say back to 'aself thinking.

I'm doing everything but pushing 'a out the door. "Thank you for bringing 'a," I call out heavy hearted to Prentice, and he get up, and start moving, getting the horses ready to pull off.

"I don't think you felt this good then, but the last time I seen you smile like you did tonight, was when you was best friends with Norma Jean, fore she got married."

"Good night, Mariella. Go getcho self some rest." I'm ushering 'a off the porch.

"Maybe we should spend the night. I left the kids with Prentice mama nem. It might be too late to travel," Ella tease trying to soften the mood.

"Nah, you cain't stay the night here." I got my hand on Ella back, lightly pushing 'a on 'a way. "We going to bed," come out wrong, and I feel it soon as I say it.

Ella get like a tree rooted on my porch. I feel 'a standing strong against my nudging. Then I stop pushing 'a, and she go on without another word.

Chapter Thirty-Three

I'm laying in the dark thinking bout Norma Jean, her step daddy and the baby. He should have to pay for what he done. Life would be so different for me and Norma Jean, if I knew sooner. Then I remember she got four kids now, and a husband. I remember Norma Jean saying it be best if we don't meet no more. I remember 'a saying she had to make decisions for 'a family now, and she wished things were different. I'm thinking bout Ella saying she know bout me.

I'm wondering bout Coley, if she sleep yet. I never ask 'a to come in here, but I miss 'a on the nights when she don't. Some nights she just crawl in bed with me after I've fallen off to sleep, and bury 'a face in my back. Something changing but I try not to think about it too much. I try not to be different with 'a. I know ain't no woman like Coley gone look at me twice, and I don't want 'a to leave me on bad terms.

I want to go knock on Coley's door, tell 'a me and Ella just needed a little time together, to say good night. I wont to apologize if I've hurt 'a feelings. Then again, some part of me feel like a man, like I'd be doing too much, knocking on a lady's door this time of night. I think I'd be intruding, maybe even scare 'a by anything I say, anything I do. I don't wont things to change. Don't wont 'a to start feeling no kinda way.

"Linny? You decent?" Coley voice surprise me and pull me out my head.

I sit right up, relieved she came. Then I'm afraid to show 'a I been waiting. So I lay down and decide to pretend like I'm sleep. Trying to make my voice deep and sleepy sounding, I say, "I'm in the bed. Is everything okay?"

"I'm fine," she say, then there's this long silence. I can feel 'a outside my door waiting, and I'm waiting, too.

"You coming in?"

She answer by opening the door. I can see 'a smiling as she walks to the bed, her head covered in a flowery colored silk scarf. Soon as she climbs in bed with me, I pull 'a close.

"I'm sorry about earlier, me and Ella just needed a minute."

She put 'a hand on my stomach, snuggling in closer to me. "It's okay, I understand. My family and I have our things we have to talk about, too, just amongst ourselves. Just sometimes, I feel like you and I are so close, and we talk so much, I can't imagine there's anything you couldn't share with me."

"There ain't," I say, half way expecting 'a to ask me what we talked about, but she don't. Ain't nothing to tell no way. We lay silent. I'm relieved that she came. After this long day, all I could think about was sleeping with 'a in my arms.

"I'm really proud of how you handled those men today and the way you stood up to them."

"I should have done something sooner."

"Everything happens in its time, the way it's suppose to. I mean, women don't tell the men in their family, especially not their elders, what they are and aren't going to do.

"You refused to let them intimidate you and took your store back. I don't think I would have had the nerve to fight back like you did. You should have seen yourself, standing there on that porch with that rifle, your hair in French braids. You looked so beautiful, and fierce," she ends all dreamy.

"You don't know what you might do if pushed." I think about all Coley done did in 'a life so far. I think about 'a being here now, a woman, travelling alone to live in a place she ain never been. Then I think about all the women in my life, Mama, and Miemay, and Ella, and Grit, Coley and me, our lives. Who we is, how we is and say, "A lot of times we stronger than we think."

"You think so?" Coley runs 'a hands over my stomach again. Everywhere she rub, feel like she stirring a pot of cold water over a fire, waiting for seasoning and vegetables and maybe some meat to become a good stew. Where 'a hand stop, be the fire right under the center of the pot, and the heat start to build right there.

"I do." I feel like all the bubbles sticking to the side of the pot getting ready to boil. The heat of 'a body next to mine making it unbearable to rest. I'm moving around trying to get some peace.

Then I feel 'a hand on my face, and its calming. She stroking my face, and I feel like I can see 'a looking at me in the dark. Don't know what possess me but I scoot closer to 'a, pull 'a so close, it's too close.

I pull 'a scarf off, and put my hands in 'a hair, rub a scalp with my fingers. She moan a little, so I kiss 'a forehead. Holding 'a so close, kneading 'a head like I would dough, making my heart race. She relax and let 'a head go with my fingers. I start to feel sore in the place I sometimes have to touch and sooth myself.

She hold on to me, and I can feel 'a lips just a ways from mine. I kiss 'a forehead again, then 'a nose, and then 'a lips. Just a little peck first. Then she moan and kiss me back. We kiss each other back and forth, and I'm starting to ache more in that place, and my nipples in knots. Feel like she breathing life into me, and I want more of 'a. So I put my hand under the cover, find the end of 'a gown and run my hands over her knee. Then she moan again, like she hungry and the food real good. Then I feel 'a hand running over my titties.

"Mmm," she moans.

I tell God if I'm dreaming, don't let that damn rooster crow. I run my hands over 'a nipples. She start to wiggle round like she on fire, too. I start to kiss 'a deeply. I want to taste 'a, put my tongue in every part of 'a. She bite my lip gently and I bite back, close my eyes and inhale the scent of the lavender soap, and the moment. Rubbing my hands over 'a titties, and over 'a stomach, I want to touch 'a like I touch myself.

Sliding my hands down in 'a bloomers, I rub over the hair there. She opens 'a legs to me, but 'a bloomers in the way. So I get on my knees, pull the covers back, snatch 'em down, then off.

"Wait," she whisper in the dark. "I've never done this before with a woman."

277

"Iain never did this with nobody." I'm scared she gone tell me to stop.

We still for a while, her laying down looking up at me, maybe thinking bout what she doing. I don't want 'a to do too much thinking. So I rub 'a stomach, and she put 'a hands on top of my hand. I lay back down beside 'a, and kiss 'a. Kiss 'a deep like my life depend on it, cause it feel like it do. She kiss back, and seem to relax.

I rub 'a hair down there again, and feel a little bit of 'a wetness on my hand. With my fingers, gently, I part 'a lips, and feel for where the wetness coming from. She moans pushing it at me, clinching my shoulder, pulling me and kissing me deeper. Gently, I stroke wetness til she start to move 'a hips so my hands find where she wont me. I touch 'a like I touch myself, gentler though. I make gentle circles in 'a wetness, and she dance with my hand.

"Harder," she whisper so I push down firmer. Then I straddle 'a leg, and move with 'a. Start to feel something rising tween my legs, too. We moving under the covers, and she moaning, then I'm out of breath when she say, "Ummm," clinching my wrist and start shaking all over. I feel 'a body extra wet, and I feel like she on a cloud slowly coming down.

I'm holding 'a close, but I can feel my heart beat painfully between my legs. So I know I got to go in the bathroom, or somewhere to relieve myself. I kiss 'a then pull away.

"Where are you going?" She holding on.

I start to say something, but stop, realizing I'm too shamed to admit I touch myself. I just look at 'a for a minute. So instead I say, "I need to go put some cold water on me, cause I'm," I stop, looking for the words and just let go of whatever come out my mouth, "I need something, too."

"Take off your bloomers and come here then." Her voice sound like scoops of warm cobbler.

"You sure?" I definitely don't want 'a to take it back.

I can hear 'a nodding 'a head yes in the dark.

So I start to pull my bloomers down. When they off and she go to touch me, I realize I ain't ready for all that. I think

I want to feel 'a leg again, now ain't nothing between us. So I straddle 'a leg, smearing my wetness on 'a. She move with me, and we kiss. Then some kind of way, she up against my leg and we both moving.

Fore I know it, the pain tween my legs start to get big and feel good, better than what I do to myself. Fore I know it, I cain't move in time, and the feeling anchoring me, pulling me away from myself. Then the soreness spread good all through my body. I bury my face in 'a neck while the feeling burying itself in me, and she holding on, still moving 'a hips, making it deeper.

Chapter Thirty-Four

The morning come like it always do, but today it's different. Yesterday I was laying in the bed with the woman who was staying with me. We were friends who were close, and she would one day go away and get married. She is beautiful, smart, college bred, she's seen more than just Zion, she reads all the time, and she was impossible.

Last night feels like a dream I had a lifetime ago. This morning, I know I what'n never dreaming. Here she is next to me, her arms wrapped round my body, her head just above my titties.

The roosters' crowing is a reminder that I'm alive and this is my life.

I get up, knowing she ain't sleep, but I don't say anything, I feel different. I get ready to bathe. I feel like I can smell 'a all over me. I get the fires started, and put some water on upstairs and downstairs. Then I go out and feed the animals while it boils. I think about the mornings Mama and Daddy nem was bathing, after they had bathed that night. I'm learning things bout things I already knew and didn't know.

I remember asking Mama why she bathing again in the morning, and getting 'aself all hot in the cool of the morning. She'd tell me I ask too many questions and worry bout the wrong things. Now I know.

I hear the men joking with one another bout how they fresh out of a morning bath. Sometimes them same men be teased when they ain't had they morning bath. All the old men say the morning baths gone get far and few between. I see how them words lay heavy on a young man, make him quiet and into whatever his hands doing while he thinking bout it.

I remember all the times men done got mad and jumped bad, after they kept saying something bout him taking baths at night, and being tucked in with the kids. I thought they was saying he what'n no man, and his wife was running the

281

house. What those men was really saying is the man what'n getting none, but as a virgin, Iain get it. They use to cut up so, sometimes I'd be laughing, and didn't even know what I was laughing at. Now I know.

When I come in from feeding the hens, Coley scare me standing in the hallway, right in front of the back door, fixing 'a robe around 'a naked body.

"Morning," she offers more than says, and it's awkward. The space between us feel like its threatening to push us closer together, or rip us apart.

I say, "I put some water on for us. I'll bathe down here."

For the first time she ain got nothing to say. She just watch me. I don't really know 'a right now. She ain't the Coley of words, and feelings, she is the Coley of silence.

"You okay," I ask nervous she gone leave me.

"I'm okay." She speaking high and loud, giving that fake laugh when ain't nothing funny, and she uneasy. I don't look at 'a, I go on about the morning chores. I start us some grits down low and do what I say, bathe.

Breakfast is silent, except for the silverware clacking against plates, spoons in bowls, and our cups being lifted and placed on the wood table. Seem like we making more noise to drown out the silence. There is so much to talk about, and I've gotten use to talking to Coley bout anything. Now, this big thing done happened, and there ain't no words.

For the first time I have so many questions I want to ask her, but I'm afraid of the answers. I try telling myself, "We'll just see what happens," like I always do. For the first time, that don't change nothing, it don't sooth my soul or stop me from wondering. I want 'a to tell me how she feels, but she doesn't look at me, and I don't look at her.

"You plan to leave," just escapes me, and I stare at 'a watching 'a squirm under my gaze, but I cain't look away. I feel how uncomfortable I'm making 'a. I'm uncomfortable making 'a uncomfortable, but I have to know.

I want to see if she lie to me, cause she too afraid to tell me the truth. I'll feel it. Breakfast sitting on my stomach heavy and nasty, like I had too much oil. Iain even hungry my nerves so bad, but I eat cause there ain't nothing else I can think to do.

"I didn't say I was leaving." She clear 'a throat, not meeting my eyes, pushing food around on 'a plate in the real proper way that she does. She is what we call a cultured woman round here.

"You afraid?" I ask gentler, still not relieved, trying to breathe easy, cause I am overwhelmed by my feelings, and they be the reason Norma Jean had to finally cut all our ties.

Truth is, I didn't just let Norma Jean go when she told me she was pregnant. I begged her not to leave me. I promised her, I would accept whatever she had left, after she satisfied her wifely duties. I told 'a my truth. Iain never think I'd have a woman of my own, but the way she made me feel gave me hope she could be all mine.

Soon as Norma Jean agreed we'd keep on doing whatever we was doing, I changed. Maybe I found out better who I am. The first time Dexter came calling for Norma Jean, I knew a day would come when I might have to share. I thought I was prepared for that day.

When I said I would be satisfied with whatever Norma Jean could give, I believed what I was saying. Norma Jean was pregnant, planning a wedding, packing to move to another town, and entertaining Dexter's family. Now I know . . . She was also dealing with being raped, and marrying a man she couldn't have loved. She needed my support and understanding. I needed her assurance. I didn't know I was starving. All she could give me was crumbs.

I became somebody Iain even know. At first I was so mad, sometimes I couldn't stand it. I couldn't eat or sleep. I was anxious. Felt like my skin was too heavy for my bones. Then I realized I what'n mad at all. I was hurt. I was devastated.

I started showing up without being expected. I was jealous. I acted out. I was possessive of her in front of Dexter. I was mean to 'a while she was planning 'a wedding. I was sad all the time and bringing 'a down. Then one day after I showed up without being expected, Norma Jean said I scared 'a. She said she was tired. That's when she told me I was no longer welcome.

Some part of me is afraid of how unpredictable I am when it comes to my heart. Me and Norma Jean ain't never get this far. Iain never felt about Norma Jean how strongly I feel for Coley. I feel so much for Coley I'm scared of myself.

Every time I see Norma Jean I remember that our kind of love was impossible. Now it feels like I'm there again, in that place where love is impossible.

"What would I be afraid of?" Coley ask sincere, putting just a bite of food in 'a mouth and then looking at me.

"Me." My heart breaks for some reason when I say it. I wait for my voice, sound and breathing, and my heart to beat on time. "I would never hurt you, never," I promise 'a. I feel like there's something I need to say to 'a, but I don't know what that is. I'm searching for the right words, reaching. Iain got nothing. Feel like I'm pleading for 'a to stay and offering to help 'a pack.

"It's okay." She touch my hand.

I feel so open and raw. I feel the way I did when I realized what'n nothing I could do to please Mama. I breathe slow, not too deep, cause there be tears in the pit of my chest, too much air'll push out. I cain't move. My hand feel numb to 'a touch.

Her chair sound like a low horn dragging over the wood floors as she scoots back. Then she get up from 'a seat and push 'a plate across the table beside mine.

My chest feel heavy like a weight laying on it.

Then she scoot 'a chair as close to mine as possible, looking in my eyes, and she kiss me a little on my cheek, like she testing to see if it's okay.

I turn around but I cain't even look 'a in the eyes, I feel anchored, and weak.

Then she kisses me on the lips. She kisses me again, and again, soft, slow, gentle, just little kisses, and it's like she teaching me to breathe.

When I can move, and I realize she here, her kisses make me sad, make me frown, but I kiss 'a back. Then I kiss her, like I'm on top of her, and she moaning and calling my name the way she did last night.

I feel like a child I wont 'a so much. My need of 'a is too big for 'a to fill, even having 'a here right now. My want of her, makes me impatient for just a little bit more. I feel how close I am to the edge. I know it could break me if she decide to just stand, and walk away.

If she decides to leave, though broken, I will silently help 'a pack, get the door, and even take 'a to where she feels safe.

All while I was bathing I was trying to prepare myself for letting go, but now she saying she will stay.

"Linny?" Coley rubbing my hand.

I realize I'm gripping the spoon needing something I can hold on to now.

She eases 'a fingers into my hand, prying the spoon out of my grip, and kisses me again and again. We kissing deep. The lights are on, the sun is up, we are dressed and we are preparing to go out into the world, but we're kissing, deep kissing.

Fore I know anything I done grabbed 'a up, and laid 'a across the table. I'm pushing things on the floor. The kissing isn't soothing me, isn't easing the feeling of losing 'a even while she promising to stay. There's a hole in my spirit I'm trying to pull 'a into.

"Linny," she moans in my mouth between kisses, wrapping 'a legs around me.

I pull 'a dress up, stick my tongue in 'a mouth, and kiss 'a deep. Moving 'a under clothes to the side, I search for 'a bloom, and she already wet, blossoming and 'a hips moving against my hand, she asking for more. I'm rubbing 'a the way I rub myself, the way I rubbed 'a last night. I climb on top of the table. I need to be rougher, but I don't want to hurt 'a. Somehow my fingers slide inside of her. Then she moan loud and frown, and sit up like a light house on the edge of the sea.

"Iain hurting you am I?"

"Um," she bites 'a lips. "You feel so good." She moans and whimpers a little like she crying. Then kissing me hungry, she start to jerk and move round, and I hold on to 'a from inside so I can stay with 'a. "Um!" She rides my hand, and I cain't believe I'm inside of 'a.

Chapter Thirty-Five

"What now?" I sit up to see if I can make out who coming, when I see and hear the automobile on my road. After yesterday, I'm on edge expecting something else to happen. The day done, and I was gone sit here reading til last light. Soon as I recognize the driver I put my book down and stand to receive 'em.

"Good evening, Madelyn!" Ms. Diamond Beaumont say, after Grover open 'a door and help 'a out, like I been working for 'a my whole life. Funny how white folks go around treating all us niggas like they own us, like they run the world we in. Whether they know a thing about us or not.

"Evenin," I say and get my bearings by finding a spot on the ground, and putting my hands in my pants pocket. Ion like talking to white folks. Never know how far ya words gone go. Wont to know why she here, but I cain't question 'a. I look out at Grover once he get back behind the wheel. He turn his face away from me, even if he know something, he cain't tell me nothing now.

I finally find the words. "How can I help you, Misses?" My voice come out too loud, too clear to me.

"I came," she say like she still figuring it out for 'aself. "I came," she start again, this time walking up to the porch.

It feel wrong, me being up on the porch while she on the ground below me, speaking. I have to look away from 'a, to keep from making eye contact with 'a where she standing.

"Being an only child and all, I've been quite pleased to learn I have a sister, whether she niggra or not." She coming up on the porch, changing the tables, probly feeling how wrong it is for a nigga to be above 'a, and for 'a to have to look up to one.

Then she start examining me all while she stepping closer, gauging how I'm buying what she selling. "And every since I saw you, and how much we look alike, you can imagine I'm as curious about you as I know you must be about me. Bet you sit around thinking about how much we look alike all the time," she say, smiling.

"Iain thought no more on us," I say truthfully.

Mostly what I been thinking bout is her daddy raping my mama. Mostly I been thinking bout how much I hate looking like Hunter Beaumont. Mostly I been sad, thinking bout how I remind Mama of what happened to 'a every time she look at me. But I cain't say none of what's really on my mind, it'd be disrespectful. Maybe she'll run tell 'a daddy, and he'll hang me and all my family.

Nigga women don't mean nothing to white men, but a way to sooth they self when they wife won't. Been that way since slavery and ain't nothing changed. Cept he cain't keep 'a in no house off to hisself, and come and go as he please. He got to rape the help he paying. Got to threaten 'a husband. Got to pretend like he don't know why some nigga got his eyes.

"Oh, come on now, girl. You don't have to lie to me. Looking almost white makes life better for your kind. All the niggas I've ever seen your color, glad they were spared from that black skin."

"I wish I looked like my daddy, the real one who raised me."

"You ungrateful wench. I bet these strong boys round here lining up to plow your fields."

"I don't know bout the boys round here, but I know every time my mama look at me she remember."

"Remember what?" She step so close to me, she push me. It's a dare more than a question.

I step back, looking off to the side and behind me. Not a word.

"What's wrong with your face, girl?" She seem shocked all of a sudden. "Word is, you down here fighting, shooting at people and carrying on. Daddy done sent me to find out what's going on. He say he ain't never knowed you to be in no trouble. You're a good girl."

"It was a family matter, and it's been handled."

"Somebody should call the law. They should be punished for hurting her." Coley come through the screen door staring at us.

Diamond look at Coley good. Coley ain't got the good sense to look down. She stare right back at Ms. Beaumont, like she a white woman 'aself.

"Be quiet, Coley," I warn.

"Well, good evening!" Ms. Beaumont put 'a hands on 'a hips and smile at Coley, hanging bees with honey. I think she was expecting me to do what Coley doing, but I know better, and I hate Coley don't. "Finally somebody know how to treat a guest. Have you seen this poor girl's face?"

"Yes, I have, but you should have seen the men who hit her," Coley say proud.

"Shut up!" I order Coley, then stare 'a in the face.

Coley silent, but she seem lost trying to find 'a place in all this. I can tell by how she acting she don't know how fragile the space is. I can tell by how she searching for something proper to say, she don't know how out of turn she speaking.

"I was just telling Madelyn that there are a lot of advantages to looking almost white." Ms. Beaumont starts fishing, and smiling.

"Linny, Madelyn, is ungrateful. I told her the first day we met, I would kill to have skin that light. You know with the right training she could pass for a blue blood."

"What's that?" Diamond asks smiling and dancing a little.

"That's enough, Coley." I cain't believe she saying all this, like she forgetting how my skin got this light.

"Now that I see my sister, I'm worried about how there aren't any laws or police to protect her. That low-life white trash over in Deweyville kill niggras for sport. If they so much as see one on the road by himself, it's a problem. Daddy been trying to talk to them. He say he don't want to scare yall away. Already so many of yall leaving for other places, where there are more jobs and you feel safer."

"Negro," Coley correct Diamond.

Diamond shocked, but she don't do what any other white woman would have done. She don't slap the taste out Coley mouth. She don't tell Coley how she ain't never wrong long as she white, and even if she is wrong ain't no nigga's business or place to correct 'a.

"Then again, ain't nothing better than what we got going on here." Diamond keep on talking like Coley ain't said a word.

"How do you figure?" Coley doing 'a best to hold 'a tongue, but the word 'niggra' done rubbed 'a the wrong way.

"They ain't got no family up north. I hear niggra men taking good niggra women and turning them out on the streets to make a profit. Heard it ain't really no jobs, and niggras starving in the streets. It's a wonder you was able to make something of yourself, girl, Coley is it, considering."

Coley squirm under the idea of being a whore or being a teacher against all the odds. I think it's good for Coley to understand who she dealing with. I hope she remembering the fair, and how she could get us hung. She sit silent while Ms. Beaumont go on talking.

"Round here niggras guaranteed work, and they got they whole family around 'em. Some of them even been able to make a nice living for themselves. Got they own land. Whenever I go travelling, I see how blessed we all are, that our niggras aren't dealing with all the problems they have to face in other places. Mothers can bring they children with them to work. In other places, they got to find somebody to watch their youngins.

"Then when niggras ain't being exposed to hard work early on, ain't no telling how they gone turn out. Here, all our niggras got a good work ethic cause they all learn to work in the fields as soon as they old enough to get around good. There isn't anywhere else in the country, where people making use of and appreciating niggas the way we do here in Georgia. Wouldn't you agree, Madelyn?"

"Yes, ma'am," I agree heartily, doing my "good nigga pose," and laughing a little, stoking Coley's fire and working 'a nerves. I'm standing while Ms. Beaumont sitting, like I'm waiting on 'a next request. It ain't legal for niggas and white folks to sit around together talking bout nothing. There's always got to be a line drawn.

"Girl, go get me a drink," Diamond speak to me then look at Coley.

"I don't have special glasses for white people, ma'am," I'm trying to keep from leaving nem alone.

"Well, what do you want me to do about that, girl, die of thirst?"

"Coley, you go get it," I order.

"No, you go get it cause I asked you to do it," Diamond insist.

I look at Coley to take notice. Coley simple ass under the notion white folks and niggas equal.

"Go on now, girl. Me and Coley will be right here waiting when you come back." Diamond smile at me, wrinkling 'a nose, and that scare me. Me and Diamond both know what she doing.

"This ain't New York, Coley," I warn 'a, staring in 'a eyes.

Coley stubbornness make me uneasy, so I snatch the screen door open and run in the kitchen. All while I'm in the kitchen, I'm moving fast as I can. I rinse the glasses, fill 'em with ice and pour them full. I'm getting hot, and decide to just take Diamond a glass. So she can drink it and go.

"Crash!" The glass breaking scare me, then I realize I've knocked the other glass off the counter. Still Ion stop to clean it up. I'm running back to the front porch with the glass. Just in time to hear Coley say, "Coloreds should have their own police."

"What I tell you, Coley?" I give Diamond the glass of lemonade. Now they sitting on either ends of the swing like old friends.

"Don't fuss at her. She was just saying how different things are here, from how they are where she's from." Diamond look across at Coley and ask, "Up north?"

"Up north," Coley agree.

"Thank you. This is good," Diamond approve, after taking a sip of the lemonade, then drinking it good. "Why Madelyn, if you were up north you could have told the police Ernest and Victor were stealing from you. You wouldn't have to be doing no policing yourself. Too bad you don't have a man to speak for you."

I feel hot, and worried. I wonder how far these words go.

"Why didn't your daddy Cash do something, or one of them brothers you got?"

"He did do something bout it."

"Did he go get them boys that jumped you in your store?"

"No, ma'am, but this is family business. We don't need no police or law. All families have disagreements. We working it out."

"Have you seen your face? Is that how niggra men work things out with they women? My daddy wouldn't never let nobody come in and take nothing from me, then man handle me too."

"Well, Iain got no daddy to stand for me. I got to stand for myself," I say to remind 'a of how me and her sisters. My mama a nigga, and she ain't laid down with Hunter Beaumont under no romantic notions. They be done hung me if I say anything directly, anything that can be seen as a attack on the head of the counsel.

"You sure you ain't got no daddy to stand for you?"

"I'm sure Cassius Remington, the only daddy I ever knew, done washed his hands of the whole situation," I promise.

"Well, that's a shame," Diamond say, standing and putting the glass back in my hand. The side of 'a palm touch part of mine.

I pull away, not soon enough, and she looking in my eyes. Everything she doing go against all the rules of niggas serving whites. She know she spose to put that glass on the bench, or the window seal, or put it down on these steps, but she put it in my hand.

"Good evening, ladies." She step off the porch.

"Iain trying to start no trouble, Ms. Beaumont. I'm a good girl," the word "girl" feel strange, wrong, desperate and necessary. "This family business." I follow her, not too close, on to the back of 'a automobile.

"Family business, it is." She stares at me, while bowing to get in the backseat as Grover holds 'a door open.

I know my words, our words, whatever Coley done said, going with 'a to a place too far to follow, or know how they gone fall.

"Watch your feet," she dismisses me, then yells to Grover, "Let's go."

"Please?" I beg, looking in 'a eyes. I keep holding on to the window frame even when her auto starts moving. I walk with it. "I don't wont no trouble."

"Your face looks like you already found some."

Chapter Thirty-Six

I'm worried when the sun start getting lazy, and the sky show she tired of shining. Instead of being a ball of fire, she spread out gentle across the sky in soft pinks, yellows and oranges. Bout two o'clock today, she was so bright you could hardly look up at 'a. Now she being real sociable.

Me and my sisters sitting on the porch watching 'a go down. It's getting late. Ella and Jenny doing needlework while Grit nursing. I'm sanding down this high chair. I'm just trying to keep my mind here, and busy. Coley usually home by now. She said she had a surprise, and she didn't wont me to come get 'a from the school house.

Dust on the road high like a auto coming. We all stop for a minute then keep on between watching it getting closer. Soon as I can make out who coming, I see Coley up front, and a strange man Ion know driving. Fore the car stop, I've stopped everything. I'm standing up looking out at 'em.

The man jump out, running round to get 'a door. Coley smile and preen like she always do, thanking him for every little assistance. He take 'a hand, and help 'a out like she some kinda queen. He bow and dance and strut. I wish another man could see this nigga putting on.

"Linny, don't just stand there staring at 'em," Ella fuss.

I cain't look away or move. The way he touching Coley and fussing over 'a making me mad. It's stirring something in me Iain never felt. Fore I know anything, I done started walking, wide striding like I'm leading a army out to the car. I'm standing so close to 'im when he turn around from getting 'a things out the car, he bump into me, and I push him back into his car. Shocked, he don't move. I start snatching a' things from 'im. I take 'a jacket and the little school bag he done pulled from the back seat.

"Good afternoon, Ms. Linny," he say, leaning away from me, probly, trying to figure out what's gotten into me, I'm sure. I cain't say, and he bet not ask. He start to snatch 'em back, but think again, when he see how I'm looking or maybe cause I'm a woman.

"Why he bring you home?" I look at Coley and this between me and her.

She start to smile, and giggle that laugh when ain't nothing funny, but she uncomfortable. She shrinking from my stare, but I don't look away or offer 'a no ease.

Ion know how long she standing there fore she start looking round, pass me.

I turn around and see all them eyes on me, on us. I see how Ella staring at me. I feel what I'm doing for the first time, and I realize I cain't be going on about Coley in public.

I shove the bag back at 'im, it feel like my face frown, then I look at Coley. Taking a few steps back, away from the stranger, I remember, she ain't my woman and I cain't fight 'im for 'a. Cain't even tell 'im she spoken for. That's her job. She know what it is between me and her.

We all stand still, silent. Then he smile nervously, looking at my sisters on the porch and then at me. He give me the bag back slow.

I give Coley 'a own bag. "Since when you cain't hold yah own things?" Remembering where I'm at, and what we doing, and how it might be seen, I say, "A woman cain't be riding around with no man she ain't married to, it don't look right. People will talk."

"I know that's right," Jenny start cosigning. "And don't be having men bringin ya to my sister's house all times of the night neither. Don't be have 'em come calling for yah. This ain't that kind of house, and she ain't that kind of woman. If a man wont to entertain you, he need to make a date, and come when it's others around to chaperone."

"Shut up," Ella say taking it all in, never moving from the porch swing, still swinging. The swinging done changed, the stride of the swing shorter, faster. Ella swinging til she can figure what else to do, with all the tension going round.

"Why I got to shut up? Everybody already saying it all over town. Look how she dress." Looking at Coley, Jenny say, "Coming down here with them northern ways, doing whatever you wont. That's yo business, but this here Zion, Georgia, where Jesus Christ rule."

"If you don't shut your mouth!" Ella stop the swing, lean forward on 'a toes and get ready to attack. Jenny don't push 'a. Ella always been a fighter, and she and Jenny done had they bouts. Jenny ain't never won.

Soon as Jenny stop talking I know I'm wrong. Anything Jenny agree with got to be stupid wrong.

Just above a whisper, Coley say, "You know how I feel about being inappropriate. You know how important it is what people think of me. You know what I've been through with a married man. Why would you treat me like a whore in front of everybody?"

Looking at my sisters pass me, she start to blink back tears, holding 'a bag close to a chest like it's a small child she hugging, like she sinking, and its keeping 'a afloat. She push against me hard, and I hear 'a sniff harder. She wipe 'a face, and refuse to cry.

I realize I done hurt 'a, and that break my heart. I want to say I'm sorry, but she done wrapped 'a arm in his. That make me wanna snatch 'im apart! I don't even hang on my brothers like that. I clinch my dress to keep from grabbing 'a.

Iain never been in love with nobody the way I am with Coley. Iain never been afraid of losing somebody so much. Every time Coley speak to somebody I think might be better for 'a I get sick, nervous, angry. Make me want to fight them for being what I cain't be, her husband, her man, her protector. Another man wouldn't never give a woman a ride home knowing she seeing somebody. But Iain no man, and don't nobody know.

"This is the surprise I was telling you about." She straighten 'a back and stand real tall. Feel like she doing this to push my buttons, cause she stare right in my eyes. "This is my friend and colleague Henry Meriwether." She hanging on 'im, hurting me back.

297

"Hank," he say grinning and offering his hand.

I just look at it, and then at him.

He take it back and wipe it on his pants like its sweaty, waiting for Coley word on what he stepped into. Then he let 'a arm go, and go on up on the porch. "Good evening ladies, my name is Henry but they call me Hank." He shakes they hands too hard.

I just look at Coley smiling and watching him. "I don't like surprises," I say, low enough only Coley hear me.

"Something sure smells good." He stops in front of my screen door, then stand looking in my house like he see somebody he know in there.

"I told Hank all about you, and how good your cooking is."

"I'm sure you ain't told Hank ALL about nothing." I stare at 'a seriously, wondering what she trying to do.

Ignoring me, she say, "I convinced him not to eat at the hotel when he was hungry." Putting 'a arm in mine like she did his, and shaking me to relax, she add, "Please, Linny, I'll be real grateful."

Turning my back to the porch, I say just so she can hear me, "I'm sorry baby."

Taking a deep breath she inhale my apology, and nod a head yes. There are new tears, she wills not to fall.

I feel like crying, too. I hate the way she moves me sometimes. I hate the way Ella looking at me when I turn around. I just pull away from Coley then start in to make 'im a plate.

"That's crazy," Grit say, kissing lil Maddy's head beneath a nursing blanking. Ella don't never stop staring at me. So I look 'a dead in the eyes, and I know she know. Grit go on, "It ain't even that late. And Linny, Iain never seen you act like this about nothing. You really upset."

"She ain prettier than you, or better, not even with alla huh schooling," Jenny whisper, walking towards me. "If you like that man, she ain't got nothing on you, honey. You could have him. Just stop wearing pants all the time, and start acting like a lady."

I look at Grit, and feel how she trying to make sense of my behavior. Then I look at Jenny, "I don't want him."

"You must think I'm a fool or something," Jenny challenge loud. "I know when a woman is jealous. And you jealous. I mean, if you don't want him, you'd have to want-," then the mouth that says anything anywhere won't finish saying that. She just stare in my eyes, and I don't flinch.

I don't know what's gotten into me but I'm tired of hiding, and watching what I say. I wont somebody to know, to understand. So I show Jenny my soul. She start stepping back, and I step with 'a. Then she stumble and fall back on the bench.

Never taking my eyes off of 'a, I say, "Excuse me while I go fix this man a plate."

"I told you to shut cho mouth, and mind yo own business," Ella scold Jenny as I pass 'a to go in the house.

I feel the silence full of questions I've left behind. I know I'm gone have to answer one day, or leave Zion soon.

*   *   *

We already done ate fore Coley came. So when my sisters come in to sit around the table, it ain't to find out if the food good, or to watch Henry Meriwether eat. He is a hundred questions, and before he swallow the last bite, they gone be done asked him ninety-nine.

"Where you from?" Jenny ain't wasting no time.

"Washington DC."

"How you know Coley?"

"She was in one of my classes, at Howard," he manages, between shoveling food down.

"I tutored him," Coley say proud, smiling at 'im, then she smile at everybody else til she get to me.

"Why you got to tell everybody that?" Hank ask, teasing.

"Cause you were a freshman and I—was a senior," she teases him, and it burns me up to watch them play.

"Why you want everybody to know you old?" He laugh, but Coley don't think that's funny. I'm surprised she don't tell 'im, "Age isn't a proper topic for a lady."

"What you come to Zion for?" I hear myself ask before I realize I'm digging into him, too. This ain my way. Me and Ella usually let people be.

"Coley invited me," he say, gulping down lemonade and shoving more food into his mouth.

"Oh, she did, did she?" Jenny take the lead. "You sweet on Coley?"

Hank spit the lemonade out, start choking and cough it up. "Oh no, ma'am." He shaking his head 'no,' too, til he finally manage to say, still clearing out his throat. "They must not know about Anson." He look at Coley.

"Anson?" We all say, cept Ella, who don't too much get into folk business less it got something to do with 'a money or youngins.

"Hank, please." Coley sit up like a stick in mud, shaking 'a head 'no,' and looking at 'im. "Don't discuss my personal affairs." Coley shifts 'a weight in the chair.

There is no stupid laugh, she just looks at me. It's the first time I've seen 'a stand 'a ground. It's the first time she ain't been all open, and wanting to talk about the odds and ends of a thing. Then she look back at Hank, before taking a mouthful of food from 'a fork. She ain never been one to eat no mouthful of food, its unladylike. Seem like she swallowing more than cornbread and greens.

"Oooh!" Jenny shout so loud it make Grit jump. "I knew something wasn't right with you, Ms. Graham."

"Ms. Graham?" Hank repeats, looking confused.

"Hank." Coley raises 'a eyebrows. "Eat your food," she orders him, and he listens.

Shoveling it in, he looks at all of us like we scarecrows, just up and appeared.

"Anson is," Coley says, searching for words, lifting 'a chin, and acting all uppity like she do sometimes. "Anson is just a man my family liked for me."

"Seem like its more to the story than that." Jenny ain taking that answer.

"He's a man of proper breeding, education, and color. I wanted to choose someone I loved." She looks over at me and then at everyone else, maybe to make it like she ain talking to me, but Ella don't seem to miss nothing. Ella look at both of us, and then she take a good look at me.

"So you running?" Ella say more than ask.

Coley turning like a cork being screwed out. "I took a job to help my race."

"Does yah family know where you—'helpin yo race?'" Ella sound like Mama.

"No, ma'am." Coley lowers 'a eyes as if she waiting to be scolded.

Ella stare at 'a, and then me, fore she say, "Henry or Hank, you need to hurry up and finish that food fore it git too late. You a stranger here, and regular folks don't even travel the roads at night."

"Yes, ma'am." He eat the hungry way our brothers do.

"Umph," Jenny say, leaning on 'a hand, but Ella hit 'a fore she could lean good.

"Don't none of this leave this room, yah hear?" Ella pointing in Jenny face. "This family bidness, and if I hear a word of it anywhere, I'm coming for you, Jenny. So you better hope ain't nobody else here talk about it neither, cause I'm gone thank it's you."

Jenny snatch away and frown.

"What you here for if you ain't sweet on Coley?" I press 'im, and Ella give me this look like she tired of this.

"I'm a recruiter for companies up north, and further east. Coley said with all the boll weevil attacks and crop failures, lots of folks might be looking for work. She said some men travel for work here already, and might be willing to move away for good with the right incentives."

Chapter Thirty-Seven

"I don't know how its possible, when I feel like I'm eating more than I ever have, but I'm losing weight. I like that," Coley say coming out the house dancing a lil with 'a school bag, and touching 'a stomach.

"You look beautiful." I'm watching 'a dance.

She pull a orange begonia from the side of the steps and put it in 'a hair, then look over at me. "You know what?" She smile, dancing a little while she talk. "I think I love Zion."

"Really now?" I laugh at 'a revelation.

"Yes, ma'am. This is the first time I've ever felt this much peace. I don't have to do anything special to be loved, or liked. Iain trying to reach anyone else's expectations, you know?"

"You starting to sound real country, using that word 'Iain,'" I tease.

"Same way you're starting to lose your accent by annunciating, 'her,' properly," she tease back.

"I can read," I warn 'a, "and I told you people round here ain't talking like they reading all the time. So it ain't no reason for me to be talking like I'm a book worm or something. They'll think I'm showing off."

"When we first met, I use to think you were so free, Linny. Now I see, sometimes you're weighed down by other people's expectations, too. Being who you are isn't showing off.

"If someone feels like you're better than them, that has nothing to do with you. That kind of thinking comes from them not being comfortable with who they are. If someone isn't comfortable with themself, it isn't our responsibility to make them comfortable by hiding pieces of ourselves.

"In fact, nothing we ever do to ourselves can truly give someone else peace. That's what I'm learning since I left New York. I'm so relieved to be away from the "Talented Tenth." Here, I'm learning to make fewer choices in fear. I'm focused on my spirit."

Skipping round me, Coley dance, touching me like she inviting me to join her. Smiling in my spirit, I just watch 'a.

"When I look in the mirror without considering what I've been told is beautiful, I love my brown skin. I love my smile. I love my full lips. When I feel how you look at me, how you touch me, I'm freer."

"Are you, now?" I say smiling completely happy, watching 'a settling with 'aself.

"I love my hair."

"You have beautiful hair."

"You were right, it is too hot and the air is too thick to be wearing my hair pressed. I am so glad I don't have to keep touching it up every other day. Now I just wash it, braid it and go. I like it easy."

"I'm glad you like it easy." I stare at 'a seriously, like I could do something to 'a right here. I forget that we outside in front of the house.

"Can it be like this forever?" she look at me, asking seriously.

"If this what you want," I tell her, and I'm hoping it will be like this forever. Me, her, and her smiling and singing with flowers in 'a hair, feeling as beautiful as she is.

"Can I ride with you?" she asks, all syrupy sweet, looking up at me on Anastasia, holding 'a hat against the sun, with 'a thick hair in plats tucked under. I notice 'a dress ain got all them slips underneath she normally be wearing. She dressing lighter, less uppity. I pull Coley up on Anastasia behind me, and start off down the main road to the school.

"Ms. Remington?" Orville, one of the hands I done hired call me from the pasture and start running towards us.

"Linny," I remind 'im soon as he get close. Feel strange having a man three times my age call me 'miss.' Then again, he probly ain never been on first-name basis with nobody he worked for.

"I cain't git old Betsy up." He talks to me like he a child, and not like the man I know 'im to be. He doing his 'good-nigga' pose on me, and that rub me the wrong way. Then I feel bad, looking down on 'im from my horse.

"Where she at?" I ask, then he point in 'a direction. When I take off riding, he run behind the horse, holding his hat.

This cow, Betsy, been round forever. I see she still looking sick. Animals get sick all the time. Sometimes they be pregnant, other times they be done ate the wrong thing. You always got to look at the cows you pumping milk from. Sometimes if they sick their milk will make you sick, too. Betsy been on 'a last leg for a few weeks now. I been hoping she'd start looking better, Iain been pumpin no milk from 'a.

"Come on, girl." I rub 'a face, run my hand along 'a ears. The bell round 'a neck ring dull. I look 'a in the eyes, and see she suffering. She moan, then shake trying to get up but it's like her body too heavy for 'a. I rub along 'a belly, and examine 'a to see if I can see what's wrong. I know she ain't pregnant.

"Oh my God, she smells horrible. It smells horrible out here," Coley complain, covering 'a face with a handkerchief.

The men laugh at Coley.

I'm listening to Betsy's heart beat, checking 'a temperature. She burning up. The bell clapper seem to be struggling, too, while Betsy trying to move around and find 'a footing. Every time she cain't get up, she moan louder and more disappointed. Then I know what I have to do.

All while I'm looking down at 'a, the men I done hired watching from the fields. I look up at the sky like maybe God know the answer to this, or can keep me from having to do it.

Iain had to shoot nothing been round a long while before. Killing pigs, chickens, and fish you bout to eat different from shooting a big cow you done been raised with. I be talking to Betsy every morning, and I done figured out how to milk 'a easy.

Usually Daddy would be the one to go out and shoot something. All my brothers done had to do it at least once coming up. So whenever the time came on they own land with they own family, they'd be ready. I remember how sad Daddy use to look coming in after putting down a horse or a cow. I spect I feel how he felt all them times right now.

I keep looking at 'a, trying to find a reason to keep 'a round. All the while knowing, if I don't do it, she'll be suffering. Might even make the other cows sick, depending on what it is she got. I stoop down looking in 'a eyes for some other option. I hear the heels of people walking round me, and they silent cause they all know what's got to be done.

"Where the rifle at?" Orville ask, looking down at the cow, too, who seems to be looking up at him and then at me for mercy.

"I'll do it. I gotta go back to the house and get a gun," I say staring in Betsy eyes. "She looks tired."

"You gone shoot this cow?" he asking with disbelief, more than asking surprised, so I look at him seriously.

Men always be offering to do things for me round here, like it's some kind of honor to be viewed and treated like I'm weaker than they is. For some reason, it makes me feel like they talking down to me. Some women like when men do what they call 'man' jobs. My sisters and family always expected me to do 'man' jobs, so it's hard not to see what's flattering to most women as being smart with me. Feel like I got something to prove all the time, and they be surprised what I take on, and what I do.

Anyhow, I jump on Anastasia, and look back at the house and cain't believe Coley done walked way back up there. She don't never walk too far pass the front yard. She scared of everything. All the animals after her, she swears.

"Are you really going to shoot that cow?" She follow me in the house, then watch me looking at the rifles, deciding which one be best.

"Ain't got no choice."

"You couldn't just wait and see what happens after a few more days?" She seem to be pleading with me.

"It's been weeks and she getting worse."

"Can I?" she ask and step up as I'm walking back out.

"No. Ain't no place for you."

My body feel heavy as I ride back, and the rifle cool to touch, warming in my hands. I load it while I'm riding, I don't ride fast. We trot, I'm thinking, listening to how the bullets and the metal click into place. When I get back, all the men are waiting, to see, if I will do it, how I do it. I think it be true to say, they ain never seen a woman kill no cow, or nothing this big.

I been deer hunting with Daddy nem a thousand times, but that's different. Deer wild, you don't feel no closeness to them. You don't think about the life you taking, you think about the meal afterwards, and the stories your daddy will tell about how good you handled that rifle. My daddy has great stories about me, laying silent and getting me one. He be proud that I'm a girl that can shoot. Still, today I feel like this the first time I done handled a gun.

Every day for years I've gotten up and milked this cow even before taking my own breakfast. We have an understanding, a trust. She been keeping my secrets, I talk to 'a while I'm milking 'a. I say good morning to 'a, and even though I milk other cows, I grew up with this one.

The rifle heavy, and I worry cause Iain shot this one in almost a year and half. I lift it silently, breath and brace myself to hit 'a between the eyes. I'm so sad I got to do this my eyes blur.

I remember being out with Zay and him shooting a horse we'd had forever. The horse didn't die right away, cause Zay was so nervous he closed his eyes to shoot, and didn't get it between the eyes. Daddy made him shoot it again, and again. If I miss, I'll have to shoot Betsy again.

Bang! My whole body jerk, but I stand stern. This gun is louder than I remember, and my ears are ringing. When the smoke clear, she jerk a little, her eyes open but then she go silent.

When I turn around, I see the dust rising all up the road to the house, like somebody coming fast. Then I see Zay coming for me. "They got 'em!"

"Who got who?"

"Did you tell your real daddy what Uncle Vick nem did?" Zay demand to know and look at me like he trying to feel if I'm lying.

"Diamond Beaumont already knew somehow."

"Well, they done went over to Uncle Victor's land and took him and all his sons down to Beaumont jail."

"What's the charge?"

"They saying he stole from yo store and attacked you. They saying, if they'll steal from they own kin and kind, ain't no telling what they'll do to white folks."

My heart start to drum fast, I try to catch my breath; I know what this mean, what's gone happen.

"You know that "Birth of a Nation" movie got them all up in arms bout niggas trying to take over. You know the Klan growing, and they been hanging folks left and right." Shaking his head looking at me, he say, "It's been a long time since they hung somebody from Zion, out of one of the counsel family slaves. Been a long time since they made an example out of somebody. This look real bad."

I turn the rifle to the ground, make sure it ain't gone discharge, then start towards the house.

"We both know ain't gone be no trial. They might not even make it til the morning if we let the sun go down and don't do nothing."

"I got to fix this." I breathe heavy, starting towards the porch.

"What you gone do? Iain never seen a nigga actually done nothing to git that noose off nobody's neck."

"I ain't neither." I look over at Coley. Some of her words done this.

Chapter Thirty-Eight

"Good evening," I offer Mrs. Silvia, Grover's wife and the Beaumont's maid since before I was born, when she opens the Beaumont's back door.

I expect 'a to tell me something about Mr. Beaumont's mood, or just about Mr. Beaumont himself. Maybe even tell me what to say, or how to say it. She just look at me from head to toe then breathe hard and heavy, waiting for me to speak. "I need to see Mr. Beaumont."

Without a word, she look out at Reverend Patrick, waiting by his automobile, then back at me again. I wonder if she know they done took my uncles. Grover and his wife don't even speak to us folks in Zion. Don't even come to our church even though they from Zion. They regarded with fear cause people say they got the ear of The Counsel. Seem to me, The Counsel might have they eye on them more. If The Counsel ever got wind a word of what they saying here found its way back to Zion's committee, Grover nem be sure as dead.

"Wait here," Mrs. Silvia instruct, closing the door leaving it propped open just enough for me to hear 'a walking away from the screen.

Mrs. Harper, Ella, Grit, Mrs. Clara and Coley got me wearing a dress, with my hair pulled back, pinned and tucked under one of these little dress hats like white women wear. The kind like Coley had pinned on 'a head when she came to Zion.

All the women I'm close to came to get me ready. We all knew I had to come. Almost every nigga woman I know at some point done had to go speak on behalf of 'a man, son or somebody. Sometimes they listen to us, cause one of us done raised one of them, maybe even nursed 'em. Iain raised nobody, and Mr. Beaumont ain never said two words to me make me think he care bout what's happening with me. For all I know, they was just looking for somebody to hang to make an example.

Most of the folks that make it to jail and the work camps, ain't really did nothing. The people they actually thinking guilty of something don't get no judge or jury. The Klan the judge and jury down here. That whip and noose be the sentence every time.

"He'll see you now. Follow me." Mrs. Silvia open the door, turn around and start walking, leaving me to close the door and catch up. We pass through the kitchen where she cleaning up from the supper she done served. I look at everything, the big wood table in the kitchen, and then the cherry wood one in the dining room.

This time when I step in The Counsel's room, I'm alone. It feels different, it's later, and darker in here. Mrs. Silvia leave me there, closing the sliding wooden doors. I don't hear 'a footsteps going away. I look at the ground and hold my hands together. I'm trying to think of what to say, how to say it, what to ask.

"What do you want there, girl?" Mr. Hunter Beaumont come in the doors behind me. I turn around collecting my words. "Come on now, Iain got all day."

"I was wondering if," I breathe and remember what Mrs. Harper told me to say. "If you could spare my uncles, sir? I don't know who told Ms. Beaumont what happened in the store. I'm glad she came to check on me, but we already got everything worked out."

"Them boys stole from you, and assaulted you in yah own store didn't they?"

"Yes, sir," I say just above a whisper.

"Well, what happens if we just let you niggas do whatever you want to each other over there? You Ernest and Victor's niece, aren't you?"

"Yes, sir. But if something was to happen to them, the whole town'll turn they back on me. They'll be saying it's my fault. They'll be saying Iain one of them. My own family wouldn't have nothing to do with me."

He take me in from head to toe, don't never sit hisself down. When I catch a glimpse of 'im, he got his shirt undone, and he bare footed. I'm thinking he was laying down or something.

"Well, I'll see what I can do," he say, his voice softer, full of thoughts.

"Thank you, sir, that's all I'm asking. Thank you." I bow the way I been taught you do when serving white people. I'm about to get out of here-

"How's yah filling station doing over there in Zion, girl?" He seem to be smiling, but Ion never look 'im in his face.

"It's doing fine sir, just fine. More folks getting they selves automobiles."

"Shoot, yall keep on, and enough folks come through, there'll be a paved road laid clear through to Savannah and Atlanta even. That'd be some more work for the men. They'll come around and be glad for you."

They'll come around and be glad for you. I repeat his words again in my head and get sick. Does that mean he expect I can work my way back into everybody's good graces after he done hung 'em? Feel like he telling me he gone hang them anyway. Iain got no way of pushing him to change his mind, but I got to try. My breathing get deep, I'm trying to control it, my mind racing, thinking of something else to say.

"Please, don't hang my uncles," come firm. I look him in the eyes, and he look back at me. Feel like my whole life in my throat. I'm scared the words putting me on the back of a horse, beneath a old tree, with my neck roped to one of its strong limbs. Still, I cain't stop them.

"If my uncle nem be hung, you might as well lynch me, too. My family will be done with me. My own mama already say I'm a curse and cain't stand to look at me. Cash Remington be the only daddy I know. I want to make him happy and he already disappointed in me.

"Things messed up so bad, with Miemay leaving me 'a things. Daddy already thinking this mostly my fault. Now if he feel I got his uncles hung he'll be agreeing with Mama, they'll both be saying I'm cursed. And you know us niggas don't want to bother with nothing cursed."

"You call for me, sir?" Reverend Patrick voice make me jump. He come in the room, sliding the doors back closed loud, staring at me, and I drop my head again. Then he come stand next to me, taking his hat off and looking at the ground now, too.

"Boy, you know anything bout why so many niggas leaving Zion? Lots of planters saying they hands moving to St. Louis, E. St. Louis and Chicago for jobs. Now folks been sending for they whole family. You know anything bout that?"

"No, suh. Cain't say I do."

"Boy, how are niggers in yah church leaving and you don't know nothing about it?"

"I mean, I know they leaving, suh, but not all the particulars, suh."

"Well, the nigger Clinton Harper ain't got no money. He barely able to pay his own land taxes. Now I hear he done settled the money he owed, and his whole family moving."

"Yes, suh, I heard the lord blessed him with a better job."

"Is it the Lord, you say?" Mr. Beaumont get in Reverend's face.

Feel like my heart skip a few beats.

"Yes, suh," Reverend answer, after turning his head to the side to keep from eyeballing Mr. Beaumont.

"Boy, I'm gone tell you this, and you better hear me good." Mr. Beaumont poke him while he talking. "It better be the Lord Jesus Christ down there taking our field niggas. Cause if not, even Jesus ain't gone be able to save you. And I bet not find out it's a work recruiter down in Zion hiring our hands, or it's gone be me and you.

"If I find out you was standing here lying to me, I'm gone take that real personal. You can shuck and jive, and Jim Crow all you want, but I know how you niggers work. The hands leaving Zion ain't got nothing, and all of a sudden they got train fair, a place to stay and jobs. I been knowing every nigger here for as long as they been born. I can smell a job recruiter a mile away.

"Let me say this, too, Patrick. You and yo family make a good bit off them niggers in that church. If everybody working move somewhere else, what are you gone do? Having niggers in

Zion don't just help planters, it helps you, yo family and Linny here. Who gone buy what she selling or pay tithes if they all go somewhere else? You think about that."

"Yes, suh," Reverend Patrick keep saying, over and over.

All while Reverend Patrick shaking his head and agreeing with Mr. Beaumont, I'm thinking on my uncles, whether they be lynched or not? I'm thinking on all the people's families be torn apart, heartbroken, and disappointed with me.

I'm thinking bout Daddy not ever speaking to me again. I'm wishing Miemay was here to help me fix this. I keep thinking bout how Mr. Beaumont don't never say whether he gone let them go or not. I think about how I cain't ask 'im again, not here in front of Reverend Patrick, not now. I'm thinking on how folks tell you one thing but don't never answer what you ask them bout. I think about how I asked Coley about Anson, and she said she ain worried bout Anson, so I shouldn't be neither.

"Maybe it's that school teacher from up north?" Mr. Beaumont break my train of thought.

"Oh no, sir, ain't her," I defend Coley fore I can think and I even look up again, then back down.

"How you know that, girl?"

"She ain even from no St. Louis, E. St. Louis or Chicago sir. She from New York, D.C. or something like that, sir. Iain never even heard 'a talk about none of them places you mentioned. All she talk about is New York, sir."

"Humph," he study me rather than get me bout sassing him.

It surprise me and Reverend Patrick he even let me talk that much, cause I done step twenty feet out of my place.

"We gone be extra vigilante around Zion. Yall niggers better stay off the streets at night. And we ain never been too kindly towards strangers, specially not no niggers. I spect I be finding me a recruiter down there somewhere. And when I do-,"

Chapter Thirty-Nine

When we pull up in front of the church, there are automobiles, buggies and horses everywhere. I take note of the men there by what's outside. Seem like everybody there, more than normal. Looks like a small service going on, but it's so quiet. If it what'n for the light coming from inside, you wouldn't know people were here.

"Still gone have a meeting tonight?" I'm getting out Reverend's auto slow and confused. When he don't answer I keep talking. "I was expecting to go back home. Even though Ion know what I was gone say to everybody waiting there. Mr. Beaumont ain't said one way or the other."

"What'n no time to cancel the meeting," he finally say, seem to be avoiding my eyes, and talking under his breath as we climb the few steps to the front door.

Soon as I open the door, the whole room of Zion's men stand. Mrs. Clara ain't here, I'm the only woman. My father is here, and all my uncles that ain't in jail, and my brothers. They staring at me with they hats off like they waiting for someone important.

Reverend and me walk to the front pews. Reverend moving faster so he can get to the podium. Still, the men are silent staring at me. I don't look away, I look at them all as I walk slowly to the front. One by one they lower their eyes. I wonder what that's all about. It's the first time I've seen all the men at one meeting. It's the first time they all standing like this. Even the older ones with they canes.

"Have a seat," Reverend Patrick says, but no one obeys, and no one turns to face him. They just keep staring at the ground, most of 'em holding they hats at they chest, facing the door like they waiting to go.

"Reverend," my daddy, calls looking at me angry, "we need you to speak with 'a on our behalf."

My heart drops, and I realize he's asking that I be treated like I'm white. Daddy speaking cause they must of decided he the only one safe. I'm being cast out.

"Wait, Daddy, why?" I walk up to him, and he looks hurt and disappointed. He stare in my eyes, at my soul, and the way he looking at me break my heart.

"It ain't safe for us to have her at our meetings no more," he say, never taking his eyes off of me. "We done talked about it, and we think this here committee was started to keep us all informed, to help each other, and to keep us all safe. I mean, she got the ear of The Counsel." He say it like he teasing, or I'm thinking I'm better, when it ain't even like that. "We won't even be able to say what's on our heart without knowing if she gone be going back telling town business. Who's next? What if somebody else makes 'a mad? If she do this to 'a own kin, ain't no telling what she'll do to somebody else, or the rest of the town."

"That's not true." I'm shaking my head 'no' and fighting the tears coming. My heart sinking, and I cain't believe all this happening. "I wasn't the one who told Diamond Beaumont what happened. Somehow, she already knew," I argue.

"Lots of niggas been wronged by each other, but the Klan ain't never thought to step in on they behalf." Daddy look at me, then over his shoulder at the men avoiding my eyes.

"I didn't ask nobody to step in. I wouldn't do that, Daddy. You got to believe me."

He don't say nothing, he just look at me, tasting my words or feeling for more of his own.

Reverend look over at me and then he start. "We'll have another meeting Tuesday, just us Zion folk, and I'll carry Linny's vote."

"I won't just give up my vote. I won't be shut out of my own town. I won't not know what's going on. That ain't no vote if you don't understand what you voting for."

"We done voted," Daddy say and wind his hand around like he counting all the men in the room.

"I don't deserve this," I say looking around at everyone. That's when they start putting their hats on and leaving. "I begged Mr. Beaumont not to let them be hung. I didn't want this to happen," I'm pleading, and they still leaving.

I've been shunned, and not the kind when someone does something wrong. Some folks still talk to them. Other folks done found the silence so hard they leave, but when they come back, Zion be home again. Not like this, Iain never seen nobody shunned out of fear. If they scared of me, or think I could get them hung, they'll never speak to me again. No matter how many years go by, they be thinking I'm after them, and my eyes The Counsel's eyes. They be raising they kids to believe that, to be scared of me.

"Good evening, ma'am," Jasper resolve taking his leave, and then Obadiah and Reynar. "Good evening, ma'am."

One by one they cast me out. My own brothers follow without so much as a word; I watch them go, until it's just me, Daddy and The Reverend.

"How you git that filling station?" Daddy pressing his finger into the back of a pew like he could crush it with just that one.

"I asked for it," I stare at him, feeling him gathering his thoughts, ready to render his verdict.

"Who you think you is? Who you think I'm is? Think I'm stupid? I'm some kinda jack cain't hardly read cause I been in the sun and fields too long to have good sense?"

"Iain thought or said none of that." I watch him move around. He stay away from me, and I feel how much things have changed. I feel the space between us. Feel like we strangers, like he don't know me no more. "Why things cain't go on being how they is, was? Why cain't you still just be my daddy like you been doing? Why you got to make everything bout what I got and what you ain't got? Everything I got I try to share, but you won't let me."

"You got to be the proudest, most selfish gal ever born. You one crazy nigga if you think I'm gone take blood money from you. You done stole the family inheritance. Now you finna git yah own uncles hung. I cain't take a dime from you, or I'll never be able to hold my head up."

"Iain take nothing. It was given to me, and Miemay left other folks money. Iain the only one got something from 'a dying. Besides that, I promised 'a I'd keep it on 'a death bed. Iain know all this stuff was what she was talking bout."

"How you ain't know she was giving you all her land, and the store? How you surprised? She started training you to run that store soon as you could read, write and count good. You ain't dense.

"She had you telling Uncle Victor nem what to do, going behind them checking they figures, and balancing them books. All the meetings and thangs she had you doing on 'a behalf, and you want folks to believe that ol' woman done got one over on you? Nall, maybe you thinkin we all some crazy niggas. Even if I believed you didn't trick Miemay, I won't never believe you ain't know or ain't have no idea."

"That's not fair, Daddy. I lived with Miemay most days. I was helping 'a out with 'a businesses, same way I was raised to help you out on yo land. You taught me a lot about fixing things, taking care of animals, planting and harvesting. Even though you what'n never gone give me none of the land, cause I what'n no boy. I what'n raised to help expecting nothing. You use to tell my brothers this yo land, and take care of this cause its gone be yours one day. You ain't never said none of that to me, but Iain never worked less or felt slighted. It's just the way it is for a girl child.

"So Iain never think nothing of helping Miemay, and learning what she needed me to know. You know she couldn't read, and you know how Uncle Victor nem is. They was always trying to get over on 'a, and she knew it, too. She needed somebody she could trust to help, who didn't want nothing from 'a and I was there. If they took too much, she couldn't help folks who really needed."

I look over at The Reverend, and I'm waiting for him to say what he know bout Miemay. I want him to go over what he told us all that one Sunday. I want him to stand behind me now, but he don't say a word.

Looking at The Reverend, too, Daddy look like he done tasted something bad. "And Ion even believe nothing Patrick got to say outside what's in that Bible. And if we let Miemay tell it, we cain't be too sure bout that neither. She ain even wont him to be pastor of this church. That's the reason why she ain't hardly come.

"Cain't prove it, but he ran that other boy out of Zion cause he what'n from here. Wonder who told the Klan bout him?" He look over at The Reverend, who acting like what Daddy saying don't even need to be honored. "That other boy was tied in to all them Negro groups. He was changing things, trying to git us some rights. He came here helping folks git jobs, and git set up to move. I what'n going but lots of folks left."

Staring at The Reverend and challenging his righteous pose, Daddy say, "You ain't wont people leaving. Trying to keep some money for yourself."

"These all lies. What Linny did and said to 'a real father ain't got nothing to do with me. Ain't no cause for you to be pulling me in yo family problems, and dragging me through the mud. Iain never used the Klan against nobody," Reverend look at me and I feel like he accusing me too, or even, like he lying on me.

Then I know. I remember him telling me that if it what'n for Miemay's vote, he wouldn't have never became Zion's pastor. We lock eyes, and he know I see him now.

Things start to come clear. Why no matter how many times Mrs. Harper said I was the daughter she never had, Iain never felt welcomed. Iain never felt like I was a real part of their family. No matter how many times they invited me to they house, I could never get comfortable. Now I understand.

I wonder if Mrs. Harper and Reverend Patrick ain't been telling Hunter Beaumont bout how they was having me over all the time. How they was raising me since my own family didn't really want me. All along they knew Hunter Beaumont was my father. They knew that if they was in good with me, it'd mean they had the ear of The Counsel and more power here in Zion.

Now all this done happen, Reverend can tell me what he wont bout Zion business meetings, and run game on me like he do all the white folks. The Harpers always knew this day would come, when no one would trust me and people would fear me. It was a privilege to have me eat with them. They never really cared about me, or how I felt. Part of me wonder if Reverend ain't told Hunter Beaumont about me and my uncles getting into it.

I start to feel ashamed that I trusted Mrs. Harper, and asked 'a advice about so many things. I start to think about what Reverend told me bout digging Miemay's grave, and I don't know what to believe no more. I remember Reverend Patrick is slippery. Miemay use to say if anybody going to hell, Reverend be the first one in line for being twofaced. Never know which one to trust. I feel lost.

"Me and Patrick grew up together. I know who he really is," Daddy say keeping his eye on Reverend. "He might be the pastor of this church and know The Word better than anybody else, but he got his own agenda. He always has and always will.

"Watch who yo friends is, and make sure they ain't cho enemies. Now he wont us all to believe Miemay asked him to watch over you, and didn't tell him why. Maybe Massa Beaumont told him to watch over you, but Ion believe Miemay got one over on him and you. That woman what'n even the kind of person to be gittin over on people."

"She outsmarted lots of folks," I defend 'a. "Miemay may not have been book smart, but she saw to running all kinds of businesses. Ain't just me. She done got others to do what she thought was right. She ain sat on no committee of men and been dumb 'aself. And what I know about expecting anything from 'a. I'm so far down the line, didn't never cross my mind she'd be leaving me nothing."

"And you spect me to believe you ain't know she was building that house for you?"

Taking in the empty church, and looking at the porch, I remember again in disbelief. I cain't hardly say it, but I didn't. "Yeah, she was good to me. Waited til it was built to die."

I take another deep breath and remember who she was, how she was, and I miss 'a right now. I wish she was here to tell 'em all what 'a plans was. Wish she was here to take responsibility for this, and say this was all her idea. Wish she was here to protect me the way she did all my life. Wish she was here to speak for me, but she ain't.

"You gone cry now. Just like any other woman, think tears gone change the truth, gone gitcho way. Ain't gone work this time. You done done too much, too much done happened. And I'm gone have to step away from you."

"Please?" I beg my daddy to love me, to stay in my life, even though I know he ain't got no cause to. Even though I know he ain't really my daddy by most folk's standards. He did more than he had to, more than most men would have if they was put in the same position. I'm hoping something I've done or said, or our relationship will change his mind.

I see it in his eyes though, that he done already decided. He ain't even angry no more, after all this talking, he just done with me. I step closer to 'im and he step back shaking his head "no." We ain never been the type of family to hug or touch each other, but for some reason I want to just put my hand on his shoulder.

He keep shaking his head, then ease off the steps of the church. "I cain't do nothing with this. It's too much. You got that filling station cause of who yo real daddy is. He wouldn't let no other nigga do that fore you come along 'just asking,' cause it woulda cut into the business of 'Ol Man Parson's station. Now he even gone have a road come through here. Then you got Diamond Beaumont coming round here talking bout how you her nigga sister. This ain't right, it just ain't right.

"I'm a man. I'm the head of this family. Iain protect my wife. Now the daughter I raised like my own, gone go to the man done did what he did, and ask him for something. How you think that make me feel?"

"Daddy, it what'n like that. I didn't know who I was, I didn't know he was my father when I submitted the proposal." I'm controlling my breathing. I breath deep. I'm trying to keep myself from crying.

"Iain cho daddy. Yo daddy got that filling station for yah. Now every time I go in town, I got to be reminded of what he put this whole family through. My family, ain't yorn."

"Iain got to have no filling station. Iain know it was this big of a deal, Daddy. I wouldn't have never done nothing to make you feel bad."

"Stop calling me 'Daddy,' girl. We ain't kin, me and you ain't nothing. You the misses living here amongst us common niggas."

"Ain't true. I'll close down that filling station."

"Cain't do that, then that be my fault, too. Town need the money, and the outsiders that station be bringing here. You and yo daddy filling station bringing a road. That be jobs for the men of Zion. That be food on they table. You good for Zion, and everybody else, but you was always a curse for me and yo Mama."

He start breathing deep, too, and I feel my heart beating fast. "Truth be told, Miemay ain't even really yo grandmother, and that's why all this so wrong. You ain't even mine, and got inheritance ain't even yorn."

"But you the only daddy I ever knew, and that man ain't said two words to me bout being no relation. Yall all I got. Miemay was all I had." I cain't help but cry. "Iain never speak to Hunter Beaumont directly bout that filling station. I just sent a proposal like any other nigga do. Iain ask for no special consideration on account of anything. Maybe he done whatever he done out of guilt."

"Well, iffin it is cause of guilt, he needed to die with that guilt after what he did to ya mama. He ain't need no way to redeem hisself. He shouldn't never sleep another peaceful night. After the way he beat 'a, and bruised 'a. Not once, but kept on coming for 'a. It's crazy how a white man can tell a nigga to work in his house, and the nigga cain't say no. She ain even tell me what was going on. Said, what could I have done anyhow, wouldn't have done nothing but got myself hung."

"Oh, Daddy," I cry gulping for air, holding my hand to my mouth. "Iain know. Iain even know it was that bad. Iain know it kept happening, I thought yall was the Hilliard house couple."

"I told 'a she couldn't never go back there when I found out. Then he came and got us, took us to the Hilliard's old place, tied me to a tree and whupped me. Then she had to go in that condemned shack with 'im to save my life. She shoulda let me hang!"

"Please? Daddy?" I cry wonting to touch 'im, wonting to comfort 'im. "Iain know that filling station would make you feel bad. I hate that I'm a reminder of what happened. I won't do nothing else to be a burden."

"You don't never thank about nobody but yah own narrow yella tail."

"I thought this would help the town. Iain know it would affect you and Mama. I already know things is bad with what happened after Miemay died. I wouldn't of never wanted to cause no more hardships."

Breathing deep and seeming to swallow every word I say he look at me. "When I fell in love with ya Mama and asked for 'a hand, I promised 'a she wouldn't never be alone. Promised I would see 'a through hell or high water." Banging his hand on the banister he say, "Sometimes I feel, that I let 'a down."

"You did all you could, Daddy."

"What'n enough. I'd rather be hung, than send my wife to lay with another man, and against 'a will. I wanted to kill 'im, but she was carrying a baby for 'im, and she begged me, saying she needed a man to help raise our kids. Said she ain wont to give birth alone. Said our kids needed they daddy. Sometimes I looked at you and wondered what kinda Daddy, I was."

"A good one."

"Nah, coulda been better."

"I won't keep the station. Just give me a few days to make this right."

"You cain't refuse his help. He be asking why, and then all this come down on the family. Then what we tell the town? Those men gone be working on the road, and all the folks in town looking forward to visitors' money?"

"I need you Daddy. Please don't leave me. Please don't turn yo back on me. I need you. I just made a mistake. I'll take all the blame on myself. I'll go to 'im and curse'm for what he did to Mama."

"This ain't about you now, what you need. Fact is, I was always worried bout what you needed. Shoulda gave you away when you was born. But after I held you, I didn't expect yah mama would hold it against you how you came to be. She did.

"You was the best child, and the rest of 'em was good, too, but you had your ways. You was strong as any man, thought a lot and didn't go round running after boys like ya sisters. You was made of good stock, a different stock, better stock some folks would argue. And when I use to think about it, I realized the only thing different from you and them, is me. Iain never know if I thought you was better, cause you was so much like me, or because you what'n mine at all.

"The Harpers, Mrs. Harper really, couldn't have nothing but boys doted on you. Begged us to give you to 'em fore you knew any difference. I what'n sure if they was doing it for the right reasons. They always got something going on, always trying to figure out a way to git over on somebody. Still it might have been better for you.

"But then they had all them sons, and they what'n no relation, and I'm thinking bout putting a yella girl in a house of men. Ya mama already had been through what she been through. Iain wont you to have to go through that, too. Just thought you'd be safer with yo own brothers.

"Now I don't know, even if they got they own reasons, good and bad, maybe I should have gave you away. Specially seeing how Pastor sons acting like they yo brothers, and he acting like ya daddy." He look at Reverend Patrick and say, "Mrs. Harper done got 'a wish."

"You my daddy."

"Nall," he say and look at me sad like he might cry, too, and say, "Nall I ain't."

"Please." I rush off the porch and wrap my arms round him. Trying to hold on to 'im. It's worse than wrapping yah arms round a tree. The tree don't fight back. I take them licks. He push me off, and I close my eyes and hold on, but he beat me, get me off of him and throw me to the ground.

"Stop crying, girl! You ain't never been no weak child, or no damned cry baby. Be strong. I raised you to be strong. This how it's gone be. And," his voice break like he crying, too, just ain't no tears, "I wish you the best with all this." He step back throwing his arms up.

Getting up, I dust myself off. "Iain crying," I say, wiping my face, pushing dirt in my eyes and it sting 'em, but I stand stern, like a tree. I lift my chin and straighten my back, and look at 'im good. This time he for real I know, and this time I'm on my own.

"You have a good evening, too, sir. Thank you for your time." I step back on the church porch, gasping for breath, letting go, feeling alone and watching him mount his horse, then go.

Chapter Forty

"Are you going to stay angry with me forever? I can't stand you not talking to me." All while Coley talking, she climbing in the bed with me. When I don't reach out to hold 'a, she start scooting into me, getting close as she can.

"Things were getting better. Folks was talking to me. Felt like I was part of this town again. This thing with my uncle nem, and what you did, talking to Diamond Beaumont, done made me a outsider again, forever."

"But they were wrong," Coley plead, like we can argue bout this.

"This about people's life. Everybody makes mistakes. People got to be able to live and come into they own understanding. Then they'll feel guilty, regret and make amends."

"They weren't ever going to feel guilty about how they treated you. They wouldn't have ever apologized, much less try to do right by you."

"We ain God. We ain got no right to be over here deciding who lives and who dies. They might be hung." I scoot away from 'a.

"Oh my God, I never thought they would hang them. I just thought," she start crying.

"You didn't think." I look at 'a, offering no comfort. She need to understand how far our words go.

"I'm so sorry, Linny. Please forgive me? I wasn't trying to get anyone killed. You're right, I didn't think. We were talking about the police, and I was just saying Negroes needed their own police force. I was asking for our own law, I was not asking Diamond to have anyone hung." Then she start to really cry beside me, and it feel like she crying for both of us.

"Ain't nobody from Zion been lynched in years. Hangings been all round and through Zion, but it what'n none of us. We been saying we safe, and now this." I'm laying on my back, looking at the ceiling. "If they hang them, Daddy won't ever forgive me. He gone hate me. It be a sure sign I'm cursed. Nobody will speak to me again." The tears fall warm, then cool in my ears. I breathe in deep.

"If they lynch them," Coley hush crying, to say, "I'll stand up at their funeral and tell the whole town what I did. Then no one will blame you."

Looking at 'a good, I see how sincere, serious and fearless she can be, when it come to me. I feel how much she love me. Then I see her bright eyes swollen and red from crying. "I love you so much. It hurts me to think anybody could be as mad at you as they are with me. I could never let you do that."

"It breaks my heart seeing you this hurt. And knowing I'm the cause." Scooting 'a head up on my shoulder she put 'a face by mine. "I'm so sorry Linny. Please touch me. Just hold me. You barely look at me. It's been two days since you spoke to me, or even hugged me."

"They might be hung." I say again, but this time I breathe slow and even, trying not to feel what I know coming in the next few days. Coley lifting my arm, getting under me, and kissing the side of my lips.

"I need you right now." She slide 'a hand under my night shirt, running 'a hand over my stomach and chest. She keep kissing at my lips, like she trying to get them to work.

I start to cry.

She wipe my tears. Climbing on top of me and putting 'a legs on both sides of me, she hold me to 'a. "I'm so sorry, baby. I didn't know." She kisses me moving 'a hips.

I turn my face from 'a. My spirit feel like it's too big for my body. I feel so powerless. Iain been able to rest. Iain been able to think about nothing else, all I can see is them hanging. I'm all over the place, mad at Coley and needing 'a, too. Wishing she ain never come here for they life, and hoping she'll never leave mine.

"Please, baby?" She follow my face kissing at me and crying. "Please? Forgive me?"

Everything hurt, to be mad, to let go, to hold on. I feel so bad it's hard to breath when I cry.

She palm my tears one by one, rubbing them in 'a skin.

I cry. I hurt. I want to stop hurting. Her weight on me making it worse.

She hold my face to her chest. I cry into her, pushing her away, she keep pulling me into 'a, clinging.

Finally, I push her away, and then pull 'a in. I forgive 'a. When she opens to me, I am open to 'a comfort.

*   *   *

The morning come like fingers striking a piano being tuned, slow with no rhythm or song in mind, just getting ready for things to come. Me and Coley take our morning bath together. I finish getting dressed first like always and go make our breakfast. We silent. Forgiveness doesn't erase the past or even change what's gone happen.

Someone knocks, and I take a sip of my coffee before getting up to answer the door. I don't ask who it is this early. It's someone I need to talk to. It's Ella.

"Come on out here so I can talk to you," Ella directs me, staring at Coley like she owe Coley something Coley don't want. When I get outside, Ella make a show of slamming the door close behind us. "They let 'em go," she say, sadly.

I'm still waiting cause the way she look I know it's more.

"But they beat 'em real bad, with the whip."

Chapter Forty-One

Me and Coley miss almost a month of Sundays, fore Grit finally convince me to come back to church.

I feel funny soon as I get to church. I expect people to treat me different. They do, but it ain't bad as I imagined. It's a distance they keeping. It's something you can feel in your spirit but you don't see in their actions. Most people acknowledge us with head nods. Mrs. Clara hugs me. Coley students glad to see her.

I'm different, dressed different. Ella told me to wear a good dress, so I do. It's a nicer dress than she or any of my other sisters own. I promise them that they gonna have to start dressing nicer if I have to. Not this Sunday, not today, but soon they agreed.

I feel hot. I take my seat with Mrs. Clara, behind the Harpers. I realize I'm sitting on the pew with all the other business owners. Suddenly I realize, I always sat here, but it was because I didn't feel part of my own family. Now I see this is kind of a family. Even if they ain't talking to me, even if The Reverend carrying my vote.

I try to keep my eyes forward on the pulpit. Uncle Victor and Ernest nem back, and Daddy's folks feeling some kind of way bout me being here. I wonder if it wouldn't be best if I don't come since everybody scared.

I think about how Diamond Beaumont already had some inkling bout what happened in my store. I wonder who told 'a, I know whoever did, is sitting right here among us. Then I don't want to think about none of this.

"Good morning." Ella sit down behind me. Her, Prentice and they kids take up the whole row behind me. Then Grit and Zay families take the row behind Ella nem. Jenny sit off with 'a own family, and my other brothers stay close to Daddy, who close to my uncles. It all says something, where we sitting, and I'm just glad that Ella, Grit and Zay behind me.

The choir come in singing "Twelve Gates to the City." We already to hear the word when Reverend say, "First a word from our school teacher, Ms. Graham."

"What are you doing?" I lean all my weight on Coley side so she cain't get up. She squeeze out of my hold and stand. "Don't do this," I plead standing up with 'a.

"She has to." Ella stand too, wrapping 'a arms round me. Then say, "Sit down, Linny," in my ear. "One day she gone go back to her world, and you gone be left here to carry the burden of all the mess she done started."

"You cain't do this," I argue with Coley pigheaded self, but Ella put 'a weight on me and I go down slow, not wanting to make a scene, a bigger scene.

"She got to do something," Ella say to me. "Now go on," she say, and fan Coley to go on, still holding me tight from behind.

"I want you all to know that Linny has been good to me. Showing me around and helping me get use to living out here. She even allows me to stay with her without charging me room and board. She's been patient as I've been learning how to best be of service to my people. Which is why when I saw her bruised face after she was attacked, I was so hurt and outraged."

"Ain't nobody attacked huh!" one of my cousins shout from behind, in the corner where Uncle Victor and Ernest nem sitting.

"She was attacked," Coley challenge firmly, looking back. "I was angry men would even be hitting a woman. In my family, the men protect us. Her brothers, her father and nobody else seemed to care about what happened to Linny. I started to worry about all of us women. What will become of us, if our husbands, sons and uncles are allowed to just beat us whenever they feel like it.

"Linny is strong. She has her own way of resolving a situation. She said it was over. She didn't have any hard feelings. She told anybody who saw what they did to her face or who asked about it, she wasn't hurt.

"Still, I heard the rumors about what happened. It seemed to me that, Linny was being painted the bad person. They were acting like they were the victims. It seemed to me, there still needed to be some legal standard applied.

"I didn't want anyone to get hurt. I hadn't thought about the possibility of the anyone being hung. Where I'm from we don't live in constant fear of being attacked or hung. We have our own newspapers and are actively fighting for our rights. We aren't bowing to whites. We have Colored police officers patrolling in Harlem. So I didn't think suggesting Zion should have it's own police force, would lead to a mob of white men coming into someone's home and dragging them out.

"When Diamond Beaumont came out to the house that evening after supper, she already knew something happened. She was coming to hear the details, or maybe to see if it was true. Then Linny's face was still swollen and bruised. I did say, 'Someone should have to pay for hitting her.' I just thought someone should be taught a lesson. I had no idea what that lesson might be. Now everyone is angry with Linny, when they should be upset with me."

"They coulda been kilt!" somebody shout.

"Well, they weren't," Mrs. Harper add, stirring in the mix. "And they ain't totally blameless in what happened to them. They did beat Linny in 'a own store. They did steal from 'a for months after Miemay died."

"They was stealing from Miemay fore she even died, if people tell the truth," Zay add.

"Umm hmm," folks start to cosign in low moans, and I'm surprised.

"I will not be called a thief in God's house," Uncle Victor growl shooting up to his feet.

"Well, you shouldn't have stole!" Grit shout surprising me and Ella, turning around and looking at him in the eyes. That's when I notice Granger ain't sitting with Grit, he sitting near Daddy.

"This whole town know you stole! But ain't nobody said nothing. When Linny came and told you to leave, you shoulda went on bout yo bidness. But you didn't!" Grit point at 'im. "You tried to beat a grown woman, the two of ya. Steada going round talking bout how she shot at yall and trying to shame 'a, you shoulda been ashamed of ya own fool selves.

"Who knows how Diamond Beaumont found out you stole from that store and beat up on Linny. For all we know, you might be the ones told the people who told 'a. Don't nobody really know who said what, but ain't nobody to blame but yah own fool selves.

"Iain gone sit here, and let people stand up and say whatever they wont whether it's true or not. Yall been stealing from Miemay forever, she knew it, we knew, the whole family knew it and the whole town knew it, too.

"When Miemay died, you tried to bury Linny you stole so much, and ain't nobody said a word. Nobody!" Grit look around at everybody in they eyes, even in Daddy's. "So you don't git to sit in here and say whatever come to yo mind cause it feel good, and cause you mad. Maybe Miemay ain't leave you nothing cause you took yo inheritance while she was alive."

"Gitcho wife," Cousin Ernest shout to Granger.

"Iain no child, got my own mind and mouth. Granger and nobody else ain't gone sit me down, or silence me no more. Yall women better start standing up for yourselves, speaking your mind. We ain't got but one life, and cain't nobody die for us, so we cain't let nobody live for us neither!

"Nobody else gone talk bad bout my sister, especially when she ain't did nothing wrong. She shoulda fought back, we was raised not to let nobody beat us and we was raised to be fair. She always did right by everybody. She ain't never been no liar, cheat, or thief. Which Uncle Victor nem all proved they selves to be and-

"Alright!" Reverend put his hands up for Grit to stop. "That's enough," he speak low like he trying to sooth Grit from the pulpit.

Grit stand silent, looking at us all, like she waiting for a challenge but don't nobody say nothing, so she take a seat.

"Iain gone feel right less there's a woman on the committee," Mrs. Clara say, then stand up beside me, looking around, like she hearing 'a voice for the first time. She take a moment to compose 'aself.

"Miemay carried my vote along with hers, and she spoke for us women here. Iain afraid of Linny gittin nobody hung. I'm afraid of a committee that speaks for and decides on all the town's business, and there ain't one woman in there to speak our piece. We need a voice, ain't afraid to stand even when people don't agree with 'a.

"Since I'm a member of the committee, and even though Iain never used my vote, I want to make a motion. I move to restore Linny's position on Zion's Committee and she cast 'a own votes, like she did before all this happened."

"I second that." Mrs. Harper stand.

"Alice, you cain't vote," Reverend say, covering the mike and looking over at his wife, scolding 'a with his face.

Then she give him a look make him silent.

"I'm carrying my own vote." I stand. "And I expect Mrs. Clara to carry her own vote going forward."

"I second that." Mrs. Clara smile reaching for my hand and interlacing our fingers.

Chapter Forty-Two

"Why you banging on this door like that, Reverend?" I open the door when I recognize his voice.

"Where you going, girl?" he asks, pushing in my house, looking at me from head to toe. "You need to stay in this house tonight. That's the devil bidness out there." He point behind him.

Bessie Smith, Ma and Pa Rainey and the Assassinators of Blues gone be at Uncle Lucius Jug Joint. It's not the regular sinful show they condemning every other Sunday. These real-life stars, so it's different, decent folks going. This be my first time being out late anywhere, and Iain delivering no baby with Miemay or nothing.

"You already know where I'm going." I won't even entertain no condemnation this evening.

"Cain't go nowhere tonight," he say leaning on the door looking in my eyes, like he my daddy or something. "You need to stay in."

"What's the problem?" Coley come down the stairs looking confused and beautiful pinning 'a hair up.

"Ain no problem, Ms. Graham. Is Hank gone yet?" Reverend come all the way in looking up at 'a.

"Finally. Linny and I have been telling him you said it wasn't safe and he needed to leave. He took a group of men with him headed to Chicago, earlier today. Not all of them were from Zion either."

I add, "And you know they have to go to Savannah by wagon to catch the train, cause they watching all the stations round here for local niggas leaving."

Breathing deep, and easier, it seem like he relaxing some when he put his hands in his pockets and say, "Well, that's too bad Hank already gone, cause if yall women ain't got no man riding with you, then you really need to stay in tonight. Zion ain't no place for women to be travelling alone at night. You know how far that jug joint is from here?

"You ain't even safe if you make it there. All them drunkards, gambling, fighting and dancing to that hoochie coochie music."

"Stop trying to scare us," I protest.

That's the thing Miemay always hated bout church. Someone was always using God, or the Bible to scare people away from living. But when I really look at him, feel like something else going on. It ain't a regular shaming.

"Less you know something we ought to know?" I'm reading him.

"He's just concerned," Coley answer, fore The Reverend can.

I'm feeling it's something else, but Coley don't give me a chance to press 'im when she go on, "At home, my entire family goes to shows. Our pastor there went to hear Negroes perform as well. The shows were usually in theatres, but that isn't an option here in Zion.

"Still, I think it's important to support our Colored performers and artists. I also think it's important to get beyond basic survival, and do more than what's needed or required of us. I think we all need to do some things just for enjoyment.

"I know some people are saying since Bessie Smith and Ma Rainey are stars, its different going to hear them sing. They're saying the show should have been held in town, at the hotel for decent God-fearing folks. Then again, everybody knows that hotel parlor couldn't accommodate all the people expected."

When Coley finish, Reverend Patrick make this face like he tasted something bad. So Coley go on, explaining 'aself too much like she do sometimes, talking 'aself in and out of things.

"Some people think everything that isn't about God or necessary to live is a sin. My pastor often invited performers to dinner at his home, and prayed for their success. He said patronizing Colored businesses, eating out, going to dances and shows makes us more balanced and cultured people. Not to mention, God blessed them with their gift. God doesn't make mistakes, so they can't be wrong.

"On top of all that, white people have been enjoying the arts, music and all sorts of entertainment for centuries, why shouldn't we? We've got to get out of that old way of thinking, and embrace different things. I don't think it's a sin to see a little singing, Reverend. Why do you?" Coley make 'a case and get ready to debate with 'im.

Reverend been nodding his head 'yes,' all while Coley talking, then he smile like it hurt. Don't look like he agreeing with 'a, more like trying to follow 'a reasoning and waiting for 'a to stop talking. Then he say, "That's all fine and well, I guess," not accepting the invitation to debate Coley points, like his mind somewhere else.

Coley too satisfied on winning this little debate, fore it even get started, to notice something else might be going on.

"Iain saying what's a sin and what ain't. I just think, if you ain't got no man riding with you, you ought to stay in."

"Maybe we will find ourselves some nice men to ride with us," Coley tease, looking to see how I'm gone react to what she saying.

I'm kinda surprised by how free she speaking, even in jest. Especially since she so concerned bout how she seen, and yet she making 'aself sound a little loose. Still I act like she ain saying nothing at all.

"Well." He look at me for a long time. "Maybe it don't make you no difference one way or the other. Maybe you'll be alright."

"What's that spose to mean?" I'm staring back, feeling him out.

"Nothing, I just wish yall wouldn't do this. I'm gone be in my house tonight and I suggest you do the same." Bowing out, he put his hat back on and frown, like he defeated. "Good night, ladies."

Chapter Forty-Three

Seeing as how late it is when we start off down the road to Lucius place, I'm glad for my new automobile. I ain't got to worry bout putting no horses away, tying 'em up or watering and feedin nem in the middle of the night. All I got to do is go where I'm going, and I do feel more protected inside my auto, too.

Then the headlights light the way. It woulda been too dark out here for horseback riding. I agree it wouldn't of been no good idea, for just me and Coley to be out here by ourselves on no horse going this far out.

"You look like you going to apply for work on somebody's farm," Coley say laughing. "You should have let me help you pick something to wear."

"I didn't even want to wear this dress." I look at 'a so serious it stop 'a from laughing. Ion care, I wont to be comfortable. I got my hair braided, pulled back and wrapped in a bun. I'm wearing a hat. I don't know what to wear to one of these things or what to expect.

For it not to be no electricity out here, Uncle Lucius place sho is bright. Soon as we start getting close, I can see all the light through neat rows of crops. The closer we get the more you feel it, the better you see, and the better you hear it.

A piano playing low, there's drumming, people talking and laughing. Seem like the cabin full of spirits dancing way the candles flickering. They spread round the yard, making the whole ground look like a full moon buried underneath the house.

I'm glad when I pull up, and all the men just wearing good shirts and pressed pants without suit jackets or ties, nothing too fancy. Ion feel out of place, but I do take my hat off and leave it in the auto. This my first time seeing this many people dressed up ain't in church.

When they see me and Coley they watch us but don't stop what they doing. Some men on the porch playing cards. I can smell the barbeque on the grill, and there is a big metal pot spose to be used for laundry, over an open fire, where they frying fish.

I can smell the scent of alcohol, aftershave, perfume and barbeque. The barbeque smell the best. I already ate but I could eat barbeque any day. I get me and Coley a plate for 10 cents each. We eat baked beans, ribs, greens, cornbread and macaroni. Iain never ate out really, not this good and sho not this late.

When we walk up on the porch, Coley say, "Good evening, gentlemen."

"Good evening to you, ladies," the men say.

I don't even see no women up front.

"And good evening, gentle ladies," one man say, then him and another man start laughing, elbowing each other.

Then I recognize my brother Zay sitting with our other brother Jeremiah. I just stare at 'em. They know I don't like when they call me a man in front of other folks.

"Shut up," I say, going to sit in they seats so I can eat.

Without a word they stand. Zay even act like a usher for Coley, holding his hand out to his bench.

"Okay, yah wife bet not see you putting on," I warn 'im.

Zay jump around like he expecting she might hear me. Then the whole porch laugh, and I remember how Zion the kind of place where no words are missed. Then Coley new, and they wanting to hear whatever she got to say.

"HEY!"

I hear a man shout from inside, then he come out to the porch.

Coley put 'a plate down and go in for a hug. When they let go of each other it's, Hank. He got a suit jacket on, and enough aftershave for all the men on the porch. Him touching Coley don't make me mad as it use to, seeing as how he sweet on Eudora, Uncle Lucius daughter.

"We told Reverend Patrick you were gone," Coley tell 'im poking 'im in the side. Now when I see them play, it kind of make me think of how me and my brothers might of been if we was raised different. Coley treat Hank like a little brother.

"I had to hear Eudora sing," Hank say and smile, then nod at me. Then he start looking around for Eudora, pass me and through Coley.

People's laughing and the piano playing right along with all the talking come through the windows. The women wearing they good boots. Everybody inside mostly dancing to the music. All they heavy footing making a rhythm of its own, kinda remind me of church, that sounds like its part of the music, too.

I don't know how long Hank looking around, tapping his foot and trying to pretend like he ain really looking for nobody, when we hear Eudora belch a note over everything going on.

As soon as Eudora sing, I know why Hank came back. She sing that song like 'a life depend on it. She feeling it too, and she making you feel it.

Eudora a handsome girl. Then she smile big as she sings out, like the sound of 'a own voice soothing 'a, freeing 'a. It's some song bout good cookin and good lovin. It's so good it make you laugh a little, like you do in church when the word hit a nerve.

Then Iain never heard nothing other than a church song. This the first time I seen a whole room get quiet for anything other than the word. I hate Iain come out here sooner. I promise myself this ain't gone be the last time I hear me some singing.

Eudora voice so strong, people stop moving, speaking and start to move inside. All the noise get quiet and everybody looking at 'a. Even I go in and stand against the wall, behind old man Frankie at the piano. I watch how he follow 'a voice.

Mr. Frankie this old man they say chose the devil. They say he use to play for the church, but the old reverend told him he couldn't serve two masters. They say, he sat for a while behind the piano thinking, then he politely covered the keys, got up and walked out. They say he ain never go back to church while that Reverend ran Zion Baptist Church.

Now there's a different man that play the piano in church, but he cain't play nothing like Mr. Frankie. People say Mr. Frankie brought the holy ghost with him every Sunday.

I learned to play the piano at somebody's house. Then every now and then Miemay would have Sister Spiller teach me some church songs. They was slow and sad. I couldn't hardly keep my mind on the keys. Even then I was reading music. Iain never just played no song.

Reading music ain't but one thing, but what Mr. Frankie can do is a skill. He can hear a sound and make it. He can hear a sound and dance with it on the piano. I want to learn to make my piano dance.

Iain never seen nobody play the piano like Mr. Frankie. Eudora tell him with 'a hands what to do. Then she start singing, and he just follow her. Iain never been able to play by ear, and Iain never had the chance to play with nobody else. I use to want to play in church but that day ain never come.

I'm watching the women backing Eudora up hum, and lead Mr. Frankie into another song. They teach him the song a bit before they get going. Then Mr. Frankie follow close to they voice. He know just what to do. Mr. Frankie could play with the best of 'em.

Soon as Mr. Frankie set the rhythm the band come in; blowing that jug, picking that fiddle, spooning that board, plucking the tub, playing the banjo, and breathing in that harmonica. When these boys get to going it's something to see. Oooh, I hate I been going this long and ain't never been over here.

I don't know how long I'm standing there when Mr. Frankie turn around and look at me, smiling, like he bout to say something. He keep looking back. When Eudora take a break, he say, "Don't chu know how to play the piana, too?"

"Nothing like what you doing. I just do it by reading music, and it's been a while."

"Come on over here and sit down next to me." Mr. Frankie smile, scooting over and leaving me space on the bench.

Soon as I sit down, I smell the snuff he chewing.

"I'm gone play this then you hit that right there." He presses on a few keys to show me. Then he do play a little and wait for me to play my part. Then we go back and forth til we speed up.

After we playing a little while, I start to feel the music in my soul. People start to cheer us on. I start to feel where I need to go next on my side, and it make me feel special to have the whole room dancing to our music.

A commotion get started. People start shouting, "That's their automobile!" People moving round, trying to get a look out the windows, saying, "It's her! It's her!"

I stand to get a good look at 'a. It's done got too dark for that.

All these men come in and they bring they own instruments, different from what they using round here. Me and Mr. Frankie moving this way and that way, making room for them to set up.

Soon as they set up, they introduce Ma and Pa Rainey. Ma Rainey belt out this note so loud, seem like she singing for today and tomorrow.

"I've never seen a woman hold a room's attention like she does," Coley whisper, leaning in my ear. "And she so black." She smile like she proud of 'a own blackness.

Ma Rainey hair nappy, too, braided smaller and tighter to 'a scalp. She looking real sharp, in 'a shiny gold dress. I ain never seen a dress like what she wearing.

I'm anchored there thinking, bout what she saying and how she moving. The songs she singing something else. They bout her and her man. She saying things make me blush, but the other women in the room seem to be use to this kind of singing.

Eudora what'n too far off with what she was singing before Ma got here.

Then Bessie Smith get to singing and speaking to the whole jug joint, like she know you want to see what she doing, and know what she bout.

The room stomp and tap. Some folks get up and dance together off on the side. I want to take Coley over there and have us some fun learning them steps. I want to hold 'a hand here. The men start inching round us, and I'm starting to feel that anger pushing itself up in me.

"Don't you want to dance?" Coley put 'a hand in mine. "Some of the other women are dancing together."

Soon as Coley say that some men come up behind them women, and start dancing, too.

"I don't wont no man holding me close." I look at 'a in a way make 'a uncomfortable. Then she start looking round like everybody can hear what I'm saying.

After Bessie Smith finish 'a first set, she give Mr. Frankie some sheet music, to thank 'im for allowing her piano player to use his piano.

He look back at me smiling all big and pleased, and say, "You think you could help me learn to read this?"

Me and Mr. Frankie stay close by each other, while Bessie Smith's man play the piano. Then he tell me to read him the names of the songs on the music she done gave him. I do, then I tell him that in order for him to learn how to read music, he gone have to know how to read, too.

Bessie Smith's man takes a break, then me and Mr. Frankie get back behind the piano to keep the music going. When I play the notes off the sheets, Mr. Frankie look at me with the same amazement I been watching him with all night. It make me laugh so hard, and I get so excited I stop worrying bout Coley and relax.

"I'm gone make you some letters and bring 'em to you, so you could be practicing sounds," I tell 'im excited I can teach him anything, and hoping he'll teach me how to play piano like him. Mr. Frankie sit up stiff, and look like he don't know me or what I'm talking bout.

"What letters you gone be practicing, Mr. Frankie?" one of the men say and laugh, full of that oil.

I realize what I done done, but I cain't take it back. It don't occur to me I shouldn't say nothing here. I'm thinking bout what Mr. Frankie say bout getting between the jug blowing, and tub plucking, but not out running the fiddle or guitar. I'm so excited about how much he done taught me, in just this little time, I forget where I'm at. Outside of Coley, I could live for

playing the piano. The words already gone, out there, when the other men start to laugh and jank Mr. Frankie.

I feel guilty, different. I think about how so many folks stop going to school soon as they was old enough to be a full hand. I think about how folks don't never think it's nothing to school, and it's more important to know how to plow the fields.

I use to be shame, going to school big as I was. All the other girls were getting married, or helping they mamas and family at home.

Miemay use to say, "Gone to school and learn much as you can. You gone need to know everything they teaching."

My last years in school I was helping Mr. Bailey, this man teacher. Women weren't teaching less they were my age and unmarried. I helped other kids learn more than I was being taught anything. I got them lessons so good in math, I still can do most problems in my head folks need paper for. I'm always breaking things down and hearing it for what it is. Reading get you to doing that, thinking about things. I'm always thinking.

I remember asking Miemay why she don't want me to stay home, in the fields. She said something like, "Them fields gone always be there, but school was just for a time. I what'n like other women, I needed to learn to read and think. Reading teach you to think."

Miemay said that's why whites ain't never wont blacks reading cause they didn't wont them to know nothing. Then right after slavery every nigga young enough wanted to know how to read. But the old people, the slaves just wanted land. They didn't understand what was going on and was always getting cheated. Still getting cheated.

"Don't other women need to know how to think, too," I asked Miemay after Jenny had teased me so, about going up til I was 18. I'm one of the few girls who graduated, over the years.

"Nah," she'd said, looking off into the fields and then at the sky kinda sad. "They already got somebody else thinking for 'em. You need to have a mind of yo own."

Mr. Bailey got tired of all the hangings and started to fear his neck would end up in a noose. After that, they couldn't keep no teachers here. Prudence Beaumont use to help Mr. Bailey out, too, over the years, cause she had so many children, and then she became the teacher.

"Aye Eee I Oh You nigga," another man sing behind Mr. Frankie's head. It's hard to believe they this disrespectful considering their ages. Then again, that jug oil might make a man say anything.

"He's learning to read, when was the last time yall learned something?" I challenge firmly, looking at them.

"We listening to this old fool, and he don't even know much as we know bout thangs," another one of them say.

"You be lucky enough to live this long, you'll find I knowed tons of thangs you ain't know, son," Mr. Frankie pout more than defend himself.

"What you gone do with reading anyhow? You cain't read them fields." They all bust out laughing like they the funniest thing ever.

"You ready?" I sit down next to Mr. Frankie.

He spin around putting his legs under the piano. He silent, and hurt.

"I'm sorry," I whisper.

"Aincho fault people don't never want no change. My own wife asked me why I was learning letters one time. She said we was too old to change, or to worry bout reading. Iain looked at 'em since.

"That's why I like music, it's always changing, and depending on who the person singing, you always got to learn something new. I like to try different things. Be nice to go on the road or something like Bessie Smith and Ma Rainey. Be nice to see some different things. I been in Zion all my life. Shoot, I was here before Zion was here."

"That's a long time." We both laugh, then I ask, "What you waiting for?"

"I could ask you the same thang. Ain nothing here for no young girl. You ain got no youngins or no man to look after. You need to take the first thang out of here smoking. See what else going on in the world.

"I always wanted to go up to Atlanta, or you know, maybe St. Louis. I hear it be better work there, and we doing good now but the boll weevil killing us. I don't know what we gone do next year if-"

Bang! Bang!

Soon as me and Mr. Frankie hear them rifle shots, we both duck. Then I shoot up from behind the piano looking for Coley.

Mr. Frankie snatch me back down and under the piano. "You know what they'll do to a gull like you?"

"Coley!" I call, snatching away from him. I study the people running up steps. Then somebody run straight into the back screen door, *BUM* and on into the fields.

"Hey hey! Nigger, you better quit running," somebody call after him.

They shooting, riding round the house.

Feel like the walls ain't even there, and we all just sitting ducks in the middle of the woods. I watch the Klansman aiming his rifle at the man's back, then another look me right in my face. I run and slam the back door shut, and lock it. Then hurry up and get out the way expecting him to shoot through it.

"Every nigger in there better come on out that God-damn house, or we gone burn it to the ground!"

"Coley!"

Lit crosses burning bright through the windows. I hear their torch flames crackling outside. We surrounded, and it's a lot of 'em. Sounds like soft thunder, way the wind whipping through they Klan robes while they riding round.

Everything silent cept for they horses, the hooves moving round outside, like too many heartbeats to be in one chest. Every door I open, the rooms lit by them, outside in they white robes and pointy hats.

I'm checking under beds, in closets and calling 'a, "Coley!" fast as I can. Every window I pass I see them robes, them torches, them rifles and they horses. I see the other niggers with they large eyes holding each other, when I peak out the window for Coley.

When I get to the gambling room, Coley behind the counter, balled up holding 'a dress. She the only one don't know the rules. If they have to come in here and get 'a, specially a nigga woman, they gone have 'a fore they go.

"I see a nigger don't believe fat meat greasy!" A torch come in the window and Coley scream.

"Come on," I say and grab 'a hand.

She pulling away from me.

"We got to get out there or they gone burn the house down!" I snatch 'a from the floor. The curtains catch fire.

"Don't say nothing. Don't open ya mouth." I drag 'a like a child's wagon behind me, snatching 'a cause if they catch us in the house we be fun fore they hang us.

Bum! The back door kicked in and the Klansman standing there turn his gun down when he see me coming.

"Get on outside, nigga! Fore you get burned up in here."

I pull Coley out the house with me and down the stairs. We run to get in the pack with the rest of the niggas.

"We looking for that nigger named Henry Meriwether. Come on out here boy or we gone burn Lucius place down and hang every nigger we don't know," a Klansman order.

Coley scream, crying.

So I bury 'a head under my arm so she cain't breathe, so she cain't scream. It be better for 'a to fall out than to scream. She ain from here. They be done hung 'a, too.

The man speaking start wielding his rifle round in all our direction. People scream and move to get out of its aim.

"Come out here boy!" one of the Klansmen order, pointing his rifle at a man Iain never seen before, and motioning for him to come out the crowd.

The man step forward, weak on his feet.

"Get over there boy," the Klansman aim at an open space, where won't nobody be behind him.

Coley push forward to look to see if it's Henry.

"Any of yall recognize this nigger?"

"Iain never seen this nigger before," another Klansman agree.

"My name ain't Henry, suh." The man gag out the words, his eyes wild, looking at all them, us, then in the barrel of the rifle, trembling.

Bang! . . . Bang . . . Bang . . . Bang they shoot him. Even after he fall, and stop shaking, they keep shooting in his body. All of 'em hollering, shouting, and cheering they going round trying to hold they horses at bay.

Coley hold on to me, crying. Now she see how serious all this is. I'm glad they ain hang him. I'm glad they shot him right off and ain't torture him.

"Come on now! We know there's a recruiter here in Zion! Yall niggers know who the hell Henry is! We could do this all night."

The man with red stripes on his sleeves, lean on his horse, resting and looking at all us. Then he say, "You niggas know you ain't allowed to leave unless The Counsel done approved it.

"What you leaving for? Got good jobs here. Got your family here. Most of you in Zion got your own land. Why would you give up everything to go up north?"

I recognize his voice, and I know that's my real father, Hunter Beaumont.

"Henry Meriwether, you bring yo black nigger ass out here. You ain gone be taking our damn field niggers and not paying. We don't take kindly to-"

"You recognize this nigger?" another Klansman aim at another man with his rifle, interrupting Mr. Beaumont. This time it's Bessie Smith's piano player.

"Nah, cain't say I do. Come on out here, boy," Mr. Beaumont order him to stand where the other man laying dead.

"Puh-please," the man pleading, looking the Klansman in the eyes with his hands up begging for his life, and looking over at the dead man. "I'm a piano player, sir. Iain no recruiter and my name ain't Henry, sir. I'm here with Ma and Pa Rainey, doing a show, sir, just passing through. Please don't kill me." He crying and begging, his face wet with tears and we all scared for 'im.

Showing he scared and bowing might save 'im, then again, it might not. I close my eyes, frowning, I cain't watch no more. I squeeze Coley even more, and the fire crackling in the silence enough to make you pee on yourself, waiting for Mr. Beaumont to make a judgment.

"I'm Henry Meriwether!" I hear from behind us. Then the crowd part. Hank walk out strong, taking big strides. His eyes wild, and my heart beating for 'im.

"No Hank!" Coley scream, reaching in his direction. I hold her back, but she still fighting in my arms, begging, "Please!"

I grab 'a face, and look 'a in the eyes. Squeezing 'a face, shaking 'a and jerking 'a, trying to force 'a mouth close. I shush in 'a mouth shaking my head 'no.' "You ain from here, they'll hang you, too," I whisper.

The other niggers round us whispering, "Thank you Jesus," and "Praise God."

"Get me a rope!" Mr. Beaumont call, and I realize he the head of the Klan with them red stripes on his arm.

Bang! Somebody shoot and Hank fall to the side, shot in the leg. He don't cry. He take deep breaths, rubbing where the bullet hit, looking over at the tree where they setting up for 'im to hang.

Two of the men get off they horse, come punch him in the face then drag 'im over to the tree. They start to beat him, and I wish I had a gun to shoot 'im in the head so he wouldn't have to suffer.

So many men round Hank, kicking and punching I cain't see 'im. All I see is the dirt rising. They pointy white hats moving round so fast, going up and down.

"Aaaah," Hank scream, and I know they stabbing him, cutting him and cutting off parts. Then I smell the gas.

I'm hurt and angry they can just come and do this to us anytime they wont, and ain't nobody to save us.

Hank start to scream and gargle, and I figure they done cut his throat, or making him drink the gas. I hear them torches crackling, and its silent cept for the screaming of cuss words over Hank on the ground.

Then all the Klansmen start moving back, and Hank is lifted up by his neck, bloody, broken and silent. I pray he already dead.

"Don't look," I whisper in Coley's ear, tears filling my own eyes. Then they put that torch to 'im.

Chapter Forty-Four

The men pull a wagon under the oak tree. Hank's body is gently pushed in position over it. Pieces fall from him, his clothes, his skin. Pieces of him are missing; ears, fingers and toes.

Some folks stare, others look away. I just hold Coley much as I can, and watch. Coley throwing up, crying and screaming like a child. People watch 'a silently, too.

The Klan gone. They brought so much fear, fire and wind it seems quiet and dark when things are almost as they should be. Coley screaming disturb the night.

The smell of 'im burning ain't bad as the bodies we done found hanging from our trees over the years. It's probly covered up some by the barbeque and fish.

When I said nobody in Zion been hung in a long while, don't mean they ain been hanging poor niggas from our trees. Hank ain't from here, and the man they shot ain't from here. Way it be told, they still ain't kilt nobody from Zion.

If they hang one person from a family here, the whole family liable to leave after the funeral. They don't wont us leaving, they need us. Travelling news say, a whole Colored town left out of some part of Mississippi, or was it Tennessee, after Ida B Wells started 'a crusade against lynching. I cain't even imagine it, but all the niggas just packed up and left them white farmers to tend they own land.

White folks scared one day all of Zion might get wise and go. They watching our newspapers, and getting weekly reports on what's going on round here. Specially with so many young folks leaving, they thinking one day it's gone be hard to find good hands to work round here during planting and harvesting season.

Miemay use to say, we still got to escape like we slaves. They'll beat a Zion nigga trying to leave, and they may hang 'im if they think he encouraging other niggas to go, too. It's like we ain't free to lead our own lives, better lives.

I cover Coley's mouth, then bury 'a face in my chest and hold 'a there. In the dark, Eudora voice calls, and some people sing the lines right behind 'a as Hank is cut down. His body still hot so they touching him easy. The Klan done watched him burn til he burned out. Water would make his body a mess. We done learned.

Tonight, tomorrow and as we lay Hank and the other man to rest, I'll be hearing this song. I've never known its name, still I know all the words by heart. I've heard it enough times. I always called it the "Hang and Surrender Song." I wonder if anybody else knows its name. Or if they just like me, done heard it so much they know it by heart, too.

Don't fight for me
Don't die for me
Don't even cry for me
What is done
Is
Already done
Now that I'm gone
I'm safe from harm
In my savior's arms

Cain't take me
Fore my time
Less it be
His will
I should die
This life
What'n never mine
I was living on
Borrowed time
So I go
With peace of mind
God has called me
Home tonight
Let me go

With peace of mind
I'm safe now
Home with Christ
This ain't forever
Just a time
We'll meet again
On the other side.

Chapter Forty-Five

"Something wrong?" I ask Coley, looking at 'a, feeling 'a out, after watching 'a staring off and pushing food round in 'a plate. She get like this sometimes now, every since Hank was killed. For a while, it was hard to get 'a to eat anything. She so weighed down with guilt. She done got so small.

For the first few days afterwards, I had to bathe 'a, and there wasn't no school. Then after a week passed, Reverend's wife and even ol Prudence had to hold class.

"You know, when I first arrived," she speak slow and think.

I don't wait for 'a words no more, sometimes they never come. Sometimes it be best I don't pry, or remind 'a what she said last, I've learned. I eat looking at 'a, worried.

"I thought I'd gotten in over my head. Still I had signed a contract for a year. I told myself it was just a year. I told myself, adversity builds character. Plus, I haven't always made the best choices. I haven't always kept my word. So I was determined to fulfill this commitment."

Lately, there's always a punch or a kick when it comes to Coley, so I don't tell 'a how good it is she kept 'a word. She might start crying, and it go from being bout one thing, to being bout something else Iain even see coming. So I just let 'a talk and wait, for the punch, or kick.

"When I first started teaching here, I didn't tell you how challenging it was. Trying to reach girls ready to be married, who thought they knew everything. Or trying to get through to boys, who were more concerned about earning enough to live and buy land, so they could afford marriage to one of those girls.

"All the teens thought they'd already learned enough. The girls were constantly challenging my authority. The boys would hardly show up. For days I was trying to think of ways to reach them, and make learning appealing.

"Then there were the babies, who were so behind for their ages. Some of them didn't even recognize their alphabet, didn't know sounds, and others weren't reading. I had so many children. They were on so many different levels, even in the same age groups.

"I knew I'd have to do separate assignments for almost every child. They all needed tutoring in some shape or form. Then I didn't have the supplies I needed. For two months I was overwhelmed.

"You were telling me I needed to work at home, and I was falling asleep making lessons for all these different students. Then I asked the girls to help me with the little ones. They didn't want to tell me what they didn't understand, so they started teaching themselves and learning to help.

"I told the older boys something you told me, about how the man has to be able to know more than his wife so he can protect his family. I told them one day their children would come home with homework, the boys, and who would help them? We all became teachers. We were all learning. I finally got things running smooth.

"Then there was a new challenge. I learned the kids would have half days during planting and harvesting season. Even worse, some of them wouldn't be coming at all. Not to mention, I needed to excuse their absences, and go on as if nothing had changed or as if nothing was wrong. How were they going to retain anything? How was I suppose to move forward educating them?

"All my hard work seemed in vain, but they were smarter than I expected," she explains and smiles. "I sent them home with little books, and they read. Some of them even started teaching their parents, and even their grandparents how to read. Then I knew I'd found my place.

"I'd found a way to make learning fun. They were so happy, and their confidence was growing as they understood things. I started to feel like I'd finally found my calling. I saw how I could help my people. I couldn't wait to see what the youngest generation of my students would become. They gave my life hope. Every time they screamed, 'I got it!', I felt like I'd accomplished something.

"They weren't concerned about my skin, my hair, or my clothes. They just loved me unconditionally. Sometimes they'd just burst and hug me. They wanted to hold my hand and help me with things. Even the older kids, who were getting ready to leave and become adults themselves, really wanted me to approve of them. They put a lot of weight on my opinions. They would bring all kinds of problems to me for advice.

"I was starting to think, I loved Zion. I loved how people worked together. I loved how their parents brought me little meals, fruit, or whatever they thought would help. Sometimes the mothers would come sit in to see what had their children excited. Then they'd come back to help, and some people asked me to help them learn to read, or add.

"I planned to start an adult class a few nights a week, with homework and all. I wanted to help people who fell off somewhere during school, get to a place where they could read comprehensively, count and add.

"Teaching is the first thing I've done well and that people really appreciated. This is the first time I felt so loved and proud. I was so content, here.

"Hank was my student. He had a hard time with word problems in math, his reading comprehension wasn't the best at first. Still he was determined, and he wasn't ashamed to ask for help. He wasn't ashamed to try. He worked harder than other students to barely pass. When he graduated from college, it was a real accomplishment. I was so proud of him. Part of me felt like I'd earned that degree, too.

"I just wanted to help the people of Zion. I wanted them to know there was something other than here. I wanted them to know what it was like not to live in fear. I wanted them to know what it was like not to struggle.

"Some of the stories my students would tell me about not eating, and their parents being too prideful to tell others . . . would break my heart. Some of the boys were talking about looking for work outside of here to help. I just wanted to help when I sent Hank that letter. Now Hank is gone."

I'm silent, exhausted. I don't know what else to tell Coley.

"It's just so much death here. I don't know . . . how much longer I can do this. I don't know how you do it."

"Death is part of life."

"Not the life I came from. People weren't always dying or being killed in New York. I don't even remember the last time someone close to me died. I've only been here a little over a year, and some women won't officially name their babies until they get to be five. Babies and their mother's dying is a common thing, around here.

"We're all walking around on our tiptoes scared somebody is going to hang or rape one of us. That's no way to live.

"Then you're shooting pigs all the time, and killing chickens. How are you even eating this meat?"

"Would you feel better not knowing where the meat you eating come from?" I take a bite of bacon, and it seem dryer now that we talking bout killing to eat.

Shaking 'a head, Coley say, "I just don't know how you can eat something you killed. I don't understand how you can go on killing all the time."

"Death is part of life, we all dying. We all changing, getting older. It's yo destiny to die. From the day we born, we dying."

"That's a sad way to think about things."

"Ain't sad at all. What's sad is worrying bout things cain't be changed. Maybe if you accepted you was gone die, too, you could think about what really matters. What are you gone do while you alive? Live? Just exist?

"Doing what other folks want or expect is existing. I watched Miemay die, so Iain afraid of death. If death is the worst thing you can think of, Iain afraid of nothing really when I think about it. I sometimes wonder what else is out there.

"Living in fear is existing. Iain afraid despite how Zion might seem to you. I grew up here and people being hung is part of life. It ain't something you get use to, you cain't never get use to a thing like that.

"We got rules. When we follow those rules, things are alright. White folks ain't been my problem, my own family has. Living my life how I want to live been my biggest problem. I worry bout my daddy speaking to me more than I think about being hung. I think about how I'm gone stay close to people I love, when they don't agree with my choices, and I done rubbed them the wrong way.

"Then I think about how Miemay ain never do what folks wanted or expected. She did what sat right with 'a own spirit. She raised more children and helped more folks than anybody else I know. She tended to other folks like it was 'a business.

"People knew when Miemay asked you about your business, it what'n to judge or gossip, it was to help." I'm smiling thinking bout Miemay. "She loved people. She healed people. She birthed babies and led spirits home.

"Still they called her a witch, and feared 'a power. She was the last person to fear, but somehow she was everybody's first. I think about 'a when I'm hiring people to help me here. I thought about 'a, when the people told me they didn't want me in the business meetings no more.

"I'm always thinking bout whether I'm living my life the way Miemay expected. You know she gave me my own dowry so I could keep myself, to follow my spirit, and do more than exist. She once said, I was the only one with the potential to really be free."

I realize I'm getting away from the conversation, thinking bout Miemay. So I say, "Death and dying, well, it's just the way it is. What you gone do while you alive, that's what you got power over, and that's what you need to be worrying about."

Chapter Forty-Six

I'm in the kitchen when I hear Coley come in the house without so much as a word, then run up the steps.

I follow her.

She just start opening drawers, and putting things in neat little piles around her room. Seem like she so deep in 'a own thoughts, she don't even know I'm here. But I know she know, she can feel me, cause I feel her, leaving.

I just wait, watch, and don't speak or ask questions, gone give her a minute. Coley a talker. When she ready, she'll tell me what she want me to know. Plus I don't want to scare 'a, by telling 'a what I need or want from 'a, when she done decided what she need for 'aself. Feel it in my spirit she ready to defend 'aself, and she done got 'aself pumped up for a challenge. I ain against 'a.

We silent for so long, I stop leaning in 'a bedroom door, and go sit in the window. I never take my eyes off of 'a, and she never look at me. She ain slept in here since Hank was hung, since she started having all them nightmares. She scared to be in the dark. She thinking she see Hank all the time. This room don't even feel lived in, just a way for 'a to have 'a things in they own place.

"Today I sent word letting my parents know when to expect me back home," she admits firm and sad. Pulling out a suitcase, she starts to pick things up and put 'em inside. "I needed to let Mama know where I was. We haven't communicated since I left.

"I have responsibilities. I've made commitments. I'm suppose to be married now. I can already feel it settling in on me, all the ways I've disappointed Mama."

She still ain never looked up, she speaking more to 'aself, but I'm here, hearing 'a.

"Soon as I dropped the letter off, I felt my hair, how thick and nappy it is. Then I thought, 'I need to get my hair done before I see Mama.' The idea of hot combing my hair made me cry. I don't want to worry about my hair so much anymore. I want to love it the way it is. Want to be loved, the way I'm is. The way I am." She corrects 'aself. Then she stops, stands up straight to take an account of the room.

Running 'a hands over the two thick braids in 'a head, she looks at me for the first time, and I wonder, if she trying to figure a way to correct this, us. But she don't say nothing to me, she just keeps on straightening, and talking.

"I mean, white women aren't going through all this with they hair . . . their hair. When I really think about it, no other race of women is going through all us Colored women go through just to look . . . . decent. What's decent anyway?" She sits down hard but proper at the foot of 'a bed.

I can see her posture already changing. She ain as relaxed as she had gotten here.

"Then again, I know Mama would say a proper lady straightens her hair. I can hear her saying how she has good hair, but me and my youngest sister have our father's genes.

"I like my nappy hair. I don't like when other people don't like it. I don't want people to think I'm ugly. I don't like feeling ugly. Mama makes me feel so ugly." She cries hard.

I want to go and hold 'a, and tell 'a how beautiful she is, but this Coley ain't the Coley that makes love with Linny. This the Coley who steps on the earth like the whole world need to be swept. This the Coley need someone else to be happy fore she is. And me and her happiness ain't the happiness she worried bout. I'm worrying now, what's gone come of us, in this place where I finally found love possible, and she feeling all out of sorts.

I want to tell 'a how she can be anything she wont, do whatever she wont. But then I already know what she gone say back. "Linny, Iain strong like you. You're different from me." She don't never see who she is, who she could be. She don't never see how happy we could both be, if she would just stop living for other people.

"Ain't nothing here for me if you go," I admit, and watch 'a turn away to pack more things. She folds everything again, sharper and lays them just so. I see 'a trying to lose 'aself in the packing, in the moving, and I'm trying to, too. But I'm losing 'a, I ain able to be absent for that.

"I can't get my hair pressed hard before I go." She put 'a hands in a lap and sit up.

I feel like Coley ain hearing me at all.

"I've gotten so dark. Mama is going to have a fit when she sees how dark I've gotten." She stand smoothing 'a dress down again, and taking another once over of the room.

Almost looks like she was never here, cept for the scent of 'a perfume. Cept for how my spirit feeling touched, and how it's on edge expecting to never be touched again.

"I think you're beautiful, just the way you is."

"I know," she say, dismissing what I said like what I think ain't enough.

That hurt me. Now I'm sad. I miss 'a being happy and feeling beautiful. I wish it was something I could do to fix how she feeling.

"I don't think I can live without you," I say, just above a whisper.

"I know," she admits and turns away, looking at the floor, her lip trembling and 'a eyes red with tears. "I don't know if there's a place there for you, for us. Never felt like there was a place for me there. For a moment, this felt like my place."

I smile at 'a, walking over to the bed. "Wherever I am, there will always be a place for you. Places aren't home, people are."

"Hank would have never come here if I hadn't wrote him that letter. He would still be alive if it wasn't for me. I should have listened to you, Linny. You warned me. You told me to shut my mouth, and think about what I was doing, before I got someone killed."

"You cain't blame yourself for what happened." I stare at 'a sitting with 'a head down. We done had this talk a thousand times, bout how she cain't change the past. Bout how the Klan responsible for what happened to Hank and nobody else.

"How can two people be murdered and nothing happen? The people didn't even say anything. They thanked God when Hank came forward. Nobody tried to fight for him," she cries harder, "not even me."

Taking a deep breath, I just look at 'a, and try to search for the words. I ask God for the words. I'm always talking to God, but it still ain't no way to explain what happened. It's unnatural to kill a young man, to force his spirit out his body fore its time. Still ain't nobody but the people who killing folks responsible.

"Ain no reason for you to feel guilty Coley. If you feel guilty, then maybe it's a little of Eudora's fault, too. She so sweet Hank couldn't leave without hearing 'a sing. Remember, he was gone, then he had to come back to hear 'a one more time fore he left.

"Maybe it's Reverend's fault. I feel like he knew they was coming and didn't tell us. Then again, he did all he could, he told us not to go. He made sure Hank was gone. For all we know his family was on the line. Mr. Beaumont did tell him he better not find out there was a recruiter in town and The Reverend was lying to him. He practically told Reverend it was his life or Hank's.

"Maybe it's Ma Rainey's fault, cause all the men leaving thought it'd be good to have one last good night in Georgia fore they headed to Chicago.

"Then again, maybe it's Hank's fault, cause he was spose to be gone. But if he hadn't of been here, how many other men would have hung in his place? His blood ain't on your hands. He is a man who made a decision. He's been a recruiter for years.

"When we told him it what'n safe here, he told us the stories bout the Klan raiding houses in Mississippi, Tennessee and Alabama, looking for 'im. Remember? He said he jumped on a cargo train in the middle of the night, almost naked.

"We laughed, but he was running for his life then. He understood the risks. He did a dangerous job, baby. If he had left like he said he was going to, he'd still be alive. But then, you always gotta wonder how many other men would have died in his place?"

"I just think," she say, shaking 'a head and crying, "I've done so much wrong in my life. Two men are dead all because of me. I didn't even know the other man. Then I had to write Hank's family, and tell them why he was never coming home. His family knows my family. It was only a matter of time before Mama came for me."

Wiping 'a face with 'a sleeve and sniffing hard, she different, changing right before my eyes. "I've disappointed so many people, and now, I know you say it isn't my fault, but it feels like more of the same."

"Baby, you got the rest of your life to make mistakes. Some of them you won't be able to correct, but the ones you can, you will."

"I have to go back then. I've made some I can correct."

"I guess you have to go back then," I resolve, looking at 'a and feeling how empty this room feels. I feel how empty this house gone feel when she gone.

"Oh Linny." She dabs 'a eyes on 'a sleeve, crying gently and laughing more than anything else in this genuine way that's new. It ain't that stupid laugh when she feeling off 'a mark.

Then she push me and say, "You know I use to think you were so simple, but it isn't that at all. You're still innocent. You still believe in first loves and forever after." Then 'a tears turn to a moan that is a grave dug too soon, to bury necessary things.

"I love you." I kiss 'a. "And if you love me, really love me . . . You seem to be the kind of woman who . . . makes decisions to make everybody else happy. You seem like the kind of woman who counts disappointing people as failure. I love you so much, I don't want you to be unhappy, and I don't want you to say things you don't mean."

I look into 'a soul, the way I do when I'm making love to 'a. "If this ain't what you want, if Iain what you want, I want you to be able to say that, and be happy."

"Oh Linny, I can see it in your eyes. You'd be disappointed."

"Iain say I wouldn't be hurt," I confess in a firm whisper, threatened to be strangled by my own feelings. "I'd be crushed, at first. Then I'd think about you being happy, and it'd sooth my soul . . . to let you go . . . cause that's what you wanted. I don't want to . . . love you against your will."

She kisses me, and looks in my eyes. "Why couldn't you have just been a man?"

"Cause it's far more amazing when a woman does a man's job." I laugh and she does too, holding my hand and leaning into me.

I stare into 'a soul. I want to feel she is telling me the truth. I'll let her go even if she says what I want to hear, if I feel it ain't what she mean, what she need. I don't want to hurt 'a even when she willing to hurt 'aself.

Closing my eyes, I rest my forehead against hers and let the words come. I want her to know how I feel, and I want her to tell me how she feels.

"I want to go home with you, Coley."

"All I can do is try," she whispers crying, and I know she is sincere. "I don't want to hurt you, Linny. Baby, I've disappointed so many people. I don't want to break your heart."

"If you leave without me, it'll break my heart anyway. Break it now, or break it later. I vote later."

"Later." She kisses me, nodding 'a head 'yes,' then kissing me deeper.

Linny and Coley move to New York with World War I brewing, the Harlem Renaissance just beginning and the Industrial Revolution in full swing.

Read on for a special excerpt.

Daughter of Zion

Available September 2014

Tailored To Fit

"Keep your arms up!" Reggie, a tailor friend of Ms. Lula Belle's orders me, when I think it's safe to rest one arm, as he's working on the other side. I'm standing in the center of a room of mirrors, with my arms out the way I've seen Jesus on the cross. My arms is tired, and I'm tired of standing like this. I'm tired of him sticking me, too.

"Would you be still? Honey!"

"Now that's it." Ms. Lula Belle puts her drink down and ease up from 'a seat, then come strut slow round me looking at me like I'm some kinda mannequin or something. "This is how a butch is spose to look, honey. Reginald, you have out done yourself this time."

"Well it helps that my subject is stunning," he slaps my behind in a way no man would dare, but it doesn't upset me as much as I'd have thought.

It's a reflex when I turn to look at him like he crazy.

"Don't worry honey I don't wont nothing you got, and you sure can't handle none of this," he puts his hands on his hips, holding the 's' long, rapping his tongue around thread and examining me for a new place to stitch.

"I've never met a man this mean, this feminine," I let slip out.

"And you never will, honey. You forgot to say gorgeous, intelligent, and just plain-

"Fierce!" Ms. Lula Belle chimes in with him laughing.

"Alright Reggie, I love it," A woman speaks like we were always waiting to hear her opinion, opening the door of the changing room, and stepping out.

"Oh now that is nice Lia," Ms. Lula Belle takes in the woman as she walks up on one of the platforms near me. Now we both surrounded by mirrors.

"Uh—Lill—Yah!" Reggie claps out every sound at Ms. Lula Belle correcting her. "Cain't cho country ass say nothing right?

You know how specific socialites, stars and butches are about their name changes."

I look at Ms. Lula Belle waiting on huh to jump full fool on'im, but she throw 'a hair back laughing, loud and hard. "Cause I shole know how we queens and sissy's is bout ours', honey."

"Now she is the most handsome butch I've ever seen. I like that a lot, too. When are you going to make me something like that, Reggie?"

I realize the woman walking round me the way Ms. Lula Belle had, and I forget my arms tired. I'm really looking at myself in the mirror for the first time. At the pin striped pants, and the shirt cut just for me, with the darts on the shirt where they need to be, steada off like they always is when I wear men's shirts. This shirt fitted too, all the other shirts I done had been like big tents stuffed in my pants. I'm always trying to iron them into something better than the big mess of material they is, so this is really something to see.

"Where the hell would you wear a tailored men's suit to A'Lelia? Madam Walker would have a heart attack if you even mentioned the notion."

"You look nice," she say staring at me for too long, making me feel uncomfortable. "Reggie you gone have to make me something like it for one of my parties," she tease. "It would drive people crazy! They wouldn't know what to think. I'd be the talk of the town. They'd be saying I'm family too. You know they already don't know what to make of me, especially considering the company I keep."

"I don't know if they'd think you was family," Reggie answers slow, distracted, staring at his work like he's trying to make sure he ain't missing nothing.

"It's always something wrong with a woman when she got huh own things, whether you in a suit or not," Ms. Lula Belle say staring off, chasing huh own train of thoughts.

"Vest!" Reggie shouts, and a man comes out of nowhere with a matching vest to the pants I have on in his hands.

He helps me put it on, and it's not completely stitched.

"Pins!" Reggie holds his hand out behind him expecting someone to fill them. Ms. Lula Belle hands Reggie the pins he was using on the pants earlier. He starts to work, humming and pinching, AND STICKING ME.

"Ouch," I warn him he got me again.

"Ain't nobody told her yet," Reggie stops, poking his lips out, like he's annoyed by my ignorance or something. "Beauty hurts," he frowns at me like something stink, "Now be still and hold your arms up."

I'm tired of standing here, and if not for being curious and wanting to see how this gone all turn out I wouldn't be taking all this. He been yelling at me since I got in here.

"Good afternoon, I'm A'Lelia Walker." The woman steps closer to me, offering me her hand over Reggie.

Reggie looks at her hand, then at me and her in the mirror daring us to shake hands.

A'Lelia take her hand back laughing a little acknowledging how crazy Reggie is.

I stare at 'a. She got deep brown skin, a solid built, bright white teeth against 'a skin and real tall for a woman. And in them boot heels even I got to look up in a' eyes cause she taller than me, and most women ain't.

"Oh excuse me for being rude," Ms. Lula Belle offers.

"I don't know why you excusing yourself Queen, you was raised by slaves. What they know about the etiquettes of socializing, honey?" Reginal tease 'a.

"Don't get started sissy," Lula Belle warn him laughing, then say, "This is Linny my neighbor."

"She a new bulldagger," Reggie jump in.

"With a name like Linny, it sounds like she's been around awhile." A'Lelia take me in, again.

I can't believe I'm being introduced to the daughter of millionaire Madame CJ Walker. I think about what Coley would think. I remember Coley going to one of Walker's shops to get her hair done. I look at A'Lelia's hair, pressed to perfection, and a hat cocked to the side like she dressed for taking pictures.

3

"Hello?" A'Lelias waving 'a hand in front of my face, and I realize I've been in a daze, staring at 'a hair. "I asked you, what is Linny a nickname for?"

"Pardon me," I say not realizing I use the word 'pardon.' Shaking my head, a little and anchoring myself I answer, "Madelyn, I'm Madelyn Remington named for my great grandmother. Some folks still called her Maddy when I was born, so they called me Linny instead of that."

"Now that's more than I knew about her," Ms. Lula Belle make this snooty face with 'a nose at Reggie, sitting back down on the counter and crossing 'a legs better than any lady I've ever met.

"Remington sounds like a powerful name," A'Lelia adds.

"It ain't," I promise 'a, "I'm just a ordinary field nigga from Zion, Georgia."

Then the whole room get silent, nobody say nothing.

Reggie creep around me silently, look in my face, and then back in the mirror like Iain been standing there this whole time. After while they all bust out laughing. Everybody looking round like I spoke too easy, and they cain't believe I said that.

Reginald get quiet like he waiting for something to happen, then he look over at Ms. Lula Belle. I realize they waiting to see how A'Lelia take it, so they know how to react.

That's when A'Lelia say, "No you aren't ordinary, and you're far from a field nigga."

"And she blue blooded too," Reggie add with a breath of relief, "whether it matter to her or not, that alone be opening doors."

"Doors even having money doesn't get me all the way in," A'Lelia admit.

"I don't know about that," Ms. Lula Belle challenge 'a.

"You're sure a handsome butch, gone have to fight'em off of you." A'Lelia seem to be admiring me over going back and forth with Ms. Lula Belle.

"Thank you," I say sincerely without looking at 'a or smiling. The word "handsome" do something to me, that I appreciate the way I think "beautiful" make most other women feel. It make me feel shy. I hope how serious I look when we make eye contact in the mirror don't make 'a think wrong of me. When I act shy, people think I got bad manners. I'm hoping I don't offend 'a.

"And your honesty is a breath of fresh air. I get tired of meeting niggas ain't got nothing pretending they have. Putting on airs and burying themselves in debt for the likes of impressing folks. Matter fact, I think, next time I have a party you should come."

"She'll be there," Ms. Lula Belle promise.

Then I can't hide my smile.

"She gone be sharp as a tack too," Reggie brag on his work moving back to get a different perspective.

"It's getting late, and I got to pick my daughter up. Me and May meeting Mama for dinner. So I'm gone git on out of here." She nod her head taking me in again.

Reggie disappear somewhere, and I can tell he somewhere helping 'a get 'a things together.

I put my arms down, looking at myself in the mirror thinking. All my life I been told how I should wear dresses, and fix my hair, and hold my tongue, and how no man would want me if I didn't. Iain never wanted no man. I always knew I wanted to be with a woman, just didn't never think one would want me back.

Standing here, I'm realizing there are other women who like women. Now somebody telling me those women ain't gone be able to keep they hands off of me. I see now, how life funny that way, and how things can be so different depending on where you at. I think I should've got out of Zion sooner, as I'm looking at myself, seem like for the first time.

Had that looking glass in my house for combing my hair, but then again it was so foggy you couldn't hardly see nothing in it. It never mattered no how neither, what'n never too keen on seeing myself back then, but now I can't take my eyes off the mirror.

"Jackson? Are you done moving those darts on her trouser jacket?" Reggie calls out, they all standing behind me, looking

5

at me looking at myself in the mirror. It's like we all working together to make me, who I'm spose to be.

Then Jackson, a dark man with a low haircut and thin frame comes from out of another room, holding the jacket up silently walking towards me. They both help me get it on, Reggie turns me away from the mirror so I can't see myself.

"Stop moving! We gone let you see when we done," he fusses.

"Yes," Ms. Lula Belle say, nodding her head, as the two men pull and tug on me. The way Ms. Lula Belle watching me so close, seem like she scared something big bout to happen and she don't want to miss it.

"Alright," Reggie say calmly then start to step back nodding his head, like he has outdone himself this time and I am some art piece on the wall.

"Alright now!" Ms. Lula Belle slap me on my thigh smiling, and start stepping back, like I need room to see myself. You'd think I had a ball gown on the way they smiling.

When I find myself in the mirror, I feel sad. To see me, who I always was spose to be after all this time, it hurt it feel so good. Feel like I'm standing outside myself looking at someone else. I look at the leather men's shoes peeking from under the hard pressed creased pants' legs and I'm afraid, she ain't me.

Then when I breathe deep taking me in, I know she me, cause she comfortable, and pleased. Then my spirit smile back at me.

"You look amazing." Ms. Lula Belle laughs, and a few tears fill her eyes. "I always knew this was you, but it's even better than I imagined. May I have this dance, sir?" She laughs, then grabs my hand.

For the first time, I actually want to dance, and I feel like crying too. We start a slow step around, and Reggie and Ms. Lula Belle hum a little tune.

We slow strut, and step, Ms. Lula Belle leading first, but then our roles start to change, and I feel her letting go. I feel myself becoming stronger and more dominant as I learn the steps. Feels like there was no learning, I always knew the steps, but I was in the wrong shoes.

Ida never had the nerve to move around like this, pushing her back and gliding this way in a dress. Humph, but if I ever have to wear one again, being in these pants gone change the way I come to dance. This suit done changed how I'm willing to be held. I lead. Something about knowing is soothing, and it changes me forever.

I start to hum the tune too. Funny how you know the rhythm of a song you've never heard, and how it's your favorite song. As I'm turning Ms. Lula Belle in the mirror, something come over me, and I go with it. I'm leaning forward, throwing her back and she dips perfect.

"Yeesss, Honey! She has got her 'Him' down already, baby," Reggie teases encouraging me. "Jackson, come look at this!"

When I pull Ms. Lula Belle up on her heels, I say, "Thank you," looking in her eyes.

"The pleasure was all mine," she smiles, "I feel like such a lady." Then she follows me closely like we've practiced dancing together before.

I don't know how long we are dancing, when I see us together over her shoulders and then take us in, from every angle in the mirrors. Then I remember Miemay's dream of me, dancing with a lady and looking like a man.

About the Author

In 2009, Nik Nicholson began research for *Descendants of Hagar*. The research exposed the challenges of masculine-centered lesbians, including how they come to terms with and express their sexuality and gender roles. *Descendants of Hagar* is Nik's highly anticipated debut novel. It is the first novel of a two-part series, which includes the intoxicatingly beautiful, *Daughter of Zion*.

Nik is an artist; in addition to writing she is also a poet, a spoken-word performer, actor and painter. To stay in touch with the artist, follow her on Twitter @artistnik. For news on the artist's projects, interviews, performances or for booking contact her team at http://www.NikNicholson.com